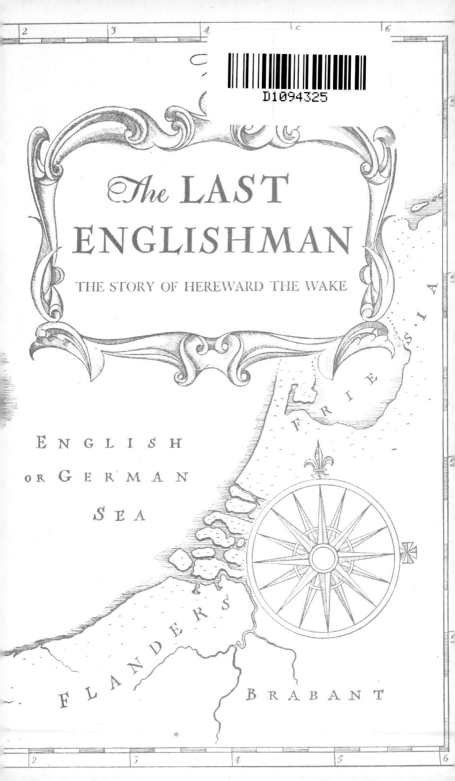

The LAST ENGLISHMAN

THE STORY OF HEREWARD THE WAKE

ENGLISH

or GERMAN

SEA

FRIESIA

FLANDERS

BRABANT

THE LAST ENGLISHMAN

The Last Englishman

THE STORY OF HEREWARD THE WAKE

BY

Hebe Weenolsen

GARDEN CITY, NEW YORK
Doubleday & Company, Inc.
1951

With the exception of actual historical personages identified as such, the characters are entirely the product of the author's imagination and have no relation to any person in real life.

My deep gratitude to
LᴇBARON BARKER
for his patient and skilled
guidance without which this book might never
have been brought to completion, and to
MAX *and* LAMBIE WYLIE,
through whose kindness the first
unfinished chapters found their way into his hands.

CONTENTS

THE LAST ENGLISHMAN

PROLOGUE

THE EVIL PORTENT appeared over England in the spring of the year 1066. In the horror of darkness at noon it flashed in the heavens, a blood-red, hairy star the size of a moon, whose immense forked tail was lost beyond the horizon and whose ruddy coronal bathed all the land below in its glare. It transformed the soaring Dover cliffs into pillars of flame; it kindled the waves that broke upon the island shore; it laid a garish flush on the turf embankments left by the Roman, the timbered hall of the Saxon, the crumbling towers of the Celt. It flooded every city and hamlet, every neatly furrowed field, every mountain peak, lake and blooming hedgerow, from Wight to the Cheviots, from Wash to Wales.

For seven days and seven nights the symbol blazed over England, a token of woes to fall upon the land; a prediction of plagues and wars, of famines and earthquakes, so that men, sleeping at night as in the brilliance of noon, arose beforetimes, and lifting haggard faces to the sky, crossed themselves and trembled.

KING HAROLD OF ENGLAND, drawn on the seventh night by the star's baleful fascination, climbed the steep stairway that led to the tower of his palace at Westminster. The battle-scarred face and arms were those of the mightiest warrior of his age, yet now his eyes were sleepless and his brow was clouded by the superstition that lay dormant in every Saxon heart. At the top of the stairs he paused, laying a hesitant hand upon the lever of the heavy oaken door, then he pushed it open and entered the room.

It was a small room, whose narrow slit windows gave out on all sides over the rippling waters that encircled the tiny isle upon which Westminster was built. It was furnished in the almost monastic sim-

plicity of its scholarly occupant and the heavy tables pushed carelessly against the cold stone walls were laden with pens and
parchments. Near the wall, to gain the full advantage of the solitary
torch, the owner of the chamber sat at his desk, his sunny head bent
in such complete absorption over his task that Harold's entrance had
gone unnoticed.

The king crossed the room and stood looking down thoughtfully
at the sleek golden hair that fell uncurled about his young brother's
shoulders, at the slender hand that had striven so valiantly to grip a
sword and wield a battle-axe, at the beautifully formed letters on the
parchment before him, legible only to the young scholar who had
written them and to the few like him who could also read and write.
But the vigorous Harold frowned at what he saw, and involuntarily
he sighed.

"Such talents were better suited to the monastery than to the
battlefield, my gentle Gurth," he said.

Gurth looked up, his warm smile fading as he noted the disapproval on his brother's face. He turned away sharply, and pushing
aside his parchments, arose and crossed to the narrow window that
looked out over the river. He stood there in silence for a moment,
leaning an arm on the stone sill and gazing down at the tossing
waters.

"Harold," he said in a quiet voice, his back still turned, "no less
than you do I prize the fighting blood bequeathed to us by our father,
Godwin, yet I fear it is not I who will attach further glory to the
name of 'Godwinsson.' "

Harold's frown had slowly vanished and now his disapproval was
mingled with tenderness as he searched the patrician profile outlined
against the cold gray stone, the slender form, the long fragile hands,
and he knew that the moment he had for years sought to avoid had
come at last.

"Speak," he said.

There was silence in the little room. The night had brought with
it a chill wind that swept down from the Scottish moors freshened
by the touch of tawny earth and gorse and heather. It swept across
the city that slumbered within its ancient walls, tossed the muddy
waters of the river, beat about the gray walls of the newly risen West
Minster and scattered the carefully written parchments in disorder
upon the floor.

"Have you not already guessed, Harold," said Gurth softly, "how much I yearn to quit my earldom, to set aside my battle-axe and sword in exchange for the chrism and the rood of the cloistered monk? Have you not already guessed how irksome to me is the coveted mail of the warrior, how little joy I find in the clash of battle? Nor do I take pleasure in the hunt, a sport which filled even the sainted Confessor with joy. For the mute plea of the stag as it sinks beneath the arrow of the hunter awakens within me no thrill of conquest, but only pity; and only pity do I feel at the tortured cry of the bittern whose plumed body is torn by the cruel talons of the hawk. Yet because of your pride in me, dearest brother, I have tirelessly striven to learn the art of swinging the mighty English battle-axe so that it cleaves a skull in twain; I have tirelessly striven to wield a sword with such cruel strokes that the lifeblood of England's enemies gushes forth from their throats like the scarlet-dyed torrents of some mountain gorge. These I have learned to do with passable dexterity. But the warrior without has failed to change the man within, for when the wounded enemy, whimpering like some poor wild creature, essays to crawl away, I still yearn only to bind his battle wounds, not dispatch him."

"It was only in Wales that we dispatched the wounded," said Harold in a hard voice, "for only in Wales did we have to match the ruthless craft of a desperate people."

"I argue not your logic," replied Gurth gently. "I say only that I care nought for the sounding clang of steel on mail, but only for the peaceful chanting of monks within their cloistered walls. I care nought for the grip of the warrior's sword in my hand, but only for the humble pen of the scholar."

Harold turned and moved thoughtfully about the tiny chamber, stooping now and then to retrieve a fallen parchment. He held them in his hands, gazing down at the delicate writing; the painted capitals, blue and gold and red; the flaming birds and flowers illuminating the chapter headings and wreathing the margins. Then he crossed over to the window and stood beside Gurth, fixing troubled eyes on the Thames.

"I have raised you from infancy," he said, "and even while I was training you to fight by my side, I had already guessed the direction your thoughts were taking. But in losing you, Gurth, I lose both son and brother. Give me but a short while longer to grow accustomed to the thought."

Impulsively Gurth slipped his arm through Harold's.

"I shall not leave you," he replied, "until you say, 'Gurth, I have no further need of you.'"

"Since you are my right hand in battle, that may not be soon."

"As you will," agreed Gurth, adding quickly, "then do you give credence to these dire portents of the future, Harold?"

" 'Tis not so much the portents that I heed as the warning voice that speaks within me," Harold answered soberly. "The fleet of William the Norman is in readiness for invading England. His ships ride anchor at St. Valery, awaiting only favorable winds to carry them to our shores."

"Be it so," said Gurth, unperturbed, "he would still have to make a fair landing and fight a winning fight. And wherefore should you, who have spent half a lifetime leading our army and beating off invaders, feel especial concern for this new attempt by William the Norman? All men know 'tis your generalship has kept England free. And who can doubt that your army, which has never known defeat, will stand firm before this new invader? Nay, Harold, your alarms are ill founded. What is there to fear?"

And Harold raised his head, seeming to seek his answer in the sky. But the blood-red star had faded from the heavens and darkness lay like a shroud of death upon the land.

THE BATTLE OF HASTINGS: The English camp crowned the summit of a hill which Harold had carefully selected with an eye to defensive warfare and had girdled with a sturdy fence of ash and oak, joined and wattled so as to leave not a single crevice.

Behind the fence, shoulder to shoulder, the Men of England awaited the Norman charge, their immense kite-shaped shields forming an impenetrable shield-wall. Inside this steel circle stood the flower of England; earls and thanes and ceorls in mail shirt and helm, and slung about their shoulders were the heavy battle-axes so feared by the Normans and with which the tall islanders, because of their superior height and strength, could cleave right through a coat of mail with a single backstroke. In the heart of the circle stood Harold the king. On his right, like an oak rooted in its soil, stood the gentle Gurth, his blue eyes calm and steadfast, his sleek golden hair falling beneath his helm to his shoulders. Behind them on the extreme summit of the hill soared the Golden Dragon Standard, rising to meet the morning sun that fired the ridge and sent its level rays across the plain.

The Normans attacked at dawn, sending up a hail of arrows which rattled through the air, only to strike this compact mass of steel and fall back harmlessly on the outer side of the palisade. Roused to battle fever by Duke William, the Norman cavalry thundered up the hill, but the luckless ones who were not turned back by a hail of English javelins were cut to bits by the English axes at the top. By noon the green plain was blood-soaked and the air was filled with the wild cries of the wounded, the neighing of horses, the groans of the dying, the clashing of shields, the clang of armor, the panting of the weary and the smell of sweat and blood.

All day long the opposing armies fought without rest and without food and so bitter was the struggle that those who were wounded refused to leave the field, but fought on till the strength was drained from their striking-arm and, unyielding still, they dropped senseless to the ground.

At length towards evening Duke William looked upwards to the west where the sun was slowly melting into a red haze. The rambling hills seemed to have slid backwards, lengthening the plain.

His moment had come!

The pirate blood of his ancestors surged hot and strong in Duke William's veins as, in a voice that trembled with excitement and exaltation, he gave the prearranged signal which would beguile the Men of England from their citadel. Obediently his captains wheeled, simulating panic in a feigned retreat. Their men, carefully coached beforehand, wheeled also and followed in what seemed to be a panic far outstripping that of their commanders.

Up on the hill, behind the English palisade, a sudden and incredulous silence prevailed as they watched the confusion on the plain below. The Normans were fleeing!

Then the Men of England made their fatal error. With fierce shouts of joy they abandoned themselves to victory. The shield-wall, which the Normans had tried unsuccessfully to breach all through the day, the English now broke of their own volition. Their shields they cast upon the ground, and seizing their mighty battle-axes in both hands, prepared to follow in pursuit of the fleeing Normans.

"Hold!" cried the voice of Harold. "Break not the shield-wall or we are lost!" But such was their joy that the men heard not their king's warning and dashed wildly down the hill into the trap so skillfully set for them by Duke William.

Once on the plain they sped in swift pursuit of the Normans, filling the air with their fierce cries of delight, wielding their battle-axes with both hands, circling them above their heads to bring them crashing down on skull and bone, severing limbs and heads, dividing trunks almost in two, striking out with such unerring skill that they clove both horse and rider at a single blow.

Yet even now, though this was part of a prearranged plan to break the shield-wall, though the English forces were divided, though those on the plain were surrounded by enemy cavalry and cut off from all help from those on the hill, still the Normans felt the fear well up within them at such a display of reckless and terrifying might. Count Eustace of Boulogne, fear-struck and rigid, failed to give the turn-about signal to the men in his command. But Duke William seemed to be everywhere on the field that day. Instantly he dashed to the fore, and in a voice which could be heard above the battle's din, he swore his favorite oath.

"By the Splendor of God," he cried, "turn and face the enemy or not a man among you shall live to fight again!"

Eustace came suddenly to life. He darted a look at the oncoming enemy, mostly Men of the Daneleagh, their free hair flowing wild in the wind, and reverting in the heat of battle to the war cries with which their ancestors had spread terror along the shores of England centuries before. Count Eustace shivered and turned back to the duke.

"My lord, these English are devils," he whispered in horror. "It were more prudent to retreat, for death alone awaits us here——"

The duke clenched his fist, dealing Eustace such a blow between the eyes that the blood flowed freely from his mouth and nostrils and he fell off his mount backwards on to the field.

Duke William raised his iron mace.

"On! On!" he cried. "By God's Splendor, the day is ours!" And he dashed in among the charging English, riding down those who were in his way, striking out to left and to right. His emboldened troops, wavering no longer, followed their duke and soon, in dreadful carnage, the English on the plain were felled and not a man among them survived.

A hard, victorious glitter was in Duke William's dark eyes as he threw back his russet head and let his gaze sweep the horizon of the hill where the tall silhouettes of the remaining English stood out lonely and dark against the fiery sky. No shield-wall now to break the charge! William's smile was a smile of triumph, because their impregnable fortress now stood open to him. He breathed deeply and felt his heart throb within his breast. Harold was up there, but nothing could save him now! Nothing!

"Harold," he whispered, "already I feel your crown a weight upon my brow. Your palisade shall check me now no more than the desperate valor of the Britons checked the arm of Hengist!"

Up on the hill King Harold leaned upon his great axe, his brow dark and gloomy. He was scanning the plain where Duke William was once again marshaling the Normans for the attack, when suddenly Gurth placed his hand affectionately on his brother's arm.

"Dearest brother and lord," he said earnestly, "it is best sometimes that courage be tempered by discretion."

"What mean you, Gurth?" asked Harold.

"While you live, Harold, England lives," replied the scholar. "Do not expose yourself to the hazards of battle against insurmountable odds. Leave me here to engage the enemy in your place, while you, gathering fresh reinforcements, retire to London. There you can safely await the issue of this contest, rejoicing with me if I conquer, avenging me if I die, so that the liberty which is the glory of England may not be threatened by your fall."

Harold turned abruptly away, deeply touched by such warlike words from the mouth of his gentle brother. For a moment he said nothing, then for answer he came forward and stood before his men.

"I shall not attempt to conceal from you the enormity of the odds the Norman brings against us," he told them. "I call upon you to put all to the death, for I know there is not one amongst you who would think to flee."

And in the thoughtful silence that followed an aging thane detached himself from the ranks.

"Where the king stands," he said, "what man would dream of flight?"

Then Harold searched the faces of these men whom he had known, each by his name, through youth and manhood, for he knew that everything for which Englishmen had ever fought and died was in their hands today.

"Invincible Men of England," he cried suddenly, passing between the ranks, "you, who have gladly braved the privations and perils of battles by sea, the toils and marches of battles by land; you, who have time and again risked all to defend this dear land, its treasures and its hearths, its fields, its humble cots, its enduring things, from all hostile nations; you, who have stood undaunted before the fierce onslaught of the ravaging Walloon, before whose terrible might the war-maddened Northmen have quailed and, fleeing to their nailed barks, have wept over the deep for their slain and sought their own land. Think not that I suppose any words of mine can add to that indomitable courage which has ever been the pride and glory of England; that courage which, tried in so many fields, can neither be added to, nor diminished; that courage which has always shone brightest when danger was greatest and which, when lesser men would have despaired, has led you exaltingly onward to certain victory. England needs that courage now, for the shadow of the Norman hovers like a bird of prey above our land. Be ours, then, the glory and ours the noble pride to thrust his flaunting banners back into the sea."

He paused, scanning the green and gentle downs about him, the mellow autumn colors of the weald in the distance. Then, as though the thought had come suddenly that he might be looking on them for the last time, his eyes slowly swept the horizon and he was reluctant to tear his gaze away. And when he turned back to the waiting ranks, his face was taut, his kindly lips were set and grim and there was an intensity in his rising voice which electrified his men.

"For myself," he cried, "I have irrevocably chosen either to conquer, which is glorious, or to die for England—which is the privilege of every man."

And the silent ranks burst forth and with lifting hearts they hailed Harold, their king; hailed Harold and England with a cry that could have been heard amongst the stars.

And the free-born Saxons tossed their yellow hair.

And the Men of Kent claimed their ancient heritage, the right to lead England into battle and so be the first to die.

And the Men of the Daneleagh gave the wild war cries of their pagan ancestors.

And again the battle began.

Through the air the fatal arrow sped, discharged by an unknown hand and aimed at an undefined target. Winged on by the hand of Fate, it streaked its course in a graceful arc, its iron tip dark against a sky left aflame by the setting sun. Swifter than Heimdall's steed it flashed across the heavens, and when at last the vagrant arrow ceased its flight, it drained the life from the mighty Harold. He fell, pierced through the eye almost to the brain. His frame was wrung in agony.

His huge battle-axe fell to the ground and he raised both hands to his face, trying to pluck out the shaft. But the iron tip held fast. For a moment he leaned against the Standard, then his hand slipped slowly down the staff and he slid to earth.

But now from the plain below came the sounds of the Norman charge, mingled with the victorious Norman battle cries of "Ha! Rou!" In agony Harold grasped the hampering shaft and broke it off from the tip, then, with both hands once again about his mighty axe, he arose from the ground to meet the oncoming Normans who were swarming up the slope in a charge that no human power could stem.

Half blinded, Harold hewed an aisle through the ranks of those who had at last penetrated to the heart of the citadel and were fighting their way toward the Standard. A Norman knight, risking all to strike at the person of the king, penetrated to the very foot of the Dragon. But again, as had happened so often in Harold's long and glorious military career, a loyal arm was there to protect him and a loyal heart was ready to sacrifice all to save him. A tall Kentishman took the blow that was meant for the king and fell at Harold's feet, and Harold himself scarce had time to sigh before he had to turn to defend his own life.

It was almost dark now. Only the jeweled Standard rose high above the shadows when Harold fell again. This time a Norman knight rushed in upon him as he struggled to rise and pinned him to the earth. He was vaguely conscious of someone springing across his prostrate form and standing protectively above him; of a flashing sword that unerringly found its mark and kept the onrushing Normans at bay; of the voice of Gurth, once gentle, now strangely changed, and filled with a ferocity that froze the Normans where they stood and held them in a vise of rigid fear.

As Harold's mighty battle-axe slipped for the last time from his grasp, he smiled with pride in the gentle warrior above him. "Gurth —Gurth——" Then suddenly the agony that racked him slipped miraculously away and Harold, hero-king of the English, had found eternal peace.

But the end had not yet come. The Men of England fought on after Harold's death, falling one by one around the Standard they had sworn to preserve; the Men of Kent, steadfast in their loyalty, staunch in battle; the brave Men of Essex, weary and war-sad; the tall Saxons from Sussex and Surrey; transfixed by spears, crushed by maces, felled at last by overwhelming odds.

And in that last quarter hour before day was gone, before the dark shadows that gripped the hilltop were dispelled by the crescent moon, Gurth, the gentle scholar, stood alone. Without hope, but without fear, he set his solitary skill against the might of Normandy. At his feet still lay the body of Harold, surrounded by the flower of England who had fallen, according to their ancient code of honor, where the king fell, and died around him.

"What shall be said of you, England," cried Gurth, "and what shall be said of your sons?"

But of England's sons let this at least be said in their defense, that not a man among them fled the field that day; not a man but stood firm and fast, facing the enemy and giving his all, till his blood spilled over to enrich for ever England's soil, as his sire's had before him.

Duke William reined in his horse on the crest of the hill and gazed in astonishment to see the Standard still flying. He gazed in astonishment at Gurth, his helmet cast contemptuously on the ground, his sleek golden hair in wild disarray, his mild blue eyes ablaze with anger and defiance and a heap of Norman corpses rising ever higher before him. Behind him, still unsullied, still untouched by the hand of the enemy, the Dragon Standard soared, glittering against the azure sky and rivaling in its jeweled majesty the glory of the rising stars.

"By God's Splendor, my lords," cried Duke William, "does a single youth stand between you and the Dragon?"

Spurred on by their duke's presence, one by one the Norman knights gave battle; one by one they went down before the seemingly bewitched sword of Gurth, who, though with each breath he drew the blood surged from his multiple wounds and dripped in rivulets down his armor, though the sweat dripped from his eyes obscuring his vision, seemed sustained by some divine power.

"By the Soul of Rou," cried Duke William, "this stripling outfights my Norman knighthood!"

"Nay, my lord," replied FitzOsbern, "no stripling, he, but the very devil come amongst us," and he crossed himself devoutly and retreated a few paces.

William looked about him, coldly scanning the strong and stubborn faces of his barons. Beneath his sleeves the muscles rose and flexed in fury, and swinging down from his horse, he drew his blade and sprang toward the heaving Gurth.

The Englishman limped forward a few paces to meet the duke and there, in the shadow of the Dragon Standard, they fought. With

every strangling breath the tensely watching Normans expected
Gurth to yield, but still he fought on. No more the gentle scholar
now, for the mildness was quite gone from his blue eyes and was replaced by the fierce gleam of one who sprang from a long line of
fighting men. Duke William's lips were set and grim when at last a
hero's death came to the gentle Gurth. The duke's sword pierced
him through and he fell. As he did so his long hair wove a golden
pattern through the air, and in falling brother fell across brother and
his blood was mingled with that of Harold, the king.

But strange it was that not a single cheer greeted William's victory.
In silence he wiped clean his blade and sheathed it. In silence the
Standard-bearer stepped thoughtfully across the bodies of Harold
and Gurth; in silence he lowered for the last time the ancient Stand-
ard of the English kings and in its place set up the banner of
Normandy.

"FitzOsbern," cried William, "have my supper table set up on this
spot beneath the Standard."

FitzOsbern started. "But, Your Grace," he faltered, "surely you do
not propose to sup here amongst a host of Saxon corpses!"

William fixed a cold eye upon him. "Why not?" he inquired
sharply.

FitzOsbern hesitated. Unwittingly he had criticized his duke and
now he sought to remedy it. He looked about him, at the sea of
mangled horses piled high amid the bodies of the slain.

"Well?" demanded the duke.

"Good my lord," replied FitzOsbern hastily, "there might be one
man among them only feigning death, waiting for the moment when
he can spring to his feet and slay the Conqueror of Harold."

Duke William turned his back upon him and when the table was
brought he seated himself and supped alone and in silence.

But later, when he had retired to his pavilion, when a brooding
melancholy had settled upon him so that he sat gazing into the darkness, he saw once again the gentle Gurth so gallantly defend the
Dragon Standard, saw him pierced by the sword, saw his long sunny
hair weave its golden pattern through the air, saw him fall to earth
and lie still. And suddenly remorse and regret mingled with the all
but vanished compassion of his youth, and the Conqueror dropped
his head into his hands and wept.

NOTE

OF THE young Englishmen left after Hastings, there were those who bowed their heads and submitted to the Conqueror; others who preferred to quit their native land for ever and take service under foreign kings; who lost their national identity, whose children never spoke their native tongue and who died at last on foreign soil still mourning their lost homeland.

A handful chose rather to oppose William and strive against desperate odds for the liberation of England. This story concerns the foremost of these, Hereward the Wake, whose gallantry was such that even the stern Conqueror came to feel for him a grudging admiration, whose fierce courage inspired the defense of the last stronghold of English freedom against the tyranny of William and whose exploits made him England's hope when all hope seemed lost. And those of his countrymen who in the bitter numbness of their hearts had not wept when England fell, wept at last, that upon the ruin and desolation of their land there shone so bright a ray.

Chapter One

NEMESIS

THERE are no traces left, now, of the ancient roadway that once struck off northeast from the town of Spalding in the English fens to end without apparent reason at a wild and lonely stretch of salt marsh, sand and sea. But at the close of a spring day in the year 1069 it remained much as it had been in Caesar's time, traversing the narrow strip of peat fen whose scattered turf pits already lay like dark and eerie chasms in the approaching dusk, then running uphill to cut directly through an ancient Roman fort. Of this camp, one of the many that had once held Britain in thralldom, little remained even then, save low embankments still tracing out the square enclosure, and, near the center, the ruins of a stone bathhouse reflected in an oblong pool of viridescent water.

From the crest of this hill the whole countryside was visible by day, the grim castle facing seaward from its lofty substructure of cemented stone, buffeted by wind and storm, aloof, forbidding; the illimitable fens, emerald above, a black morass below, from whose treacherous depths arose a host of solid islets where the fenmen built their mud and timber huts; shining meres above which wheeled a million screaming fen fowl; the forest in the distance. But at night, when the resolvent skill of the Roman was shrouded in darkness, the spot seemed somehow invested with a restless, watchful melancholy, as though the fallen legionaries had found no peace beneath the green sod of Britain, but would stir if the war trumpet summoned them to walk again shoulder to shoulder with their comrades in the shadow of the Roman Eagle.

Obscure though their reasons were, the scant population of the countryside feared this spot, called, in the ancient British tongue, "Cruc Maur." Returning home at dusk from fishing or fowling, the fenmen would sing lustily as they crested the hill and passed through the green levels of the fort. If here, on moonless nights, the deeper shadows harbored unfamiliar forms in corselet and shining helmet, they were not aware of it, for they glanced neither to left nor to right. With eyes fixed straight ahead, they walked noisily in their wooden clogs, striking with defiant heels at the fragments of Roman pavement washed up by the rain, yet, for all their defiance, lengthening their stride till the hill was left far behind.

On this May evening dusk had come early to the hilltop as a gray day gave place to that expectant and ominous gloom which preludes a storm. In the vague light the tracts of open country below looked suddenly naked, unclothed. The sea wind moaned above the treetops, bending their tips in unison as though brushed by the shapeless hands of the jinn. Down on the beach the tall, dry grasses of the dunes nodded endlessly. Their rustle was a plaintive, lonely sighing. Further out, deep in the opaque infinity of sky and sea, thunder snarled, low, brooding.

Beneath such an imminent threat, therefore, there was something odd in the sluggish pace with which a group of horsemen moved uphill through the dusk. As the leader topped the hill, both horse and rider were for an instant revealed in bold silhouette, to be followed immediately by the more arresting spectacle of a man afoot, reeling, stumbling, his head lolling drunkenly on his breast. Such was his evident state of exhaustion that his ability to remain upright seemed momentarily in doubt. Indeed, his forward motion would certainly have ceased entirely were it not for the propulsion of the rope about his throat that tethered him to the rider and threatened to strangle him if his feet should become too laggardly. Behind the prisoner, a low black carriage hove into view, followed in due course by a solemn procession of some twenty mounted men-at-arms.

The leader of the cavalcade was, judging by his accoutrements, a Norman of noble birth, and, judging by his face, a man of cruel inclination. There was something infinitely fiendish in the way he played the rope, keeping it taut as though it was in his mind to deny his victim a moment's surcease. He was short of stature, being barely five foot six. His head was inordinately large, pedestaled upon a squat and massive neck which seemed somehow estranged from the puny body to which it was wedded. Of this physical imperfection Sir Guy de Lussac was all too well aware. In an age when virility was absolute, he had learned to detect in the eyes of his fellow men the faintest sign of contempt, displaying toward those who were guilty of it the malevolent and tight-lipped scowl which foreboded future quittance. For Sir Guy, revenge for every grievance, real or imagined, was a wellspring of life.

The wrong he planned to right this night, however, was not concerned with his accursed physical inelegance. It was of a deeper, more cancerous nature. As he rode, his black eyes beneath their heavy brows were hard and bright, reflective of the vengeance he had waited two years to achieve.

As for the object of that vengeance, he had obviously passed beyond all caring, probably beyond all feeling. An oozing knife wound had bloated one cheek, causing the eye to sink back out of sight. He was half naked, for his blood-clotted tunic hung in tatters, flapping crazily about his thighs. One brogue was worn through, its upper now encircling his leg like a clumsy anklet, whilst the foot it had once shod left a bloody trail upon the rough roadway.

Just as the cavalcade reached the center of the fort, the prisoner finally succumbed to exhaustion. Straightening up, he teetered for an instant uncertainly upon his heels, then pitched forward and lay sprawled face down in the dust in a blessed state of insensibility from which the violent jerkings of the rope and the torrential curses of his captor failed to recall him.

"Espèce de chameau!" bellowed Sir Guy, reining in his horse and turning in the saddle. "Pig's bastard! Devil's spawn! Is it your whim to keep us here till the storm breaks?"

By now the driver had brought his vehicle to a stop, halting the cavalcade. Within the carriage its solitary occupant, a young girl of some seventeen years, listened to Sir Guy's abuse with rising fear and apprehension. Warily she slid along the seat to the window and thrust forth a cautious head, her eyes probing the darkness. De Lussac had descended from his horse and was bending over the prostrate man, lashing out savagely with a whip. As he heated to his task the puny body seemed to become possessed of a diabolical strength, as though the pent-up hatred of years was at last unleashed.

"Whoreson!" he raged, repeating the invective with every fall of the whip. "Whoreson!—whoreson!—whoreson!"

The girl watched, appalled at such an exhibition of brutality, flinching as the rawhide hissed through the air and struck again and again at the half-naked flesh. For a moment her fear was stronger than her anger, then, with a sharp little cry that dismissed all caution, she threw open the carriage door and leaped out. Swiftly, before the astonished driver could gather his wits or frame a word of warning, she had reached Sir Guy and flung herself upon him, restraining his arm from further violence by the sheer weight of her body.

"You misbegotten fiend!" she cried. "You poor mockery of a man! If he were not already half dead you wouldn't dare raise that butcher's arm to him."

Before so fierce an onslaught from such an unexpected quarter Sir Guy de Lussac stood amazed. He forgot his victim, turning his attention to the girl. The hood of her cloak had fallen back, revealing a profusion of copper-colored hair which looked almost black in the half-light, and a pair of gray eyes that blazed with wrath and defiance. Sir Guy dropped the whip, bringing his arm around behind her to seize a handful of hair close to the scalp in a grip that made her wince. Jerking back her head, he held her fast, lowering his sweaty face to hers so that the stench of his winded breathing sickened her.

"Well, what have we here?" he asked with a pleasantness that managed to be thoroughly unpleasant. "The young bitch has considerably more spirit than the father!"

His black gaze passed unhurriedly over the lovely young face with its many cuts and scratches, pausing briefly at an ugly welt above the delicately pointed chin. It traveled downwards, appraising the slight form, noting the many rents in the cloak of mink-trimmed cobalt velvet, and finding malicious amusement in each. The little vixen had put up a spirited fight before she was taken. It had needed five men to subdue her.

"Pardex!" he exclaimed. "If you are the lady Althya, then my spies shall be severely chided for lack of punctiliousness in describing you. A seductive little wench, without a doubt. Forgive me, my dear, that I have not yet had time to formally present myself, but as you can see, your father's welfare has been my primary concern."

She met his gaze with scorn.

"Only one man could so perfectly personify his foul reputation," she replied with vigor. "You must be Guy de Lussac."

His laugh was entirely devoid of mirth.

"Is it possible that the amiable Turgis begat this little spitfire?" he asked. "I find it hard to believe him capable of such a feat. Aye, doubly hard, seeing him lie there like a hog in the muck!"

"Guy de Lussac, you are a fool!"

"From your lips, lady, the epithet falls like a benison."

The girl pulled away, and upon feline impulse he released his grip on her hair, half expecting her to turn and flee. Instead, she stood her ground and faced him squarely.

"My father never told me that you and he were enemies——"

"An unpardonable omission, my dear," he interrupted.

"Nor do I know of any injury he has ever done you that would justify this inhuman treatment of him, or the criminal slaughter of our escort. But this I do know. News of this kind eventually reaches the ears of those whom it most concerns. My brother Toustin will hear of it, and when he does he will lose no time in petitioning King William for your arrest. You will be called upon to justify today's outrageous actions, and let me tell you that if you cannot, your punishment will be retributive!"

"The lady Althya's tongue is more nimble than her wits," he answered. "Permit me to point out that all hostile witnesses to our little ambush have been carefully removed. As you say, your own retinue was wiped out. You and your father will be held by me at my castle—incommunicado. How, then, ma petite, will your brother know where to start his search, or upon whom to place the blame for your total and inexplicable disappearance?"

Althya frowned, puzzled at first by Sir Guy's words. Then she drew a sudden, sharp breath. Sir Guy smiled.

"You see?" he asked.

Agile as a pantheress, she sprang, a knife flashing in her hand. So swift were her movements and so lithe the young body that de Lussac, caught unprepared, scarce had time to dodge the blow. As the weapon pricked his throat he veered to one side and the blade carved out a bloody crescent before plunging into the loose flesh between neck and shoulder.

"Devil take you, you little wildcat!" he gasped. "You'll pay for that!" Gripping her arm, he twisted it till the knife fell to the ground, then gave her a vicious cuff that sent her sprawling and knocked the breath out of her. Whipping out a kerchief, he dabbed furiously at the blood on his neck. "François—Pierre, throw this she-devil back in the carriage."

"Yes, my lord."

Instantly two men advanced upon her through the darkness. She lay waiting, her bosom heaving, eyes steadily measuring their approach. As they reached her they paused, uncertain as to just how to proceed with their task.

"Come now, m'lady," said one of them, an aging trooper with a white stubble of several days' growth on his chin. "Orders must be obeyed. Will you walk or shall we carry you?"

"Don't you dare come a step closer," she gasped. "Don't you dare lay a hand on me!"

The older man glanced at his companion, then cast a hurried look over his shoulder in the direction of Sir Guy.

"Pierre, you take her legs," he said, then turned with casual respect to Althya. "Sorry, m'lady, it can't be helped. A soldier has no choice."

With that he moved over and laid a firm grip on her shoulders, whilst Pierre stooped to grasp her ankles. As he did so she braced herself on her elbows, shooting one foot forward with the force of a blacksmith's hammer. It caught the stooping Pierre full in the groin, doubling him up with unreserved howls of agony before he fell, convulsed and writhing, to the ground. The older trooper forgot the girl and rushed to Pierre's assistance, where he was quickly joined by de Lussac and two or three eloquently sympathetic mates who leaped from their horses and came up at a trot. Althya, having estimated the ensuing confusion at a glance, arose warily to her feet and slipped away like a wraith through the dusk. A moment later she was speeding down the road, her voluminous skirts hoisted well above her knees, her legs churning with every ounce of energy she could muster.

Sir Guy turned suddenly and let fly a string of curses.

"B'God," he raged, "the wench has more fight in her than a score of you yellow-bellied bastards. After her, my saucy pretties. If she escapes I'll skin the living hide off each one of you and stake you out for the ravens!"

Instantly five or six mounted men took off in pursuit. The girl heard the horses coming up behind her, their flying hoofs eating up the short stretch of ground. She swerved sharply, heading for the low, broken walls of a ruined building. Agile as a doe, she vaulted the wall and took off across the rubble. This maneuver brought the horsemen up sharply. Glancing furtively at one another, each man declaimed loudly upon the inexpedience of crippling their mounts on such treacherous terrain, at the same time stoutly ignoring his neighbour's very obvious desire to eschew this specter-ridden area. Whilst they were vociferating, Althya reached the other side and started up a grassy slope fringed by a thicket. At the top she plunged into the dense undergrowth of shrubbery and was lost to view.

A moment later, however, spurred on by Sir Guy's savage threats, the horsemen swept in unison down a winding, rutted path they had at first found it convenient to ignore. Urging on their mounts, they took the snakelike curves at full speed and climbed the slope. At the thicket they divided up, sweeping around it in two columns and converging on the other side in a pincerlike formation. The girl was already clear of the woods and was making for a high turf embankment which had once walled in the ancient fort. A whoop of triumph went up as they sighted her. Above her own labored breathing she heard it and glanced apprehensively back. As she did so she tripped on a fallen tree trunk, somersaulted, and lay still.

Dazed, yet prompted by a frenzied sense of urgency, she shook herself and struggled to her feet. She was vaguely aware that they were closing in, shouting to one another as they flung themselves from their mounts. With buckling knees she tottered forward a few paces before a dozen hands reached out and bit into her flesh. She swung around, fighting desperately, showering them with blows from small clenched fists, striking out at the pale blur of faces. From behind, a sharp slicing blow cut across the back of her knees, knocking the legs from under her. She went down on her back, engulfed in a sea of sweating bodies, kicking and clawing, till one of the men caught a flailing fist with his boot, grinding it beneath his heel into the ground so that her tightened lips involuntarily let out a short yelp of pain.

Old François pushed his way through the melee and bent over her. She had ceased to struggle and lay spent and vanquished on the grass, inert save for the spasmic breathing which racked her bosom like hard, dry sobs.

"Easy now, boys," he said, "she's all done in. She'll give us no more trouble. Stand back now, all of you. Out of my way, so I can get her back to the carriage."

He stooped, and lifting the limp form from the ground, started back up the road, carrying her with stolid indifference, her head dangling lifelessly, her arms swinging to the rhythm of his gait, one knuckle mashed and bleeding. At the carriage Sir Guy was awaiting them, an almost jocular expression on his dark face. He reached out and took the girl from François's arms, then flung her on to the floor of the carriage with intentioned roughness and slammed the door.

"Good work, men," he barked. "There's wine and meat awaits us at the castle and a butt of brandy to beguile the night away." He strode back to the girl's father, who still lay sprawled in the roadway where they had left him. "Auguste, some water here. Revive this swine! The rest of you help Pierre to his horse."

Auguste crossed to the pool where he filled his casque with water, returning to splash it over Turgis, who responded by moaning softly. Dragging him to his feet, they held him up by the tunic and slapped his face. He swayed for a moment and seemed about to come to, but as soon as they loosed their hold of his garments he again plummeted to earth, where a savage kick from de Lussac's boot drew from him no further evidence of returning consciousness.

Sir Guy glanced hurriedly about. The wind had reached galelike proportions. Over the hilltop a driving rain edged forward like a moving wall, its raucous patter drowning out the plaintive crying of the gulls who fled before it. The low muttering out at sea was more audible now, accompanied by brilliant flashes that split the darkness and zigzagged down the sky. With a gesture to Auguste, Sir Guy bade him hoist the prisoner before him on his horse, then, reclaiming his own mount, he rode briskly off.

Fifteen minutes later the cavalcade thundered across the drawbridge of Guy's stronghold, a half-ruined castle which took its name, Cruc Maur, from the nearby hill. It faced the open sea whose waters rose at high tide to surround it. Rich green ivy clung to the very tips of its lofty towers, hiding their gauntness and concealing its gaping scars of decay. Below, the huge stone courtyard was tufted with grass and blood-red poppies. Here and there a fallen boulder from the crumbling towers above lay where it fell, to sprout its own crop of weeds. To the left of the courtyard stood an ancient ivied chapel, its cross long since vanished, its oaken doors swining on rusted hinges and choiring the wind with their creaking.

Sir Guy leaped from his horse, and throwing the reins to a squire, watched Auguste shoulder Turgis as he would a dead buck.

"Hold the girl in the dungeons until I send for her," he said, turning to François, who was descending stiffly from his horse. "Take no chances with her. The wench is uncommonly resourceful."

With that he beckoned Auguste to follow with his burden, and turning on his heel, mounted the steps and disappeared into the dark and musty recesses of his stronghold.

Some thirty minutes later Turgis de St. Denys opened his eyes to find himself lying on a straw pallet in a tiny tower chamber almost circular in shape. From the sparse severity of its furnishings the room might at one time have served as a prison for some former occupant, though now cobwebs hung from every available protrusion and the air was heavy with that peculiar odor of decay which betokens long abandonment. Upon a low table stood a cracked clay pitcher and a metal trencher, green with the patina of years. The thick carpet of dust upon the floor was smooth and untrodden, save for a succession of fresh tracks between the pallet and the door. The door itself was of solid nail-studded oak, beyond which a sentry measured off his monotonous paces. A single torch flickered querulously in its rusted iron wall bracket, casting a murky half-light on the concave walls and intensifying the irregularity of the great blocks of rough hewn stone.

There was something frightening in the massive power of these formidable walls. Turgis, emerging slowly from his state of coma, was instinctively aware of this. His half-stunned brain struggled with a confusion of nameless fears, then, perhaps beneath the influence of a rising fever, his fancy distorted the dark lichen growths upon the walls into shadowlike forms which were further quickened into animation by the fitful flickers of the torch. Their motions dizzied him, but he could not withdraw his gaze, repelled, yet fascinated by the monstrous appetite of a witch-wolf with dripping jaws, stalking its prey with infinite patience, devouring in turn a saltman stooping at his pans, a grazing antlered buck, a black-cowled monk chanting in his stall——

"Jesu!"

A searing stab of pain running the length of his swollen cheek brought Turgis abruptly back to reality. He tried to raise a hand to his face, only to discover that his wrists were chained to his ankles in such a way as to deprive him of the use of either arms or legs. He lifted up his head and examined the fetters in amazement, trying unsuccessfully to recall the events that had brought about his present dilemma, then sinking back as his muscles, taut and stiff, shot pains throughout his body.

Turgis lay still, breathing hard and listening to the regular pacing without. After a moment he managed to pull himself up to a sitting position, moving slowly to ease the pull of his blood-clotted tunic on his countless wounds. Squatting cross-legged on the pallet, he scanned the room. The slit windows were too narrow to permit the passage of a man, but up beyond them, reached by two or three broad steps, was an aperture of unusual dimensions sunk deep in the indented walls. Its function was apparently that of a lookout, for Sir Guy, being a coastal lord, replenished his empty coffers from the ransoms of those unfortunates who were unlucky enough to be wrecked and stranded on his inhospitable shore. The lookout faced the open sea, being some four feet broad and three in height. Hanging from it by one rusted hinge was an iron grating made of sturdy crossbars which must at one time have fitted directly across it. On the floor beneath, two iron locks lay where they had fallen long ago, their corrosion hastened by fountainous spray from the breakers which lashed at the sea wall below.

By now the storm was near its height. The wind screamed through the loops in icy blasts, whipping through Turgis' tattered garments. A thunderclap directly overhead jarred the castle to its solid foundations. A lot of ships would be wrecked this night; a lot of cargo would bestrew the beaches in the morning—a lot of broken bodies and dead and dying men——

The chill air had started to clear Turgis' head, recalling to him, with a sudden harrowing rush of memory, that Althya had been with him when he was taken. Holy Mother of God, where was she now? What had they done to her? The thought set him to working frantically at his shackles. Perspiration burst from his brow and streamed down his throbbing temples, yet his hands as he worked were stiff with cold.

Some sixth sense made him pause and raise his head—and he saw de Lussac.

Sir Guy sat near the foot of the pallet, just outside the limits of the torchlight. He was motionless, his arms folded stoically across his chest. His head seemed to balance grotesquely above the absurdly narrow shoulders and puny frame. He had not yet changed his tunic, which was bloodied from the crimson crescent left by Althya upon his neck. His face was as expressionless as a mask, and possessed of a shocking deathlike pallor. He seemed almost to be asleep, except that his eyes were open. They were staring unblinkingly at Turgis, riveted upon his face with soul-searching intentness and brilliant as though with some long-harbored obsession.

Turgis gave a start upon perceiving him, then strained his eyes to penetrate the semiobscurity in an effort to convince himself that this was not another hallucination. Reassured at length that he was in his right senses, and having identified his visitor, he leaned anxiously forward.

"Where is she, Guy—where is Althya?"

Guy didn't stir. To Turgis the moment of waiting was an eternity.

"Guy, you forsworn devil, you heard me! Where is she?"

At last Guy's lips moved.

"I trow the wench is safe enough."

At another time Turgis would have been angered at this unmannerly reference to his daughter, but now he only sighed with relief.

"Then see that she stays safe, Guy de Lussac," he replied. "If you or your men harm her, you shall live to rue it."

If Guy heard the threat his face gave no sign. He was seemingly immersed in his own thoughts.

"Turgis," he said in a colorless voice, "I have waited a long time for this day."

Guy's manner was totally bereft of its former malice. Turgis was quick to note this as he carefully explored the other's countenance. The information he gathered from his short scrutiny sent across his features a flicker of understanding, which was followed immediately by an expression suggestive of the furtive wariness of a trapped animal. This, however, he almost succeeded in concealing beneath a demeanor of frank innocence, even forcing a faint smile as though to prove he had nothing to conceal. When he spoke he chose his words with the extreme care of a man who had good reason to shrink from the discussion into which he was about to be unavoidably propelled, and with the alertness of one who, being forced to prevaricate, had much to lose if his diplomacy should fail.

"My old friend," he began soothingly, "you and I have known each other since childhood. As youths we quarreled, bitterly at times, yet as men none have ridden into battle with a greater sense of comradeship than we two; none have more gladly shared a campfire, nor stanched each other's wounds with more solicitude. We fought at Hastings side by side and even took our guerdon in estates close by each other. Our friendship has indeed been an enduring one. Looking back upon it now, I cannot believe that you would wittingly injure me, or any member of my family. Your present actions, therefore, confound me. You have this day criminally waylaid me, captured my daughter, massacred my men, and have yourself deliberately inflicted upon my person untold suffering. Why? Are you utterly deranged, my poor Guy? Do a few gray hairs so befuddle you that you can no longer distinguish friend from enemy?"

"You are a clever man, Turgis," Guy replied. "You have learned to cover your traces well."

"My traces?" Turgis' well-feigned astonishment was almost convincing. "Come, Guy, if there is some imaginary grudge rankling in that unfathomable brain of yours, then out with it. Do not leave it to putrefy, like offal, in the dark."

"The suggestion is timely, since it was with the express intention of airing it that I brought you here."

"Splendid, mon vieux," exclaimed Turgis. "You will find me amenable, eager to listen to your grievance and anxious, if I have unintentionally injured or offended you, to make amends. What could be fairer? What more can I say? But before we enter into any discussion there is a point I wish to settle. My daughter Althya is too young for involvement in men's quarrels—today being in fact her seventeenth birthday. Since she has only been in England a short while and since you yourself have never before set eyes upon her, it follows that she is not included in your enmity. I therefore demand that you immediately release her, that you provide her with a trusted escort and send her home."

"I see that I must enlighten you concerning one most important factor."

"What is that?"

"That I would have little use for you, if I did not also have the girl," replied Guy. "She is the very essence of my plan. I need her as the grape needs the vine, as the vine needs the soil."

Turgis swallowed hard.

"What," he asked, "do you mean by your 'plan'?"

Guy's face had assumed a distinctly feline appearance, like that of a cat playing with a mouse.

"It should have been immediately apparent to you that I had a plan," he replied. "The ambush was obviously premeditated. Nor could our knowledge of your movements have been the result of chance. How did I know, for instance, that you and your daughter were planning a trip to London? Because my spies have watched you night and day for months. How did I know when you planned to leave? Because my spies informed me of it. And how was I aware of the existence of the conveniently narrow defile in the forest through which you would have to pass? Because months ago I personally inspected the terrain."

This time Turgis' astonishment was sincere.

"For a man reputed to be penniless," he said, "you seem to have gone to considerable expense to indulge some obscure caprice."

"Hardly a caprice," replied de Lussac. "I have given the matter much forethought. It has been my chief concern, nay, my obsession, for almost two years."

"Two years is a long time, Guy."

"Two years is an eternity!"

There was a pause. Turgis had succeeded in manipulating the conversation with sufficient adroitness to have confirmed his earlier suspicions. To pursue it further could add little to his enlightenment, and might provoke an outright discussion of a subject which for the present should be avoided at all costs. Now he must temporize. He must somehow defer an overt clash until it seemed certain that Althya was safely away. After that he could look to his own skin.

"Mon ami," he said, "I am confident that whatever differences exist between us, we can find a means of settling. You claim to have a grievance against me. Today you have given me ample reason to make the same claim against you. At this moment I am so overcome with pain and weariness that I can think of nothing but sleep. To-morrow, however, after we send the girl home, we shall sit down like the old comrades we are and weigh our differences on the scales of Justice."

Guy's dark eyes snapped.

"A pretty speech," he observed, "and one which betrays an underlying anxiety for the girl's welfare. Such paternal devotion is commendable in any man, but in you, Turgis, I have reason to regard it as a source of personal gratification."

Guy's words were calculated. They were intended to convey a threat, a sinister portent, and in this he was entirely successful. Beneath the flush of fever, Turgis paled. With a shudder his mind awakened to the peril that threatened Althya, to a brutal realization of her utter helplessness in the present circumstances, and a look of fear crept into his eyes.

"I warn you, Guy, you have gone far enough today," he broke out. "I shall hold you responsible for my daughter's safety. If you value your hide you'll see to it that no harm befalls her."

"You mean—such as befell my wife?"

Turgis tensed. Below the lookout the breakers hurled themselves with renewed violence against the sea wall, sending up a heavy spray which looked like a flock of floating gulls taking to flight. To Turgis de St. Denys there was something prophetic in the increasing fury of the storm. He licked lips gone suddenly dry.

"Come, Turgis," urged Guy in a silky voice, "do you deny your infatuation for my poor, dead wife?"

"My infatuation!" exclaimed Turgis. "Are you so far besotted, man, that you forget I was your wife's kinsman?"

"A most solicitous kinsman, to have visited her so regularly during my absence."

"I came here a few times, it is true," admitted Turgis, "but each time it was at her own request and in connection with the management of your estates. A woman is a poor hand at such matters, and whilst you courted favor with King William, engaging for prolonged periods in his interminable military campaigns, neglecting your domain for a hunting ground of slaughter and mutilation, your wife—my poor kinswoman—was at her wit's end to provide the scantiest provender for your menials here at home. Your return was long overdue. It must have occasioned great rejoicing by all your dependents, most especially your wife."

"On the contrary," replied Guy, "for her my return was most inopportune. It surprised her in a suspiciously robust state of health."

Turgis gave a negligent shrug.

"It is said that no woman remains inconsolable for ever," he murmured.

"Then my wife proved the truth of your maxim," replied Guy, "though I admit that at first my implicit confidence in her made me incredulous, disposed to doubt the evidence of my eyes. I waited, watching her daily till at last there was no longer room for doubt. She, too, seemed to be waiting, expecting me to question her—to accuse her. This, of course, I did not do. Call it pride, if you will, that restrained me. As the months passed, my continued silence must have forewarned her, must have provided some inkling of my intention, for her eyes took on a look of dumb fear, like those of a stricken doe. The premonition of her ultimate doom drove her to feverish attempts at escape. When these were blocked, she turned to suicide, which happily we also succeeded in preventing."

"Suicide? Man, you're addled!"

Guy glanced wearily about the little chamber, apparently unaware of the interruption.

"This is where she spent her last days," he continued. "I dismissed her women, attending personally to her immediate needs. She seemed to know that this was the end, that from here there was no escape. Even the lookout, from which she could have plunged to instant death on the wall below, had been heavily barred."

Turgis' face had slowly assumed a look of horror. The instinctive knowledge of what was to come sickened him. "What monstrous talk is this?" he faltered, trying desperately to get to his feet, sinking back only after the fetters had cut deeply into his chafed flesh.

But a subtle change had come over Guy. He was now totally oblivious to Turgis' presence. His nostrils dilated. His voice drifted tonelessly on. He seemed to be repeating the events by rote, as though he had already recited them countless times, using the self-same words.

"I had not long to wait. She lay here on the pallet, her knees lashed together with leather thongs which would destroy that mis-begotten spawn of Belial. My purpose was achieved. It died in its own sepulchral world of darkness—unborn. But a vigil is long in the night. For me it was endless, sitting here on the stool, listening. All night I watched her writhe in agony. All night I heard her pray for death. At dawn I watched her die."

Turgis' voice was hardly more than a hoarse whisper. "You're mad!" he gasped. "Insane!"

Guy's dark gaze returned abruptly from its roving, passing list-lessly, without envy, over the splendid frame of the man before him. Turgis was still a fine brute of a man, massive of chest and arm, sheathed in muscle.

"Turgis de St. Denys," he said, "you will never again abuse an-other man's home. You will never again beget a bastard on another man's wife."

Turgis drew a sharp breath.

"A woman can be paid for, Guy," he whispered. "I will make res-titution."

"So?"

"Yes, Guy, you'll see—I'll tell you everything, I'll make a settle-ment. I am a rich man, Guy, you know that. You can keep me, but let my daughter go!" His voice was rising, broken and stifled. "Yes, let the girl go, that's all I ask. Just give me your word that Althya is released, that she is safely on her way, and I'll be generous, Guy, more than generous."

The intentness gathered in Guy's black gaze.

"Let the girl go?" he echoed. "Turgis, you are dull."

"Dull?"

Below the lookout the breakers ran amuck, lashing at the sea wall in seething fury. Their onrush had a deafening, clamorous urgency which rose to frenzied heights, only to break and trail off like a fading melody. Guy's face was stony, expressionless, yet about his lips there was a faint smile. His meaning was inescapable. Turgis understood, yet struggled against his sure knowledge. His heart hammered at his ribs. Horror slimed his mouth.

"Guy, you cannot mean that—she's so young, so innocent," he gasped. "Guy, I'll make amends, by the Cross, I swear it. Take your vengeance on me for what I've done, but let the girl go. Guy, do you hear me? Let the girl go, and in an hour you'll be a rich man!"

The half-smile was gone from Guy's face. All that remained was the gray pallor, the stony inertia. His tired voice was somehow estranged from his body. It seemed to come from out of nowhere.

"Of course," he said, "I shall keep you here. You shall see the girl daily. You shall watch, as I watched, knowing all the time what the end will be."

Turgis' whole frame was shaken by violent tremors. Summoning all his strength, heedless now of flesh torn by the fetters, he dropped from the pallet and dragged himself painfully across the rough stone floor to Guy's feet.

"Guy, you cannot mean that. I refuse to believe that even you could be so inhuman. The girl has never harmed you. Such an act would be deliberate murder. Let her go, Guy, I beg you. Yes, on my knees I beg you to let her go and I'll make you rich. Half my vast wealth will be yours, nay, all of it, my castle in Normandy, my forest lands, my meadows, all are yours. I give them all to you, all of them, all—all——" But nothing could have been plainer than the futility of his entreaties. In despair he dropped his swollen face to Guy's knees. "Oh, God, make him do it," he sobbed. "Make him do it, make him——" His words became incoherent, breaking off into a wild muttering as the tears coursed unashamedly down his cheeks.

Guy sat for a moment looking down at the distraught man, then, pushing him roughly away, he arose from the stool.

"Cease your babble," he said dully. "I have too often rehearsed this moment, I have too long directed the course of my life in a single channel, to be swayed from my purpose now by a few noisy laments. What have you thought all these years? That you, like a wary old fox, had completely covered your tracks? That my arm would not be long enough to reach you? Or did you think I would be satisfied to do as other men do, cut off my wife's nose and so advertise my dishonor to the world? No, mine is a prettier scheme, a sweeter scheme." He strode to the door and flung it open, summoning François, who was hovering uncertainly on the landing. "Bring the girl now," he ordered.

François hesitated in the doorway, an expression of complete bafflement on his rustic face.

"But, my lord, that is what I came to tell you. We have searched everywhere, but have found no trace of her. I do not know where the girl is."

Guy regarded him in dumb surprise.

"Not know where she is! How can you not know where she is?"

The question seemed only to add to François's confusion.

"Good my lord, I'm sure I cannot say——" and he extended his open palms to indicate his utter bewilderment.

"Pardex!" swore Guy. "Are you still a suckling, that you cannot explain yourself? What is it you cannot say?" He gripped François by the forearms, his small frame quivering with passion. "Did you not hear the orders I gave you a while ago in the courtyard? Did you not incarcerate the wench in the dungeons as I ordered?"

François quailed before Guy's fury. He tried to disengage himself and back away, but the pressure of Sir Guy's grip only increased.

"My lord," he mumbled, his face blanching, "I heard your orders well enough, and most assuredly expected to execute them. But when I got to the carriage, my lord, it was empty. The girl was no longer there, my lord."

"Impossible!"

Guy's face was livid. He let fly a string of curses that ran the gamut of all the saints in heaven and all the devils in hell. He was acutely aware of a lull in the room behind him and knew that Turgis was listening, muffling his sobs in an effort to catch every word.

"Well, you spavined bastard," he shouted at François, "what are you waiting for? Be off with you. Take ten men and get the girl, d'you hear me? Scour the countryside. Don't return without her, or, by Beelzebub, I'll have you hamstrung!"

François turned and scuttled off down the turret steps, glad to be gone. Guy watched his descent, shouting after him every possible obscenity and malediction, until a sudden sound behind him caught his ear. He swung around.

Turgis had somehow risen from his knees and was standing as best the fetters would allow. His exertions had reopened the gash on his cheek, from which oozed a scarlet runnel which dripped slowly down his chin. His inflamed face, now little more than a shapeless mass of flesh, cradled the one eye that glistened in exalted triumph. He was choking with an uncontrollable laughter which gurgled resonantly in his throat, like the welling up of spring water between naked stones.

His jubilance stung Guy beyond endurance.

"Save your mirth," he shouted. "They'll find her, have no doubt of that. There's not a man or woman in the entire fenlands would give succor to anyone of Norman blood and how far can a girl get in this lonely countryside, afoot? I'll have her before morning, you'll see—you'll see!"

But Turgis was momentarily beyond all threats. The shock of relief was more than he could stand and his tormented nerves lost control. Hunched over by the fetters, unable to straighten his spine, his ragged garments whipped by the wind, his matted hair tossing crazily, he was convulsed with reasonless mirth. The gurgle in his throat had changed to outright laughter which shook his frame in successive, increasingly violent tremors. Swept on by irresistible currents, his laughter rose, peal upon peal, growing wilder and more raucous, till the tiny room rang with it, till it rebounded from walls and masonry, till it filled all the spaces.

But already a new thought had quite chased away Guy's anger. He was watching his prisoner with an expression in which malevolence merged strangely with jocularity. His curious half-smile had returned to his lips as he hurried from the room, shutting the door with infinite care and shooting the bolt firmly into its socket. Outside he stood a moment, his head cocked to one side, listening to the wild laughter, then he turned to the pacing sentry.

"Neither food nor drink to the prisoner, d'you hear," he ordered, "nor is this door to be opened at any time. We'll see how long he can laugh on an empty belly. I'll visit him in a week. He won't be laughing then!" He turned and hastened down the stairs, calling back over his shoulder as he went and sharing, in a moment of unwonted generosity, his soaring elation with the astonished sentry. "I know how the wench escaped. I know where to look for her. I'll have her back here in an hour. B'r Lady, I'd take any wager on it!"

He was still smiling when he reached the courtyard and called loudly for his tracker and his horse.

Chapter Two

HOMECOMING

THE lonely beach stretched with seeming endlessness in the aftergloom of the storm, its firm ripples strewn with seaweed, drift logs and the coral fragments of discarded crab shells. Wedged deep in a sand bar lay an ancient wreck, whose waterlogged hulk with its clusters of barnacles gave off a sea smell at once stagnant and fresh. The curlews swooped low about it, then glided off as evening neared and disappeared among the tall grasses that fringed the hilly dunes.

From seawards the plaintive cry of a sea bird echoed three times above the pounding of the surf, and after a moment it was repeated from the beach. A man had arisen from his place of concealment in the wreck and was moving stealthily along the water's edge, heedless of the waves that seeped through his buskins and drenched his hosen to the calf.

The cry came again, nearer now. Again the man answered and soon his searching eyes discerned a light skiff being brought swiftly to shore as two pairs of oars plowed through the heavy sea with skill and vigor. A moment later the prow of the tiny craft grated on the wet sand and its two occupants leaped out. The first one stood, his broad back to the sea, his eyes scanning the reed-ronds, the sloping shoulders of the dunes, the dark patch of pine woods in the distance. His companion stretched his lanky form and brushed the unruly elflocks from his eyes, then he stooped, and lifting the skiff above his head, carried it over to the flats and concealed it with the utmost care among the grasses.

Then, in unison, as though their plan was so perfected that it needed neither speech nor gesture, the three men pushed their way inland toward the pine woods and as silently as they had come, they melted in among the trees and were gone, leaving nothing but the lonely beach, nothing but the reeds rippling in the flats and the night twitter of the nesting birds.

Deep in the pine woods stood an abandoned fisherman's hut. The trail that had once led to its sagging door was now completely overgrown with spiked dune grass, for few people ever passed this way and no voice other than the hoarse shouting of the wind and the crying of the gulls disturbed the eternal silence. The hut had long since fallen into decay, for it received scant shelter from the ragged pines about it. Indeed, they themselves seemed drained of all sap and vigor, leaning as they did all in the same direction, as though making a last desperate effort to escape the merciless pummeling of the spiteful north wind.

It was to this lonely hut that the watcher on the beach guided his companions. Once inside, he glanced hastily about the tiny hovel searching for alien footprints on the sandy floor, peered through the chinks in its walls, scanned the aisles between the trees, the desolate sand ridges, the scattered clumps of dune grass. Then he turned.

"You are welcome home, my lord Hereward," he said.

The man to whom he addressed his words unhooked his long dark cloak and threw it carelessly in a corner. He appeared to be somewhere in his late twenties and was of exceptional height, with long yellow hair that fell to his shoulders and a face deeply tanned by the desert sun. His chin and lips were firm, his eyes of a pale blue, searching and clear, whilst his manner implied a restlessness of spirit born of prodigious energy and physical strength. He dropped his jeweled sword belt to the ground and divested himself of his scarlet tunic, and in doing so exposed the massive welted arms of a fighting man and a chest upon which the flaming tip of a Saracen dart had burned away the flesh and left its indelible scar.

He smiled at the other's welcome.

"Thank you, Dirk," he said. "I wonder you recognize us, we've been away so long."

"Ten years, lord," answered Dirk. "But you have not changed too much—nor has Lightfoot," he added, glancing at Hereward's companion.

Lightfoot, who had been Hereward's confidant and servant since the boyhood days when they roamed the fens together in search of herons' eggs and bullfrogs, shook his dark head somberly.

"No," he muttered, "we have not changed. It is England that has changed, with William the Norman in the saddle."

"Aye," said Dirk. "The tyrant calls himself our king and expects us to do likewise. The more we struggle against him, the tighter he draws our bonds."

"How are things with you, Dirk?" asked Hereward.

"Well enough, lord," Dirk replied. "So far the Normans suspect nothing. I come and go as I please."

"Have many Normans settled hereabouts?"

"The fenland teems with them, lord," Dirk replied. "King William's vaunted Norman knighthood seems, in less than three years, to have turned into a band of brigands, fighting among themselves for the possessions of the conquered English. They have seized everything of value in the fens—lands, goods, cattle, leaving only that which they scorn to take or what has been too well hidden for them to lay hands upon. It is a fair measure of consolation, however, that they have come to live in constant fear of us, for many a house has gone up in flames at night above a Norman head. Now they garrison their new domains with huge bodies of men-at-arms who periodically swarm over the countryside on sprees of wild debauchery, thinking nothing of stringing a man to a tree for no crime other than that he is an Englishman. We fenmen keep mostly to our islands in the fens to avoid molestation. Our women dare not show themselves."

As Dirk talked he had scraped away a hole in the sandy floor of the hut and now he drew forth some faded fenmen's garments which he handed to Hereward and Lightfoot.

"God's blood!" exclaimed Hereward angrily as he thrust his muscular legs into a pair of worn blue hosen. "Is it possible for England to have sunk so low? Is it possible for so many evils to fall upon one nation?"

"Unhappily for us they have fallen upon you, too," answered Dirk regretfully, "for you are no longer our lord. You have been disinherited by King William, who has granted out your castle at Bourne to Oger of Bayeux."

"What sort of an overlord is Oger?"

"His objective apparently is to reduce us to despair," answered Dirk. "But that is still not the worst, for your domain of Cruc Maur has been granted to one Guy de Lussac."

"And is he no more kindly than Oger?"

"With every passing day he becomes increasingly violent and oppressive, lord," answered Dirk. "He intends to restore the ancient castle of Cruc Maur where he is in residence, though fortunately for us he frequently waits upon the king at London. He has recently installed fiendish machines of torture in the dungeons below the castle, which he does not hesitate to use at the slightest provocation."

"Upon whom does he use them?"

"On the fenmen, lord," Dirk replied. "His short visits here are spent in cruelty beyond my power to describe, for he maims what cattle are left to us or breaks the backs of our sheep before leaving them along the roadside to die."

"De Lussac is a name I shall not forget," Hereward promised grimly. "What he has taken or destroyed, he shall someday replace."

"That will make an impressive score," said Dirk.

By now both Hereward and Lightfoot were clad in the thigh-length, hooded tunics of the fenmen, with rough woolen hose and leather brogans cross-laced at the calf. Around their waists they wore stout leather belts into which were thrust long hunting knives.

"Dirk," said Hereward thoughtfully, "what of the young men? Do you think they would be inclined to rise against William Bastard and fight for freedom if they had a leader?"

A faint smile flitted across Dirk's taut and hungry countenance.

"It is not for nothing that we talk among ourselves of your military exploits in the East, lord," he replied. "It is not for nothing that we enumerate the battles you have fought and won, the cities stormed, the castles taken. We keep them listed chronologically in our memories, which doubtless you yourself have not troubled to do. A hundred campaigns—and every one victorious—you have undertaken for princes able to pay your price. You have won new laurels and rich booty wherever you have passed, from Jerusalem to Sicily, from Constantinople to the Saracen land of Africa. To the young men, all of whom are eager to fight, it was happy news that you were coming home, lord. We fed our courage on the thought that you could not stay away for ever."

"The Godwinsson did not die," reflected Hereward. "His heart beats on in every English breast." Aloud he said, "And Godrith, is he well?"

"Well enough, lord. The old man is clear of mind and sound of limb."

"And Hugh?"

"He will be at Godrith's cottage tonight after moonrise as you directed, lord. The signal will be a lighted taper to the right of the casement if all is well."

"Then Lightfoot and I had best be on our way," said Hereward. "The skies will be clearing. We can cross the fens before nightfall if we hasten. Will my sword be safe here?"

"Aye, lord," Dirk replied. "I shall wrap it carefully in your garments and bury it in the sand. When the moment is opportune, I shall convey it to a safer place." So saying, he picked up Hereward's sword and belt and reached for Lightfoot's little axe lying near by.

"No, no," cried Lightfoot, snatching up the shining weapon. "She is my sweet, my bride, my wife. We are never parted—by night or day," and to Dirk's astonishment he proceeded to conceal the strange but exquisite little axe in the folds of his tunic, exerting the most loving care.

Hereward smiled at Dirk's bafflement.

"If you still think of Lightfoot as a peaceable man," he said, "you will find he has picked up some barbarous customs in the East. 'She' is no idle ornament."

"Such accomplishments are handy in this new England," answered Dirk, as he followed them to the door. "Nevertheless, if you should chance upon a Norman, it is best to do as we do—make a detour to avoid a direct encounter. Farewell, my lord. God keep you. Farewell, Lightfoot."

The sky was beginning to clear as Hereward and Lightfoot set off through the pine woods. Between the upper branches they could see small patches of blue, and a pale yellow light illumined the green gloom as though the sun was breaking through the storm clouds. They moved noiselessly in their soft leather brogans, Hereward with the easy stride of one accustomed to long marches; Lightfoot with a curious awkwardness which belied his exceptional nimbleness and speed. He was as tall as his master, but rawboned and dark, and beneath the tight woolen hose the thigh and calf muscles undulated like those of a stalwart blacksmith. Soon the pines thinned out and gave place to a low scrub thicket climbing a gentle slope of firm soil. Here, with the aching eagerness of those who have been away too long, the men increased their speed to a trot, until, at the summit of the ridge, they halted and stood side by side in silence. Below them, separated only by a stretch of woodland, lay the fens.

For miles along the coast to the south the sea overran the land, creating a strange miry region, neither land nor sea, but a commingling of both. The fens possessed all those who were bred to them. This Hereward knew when the sight of them made his pulses race as they did at the spring's wild urging; when the old nostalgia rose up within him, the ineffaceable love for this small green plot of sea and soil which, subordinate for a while to wanderlust, had been forced into the background, hidden deep, quiescent, half forgotten. Soon, he knew, the sun would sink into the fens, twilight would rob them of their vibrant hues and a thin mist would curtain them until the moon arose to dispel the mist and light them with her clear, celestial light.

But now they stretched away with seeming endlessness until somewhere in the boundless distance they reached up and touched the sky. Their velvet greenness was dotted by sky-reflecting meres whose open waters were a haven for the millions of wheeling, screaming fen fowl that plunged from time to time to float, in sudden stillness, like water lilies on a pond.

Scattered clumps of trees seemingly bedded in the morass marked the islands of firm soil where the fenmen made their homes, islands reached only by means of long poles with which they vaulted the impassable marshes, by dikes, or by hidden footways cleverly sunk out of sight below the surface. Only the fenmen were really familiar with these paths and knew just where they lay, or where they led. All others wisely eschewed them, for the fens wore a chameleon face. Beneath their lush green mantle lay oozing, bottomless depths into which, if a man were luckless enough to make a single misstep, he would be relentlessly drawn to his doom. Those new to the region, therefore, kept to the causeways of clay and sunken tree roots built centuries before by the Romans, or used small skerries which could be poled through the dikes.

By day the fens were a tumult of sound and motion. Their smooth green levels were mottled by the questing shadows of the fen fowl and the air was filled with their jangled pipings. But at night, after the last bullfrog had wearied of his own deep-throated dirge, they were gripped in a weighted silence, save only when the changeling breeze blew across them from the forest of the Gronnaswald and carried with it the plaints and strange murmurings of the forest creatures.

"I doubt," said Hereward at last, "that a single reed has either grown or withered since the day we left."

Lightfoot indulged in one of the rare grimaces that passed for a smile.

"Who should know better than you, lord, that the fens change only with the seasons, from white to green, from green to gold, from gold to white again."

But with Dirk's words fresh in his memory, Hereward's gaze drifted away to the southwest where in the distance could be seen an island larger than the rest, connected with the mainland on either side by a broad causeway. This was their objective, the village of Bourne, whose ancient castle had been held for generations by Hereward's forebears but which, according to Dirk, was now no longer his, but the property of Oger of Bayeux.

"The changes here are not seasonal," Hereward answered. "Yonder lies our home, yet tonight we are homeless."

Lightfoot spat savagely.

"God's curse upon all Normans—and Odin's, too!" he exclaimed.

"They do but borrow it, son."

"Aye, but with too much show of force. Will they have garrisoned the castle, do you suppose?"

"Yes, but that need not concern us, since in any case we'll give it wide berth. The thing we have to watch for are the sentries posted there to overlook the fens."

"—and the causeways, too, lord. They might speculate upon an unfamiliar face."

"We won't risk the causeways," Hereward answered. "We shall cross over to the Gronnaswald from here, wait till the mist falls at dusk and then go by fen path to Bourne. From the other side, hidden from the castle by the woods, we can approach the isle unseen and be at Godrith's cottage after moonrise as planned."

"Ah, that is solid wisdom."

"Come, then."

Rapidly they descended the slope into the woods and threaded their way among the trees. The late evening sunlight sloped through the gloom, pointing long yellow fingers at the blossoming May and the bluebells nodding in the turf below. The atmosphere was warm and lazy, its stillness broken by the furtive rustlings of creatures in the underbrush; by the hornet's drone; by the mumbling of a brook close by and the high-pitched call of a robin hanging briefly on the air.

It was instinct first warned Hereward that the lower woods were

full of Normans. He drew up suddenly, listening. He could hear
nothing unusual, but the vague sense of uneasiness persisted.

"Keep low," he warned.

"Normans, lord?"

"Aye."

They glanced skywards. Above the treetops to the west the
frightened birds were rising up and circling overhead, cawing and
screeching. A moment later they recognized the soft thud of horses'
hoofs on the loose earth, followed almost instantly by the voice of the
captain rasping out his orders.

Lightfoot turned his head slowly in a semicircle.

"They seem to be coming up from all sides," he said.

"They've fanned out. It sounds like a searching party. This way,
quick!"

They plunged into the underbrush and ran a zigzag course, veer-
ing slightly west. They bent low, covering the ground noiselessly,
dodging continually to avoid stirring the upper branches as they
passed. Soon the earth grew moist, squelching softly beneath their
shoes, and they came out suddenly at a sedge-grown pool surrounded
by heavy foliage. The reeds grew tall and dense in the center, their
matted roots lost in the slime below.

Hereward and Lightfoot took a long leap from the underbrush
and landed in the water, leaving the mud rim clear of tracks. Plow-
ing knee-deep through the mire, they reached the reeds, moving
now with extreme care to avoid sending up a telltale flight of water-
fowl. In the center of the reed-rond they found solid footing and
crouched low, listening to the bullfrogs, waiting.

"Do you suppose the quarry is a fenman, lord?" whispered Lightfoot.

"Be ready, son, in any case," answered Hereward. "If it is, we
shan't leave him to be slaughtered by the Normans."

Lightfoot grinned, affectionately patting the little axe that lay
hidden in the folds of his tunic.

"I'll be ready, lord," he murmured happily. "I'll be ready."

The horsemen were approaching rapidly. They could hear them
sweeping up from the fen bank, wheeling, leaping over shrubs and
bushes and lashing out on all sides with their long whips in an effort
to flush the quarry. The earth trembled as they crashed through the
underbrush, circled the swamp and passed on, cursing as they rode.
But apparently there was no sign of the game they sought and soon

the thudding of hoofs faded as they reached the ridge, swept through the pine woods and out over the dunes.

"Let's move fast," said Hereward.

They left the swamp and strode on with long, easy strides, traveling in silence, halting occasionally to cock an ear or glance back over their shoulders. The breeze blew directly toward them, pungent with the familiar smell of the fens, and they inhaled deeply of the moist, earthy air. The trees were thinning. In the vague distance they had already begun to catch glimpses of the vast, open expanse beyond, when their eyes lighted on a sight that made them draw up abruptly and gaze in astonishment.

"The quarry!" whispered Lightfoot.

"God's blood! A girl!"

They stepped behind a tree and watched as the girl started to slither, none too expertly, down the side of the oak in which she had taken refuge. So concerned was she with the difficult descent that she paid no heed to her clothing and was therefore totally oblivious to the fact that the hem of her full skirt was firmly caught on one of the branches, with the inevitable result that the lower she climbed, the higher rose the skirt.

"A pretty ankle," murmured Hereward.

"A pretty calf," replied Lightfoot.

"—and a well-rounded knee."

A moment later Lightfoot laid a tight grip on Hereward's arm.

"Holy St. Peter, what next?" he gasped. "Has the wench no modesty at all?" and with a merry little twinkle that was scarcely visible behind his fringe of scraggy black elflocks, he piously averted his eyes.

The girl, meanwhile, having still not felt the pull of her skirt from above, had lowered herself gingerly from the bottom branch and was swinging by her hands in preparation for the final leap. Having carefully gauged the distance to the ground, she dropped, expecting to land on solid earth, but instead found herself suspended suddenly in mid-air, her skirt wrenched up about her shoulders, her toes kicking futilely at the bark of the tree about three inches from the ground. Realizing her plight, she tried first to recapture the branch, then, perceiving the impossibility of this, began to wrestle with the skirt, tugging at it feverishly in a vain effort to tear it loose. But her fierce struggles exhausted her and soon, having reached the extreme limit of her endurance, unable to go either up or down, she just hung there in mid-air with her face drooping forward against the rough bark of the tree, sobbing with anger and frustration.

Hereward curbed the amusement on his features and stepped forward.

"Women shouldn't climb trees," he said solemnly, and with one arm encircling her waist, he raised her sufficiently to relieve the tension on the skirt, freed it, and set her on the ground.

She swung around, pressing back defiantly against the tree, hastily brushing the tears from her cheeks and leaving behind a patchwork of dirty streaks. Her eyes dropped quickly to his fenman's garments.

"Who are you?" she demanded in English.

Her Norman-French accent was unmistakable. At the unpleasant sound of it the muscles of Hereward's lean mouth tightened.

"Who are you?" he countered.

"You're not one of de Lussac's men!"

"Lady, I'm nobody's man."

"Are you crossing the marsh?"

"How can that concern you?"

"You must be—or you wouldn't be down here. Will you take me with you?"

His laugh was short and caustic.

"Help a Norman!"

"I'll pay you well."

"I have an ineradicable antipathy for Norman gold."

His manner clearly indicated that his antipathy embraced everything Norman and to the girl, accustomed only to subservience on the part of the conquered English, his easy air of independence and supreme self-confidence were quite bewildering. She frowned, shifting uncertainly from one tired foot to the other.

"I'm in grave trouble," she said at length. "The fact of my being Norman shouldn't prevent you from helping me."

"So it *is* you they're hunting?"

"Yes."

"Why?"

"I don't really know. They ambushed us. They slaughtered our escort."

"Who are 'they'?"

"De Lussac and his men. They almost killed my father. They've taken him to Cruc Maur Castle."

"And left a witness loose to report their crime?"

"No, I escaped."

"From de Lussac!"

"Yes."

"Did you now." He regarded her with new interest. "And how did you manage that?"

For an instant a half-smile played about her mouth, but quickly faded as she plunged into a hasty account of the ambush and Guy's strange behavior of that afternoon.

"When de Lussac threw me back into the carriage," she concluded, "I crept out again through the other door. The men-at-arms were not watching me. They were too intent upon de Lussac's brutal treatment of my father. A broken column stood near the carriage door. I crouched down behind it and waited until they had all ridden off."

Hereward appraised her thoughtfully.

"What's your name?" he asked.

"Althya de St. Denys."

"Do you live in the fens?"

"Yes, on Orchard Isle."

He raised an eyebrow. It had been part of his own domain.

"I know it well," was all he said.

"I dare not go home by causeway. They'd overtake me in no time."

"They likely would."

"Though if I stay here," she continued hopelessly, "they'll catch me sooner or later anyway."

"They likely will."

He continued his unhurried appraisal of her, standing with his long legs apart, thumbs hooked in belt. She certainly presented a most bedraggled appearance with her clothing torn and wet from the rain, hair in wild disarray. Her face was so begrimed it was difficult to make anything but a rough estimation of her features, except for her eyes, which he observed were of a soft, clear gray. She held one hand cradled in the other and the palm, which lay uppermost, was smeared with blood—mute evidence of the truth of her story.

Her plight was a nearly hopeless one. Since she was the only witness against de Lussac in this little matter of personal vengeance it was imperative that he recapture her, and that, hemmed in as she was in this tiny space between sea and fen, would not be too difficult. From what Dirk had said of Sir Guy, he was a merciless man. He would pursue his search for the girl with grim resolution, and once he had her and the doors of his dungeon closed upon her, she would vanish without a trace.

Hereward, despite his natural repugnance of everything Norman, found himself assailed by a sudden unwelcome compassion.

"Well," he said at length, "your method of escape was effective, but not too original. It won't be long before de Lussac realizes just what happened and when he does he'll be out after you."

"Then you don't think he was with the searchers?"

Hereward shook his head.

"I doubt it," he replied. "De Lussac would have been more thorough. He would never have conducted so desultory a search as that one proved to be. You must have left tracks all over the woods which the searchers could only have failed to find because they failed to look. But Sir Guy will look."

"Oh!" Althya shivered and glanced hastily about at the first shadows that had started to fall among the trees, as though expecting them to suddenly produce the dreaded form of de Lussac.

"I suppose you had better come with us," Hereward continued reluctantly. "We'll get you to the other side of the fens where you'll be beyond de Lussac's reach, but that's all we can promise." He turned to Lightfoot. "With the girl along, though, we had best forget the fen path. It lies too far north."

"Aye, men on horseback could overtake us long before we reached it."

"There's another way."

"How?"

"The ea."

"By skerry."

"To Hog."

"Etheldreda!"

The latter part of this conversation made little sense to Althya, but when, with a curt nod in her direction, the two men turned and strode briskly down to the fen bank, she trotted confidently behind them. On the low bank they turned south, pausing occasionally to wait for her to catch up to them or to help her across the more treacherous, miry spots. Soon they came to a narrow ea, or river, running from the woods out into the heart of the fens where at times it burst from its muddy confines to further inundate the morass and form its own broad, shining pools. About two miles out it veered past a large isle, then twisted abruptly to continue on a wayward course between a host of smaller islets.

Tied to the fen bank at their feet were several tiny boats known as skerries, flat-bottomed for fishing the meres and built to carry only two men. Into one of these Hereward, without explanation, lifted Althya. The two men leaped aboard as they shoved off, and beneath Hereward's vigorous poling the skerry darted away from the bank and out into the green, sunlit levels of the fens.

Sir Guy de Lussac, meanwhile, favored by a clearing sky to expedite his search, was speeding back to Cruc Maur Hill where he felt certain of picking up some trace of Althya. He was accompanied by his tracker, Hubert, a six-foot Angevin whose fleshy red face was surmounted by a cap of soft brown felt pulled down jauntily over one brow, and whose brawny frame was clad in a short leather tunic of the same hue. In one hand he carried a sturdy longbow, on his back a sheaf of arrows.

The two Normans slackened speed when they reached the Roman encampment and Hubert surveyed the terrain with a professional eye. As they came abreast of the pool he pulled up suddenly, then descended from his horse and stooped to examine a group of small footprints clearly visible in the rain-soaked earth. After a moment he straightened up. His glance traveled unhurriedly along the road for a space, following the tracks until they sloped out of sight beyond the hill, then he glanced up at Sir Guy and grinned.

"You were right, my lord," he said. "Here is where the wench quit your company, but if she had paused to light a beacon at every step, she could not have left behind a clearer record of her flight. I think I shall earn my pay with ease today."

"Then move, man," cried de Lussac impatiently. "I want her back before sundown."

Again the tracker grinned and hoisted his bulky form back into the saddle.

"Patience, my lord, and you shall have her," he promised confidently. "If she has been witless enough to attempt the causeway, we shall overtake her long before she reaches Bourne. If not, these tracks will lead us straight to the covert." With that he spurred his horse and cantered off down the road, followed closely by de Lussac.

As they neared the marsh the tracks left the road and struck off across the peat fen in the direction of the woods. Here, the peat being hard in spots, they became more difficult to follow and once again Hubert was forced to dismount and lead his horse by the bridle. Slowly they edged toward the marsh, sometimes losing the trail completely and being forced to thread back and forth a dozen times before recovering it. At the point where the trees ran down to make a juncture with the fen bank it swerved sharply, as though the girl, alarmed perhaps by the clatter of approaching hoofbeats, had abandoned all hope of escaping via the Bourne Causeway and sought quick sanctuary in the woods.

De Lussac, following in Hubert's wake, had just reached this spot when he let fly an oath which caused the tracker to turn in surprise and retrace his steps. Sir Guy was shading his eyes against the glare of the evening sun and staring hard at a skerry that had just pulled out from the cover of the trees a short distance up the bank. It was poled, he noted, by a tall, yellow-haired fenman who stood in the stern, whilst a second man sat in the fore. But Sir Guy's concentrated interest was not centered upon either one of these. It was directed solely toward a rounded object in the waist of the tiny craft which was clearly visible against the background of green fen and which, it occurred to him, might well be the crown of a girl's head.

With the boat rapidly pulling away from shore, Sir Guy wasted no time in speculation.

"Call across to them," he barked to the tracker. "Order them to return. If they fail to obey, loose your arrows!"

Hubert cupped his hands to his mouth and sent a resounding "halloa" across the marsh. The two fenmen turned their heads in unison and scanned the shore line, but the speed at which the skerry moved continued unabated. Hubert stepped to the brink of the fen, readied his bow and stood poised to loose the shaft.

"Pull ashore," he roared, "or you'll get an arrow in the belly!"

The fenman in the stern stopped poling. He stood clearly silhouetted against the sky, gazing shoreward as if gauging the distance between the threatening form of Hubert and his own exposed person. Apparently his eye was keen for such matters, for a single instant sufficed to assure him that he was well within range of the bowman's shaft. He replied with a pleasant "Aye, m'lords," and after exchanging places with his companion, started poling back to shore at full speed.

Something in his actions aroused de Lussac's suspicions.

"Now why," he asked in a puzzled tone, "the overly eager compliance with my orders? Why is that churl in such a deuced hurry to return to shore?"

"A trick perhaps, my lord?"

"Then these bastard English will find they can't trick me," snapped de Lussac. "You stay here. Keep your shaft drawn to head lest he take the sudden notion to turn about again. When he pulls in he's going to find me waiting at the riverbank. Follow me there."

"Very good, my lord."

De Lussac sped away, intending to follow the shore line to the ea and thus keep a vigilant eye upon the skerry, but his horse foundered repeatedly on the fenny bank, almost throwing his rider, and Sir Guy was finally forced to make a wide detour back through the woods.

By the time he reached the ea the skerry had already pulled in. The two fenmen sat awaiting his arrival, filling in the time by working industriously on their fishing tackle and apparently quite unperturbed by the sudden interference with their quiet business. Sir Guy drew rein upon the riverbank and peered down eagerly into the tiny craft. Not only was there no sign of the girl, but clearly there was no place therein where even a child could hide. He looked about on all sides, letting his searching glance sweep every scattered tree and bush, then he turned back to the fenmen, an expression of angry bafflement on his dark countenance.

"What have you done with your passenger?" he demanded.

The yellow-haired fenman set down his tackle and arose from his seat. His companion, however, seemed to have remained in total ignorance of Sir Guy's arrival. He just sat there working at his line, his fingers steady, his unruly black elflocks falling about his eyes. De Lussac got the impression he was quite deaf.

"Passenger, m'lord?" repeated the fenman in the stern.

"Yes, I saw three persons in this boat."

"Three, m'lord? The skerry fits only two."

"Then where were you off to in such a hurry?"

"Home, m'lord."

"Where is 'home'?"

The fenman turned and the generous sweep of his arm seemed to envelop the entire fenlands. He could have been indicating any spot on the vast horizon.

"Yonder," he answered comfortably.

Sir Guy studied the fenman closely, vaguely disturbed by something elusive in his manner, something which was not immediately definable. Perhaps it was the faint, incalculable smile upon his lips, or the aggravating ease with which he stood there, his tall, muscular frame straining at the flaxen knit of his snug fenman's garb. His demeanor, however, was suitably respectful and combined with an eager willingness to please which was a rarity these days in any Englishman. If he was lying he certainly evinced no trace of either fear or guilt. On the contrary, his light blue eyes were as clear and tranquil as if he had been weaned but yesterday. Besides, these fenmen were said to be abominably stupid and Sir Guy felt somehow reassured by the thought that this fellow, like the rest, was no doubt totally incapable of artifice or guile.

But de Lussac's suspicions were still not entirely lulled. His face had a tight, closed expression as he leaned forward to observe the effect of his next question.

"Have you," he demanded slowly, "seen a girl pass this way?"

To his surprise the fenman's reply came without hesitation.

"Would my lord perchance mean a Norman lady?"

De Lussac leaped in the saddle.

"That's the one!"

"Wearing a blue cloak, m'lord?"

"Christ's beard, man, don't quibble. Which way did she go?"

"Across the marsh."

"Across the marsh! How the devil could she get across the marsh?"

"M'lord, it was easy."

"How, 'easy'?"

"I took her."

De Lussac felt a sudden savage upsurge of anger which, however, he carefully controlled.

"Exactly where did you take her?"

"To my isle."

"Where is your isle?"

Again came the vague, airy gesture.

"Yonder."

"Why did you take her there?"

"M'lord, she asked me to."

"What did she want at your isle?"

The fenman shrugged amiably as though to imply that it was not his place to question the idiosyncrasies of the Normans.

"She paid me well to take her home and lodge her with my wife for the night, m'lord."

De Lussac breathed hard.

"Did she say why?"

"No, m'lord. She kept hurrying me, though, glancing behind her all the while as though the Devil himself yapped at her heels."

"Who else lives on your isle?"

"Only myself and my wife, m'lord."

"Is there a fen path from here?"

"No, just the watercourse. I took her in my skerry."

"So?"

De Lussac turned to the tracker who had ridden up in time to overhear the latter part of the conversation.

"Examine the earth here for tracks," he ordered sharply. "See if this churl is telling the truth."

Hubert swung down from his horse and carefully inspected the soft earth of the fen bank. Here clearly were the girl's tracks moving toward the river. They ceased abruptly a couple of paces from the water as though someone had lifted her down into the skerry.

"My lord," said Hubert at length, "it is true that the wench was here, for the footprints are identical with those on the hill. There is one set only and they are headed toward the skerry. I can find no reverse tracks to indicate that she returned this way."

De Lussac turned back to the fenman.

"Can it be," he gibed, "that you were speaking the truth?"

"So the evidence seems to prove, m'lord."

"Evidence?" De Lussac's voice was smooth and a cunning smile flickered over his dark visage. "The only real evidence is the girl herself, but she, you claim, is on your isle, and that is exactly where you are now going to take us. It is well for you to bear in mind, however, that if by chance you fail to produce her, Hubert here will put an arrow cleanly and neatly through your lying heart."

The fenman's quick glance seemed to size up Hubert's weight and brute strength, then dropped for an instant to the bow and one loose arrow still gripped in the brawny fist. But it was hard for de Lussac to read the man's thoughts, the more so since his next words seemed to indicate concern, not for himself, but solely for the tiny craft bobbing lightly on the water.

"Three in my poor skerry," he was saying, "when it fits only two."

"I'll pay you," snapped de Lussac.

"Pay me! Oh, in that case—how much, m'lord?"

De Lussac plunged his hand into his purse and drew forth a large gold coin which he flipped into the fenman's waiting palms.

"A thousand thanks, m'lord," said the fenman, and nudging his companion to vacate and make way for the Normans, he went about the business of readying the boat as cheerfully as if the thought had not crossed his mind that Sir Guy was scarcely a man to dispense so large a coin if he did not intend later to retrieve it, or that, however the game played out, the only reward de Lussac surely planned for him was one of Hubert's arrows through his heart.

As the skerry pulled away from shore de Lussac became aware of an almost imperceptible tensing of the muscles. Hitherto, whenever the need carried him across the fens, he had always kept to the well-beaten causeways, being careful to ignore the disturbing solitude of the flat wastelands lying to the sky, and concentrating his attention instead upon the narrow ridge of tree roots and embanked clay which bore him safely to his destination on the other side. On these occasions the knowledge that there were at least a dozen men-at-arms at his back had always been of singular comfort, and the eerie whispers of the wind and the crying of the birds were forgotten in the familiar clatter of the horses' hoofs.

Now, however, he was forced to look upon the fens as his immediate field of action, and seeing them consciously for the first time, he found himself shaken by their strange and chilling loneliness. As the distance steadily widened between the skerry and the shore he was disturbed by an overwhelming sense of his own smallness and helplessness when deprived of the great pile of stones that sheltered him and the ruffian band of men he paid to protect him. Between them and himself he had, of his own volition, placed a treacherous expanse of deep black slime and in doing so, he now reflected, he had perhaps been a little precipitate. Not that he would have considered relinquishing the girl, of course, but he could always have sent Hubert.

Soon Sir Guy caught himself throwing hasty glances back over his shoulder. At what? he asked himself uneasily. There was nothing out here, only the marsh—and the reeds—and the water. Even the fen fowl had fled at their approach, wheeling and screaming as they darted up from the nearby meres and took off for distant places. In their wake they had left only silence, a silence which was somehow intensified by the dull thudding of the water against the boat and the muted dirge of the wind in the reeds. It was surely this uncanny quiet that unnerved him and produced an unaccountable craving for the sound of a human voice.

He shifted his attention to the fenman, who was poling with effortless rhythm, standing in the stern with feet apart, easing his body to the motions of the skerry. The wind caught his long yellow hair and ruffled it, whilst his eyes, pale against his bronzed skin, roved reflectively over the fens as though he loved each inch of them.

"You have an uncommon tan for a fenman," Sir Guy observed suddenly.

"Aye," agreed the fenman, changing neither the direction of his gaze nor the rhythm of his motions.

"I have seen men burned like that before—but only by a desert sun."

"I misdoubt that the desert sun travels this way, m'lord."

Sir Guy searched the other's face, thinking for an instant that he detected thereon the faintest smile. But no, he was mistaken. The man's countenance reflected only the serene artlessness that had prompted his retort.

"How far is it to your isle?"

The fenman glanced toward the west where the sun was fast dropping down to meet the horizon, gilding the meres and the winding waterways so that they lay like fluid gold in the green morass.

"We shall be there by sunset," he replied.

"By sunset! Then when do we return?"

"Tonight, if m'lord wills."

Sir Guy frowned and was once again conscious of the vague misgiving that had disturbed him back on the shore.

"I thought," he said slowly, "that you fenmen were afraid to set foot on the fens after dusk."

"There is surely nothing strange in that, m'lord," the fenman answered, "for when the night mist hangs low upon the marsh a man is liable to take leave of his wits and see things there that were never meant for human eyes."

De Lussac leaned forward, his eyes hard, his suspicions clearly written on his face.

"And yet you yourself are offering to make the return trip tonight. Why?"

"On spring nights like this, m'lord, the moon lights the fens as bright as day. By moonlight it is different. The fen beasties are shy of the moon."

"The fen beasties?"

"Aye, the creatures that come out at dusk to prowl the marsh."

"Sapristi! Are there such things?"

The fenman gave a low laugh.

"Phantasms, mostly, m'lord," he said. "Certainly at dusk, when the sea fog closes in and moves wraithlike across the fen, it is easy enough for a man to fancy he sees therein nixes arising from their dark pools, giant trolls prowling the wastes or demons of the unseen world dissolving into the opalescent gloaming of a marsh mist."

"The gibberish of fools!" scoffed de Lussac, glancing behind him once again and noting, as he did so, that the burly Hubert was hastily crossing himself.

"Gibberish it may be," the fenman allowed, "but then, every region has its legends and superstitions. Isolated as we are from the outside world, we have perhaps more than most, and cling with more tenacity to the traditions of our ancestors. Who is to disprove that the demon Hymir fishes the meres at dusk, baiting his hook with an oxhead which he straightway throws at any human who chances upon him? Who is to disprove that Thor's Hound roams the marsh on nights as black as himself? Large as a cow he is, too, by all accounts."

"You fenmen must be half-wits to believe such tales."

"Being Christian, m'lord, we stoutly deny that we believe them at all."

"Then," snapped de Lussac, "don't waste your breath repeating them. Save it for poling, since that's what you're paid for."

"Aye, m'lord."

They moved on down the quiet ea. A few billowy clouds on the horizon had turned to crimson and the sun was poised like a fiery ball on the distant rim of the marsh. A flight of ducks passed overhead, dark against the glowing sky. Far off a dog barked and the sound carried sharp and clear through the tranquil air. In the meres the fish were jumping, making surface ripples that rocked the shining lily pads, and all around the brittle reeds swayed and whispered plaintively as the wind brushed them and swept on.

"We are there, m'lord," said the fenman suddenly.

Sir Guy turned to find that they were entering a broad mere formed by the overlapping waters of the ea. To the north, where the mere met the fen, a thickly wooded isle reared itself sharply from out of the morass and it was toward this that the fenman steered his course. A few moments later the skerry scraped the bank, and grasping an overhanging willow branch, the fenman steadied the boat whilst his passengers climbed ashore, then set about tying it to a tree. Sir Guy took advantage of the Englishman's momentary preoccupation to make a covert sign to Hubert to be on constant guard, then he himself turned and searched about on all sides, taking careful stock of their surroundings.

They stood at the foot of a steep incline which, with the exception of a single rude trail, was completely covered with trees and tangled underbrush. The trail itself was so narrow that it seemed at first to be nothing more than a deer run, whilst the trees that flanked it were curiously gnarled and dwarfed, their branches meeting overhead to form a tunnel whose thick foliage shut out the evening sun and left it in a spectral half-light. At the skerry's approach the wild life had quickly taken cover. The pheasants whirred up from the nearby brakes and abruptly vanished, the hares scampered for their burrows, the birds ceased their pipings. Now only the wistful soughing of the boughs disturbed the silence and Sir Guy found himself in some measure reassured by the island's atmosphere of deep and utter tranquillity. But instantly the thought of Althya returned to overwhelm him with an unendurable impatience and he turned on the fenman, cursing him savagely for his slowness.

"Espèce de chameau!" he shouted. "Stop dallying with that boat and get us to the girl."

"Aye, m'lord," answered the fenman complacently, slipping a last knot in the rope. "It is finished."

He led them single file up the slope and along the narrow, tunneled path, striding ahead of them and stooping his tall form from time to time to avoid the low-hanging branches. Sir Guy, following in his wake, moved warily, careful at all times to maintain a safe distance between himself and the fenman. The fellow would be a fool, he reflected, to try out any ruse on them. Both he and Hubert were fully armed, and he had seen the tracker fell many a recalcitrant fenman with a single blow of his sledge-hammer fist. With a rapid glance behind, de Lussac again warned Hubert against relaxing his vigilance for a single instant and motioned him to keep his arrow aimed constantly at the Englishman's broad back. But the precaution proved to be an unnecessary one, for soon a circle of light ahead told him that they were nearing the end of the sombrous path and Sir Guy relaxed somewhat.

"Where is your cabin located?" he demanded of the fenman.

"On the other side of the isle, m'lord, just beyond yonder knoll."

"Then," retorted de Lussac, "why didn't you land us on the other side of the isle?"

"M'lord," answered the fenman blandly, "a skerry must needs keep to a waterway."

Sir Guy scowled.

"Well, no tricks," he warned. "Hubert here knows his job. He doesn't often miss a target."

"No tricks, m'lord."

At the end of the trail they found themselves in a clearing from whose center rose a knoll of such turfed smoothness that de Lussac was instantly reminded of an ancient earthwork. The impression was forgotten, however, as they started the uphill climb. A moment later, above the stunted trees, they could see the broad sweep of fenlands, the bright green reed-ronds, the darker alder beds, the meres with their interlacing waterways. Above it all flamed the sunset sky, fading eastward into purple and a deep night-blue and scattered with its ever-changing cloudscapes.

They were already halfway up the knoll when the fenman let out a cry and pointed his finger down toward the ea.

"The skerry, m'lords," he shouted. "The skerry—she has slipped her mooring!"

De Lussac swung around. Following the direction in which the fenman pointed, he saw the skerry drifting leisurely away on the quiet bosom of the ea.

"You witling!" he cried. "Didn't you secure it?"

"Yes, m'lord," the fenman answered, "but you hurried me. Perhaps my fingers were skittish, m'lord, and failed to tighten the knots."

"Then, devil take you, don't stand there driveling. Go after it. Bring it back!"

The suggestion clearly startled the fenman.

"Go after it, m'lord?" he repeated. "I can't do that."

"By Christ, you can—and will!"

"How, m'lord?"

"How? How should I know? Find a fen path."

"M'lord, as I have already said, there are no known fen paths to and from this isle. There is only the ea."

"Then swim that!"

The fenman shook his head.

"M'lord, I cannot swim."

"Ventre St. Gris!" raged de Lussac. "What a dolt! Can a man live and be so stupid? Don't you see, you fool, we can't stay here? It may be hours before anyone passes close enough to hear us call for help."

The fenman's eyelids fluttered.

"It may be days, m'lord," he murmured, "—or even weeks."

"Then you'd better find some way to get the boat back," de Lussac shouted, his face purple with rage. "I don't intend to spend the night on this isle through your accursed stupidity. You're the fenman. You know the hidden paths. You know how to cross the marsh. So get out there. Swim—walk—crawl, but return with that boat or you'll find yourself stuck with as many arrows as a boar at bay."

The fenman was silent for a moment, standing irresolute, his glance dropping to Hubert's longbow, then moving out again across the marsh to the drifting skerry.

"I'll see what I can do, m'lord," he answered. Then he turned and left them.

He moved slowly down the hill and plunged into the thick undergrowth, reappearing a few moments later along the shore where he seemed to be testing out the fen in spots in an effort to locate a path. This, after many fruitless attempts, he finally succeeded in doing, but it was so deeply submerged that at times he was up to his thighs in mud. A short way out, however, it rose nearer the surface and he started to trot, then finally to run at such a lively speed that he began to overtake the skerry. From the hill the Normans watched him, standing side by side in silence, listening to the sloshing of his feet in the mire and conscious suddenly of the unnatural clarity with which the sound carried back to them.

"Those footfalls make eerie listening, my lord," observed Hubert at last.

"Yes, the fens are apt to play many a trick upon eye and ear," de Lussac replied. "But come, the fellow said his cabin was just beyond the knoll. While he is out chasing the boat, we'll find the girl ourselves."

Once again they started uphill and upon reaching the summit were surprised to find themselves on a broad, grass-grown tableland of such circular smoothness as to indicate that it was man-made, whilst in the center of this plat stood an object which instantly attracted their attention and made them draw up with a start.

It was the statue of a hound as large as a cow and seemingly hewn from a single block of ebony stone. It must have been of great antiquity, for its flanks were worn by the elements and the workmanship was both crude and paganic. Its face was unspeakably evil. Even now, mellowed by the warm light of the setting sun, its whole expression was one of unbridled cruelty, whilst the lichen growths upon its cheeks gave it a lean, cadaverous look.

Hubert, pausing beside his master, laid a tighter grip upon his longbow and muttered a hasty invocation to the Virgin, whilst upon de Lussac's face there dawned an expression of bewilderment. Thor's Hound, without a doubt, he reflected, but what did its presence on this island signify? Why was this monstrous likeness set here to overlook the fens from its man-made eminence? As his questing eyes took in the remainder of the scene he saw that up beyond it lay a group of low green hummocks surmounted by weather-beaten stones, which, he thought with rising apprehension, looked uncommonly like ancient barrows of the dead.

De Lussac came to life. Racing across the clearing, he searched about on all sides for the path that would lead them to the fenman's cabin, but found only an impenetrable wall of underbrush. He cast about for signs of a roof. There were none. With an upsurge of blinding rage he knew the truth.

This isle was a shunned and legend-bound wilderness!

Sir Guy swung around and looked out across the marsh. The fenman was some two hundred yards out by now, running with long, easy strides and seemingly knowing just where the path lay. An arrow could still reach him, but since with every step he was gaining on the skerry, Sir Guy held his order. Even as the Normans watched, the path veered sharply, bringing him right alongside the ea and a few yards ahead of the boat. He gave it no heed, however, passing it by without a glance as though already his errand had slipped his stupid fenman's memory.

De Lussac turned on Hubert.

"Kill the bastard!" he shouted. "Put a bloody arrow through his back! Riddle him! Sink him in the marsh!"

Instantly Hubert raised his bow. The string twanged. With a great humming the arrow sped on its way, but the wind was against it and it fell short by several yards. Exerting the greatest care, Hubert measured the distance with his eye and loosed another shaft, then a third, but with the same result. Finally he lowered his bow.

"The wind is contrary, my lord," he said with an oath. "He is well out of range."

Out on the marsh the fenman sped on his way. With uncanny instinct his feet found the sunken path, clip-clopping swiftly through the mire, and the dark-eyed Normans stood still and watched till he shrank to a moving speck on the vast, sun-swept landscape; till even the eerie footfalls faded into the distance and all that came back to them over the marsh was the screaming of the fen fowl and the hollow boom of the bittern as it stalked its prey on the desolate edges of the morass.

Chapter Three

BY THE CAMPFIRE

THE great forest of the Gronnaswald lay to the north of the fens on the far distant horizon, a dark blot on the earth's rim. No man dared hunt beyond the fringes of the forest, for its streams were guarded by jealous water sprites, and the tree fairies conjured up choking fever mists to haunt the path of the trespasser so that he was never seen again. And the fenmen said that sometimes in winter, after a wild snowstorm had frozen the sheep in the drifts and left cattle lost and struggling in the mire, huge footprints could be seen entering the forest, yet none returning, though why this should be, no man could say.

And so, save upon its outermost fringes, the mighty Gronnaswald remained virginal, since even the most desperate fugitives from Norman oppression still feared to take refuge there.

Althya, however, knew nothing of these wild tales, for she had been kept in ignorance of all local legends and superstitions by the insurmountable racial barrier which separated English from Norman. She was in no way surprised, therefore, when Lightfoot, having helped her from her hiding place and having appropriated Sir Guy's own mount for her use, took the horse by the bridle and headed straight for a fen path leading to the forest.

As she rode, Althya's thoughts were centered upon the yellow-haired fenman who had befriended her and who, she clearly recalled, had seemed in no way perturbed by the tracker's orders to return to shore. At the time she had attributed this to the fact that it could matter little to him whether she again fell into de Lussac's hands or not, but she soon learned that he had no intention of turning her back to Sir Guy. As he poled at top speed back to shore he issued instructions to his companion in a low voice, having apparently estimated the length of time required by Sir Guy to make the detour back through the woods as against the time required by them to reach the shore line where the trees would screen them from the tracker's view. There would, he said, be an interval of only a few moments during which they would be unobserved by both Normans at once, but those few moments were all they needed to deposit the girl in one of the many reed beds that swarmed along the shore.

Looking back upon it, Althya was struck by the ease which the fenman formulated and carried out his plan, then she reflected for the first time with growing uneasiness upon the predicament into which she had unwittingly plunged him. What would his fate be, she wondered, if he did not succeed in escaping before Sir Guy suspected the truth? How could a simple fenman outwit the shrewd de Lussac? And how could he possibly hope to elude an expert tracker armed with a longbow and a sheaf of arrows?

This latter thought filled her with dismay and an overwhelming self-reproach. She turned to her companion, eager for a few reassuring words concerning his friend's safety, but was repulsed by a single glimpse of his enigmatic profile. She looked uneasily about her at the illimitable morass, awakening suddenly to the realization that she was sole alone on these wild fens with this creature whom she neither knew nor trusted, whose face was a grotesque mask which she had not yet dared to look upon, and who now trotted, sphinxlike, by her side.

The evening was drawing to a close as they neared the Gronnaswald. The uppermost tips of the trees were still lit by the fiery rays of the setting sun, but below there was only a silent, misty half-light, the perpetual twilight of the forest. The trees grew sparsely on the forest's outer fringes, springing up from fern-spread glades and boggy hollows. Further in, tangled thickets formed a screen too dense for curious eyes to probe, but above them could be glimpsed giant oaks of extreme antiquity, their branches hung with trailing mosses which stirred restlessly in the evening breeze, their cankered trunks soaring like dim colonnades, indistinct in the lengthening purple shadows.

Althya was oppressed by the extreme loneliness of the vista. No sign of a trail or rutted ox path showed along the bank, no sign of human habitation. Here was just the vast and hushed solitude of an unfrequented region. Again she searched the fens for the sight of another man or woman. Again her uneasy glance swept the forest, then, as it dropped to the silent man by her side, a slight shiver passed through her.

"Are you cold, lady?" asked Lightfoot.

"A little."

"Then while we are awaiting the arrival of my master you shall have a fire to warm you."

"You think he will come?"

The man looked up sharply.

"He said he would come. He will come."

His words, despite their curtness, reassured her somewhat, and a moment later he led her horse up the bank and across an open glade. He seemed to know just where to penetrate the seemingly impenetrable forest wall, making straight for a trail worn by the deer. After following this for a short way they came out on a little heathy clearing from whence a fire would not be observed across the fens. Here, silently, he helped her to dismount, tethered the horse to a tree and instantly set about gathering firewood.

Althya stood and watched him for a moment, then slipped back down the trail to the forest edge where she anxiously searched the fens for Hereward. But the fens were still empty. The sky, too, was empty, quit of the nesting fen fowl. A solitary swift cut through the air with the speed of a dart, jet-black against the crimson sky. A hungry bat swooped low. The sun seemed to be sinking into the marsh, and as Althya stood upon the fen bank, it slipped from view, leaving behind a vast arc of auroral light.

She did not hear Lightfoot move up behind her. When his voice sounded suddenly close to her ear, her heart throbbed in her throat, but he made no effort to touch her.

" 'Tis not really the setting sun you see to westward, lady," he said softly. " 'Tis the scarlet sail of Odin's long-ship you see mirrored in the sky. *Skidbladnir*, he calls his vessel, and with such cunning is it fashioned that when Odin is not at sea he folds it like a kerchief and slips it in his pocket."

Althya turned in surprise and for the first time was able to bring herself to look directly up into the strange, misshapen countenance so close to her own.

Lightfoot's face was, like his body, long and lean. His raven hair fell in a scraggy fringe about piercing black eyes, almost concealing them. The nose was high-bridged and bony, the chin so elongated it almost hid the scrawny neck with its bulbous Adam's apple. The monstrous crooked mouth seemed to cut his face in half and from it his tongue hung down, long and thin like that of a wolf and bright against his mahogany skin. There was about him something remote, something fey, something utterly other-worldly. It was as though his chafing spirit could at times divorce itself from his body and take off alone on some mysterious ethereal expedition.

The man seemed unaware of Althya's scrutiny. He continued to gaze past her until the red glow melted from the sky, until the farthest distances began to fall away into the night, until the first veil of pearl-pale mist rose slowly from the marsh and hung wraithlike on the air. Then reluctantly he withdrew his gaze and stepped back a pace.

"Come, lady," he said. "The fire is lighted. Sit and warm yourself until my lo—" he checked himself at the word "lord"—"until my master comes."

Althya hesitated, loath to return with him alone into the forest, feeling somehow safer here in the open. And he, sensing himself to be the cause of her disquietude, turned without a further word and left her. She watched him as he moved toward the trail with his noiseless, lumbering gait, his arms hanging awkwardly by his sides, the corded leg muscles writhing beneath the clinging hose. She was distinctly glad that he had left, yet at the same time she mentally held back the moment when he would disappear and leave her quite alone in this vast solitude.

And when at length, without a backward glance, he passed from sight, she stood upon the fen bank, disconsolate and lost. A little stream ran close by and here she washed the mud from her face and straightened her tumbled hair, then she leaned over and let her injured hand trail in the chill water until the pain abated. But in a little while the night crept over the fens and closed in tight about her. An animal moved somewhere in the bushes and she started up. She searched the wall of underbrush for the path the man had taken, but could not find it. Then she saw him standing there, framed in the opening, showing her the way.

When they reached the clearing she found he had piled dry leaves in a little mound beside the fire for her to sit upon, but he himself moved off to a respectful distance and dropped easily to his haunches. He sat without stirring, completely withdrawn unto himself, his long, bony hands hanging in relaxed peacefulness from his bony knees, his black eyes staring abstractedly into the flames. He appeared to have quite forgotten her, and soon she, too, relaxed, listening to the forest's furtive rustling, to the cry of the nightjar, to the wind hunting in the treetops. Her gaze swept the dark world outside the limits of the firelight, probing the deeper shadows as though expecting to glimpse some forest creature moving silently within. She watched the mist drift in from the marsh and creep serpentlike from tree to tree, twisting, turning, wreathing the whitening thorn and the polished leaves of the holly thicket.

"Do you still think he will come?" she asked suddenly.

The man emerged from his trance.

"My master, lady?"

"Yes."

"He will come."

"But it is so dark, now. How can he cross the fens?"

"He has likely crossed already."

"Then why isn't he here?"

"He will be here."

"Perhaps he can't find us."

"He will find us."

"But how?"

"He will know."

"Listen," she burst out, "I think it was unwise of him to attempt to deal with de Lussac and the tracker singlehanded."

"He knew what he had to do, lady. He doubtless also knew just how he was going to do it."

"But something may have gone wrong. De Lussac may have suspected the truth before he was able to get away from them. Besides, how could anyone possibly escape from a skerry? If he leaped out they'd shoot him down before he had gone ten paces."

"I doubt he would ever think to leap from the skerry, lady."

"But if he planned to meet us here, why hasn't he done so? It must be because his plan has miscarried. If he isn't here soon I think we should try to get back across the fens tonight."

"What for, lady?"

"Because he may have been hurt. They may have left him wounded by some wayside."

"My master was born in these fens, lady," the man replied. "I'll warrant that wherever he is at the moment, he is safer than de Lussac."

She watched him across the fire. The flames leaped up, imparting a ruddy hue to the strange, wolf-like face and she realized now that even when he talked he felt no need to pull in his tongue, so it just hung there, moist and bright, from the side of his mouth.

"What is your name?" she asked.

His reply came slowly, the considered words of a man who knew when to keep his own counsel.

"Lady," he said, "I have no name."

"Everyone has a name."

"Then call me what you will."

"Are you afraid I'll tell it to de Lussac?"

"Perhaps."

"Then I suppose your master, too, is nameless."

"Aye."

"Have you been with him long?"

"All my life—and all of his."

"Were you born in his parents' household, then?"

"No, lady. I was a babe of a few weeks when my master's mother found me by the wayside and took me home. No woman could be found to suckle me, though, for, seeing my face, they all feared me to be the Devil's own spawn. But my dear lady had compassion and wouldn't let me die. She fed me at her own breast along with her own son. From infancy I was my master's playmate. From boyhood I have been his servingman, though in truth he counts me more his friend."

"And have you never been separated?"

"Never, lady, though we have roamed the world together. We have prayed at the Holy Sepulcher and bathed in the hallowed waters of the Jordan. We have beheld the wonders of far-off Mickelgaard. We have scaled the wild mountains of Oman and have even crossed the sandy wastes of the Saracen Land."

"Your master must have an adventurous spirit."

"And a bold one, too. De Lussac grabbed himself a pretty hornet's nest when he tangled with my master."

"And what about yourself?"

"Myself, lady?"

"Yes, what made you leave England to follow your master to all these distant places?"

The man was looking straight at her, but Althya had the impression that he was not seeing her at all. She was reminded of the moment when he had stood entranced upon the fen bank, gazing into the sunset.

"Is it strange," he asked, "that I, too, lady, should yearn to stalk the enchanted white sea-deer that sails the floes, or ride the witch-whale and feel her spray upon my face? Is it strange that I, too, lady, should yearn to follow the sun to see whither it goes when it leaves our heavens, or watch the fairies bathe in the moonlit fountains of Brocheliaunde? And is it strange that I, too, lady, should yearn to journey beyond Cathay, to behold the earth's farthest rim, or, companioning the wind, learn what it is hulls down the world in the nameless sphere betwixt heaven and hell? That, lady, is why I followed my master—because I, too, knew the restlessness that caused him to leave his father's house."

Althya considered his reply, not quite sure what to make of her odd companion.

"Then how, after such adventures, can you both be satisfied with the tranquil life of the fens?" she asked at length. "Do you not sometimes feel the urge to take off again on your travels?"

"What, leave England now—with poverty stalking the land and Tyranny ruling her?"

"Tyranny?"

"William Bastard!"

Althya was startled by the vehemence with which he spat out the name. It was clear that, like his master, he carried in his heart a deep and bitter hatred of everything Norman, most especially the Conqueror. She sought for words that would soothe him, but finding none, she just sat there, held by the smoldering fierceness of his gaze.

Then slowly she became aware that a subtle change had come over him. His anger had departed as abruptly as it had come and he seemed now to be alert, listening, though Althya had heard no sound above the nocturnal forest noises. His gaze had shifted almost imperceptibly. It was no longer fixed upon her, but upon something directly beyond her, where the thickets hemmed in the clearing at her back. Quickly she turned, but could discern nothing in the deep black shadows of the holly thicket. She glanced back at the man.

"What is it?" she whispered.

If he heard her question, he ignored it. He continued to stare intently ahead, as though his eyes could penetrate the night and perceive therein something beyond the scope of ordinary vision. Then, quite without warning, without rustling either leaf or bough, Hereward advanced from out of nowhere into the circle of light. Despite the fact that he was caked in mud to the thighs, he evinced no sign of fatigue. As he moved toward them he smiled broadly and held up one hand to exhibit a large haunch of deer meat.

"Food," he said, as he passed the meat to Lightfoot. "And let us sup soon. I'm damnably hungry."

"Aye, it shall be quickly done."

Instantly Lightfoot arose and searched the edge of the clearing until he found a large stone slab. Returning with this, he spread the meat upon it and sliced it into thin strips, then, using his own hunting knife and that of Hereward, he speared the meat on the blades and set it over the low embers to broil.

Althya, meanwhile, was directing her entire attention toward Hereward. She had expected, if he reached the rendezvous at all, that he would show signs of a struggle, perhaps even a wound or two. Instead, he had apparently suffered no ill effects whatsoever from his adventure with de Lussac. She sighed with relief.

"I'm glad to see you're safe," she said.

He looked down at her in surprise, then gave a short laugh.

"Did you think I might not be?" he asked.

"I didn't know—I naturally wondered."

"How does your hand feel?"

"A little better, thank you."

"As soon as the moon rises we'll take you home, then you must have your women dress it."

He dropped to the turf on the opposite side of the campfire, clasping his hands about his knees, and for the first time Althya really saw him. She noted the long, well-proportioned limbs, the unconscious self-assurance in the set of the shoulders. She studied his face, observing the way the deeply bronzed skin contrasted the light hair that framed it, the way the firm lips relaxed into a contented little smile as he idly watched the venison turn a delicate brown.

"What have you done with de Lussac?" she inquired.

"De Lussac? Oh, he's on an island surrounded by fen." He glanced across at her and Althya caught the little twinkle of merriment. "It's a deserted island—and haunted, too, according to legend. The only men who ever dare set foot upon it are murderers and such who are attempting to evade justice."

"Hound Isle?" asked Lightfoot.

"Aye."

There was a momentary pause as Lightfoot handed them both their meal. He served it up as he had cooked it, upon the knives, having first slipped from the tip of each a fair portion of meat for himself.

"I suppose he can call for help," observed Althya at length.

"Who will answer if he does? The fenmen would detect his Norman accent and leave him there to rot."

"What about the river?"

"He has no boat."

"Couldn't the tracker swim it?"

"He'd have a long swim."

"Aye," added Lightfoot with relish. "It's quite a distance."

"Then what are you going to do?" asked Althya. "Just leave them there?"

Hereward's face was quite expressionless, yet somehow she was certain that, whatever his thoughts were, they were causing him great amusement.

"I think," he said, "that I shall return tomorrow and ransom Sir Guy."

"Ransom him!"

"Aye." He looked up and again she caught the merry gleam. "Tell me, what would you judge to be the limit of his coffers?"

Suddenly, despite the fact that the joke was on one of her own countrymen, Althya found herself laughing.

"I don't really know," she replied, "but I should think Sir Guy is the kind of man who sets a high price on his own neck."

"Good! Then so shall I."

"I thought you had an ineradicable antipathy for Norman gold."

"I'm sure I could grow to like de Lussac's, once the habit is more firmly rooted."

"What habit?"

"Of sharing with him the contents of his strongbox." He drew forth the coin Sir Guy had thrown him that afternoon, flipped it into the air and caught it again. "Only this morning this gold mark was de Lussac's very own. Now it's mine. He gave it to me for marooning him."

"Wasn't that a very generous fee for what you were supposed to do?"

"Oh, he didn't intend to let me keep it. He was going to reclaim it later by playing the ghoul to my lifeless body."

"You can't really mean that!"

"Of course I mean it, it happens every day. When the victim is an

Englishman, it's no longer murder. It's justifiable self-defense." He could read the doubt upon her face. "You haven't been in England very long, have you?"

"Only about ten months."

"Has all that time been spent here in the fens?"

"Yes."

"Then you have a lot to learn about England and the Normans who claim to have conquered her." He ate thoughtfully for a moment. "What is your quarrel with de Lussac?"

"Until this afternoon I had never laid eyes on de Lussac, so I personally had no quarrel with him," Althya replied. "If one existed between him and my father, I have never heard of it, nor have I ever heard my father mention his name."

"An old score, eh?"

"Perhaps." She paused. "I seem to recall, now, having heard that de Lussac was married to one of my father's numerous cousins, though that would hardly account for what happened today. What do you suppose Sir Guy has in mind?"

"Money, perhaps. Is your father wealthy?"

"He's reputed to be one of the wealthiest men in Normandy with a fortune estimated at more than forty thousand marks."

"That could be it," said Hereward. "In any case be prepared to take strong measures to have your father released. De Lussac is a man to hold on to a prisoner once he has captured him."

"What kind of measures should I take?"

"Have you any other male relative living in England?"

"Only a brother, Toustin, who is at King William's court in London."

"Then get word to him immediately. Have him place the matter before the Bastard."

"But such a procedure may take weeks—perhaps months," protested Althya, "and if you had seen de Lussac's cold-blooded massacre of our escort and his brutality to my father, you would know that the matter can't wait that long. There must be a quicker way."

"Not unless you can raise an armed force strong enough to storm Cruc Maur."

"That's out of the question," replied Althya wearily. "I doubt if we have a dozen men left at home, and Cruc Maur is heavily garrisoned." She sat still for a moment as a fantastic thought took shape in her mind. This Englishman—who was he really? She was beginning to suspect that a glimpse beneath the flaxen sleeve might reveal, not the smooth arms of a peaceful fenman, but instead the scarred and welted arms of a warrior bred to battle. "I think," she continued slowly, "that if you wanted to, you could find the necessary men. I think you could find the way to storm Cruc Maur."

"I?" All the quiet courtesy of a moment ago was gone. His features were set and grim, his voice was hard. "I wouldn't raise a hand to help your father or any other Norman."

"Why not?"

"Because frankly, my dear, I care not if all the Normans in the fens cut each other's throats."

"But I'm Norman. Why did you risk so much to help me?"

"Because you're a woman and because the odds were so hopelessly against you."

"Otherwise you'd have left me to de Lussac?"

"Without a qualm."

A heavy silence fell about the campfire, broken only by the peaceful cropping of the horse and a strange, gruntlike sound from near by. Lightfoot had quietly slipped away, and having rolled over on his side beneath the thicket, was snoring comfortably. The fire was low now, no more than a mass of crimson embers, and above it a moth fluttered indolently, then vanished into the surrounding darkness.

"Forgive me," said Hereward in a little while. "I shouldn't have spoken so harshly, but perhaps you can understand something of how we English feel."

"I'm afraid that until today I have not had the opportunity to find out," Althya admitted. "Living as we do on an island in the fens, surrounded only by Norman women and Norman men-at-arms, is a little like being back in Normandy. Your servant was the first Englishman I've ever really talked to."

"And he is anything but typical."

"I did find him rather odd."

"The surprising thing is that he talked to you at all," observed Hereward. "He's usually quite taciturn in the presence of strangers. Once he gets started, though, he's a mighty talker and, if he's in the proper mood, a gathering of as few as two persons suffices to evoke an authoritative discourse on almost any subject."

"It must be hard on him when he's in the mood, but lacks the audience."

"Oh, no, he can adapt himself to almost any circumstances. At need he can become both orator and audience, listening with rapt attention to the eloquence of his own words. But that is by no means his only accomplishment," Hereward continued. "He has never ridden horseback because he can outrun any horse for speed and has twice the endurance. In our travels we learned that just such a race of men once lived somewhere in northern Ireland. Since nothing is known of his parentage, he could be the last remnant of that race."

"Did he travel on foot all over the world?"

"For the most part, yes," answered Hereward. "In the desert he consented to ride a camel, but only after he had said a few earnest prayers and commended his spirit to the proper deities."

"Who are the proper deities?"

"As to that, it seems he regards religion with a cautious eye," replied Hereward. "To insure salvation he worships the heathen god, Odin, no less than the true God, and prudently attributes to them co-authorship for the creation of the earth and the guidance of his personal destiny."

Althya laughed. "Then he isn't really Christian."

"Indeed," replied Hereward soberly, "I hold him to be more Christian than most men."

"Then how did he come to adopt the Norse religion?"

"He claims, though his reasoning has always been obscure, that his mother was a Norsewoman." Hereward smiled at her suddenly. "I discount the theory, though, that he ever had a mother at all. I claim he was sprung from the wind and the earth and the rocks."

"In any case, he is quite devoted to you."

"Aye, we are like brothers."

Althya leaned forward.

"I'm glad you don't look like brothers," she whispered between snores.

By now the fire had burned itself out and had shrunk to a tiny heap of white ashes. The dense, gloom-haunted jungle about them had been transformed by the rising moon, whose mercurial light flooded the forest and revealed all its native wildness and beauty. Even the ageless oaks seemed to have taken on greater height, their trunks black and silhouetted with crystalline sharpness, their boughs more intricately patterned against the sky. Roofed in foliage, the scene called to mind the columned aisles and transept of a vast cathedral, and here, Althya reflected, one's fancy could easily take wing, traveling unobstructed into the farthest distances to where the outlines of the trees grew vague and dim and were lost at last in an opalescent haze. A gust of wind sweeping in from the fens stirred the trailing mosses and set the whole forest to murmuring, then somewhere in the foliage above the clearing a nightingale sang, wild and sweet, and the murmuring ceased, as though even the forest had paused to listen, awe-struck at the sharp agony of his love song.

Althya became aware suddenly that the fenman had been watching her closely across the short space that separated them. She was glad, now, that she had thought to wash her face and smooth her tumbled hair, though that this should matter to her was something she realized with no little surprise.

"What did you say your name was?" he asked.

"Althya de St. Denys."

"Did your father fight at Hastings?"

"Yes, our island here in the fens is his Hastings guerdon."

"Orchard Isle, you said." He paused. "That is rightfully the property of an Englishman whose family has held it for generations."

"His name was Hereward Leofricsson, but he was dispossessed by King William."

"On the grounds of being an Englishman?"

"I know very little about these confiscations," answered Althya, "but my father risked life and limb for William on the battlefield and in such cases a land grant is both just and legal."

"In English eyes it is neither just nor legal that one man should be dispossessed of his patrimony so that another may be invested with it," said Hereward. "But, to indulge in conquest, William has had to close his eyes to law and justice. Even his so-called kingship is nothing but a brazen-faced piece of legal fiction, since according to English law our kings must be freely elected by the people. William the Norman was never so elected. He usurped the crown by military force. He neither speaks our tongue nor knows our laws. He looks upon England as one vast heap of booty with which to enrich himself and reward his followers according to their merit and their rank."

"What you're saying," cried Althya hotly, "is that William has committed himself to wholesale robbery."

"Aye, the robbery and oppression of an entire nation." He spoke quietly, but there was an intensity in his voice that held her. "Have you ever wondered what became of those dispossessed Englishmen?"

"They were taken into service by the Normans."

"Being stripped of all they possessed," he told her, "and having no way to provide the merest crust of bread for their starving wives and children, they were driven to commit themselves and their families to the 'protection' of some Norman overlord. Thus they bound themselves to serfdom on what, in many cases, was their ancestral estate. Today a Norman owns an Englishman as he would a horse or a cow or a pig. He uses him to plow his fields or make him over to a creditor in payment of a debt. If the debt is small, the creditor may find himself in possession of one half an Englishman, for any quantity of English flesh is considered to be lawful tender."

"The oppressed state of his English subjects no doubt causes the king great anxiety," retorted Althya, "and may take time to correct. But however bitter the truth may sound to you, it is nevertheless a fact that William won England fairly on the battlefield of Hastings and England is now unequivocally his."

Hereward leaned over and picked up a handful of loam in one large brown hand. Thoughtfully he crushed it, letting it run out through his fingers.

"This," he said, "is England, and it cannot be won on any battlefield. William may dispossess every last Englishman. He may rewrite our laws and bastardize our tongue. He may seize our gold and lock it in his treasure chest. He may deprive us of every national heritage except the one we prize the most—the soil our fathers died to defend. It is the one thing he cannot take from us because he cannot gather up every clod of earth and place it under lock and key. This soil may be all that remains to us, but it is the weapon that will defeat him in the end."

"Such a hope is futile. William knew how to conquer England and he will know how to hold it."

"How long," asked Hereward, "can he hold it? For the duration of his lifetime? Until seven feet of ground is the utmost limit of his holding? And can he ever really feel the land is his? No, my dear Norman lady. Even William cannot kill a nation. Even William cannot completely crush the English spirit. So long as England lies stretched out beneath the English sky, so long as her own sons can kneel and plunge their hands into her soil, there is something left for Englishmen to fight for and to love."

For once Althya could find no answer. She had never before asked herself what it felt like to be English—and oppressed. It had never occurred to her to question either the justice of the Conquest or

William's right to hold by violence and bloodshed the land he had taken by violence and bloodshed. Now, however, the Englishman's words confused her and left her with a vague sense of doubt that admitted of no verbal elucidation.

"Your man wouldn't tell me your name," she said gently. "Will you?"

"What is a name? I am an Englishman."

"An Englishman——"

"Aye, can William say as much?"

They smiled at each other suddenly across the dead campfire, their national enmity once again forgotten, and just then Lightfoot approached, leading Sir Guy's horse by the bridle.

"The moon is high, master," he said. "We have tarried overlong. It is past time for us to leave."

So Hereward took Althya up behind him on the horse, and with Lightfoot trotting at his heels, left the forest and set off in a southerly direction. The starlit sky hung low above the fens and the moon, round and bright, silvered the meres and lit the landscape to its vast sky-skirted horizon. On all sides could be seen the dim shapes of islands firmly bedded in the morass, upon which stood an occasional fenman's cot, its roof thatched and left with fringes hanging ragged like a stubby beard. In a tiny island meadow a few scattered sheep lay like white boulders beneath the blossoming cherry trees. The warm night breeze was fragrant with mint. It played over the reeds and bog grasses and stirred the golden flag iris dreaming by the waterside. It ruffled the meres and set them to glittering, then in a moment it was gone and the land was still.

And as they rode Hereward told her of the fallen forest that lay beneath the fen, of the hulls of ancient boats which had been found buried in the silt, together with battle-axes and war shields of curious design whose runic inscriptions were undecipherable. He told her of the fenmen's mighty forbears who, plunder-bent, had set out centuries before from the tall fir forests of their native Denmark to roam the seas in their dragon-ships. Wild and reckless men they were, too, he said. They laughed at the storm blasts that blew them off their course; they laughed at the ocean's wrath that shivered their long-ships on the rocks and left them stranded on some hostile beach. "Kings of the Sea," they called themselves and went down in battle with the name of their war god, Thor, upon their lips.

"Many a dragon-ship," he told her, "found its way into these fens in those far-off days when England was still known to mariners as the Isle of Honey. And springing from their crafts, these fierce men, with flowing hair and reckless laughter, pushed inland, intent upon conquest. Fierce they were, but gentle, too, for the ever-changing beauties of the Isle of Honey soothed their restless spirits, and hanging up their ivory war horns and shields of polished steel, they stayed to make their homes here, tamed at last by the very land they had come to conquer."

And as Hereward talked Althya watched him from beneath her hood, observing his every mannerism; the way he sat his horse, his profile etched against the sky, the strange lilting quality that came into his voice when he spoke about the fens. But she listened in silence, for she was coming to understand by slow degrees what it meant to this man to have lost to an alien race the land he loved so well.

And when at last they reached her home, approaching it, not by the new causeway, but hidden from the guards by a grove of willow trees, Lightfoot stood silently by whilst Hereward lifted her down from the horse and set her on the ground.

"Good-by, Althya," he said.

"Good-by," she answered, thinking as she spoke that it was the first time he had called her by name. "You've both been very kind and I'm so grateful. I should like to see you again."

"At present," he said, "our paths lie far apart. But I shall be back."

"When?"

"Before too long."

He tarried a moment, smiling down at her, then he turned, and remounting his horse, started back across the fens with Lightfoot at his heels. He rode slowly, easy in the saddle, his long hair flying free, his face lifted slightly as though to scent the rushing breeze.

And Althya stood alone upon the shore and watched him go, and wished herself back again by the campfire in the forest.

Chapter Four

ACTION BY MOONLIGHT

AN HOUR later an old man sat alone in his cottage in the village of Bourne, his fingers busy with the tunic he was mending. He did not seem to be aware that the patch was red and the tunic blue. Indeed, his mind was obviously not on his work at all, but on the thin taper that weakly lit his little room; on the window; on the sound of footfalls approaching and receding on the cobblestones without. His skin was brown and weather-beaten, and where his silken beard had once been there now grew a stubble which looked like a soft white fungus on the bark of an ancient tree.

He turned his head slightly to make sure the taper was at the correct angle. If its light fell to the left of the street without, "he" would know there was danger and would go away. But if it fell to the right, then "he" would know all was well and would enter. And so the minutes passed.

No sound split the heavy silence of the night. No movement. Not the slightest rustling. Yet the old man knew "he" was there, standing in the doorway. For an instant he raised his eyes to meet the other's gaze. Cautiously he laid aside his work and blew out the taper so that no passer-by could glance within. Then he spoke.

"Hereward Leofricsson," he said softly, "the years fall away at the sight of you."

Hereward came into the room, and clasping the old man's hands in both his own, smiled down at him.

"Then I have not changed too much since you taught me the craft of the forester in my youth?" he asked.

"Only that the boy went away, but the man returned."

Hereward laughed. "Ah, Godrith, it's good to be home."

"Though 'tis not the homecoming we could have wished for you, my young lord," the old man murmured regretfully.

"What matters? I have already been in England long enough to have become inured to the state of things."

"So I guessed a week ago when your messenger arrived and I learned to my surprise that he was a Yorkshireman. How long have you been in England—and where?"

"Three months—in Northumberland."

"Why Northumberland, lord?"

"Because the north is the chink in the Bastard's armor," answered Hereward. "William has been unable to consolidate his position north of the Humber. As yet his new fortress at York is the extreme limit of the Conquest, for beyond that the terrain is wild and trackless, sparsely populated by men who are savagely hostile to him, or to anyone else who threatens their independence. The Bastard has so far feared to invade this portion of his so-called kingdom, realizing the insurmountable obstacles that would confront an army unfamiliar with it."

"So?"

"Such terrain is the natural springboard for revolt."

"Ah!" Thoughtfully Godrith crossed to the closet, returning with two horns of heather ale. "From whence would you recruit an army? A general movement of men from the south or the midlands would be instantly noted by the Normans and act as a forewarning."

"We will have to rely at first on the Northumbrians."

"But they are staunch partisans of the House of Siward," objected Godrith. "It seems unlikely, lord, that they will heed the call to arms of a Leofricsson."

"The call to arms has already been issued—in the name of Waltheof, Siward's son. The Northumbrians are obeying the summons and flocking to the muster."

"But what will happen when they learn that Earl Waltheof is not there, but is still the Bastard's prisoner in London—his willing captive-guest, so it is said, and glad enough to exchange an impoverished freedom for the physical comforts of the royal court."

"Word has passed between us," Hereward answered. "Waltheof has agreed to find a way to join us as soon as I send him assurance that plans for rebellion are complete."

"He expects to escape!" exclaimed Godrith. "Then have you not heard, lord, that fear of the Londoners has recently forced the king to transfer his court to the Tower? How can Earl Waltheof escape from there? How is it possible for you even to get further word with him?"

"There are ways, my friend, for a man of courage and nimble wits to penetrate the Tower precincts and gain the earl's ear," answered Hereward. "Hugh has courage and wits aplenty, but above all he has a loyal English heart. Hugh is the man to carry the message, Godrith, which is why I sent word for him to join us tonight. Is he not here?"

"Hugh?" Godrith was silent for a moment, then he shook his head. "My son cannot carry your message, lord," he said at length.

Something in the old man's voice made Hereward search his face through the dimness. "Why not?" he asked.

For answer the old man led Hereward over to the window that looked up to the massive pile that was Hereward's childhood home, the Castle of Bourne. Its massive outlines were stark against the night sky and the moon's clear light illuminated the castle keep.

The tower stood gaunt and stern, the work of primitive Celtic hands having little care for the uniformity of their stonework, yet a whimsical delight in the unusual, for they had fashioned windows of a curious pyramidal shape, from above which the stone face of some strange and forgotten deity kept its watch. Above its flat roof and rising high above its battlements for all the world to see hung the mangled, limp form of a man, suspended from a gibbet erected hastily for the purpose. There was a gentle breeze and the chains that held him creaked plaintively in the clear night air.

Hereward turned from the window, scarcely able to believe what was so clearly there for him to see. The old man had moved up behind him and in the hard moonlight Hereward was shocked to see how grim and terrible were his eyes.

"How did it happen, Godrith?" he asked.

"Hereward Leofricsson," replied the old man sadly, "this is spring, a time of plenty. This is a time when the fledgling quail abound in every bush; when the white-coated ewes our fathers bred crop the rich meadow grasses, while a lamb on trembling legs bleats by her side, and yet we starve. This is a time when the fish dart like myriad silver arrows through the sun-flecked streams; when the sleepy pike and perch await the angler in every grassy-margined mere, and yet we starve. This is a time when the hart and the roe pause, heedless of danger, to scent the languorous air of every dim forest hollow, and yet we starve."

Hereward turned in sudden anger and strode about the little room.

"You starve because the streams and the forests, which were always free, are free no longer," he cried. "They are trying to drive you by hunger to fling yourselves at the feet of your Norman overlord, and placing your hands in his hands, take him for your lord, and his king for your king."

"Aye, lord."

"And Hugh was caught hunting?"

Godrith nodded his white head sadly.

"Our shelves were bare, lord, but our pride was stubborn."

"When did it happen?"

"Yesterday," replied the old man. "Hugh had been gone since dawn, and as the morning advanced I felt a great fear within me. About the hour of noon a silent crowd gathered in the square before the castle. Something drew me to the spot."

Godrith paused. He turned and walked back into the room, and when next he spoke, his voice came to Hereward from out of the darkness.

"The midday sun was hot, lord, hot and bright. I pushed my way through the crowd and there on the cobbled square before the castle gate a shadow was cast by the sun, the shadow of a limp and swaying form hanging from a gibbet. I stood quite still, afraid of what I'd see if I raised my eyes."

"Go on."

"You know the rest. His hands were tied behind his back. He wore no shoes, for the torturer had removed them. His green tunic, torn and ragged, hung about him, barely concealing his once sturdy frame. They say he had been put in the crucethouse before they hung him up there."

"The crucethouse?"

"Aye, lord, a machine their fiendish minds have conjured up. A chest, short and narrow, filled with sharp stones so that the man within is crushed and his limbs broken."

"I have seen the like in the East," murmured Hereward.

"But those who killed Hugh knew nothing of the stoutness of his heart, for in that limp and swaying form there was no surrender, only defiance. And defiance was mingled with the silent mourning of the crowd."

"They shall pay for this, Godrith," said Hereward. "That I vow!"

"Nay, Hereward Leofricsson," cried the old man in alarm. "There must be no mischief at Bourne on this account, for the castle is garrisoned with from twenty to thirty men. There would be no hope for a man alone."

"I shall not be alone," replied Hereward shortly. "Martin Lightfoot awaits without."

At this the old man sighed, for he knew of old that it would be useless to argue with Hereward Leofricsson.

"Then let me at least find you two good horses with which to make your escape," he begged.

"Ah, Godrith," cried Hereward, "did you not yourself teach me to know the fens, to know each hidden path? How far apart each bulrush stood from his brother? The depth of every mere? The exact contour of each reedy isle? And think you that I have been able to forget them in these ten years? No, it is not a horse I have need of now. It is a trusty man to take my message to London."

"Then your need is already filled, my lord. A man awaits without, Letwold by name."

"Letwold? The name is strange to me."

"Aye, you would not know him, for he is not from these parts, but hails from Sussex. He is a freed serf of Harold Godwinsson."

"How long has he been free?"

"He was freed on the eve of Hastings," replied Godrith. "The story goes that the traditional ceremony of freedom was not performed, for, it being the eve of battle, Harold could not take him to a spot where four roads met, and placing within his hand the sword of the freeman, bid him go whither he would. But just as truly as if the ceremony had been performed, Letwold is a free man."

And Hereward listened with interest as Godrith rapidly told him a strange tale; of how Harold's serf had visited the English camp on the night preceding the great battle; of his meeting with the king; of how Harold had freed him from serfdom, placing his own jeweled chain about Letwold's neck to prove the serf's new freedom in the event that he himself should not survive the battle.

"Happily for the success of the many missions Letwold has already performed for us," continued Godrith, "he clearly exhibits the marks of his former serfdom, which, combined with a cleverly assumed attitude of servility and gratitude, quells any suspicions the Normans might have concerning him. Many are the services he has wrought for us in the name of Harold, his lord, for great was the love he bore him."

"And this jeweled chain?" asked Hereward. "Where is it now?"

"He carries it faithfully upon his person and never parts with it."

"That is strange," said Hereward, "for in truth there would be nothing to prevent him from taking ship to Flanders where men from all walks of life are made welcome, and there living in princely style upon its proceeds. Is he well known to you?"

"Aye, for these past two years," replied Godrith. "And when he is away—a manor to be fired above a Norman's head or a lordly food train to be ambushed—he leaves his son here and my granddaughter, Edgitha, cares for him; a poorly, witless child of eight who utters never a word, but of whom this Letwold is passionately fond since it is all the Normans have left him."

"Call him in," said Hereward suddenly.

Godrith went to the door and beckoned to a beggar who had been sitting miserably on the cobblestones. Slowly he arose and shuffled into the cottage, but once within the room he dropped both shuffle and stoop. Hereward appraised him; the tall and wiry form; the large, coarse hands that told of serfdom; the filthy clothes that barely concealed his muscular frame. But serfdom had in no way dulled the independent fire of the Celt that lingered in his eye, or the native intelligence that lighted the nondescript features.

"Godrith tells me that you are from Sussex," began Hereward.

"Aye, my lord," Letwold replied. "As the Normans progressed I fled before them, bringing my son to the safety of the fenlands."

"He tells me also that you are in possession of a chain given to you by Harold Godwinsson."

For answer Letwold unfastened the filthy garments at his throat, revealing to Hereward's astonished eyes a massive golden chain upon whose every link sparkled a precious gem. Suspended from it was an amulet; a single sapphire of fantastic size, upon which was graven, in strange and unfamiliar hieroglyphics, the timeless magic of the East.

"Why do you carry such a treasure with you?" asked Hereward in amazement.

"My lord," replied Letwold, "who would think to search a beggar? Besides," he added with a sly, gleeful smile, "they would have to catch him first."

"He is quick-witted," reflected Hereward, "and undoubtedly has the courage needed for such a perilous task. But would it not be wiser to delay a few days until I find a man who is better known to me and whom I can more safely trust?" Aloud he said, thinking to discourage him, "The mission at hand is a dangerous one."

"Then have no qualms, lord," replied Letwold promptly, "for if I fail in its performance you can dispatch another more skilled than I. But if I succeed, I shall have avenged my father whom the Normans murdered, a man so ancient there were none who could recall his youth. I shall have avenged my royal master; nobler, he was, than the noblest earl; more knightly than any king."

And Hereward knew from the grim aspect of this man's face that there would be no solace for him anywhere, save in action.

"Then the mission is yours," he said suddenly, all hesitation vanishing. "The task will be difficult, for you must find a way to get word to Earl Waltheof at King William's new fortress in London which they call 'the Tower.' Here the earl resides as an enforced guest of the Bastard, who undoubtedly calculates to attract many other Englishmen to his fold by his seemingly affectionate regard for this foremost of English earls." He scrutinized Letwold's tatters. "Such clothes would not be quite appropriate, for these Normans claim to have dainty nostrils. These can easily be changed. It is effecting an entrance to the Tower that will be difficult."

"Perhaps not, my lord," replied Letwold, "for I play the ghittern with reasonable skill, and by shaving my hair and my beard, I shall pass among them as a minstrel, singing the ancient ballads which may perhaps afford the court some amusement."

Hereward hesitated, but Letwold grinned.

"The strain of prolonged watchfulness tauts the Norman nerves, lord," he said. "They always have need of a simple gleeman."

"So be it," said Hereward. "Such a device would make it unnecessary for you to address the earl directly. The Normans know little English so you could perhaps insert the message in your song. As for recognizing Earl Waltheof, that should not be too difficult since there are few Englishmen at the Norman court."

"But I know him well, lord," replied Letwold eagerly, "for I have seen him in the company of my royal master. Ofttimes I have watched him show with pride his furry, pointed ears, which he claims prove his descent from the Fairy Bear."

"Good!" said Hereward with satisfaction. He plunged his hand into his pocket and pulled out a small object which he placed in Letwold's palm. "You will find a way to give him this," he said, "as proof that you are the messenger he awaits."

Letwold dropped his eyes and gazed at the object in his palm. It was the upper half of a silver penny, upon whose reverse side was a cross formed of double lines. These were placed there to facilitate the operation of cutting the coin neatly and exactly where half-pennies and forthings were required for small payments. Thus the coin in Letwold's palm had been cut from left to right across the center.

Slowly Letwold turned the coin, holding its obverse side upper-most, and gazed down upon the thoughtful profile of Harold, his long ringlets graved about his face, the gem-encrusted diadem of Britain reposing on his brow. The lower half was missing, it being in Earl Waltheof's possession, but well Letwold knew it; well he knew the pitiful word PEACE written in Latin, the word which Harold, of all England's kings, had invariably spelled aright, owing to the vigilance of the scholarly Gurth; the PEACE for which Harold had so ardently striven, but of which he had enjoyed so little in his nine short months of kingship.

Letwold's eyes were moist as he met Hereward's kindly gaze.

"I regret that this should be the token," said Hereward gently.

"Regret it not, lord," replied Letwold, "for the journey ahead is long and difficult, and when the feet lag and the courage fails, this image will spur me on."

"Then memorize the message carefully," continued Hereward. " 'The men of the north are united. The time is now.' "

" 'The men of the north are united. The time is now,' " repeated Letwold faithfully, then, bowing low, he disappeared through the door and shuffled into the night without a further word.

Hereward listened thoughtfully to the footsteps receding on the cobblestones, then he turned to Godrith.

"I left my sword in Dirk's care," he said briefly. "I must borrow one from you."

Obediently the old man left the room, returning in a moment with a goodly sword and belt. Carefully Hereward inspected the blade, then, satisfied, proceeded to buckle the belt about his waist.

"My young lord," wept Godrith, "it is not hard to guess what you have in mind. How can I dissuade you from your purpose?"

But Hereward simply reached out and shook his hand. "Contrive to have de Lussac removed from Hound Isle," he said. "We want no trouble in the fens." Then he turned and strode away. A moment later he, too, had disappeared.

In the woods behind the cottage Martin Lightfoot reclined at ease on the stout branch of an oak tree, but the alert black eyes behind the scraggy fringe ceased not for a moment in their restless vigilance for his lord's safety. As Hereward approached he slid to the ground, instantly falling in step with his master, and together they moved swiftly through the sparse woodland, keeping well under cover.

From his master's moody silence Lightfoot knew that something was afoot, and coming at length to a small clearing, he took advantage of the moonlight to scan the countenance that was now so clearly presented for his inspection. What he saw there made the dark eyes behind their impenetrable screen sparkle with anticipation and humor.

"Strange, lord," he said, "that I should have the sudden urge to pause awhile and sharpen up my little axe. Mayhap I neglected to do it this morning—being a peaceful man."

Hereward shot him a sidelong glance.

"Like as not," he replied, his face momentarily losing some of its grimness, "you've earned this peaceful way of life by killing off your personal enemies."

But Lightfoot admitted nothing, only shrugging modestly and smiling his strange, secretive little smile into the darkness.

Soon they had circled about the village and found themselves on the other side of the castle. From time to time small white clouds were driven by the breeze across the moon's face, veiling in their momentary shadow the countryside beneath. Hereward and Lightfoot took advantage of this to cover the expanse of open ground between the woods and a small clump of pines on a hillock; Hereward stooping and taking cover wherever possible; Lightfoot doubling his gaunt frame and moving with spasmodic, graceless jerks like some strange night creature in pain.

The pines that offered them momentary concealment stood tall and motionless. The ground at their feet was devoid of grass, with only an occasional stubby bush bedded in pine needles. Hereward and Lightfoot lay upon their stomachs inhaling crisp night air sweetened with the clean fragrance of gum.

From where they lay they had an almost uninterrupted view of the island. Directly below them lay a gently sloping valley divided in the center by a small stream which rushed down from the castle and passed on its way through fields that were golden; fields brown and neatly furrowed; fields green and filled with fat herds behind brow-worn fences—once Hereward's, the Normans' now.

The castle itself was perched upon a hill augmented by earth banks, giving the illusion of extreme height against the surrounding fen-lands. The round tower, with its pyramidal windows surmounted by their stone-faced deities, was wreathed in a haze that rolled in across the hollow lands from the sea. The haze was silvery, lighted by the clear moonlight behind it, and the terrible form above the keep seemed to hover in its translucent motion like a huge bird of prey about to spread its pinions in flight.

The defensive wall about the castle had been raised several feet by Oger of Bayeux and the new masonry looked stark and naked against the lichened wall below. Upon each corner of the wall a small tower rose, round and with a tiny pointed roof, from which the sentries looked out across the fenlands from time to time.

For a moment the two lay quite still, gauging with experienced eyes the height of the sleek walls upon their grassy embankments, walls which curved inward slightly about the middle so that in time of siege its defenders could better protect the solid buttresses below. Behind the wall the tip of the sentry's helmet moved rhythmically as he paced his beat inside the courtyard.

"He moves with too much energy," whispered Hereward.

"Aye, lord. I fear he must be fresh upon his beat."

"Patience!" said Hereward lightly. "The French wine he surely guzzles behind his captain's back is a slow ally."

They lapsed into silence, each occupied with his own thoughts. The only sounds that disturbed the calm night air were the creaking of the hangman's chains above the keep and the laments of a mother-less calf grieving in the marsh.

Hereward was able for a moment to forget the grim task that lay ahead of him and instantly his thoughts reverted to his meeting with Althya.

It was an easy thing to summon her face to mind. In the firelight her every feature had been clearly visible and he had had ample time to study them, the wide brow, the gray eyes, the chin which was somehow purposeful for all its femininity. It was a curiously provoca-tive face, possessed of a mobility that had held his attention from the first and a mouth which, if overly large, betrayed a spirited and im-pulsive nature. Even in that disheveled state she was damned pretty, though her hair was undoubtedly her real beauty, being thick and lustrous and of a brilliant copper. She was small of stature, slender and delicately formed. Was that why he had snatched her from de Lussac?

As he thought of her, Hereward became aware of a soaring elation which had the effect of overshadowing all those things which only this morning were paramount in his life. His thoughts wandered blissfully back over their brief meeting, recalling a gesture or an intonation with a vividness that was startling and which made even his careful plans for the liberation of England seem now like illusory shadows in the very distant past. But soon, as suddenly as it had come, the elation faded and he was oppressed in turn by an overwhelming loneliness, a sense of utter loss that he must leave tomorrow without seeing her again, or without even knowing when he could return.

And now the struggle was about to begin which would rid England of the Bastard's mailed grip. But this he knew. When it was over, when William the Norman was no longer master of the land and he himself no longer an outlaw, he would come back to Althya. He would teach her to know the fens, would teach her to love the vast sky and the silvery meres; to glimpse through the haze the shining spires of the holy isle of Croyland, from whence on a summer eve the vesper bells sounded across the wastes and the chanting of the monks fell upon the peaceful air like the low rolling of the sea.

Here Hereward's reverie was interrupted by Lightfoot, who leaned towards him.

"Look, lord," he whispered, pointing a long, bony finger toward the castle well.

"The sentry tires of his vigilance."

"Aye, his speed slackens."

A few minutes later, in the shadow of a drifting cloud, they left their cover and sped across the last patch of open ground between them and the castle. With a leap they gripped the ledge of the wall and pulled themselves up slowly, till they peered above it.

The sentry was sitting on a pile of boulders that had been brought from the ancient Roman ruins of Cambridge across the fens for the purpose of heightening the wall. He appeared to be in a drowsy reverie, for his unblinking gaze was fixed upon the rushing waters of the little stream that emerged from beneath the castle, crossed the stone courtyard between mossy banks and cascaded down the em-

bankment to the meadows below. They waited, hanging to the side
of the wall till their arms ached and their fingers were numb.

"Will he never sleep?" whispered Hereward.

"Methinks he has a lidless eye, lord," Lightfoot replied.

Again they lapsed into silence and the minutes passed. But soon
the ceaseless rushing of the brook and the croaking of the bullfrogs
lulled him to a sense of quietude, and almost without it being apparent the sentry's lids closed over his eyes and he sank into a light
slumber.

Soundlessly they slipped their legs across the wall and dropped
into the courtyard. Soundlessly they glided forward, their eyes upon
his face to detect the slightest sign of awareness. Forward—forward
—then they sprang. Hereward's hand closed like a vise over the
sentry's nose and mouth, stifling his cry; his dagger flashed, then it
was over.

Moving like wraiths, they skirted the castle, keeping well within
the shadows of the wall, and when some fifteen minutes later they returned to wipe their daggers clean upon the mossy banks of the
stream there was not a sentry left on guard at Bourne Castle.

"Like as not the doors are barred and double-barred," whispered
Hereward above the rushing of the waters.

"Aye, lord," replied Lightfoot. "To batter them down might perhaps excite suspicion, yet it would not be good sense to knock
politely and request admission."

Hereward gave a low laugh.

"Then I shall enter without disturbing them," he said.

" 'I,' lord?"

Sternly Hereward eyed the disapproval on Lightfoot's face.

"Lightfoot," he said, pointing to a straggling row of buildings
somewhat apart from the castle proper, "those who escape my sword
will have but one thought, to reach the stables. You will post yourself at the side door leading to them, cutting down any who attempt
to flee."

Lightfoot's disappointment eased somewhat as he drew his little
axe from the ample folds of his tunic and patted it affectionately.

"Odin sent me this for no other purpose than that which con-
fronts us now, lord," he said, "to see that not a single Norman at
Bourne tonight feasts his eyes upon tomorrow's sunrise."

Hereward touched Lightfoot's arm.

"And in you, lad," he replied, "Odin sent me the best of friends."

For a moment Lightfoot looked at his master, his dark eyes shining, his long pink tongue trembling on his grotesque chin like that of a happy dog. Then swiftly he turned away, leaping agilely across the stream, and when a moment later he glanced behind him, Hereward had disappeared.

But there was nothing strange in Hereward's sudden disappearance. He had simply stepped down into the bed of the stream, and stooping, had started rapidly removing the boulders which were piled to one side of the culvert through which the waters of the brook escaped from beneath the castle keep. In doing so he exposed a flat surface, mossy with disuse. After making a few cursory scratches with his dagger, he quickly scraped away the embedded earth from the crevices, then placing his shoulder against the flat surface, he pushed.

The small door gave, only slightly at first, but after successive tries it opened far enough to permit his entrance. Bent almost double, he passed through, closing the door behind him.

The tunnel in which he found himself was exceedingly low, making progress difficult in the inky blackness. The rough boulders of which it was built protruded unevenly and from them the water dripped, lying like drops of dew on the shoulders of his tunic. The air had a pleasant earthy smell, but the wall along which he passed his outstretched hand was slimy and chill to the touch. In terror the rats scampered across his feet, scurrying back into their holes deep in the castle's foundations, and the huge cobwebs caught in his sunny hair as he broke through them in the darkness.

He was moving carefully, evading the frightened darting of the bats, when he came suddenly to what seemed to be the end of the passage, for a blank wall barred his progress. With both hands extended before him, he stood quite still, recalling that the lever which operated this hidden door was on the other side of the wall. But his dismay was only momentary, for, suddenly alert again, he started groping among the crevices of the rough boulders above his head till his eager fingers found a rusted chain. He pulled it.

The wall swung slowly away from him on creaking hinges and he stood at the foot of a long flight of stone steps in the base of the keep. The steps were worn and steep, but from the thick dust that carpeted them it was evident that the Normans had not yet discovered this secret exit.

Moving more rapidly now, he felt his way upwards, guiding himself by the rounded, windowless wall. He left the stairs, however, before he reached the top, pausing at a little ledge and groping again in the darkness. His two hands closed firmly about the large iron ring and he pulled. He uttered a soft exclamation of satisfaction as he felt the small aperture swing inwards. Bracing himself against it so that it opened no more than a crack, he slipped one arm out to turn back a corner of the tapestry that screened it and waited a moment for his eyes to become accustomed to the light. Then he slipped through.

He stood on a low balcony overlooking the main hall. The domed roof of this immense chamber was supported by square stone columns, etched and scrolled with figures of Celtic deities and animals of the chase, gracefully intertwined with fruits and foliage. At either end of the hall was a huge stone chimney, and upon their mantels rested the Roman urns of fine red and white earthenware which had been plowed up in the fields about Bourne and which had been so treasured by Hereward's father, the great Earl Leofric. The shining timbered walls were hung with the rare tapestries for which the Englishwomen of the age were so famed, and the long table was laden with chasened vessels of gold and silver, and drinking horns trimmed with precious metals and studded with jewels.

A feast had evidently been in progress for some hours, for the table was littered with the carcasses of fowl, and the bones of sheep and cattle. Wine ran freely from overturned flagons across the table, forming little red pools on the floor, and from the twelve men seated at the festive board came hilarious sounds of merriment.

But it was not the revelers in the hall who engaged Hereward's immediate attention. Swiftly he moved along the balcony, descending to the kitchens and the apartments of the men-at-arms, and there his dagger worked in such skillful silence that when he stood once again looking down upon the merrymakers in the hall, they still had no suspicion of his presence.

Oger of Bayeux, the new lord of the castle, arose from the old earl's chair at the head of the table. He pushed the lank hair from his wine-flushed forehead and slapped his fat thigh.

"A toast!" he cried, raising his horn. "A toast to the English guest who enjoys our hospitality atop our keep."

His companions roared with laughter at this witticism and raised their horns for the toast.

But the wine never reached their lips.

With a bound Hereward vaulted over the balcony to the hall below where he stood before them, a yellow-haired giant in fenman's garb, the cobwebs that mantled his shoulders aglow with rainbow colors in the torchlight.

"Of your courtesy, sirs," he cried, "do not neglect the English guest who enjoys the hospitality of your hall."

Oger of Bayeux, horn in mid-air, seemed to freeze on the spot. With blanching lips he perceived the cold glitter in Hereward's eyes and his upraised hand trembled so that the wine in the jeweled horn heaved like a tempest-tossed sea.

In stony silence all heads turned to follow the direction of Oger's glassy stare. They gazed in inert fascination at the blade of the sword that Hereward brandished in the air, then their attention shifted to the fierce face of the Englishman, upon which was clearly written the grimness of his intent.

"Unsheathe, sirs," cried Hereward, "for I come to avenge the man you were about to toast."

At this the warmth flooded back into Oger's frozen veins, for he realized that this sudden apparition was alone; he realized that there were eleven men with him in the hall, and twenty men-at-arms in the outer apartments within reach of his voice.

"A moi, mes hommes d'armes," he cried, licking lips suddenly gone dry. "A moi!"

But no running footsteps of his men-at-arms answered his summons. Instead the Englishman threw back his head and gave a laugh so fierce that there were none who dared rush in upon him.

"At him, men," cried Oger in a hoarse voice, retreating cautiously to the rear. "At him!"

But the only one who sprang into action was Hereward, who, with a broad sweep of his sword, lopped the head off the man who stood nearest him.

During all this time Martin Lightfoot had been waiting with increasing apprehension outside the door leading to the stables as Hereward had directed. With the passing of time his fears for his master's safety had grown upon him so that now, as he brushed aside the tangled hair with a bony hand, the dark face behind it was wrapped in the deepest gloom.

"One lord had I," he explained to himself, "one dear-loved lord. But now he is surely gone, cut down by the sons of wretchedness who slay our heroes and usurp our land. May Hel, the dark goddess of the damned, claim them for her own! May she bear them down to her vermin-haunted caverns where the gluttonous worms can feast for evermore upon their bones!" Then suddenly his ferocity left him and his mood became more melancholy. "Ah, miserable am I," he told himself, "to be left to live out my life in the shedding of water-less tears and the one dear hope that I may be deemed fit to be my lord's man again in the mist-world."

He cocked his ear and listened in the hope that his lord would make it known to him if he still lived, but the only sounds that came to him were those of the revelers in the hall.

"Ah, 'tis true I have not always lived worthily," he admitted to himself, an admission wrung from him now only by the abysmal depths of his suffering, " 'tis true the inner man is scarlet with many a secret crime. Yet if to teach me penitence the gods have bereft me of my lord, then truly I say that I am harshly dealt with."

But at that moment the sounds of revelry were shattered by the chilling death cries of the Normans in the hall. Lightfoot's long pink tongue trembled with joy on his tanned chin, for well he knew the meaning of each despairing shriek; well he knew what meant the sudden fierce laughter of his lord.

A moment later came the frantic footsteps of the few who had escaped Hereward's terrible blade. The door was flung open and the shameless Lightfoot, caring nothing for chivalry, cut down the flee-ing Normans with their backs turned as they ran past him, hastily tossing their lifeless bodies aside so as not to serve as a warning to the rest.

Then again Lightfoot cocked his ear, for a deathly silence had de-scended upon the castle, broken only by the unmistakable footsteps of his approaching lord. And as he carefully replaced his little axe in the ample folds of his shapeless tunic, Lightfoot's heathen face held a look of supreme joy.

After that there was less cruelty to the English on Hereward's sequestered lands, and much fear of him in Norman hearts. For they knew that soon he would return, sword in hand, avenging the free-man who looked to him for protection, or the humble serf who claimed him still as lord. They knew that from Hereward Leofrics-son they could expect no mercy; that he would relentlessly repay in kind, then vanish as he had come, leaving only the echoes of his fierce laughter to mingle with the moonlit haze above the fens.

Chapter Five

THE TOWER OF LONDON

UNHAMPERED by embankments, the restless waters of the Thames overlapped their spreading shores, reaching almost to the solid mass of cemented stone upon which the Tower was built. The southeastern angle of London's ancient wall had been demolished, and in its stead the Conqueror's mighty fortress stood guard upon the river's bank, defending on the one hand the maritime approach to the capital, and on the other quelling the sullen, rebellious spirit of the Londoners, whose city he so zealously defended.

More than a thousand years before another conqueror had built a tower upon this same site, for Julius Caesar had also remarked the advantages of the low hill on the riverbank. To the west lay the city. Northwards, beyond a broad strip of open meadowland, the fierce boar and wild white bull guarded a belt of dense forest. On the east the fortress was made unapproachable by pathless marshes, bottomless, terrible, creeping up almost to the very base of the Tower, till the solid motte or mound of stone which formed its substructure turned back the encroaching waters. Into this marsh in ancient times the Londoners would lure the enemy, escaping themselves as best they could or grappling with their horrified victim till the inky morass closed above them both, and the tangled roots of rush and reed gave them resting place.

The upper levels of Julius Caesar's fortress had long since crumbled and vanished. Now upon the Roman foundations rose the grim Norman keep, in whose base could still be seen patches of crushed Roman red tile which gave rise to the superstition handed down by the English that the Normans mixed their mortar with blood. Other remnants of Roman handiwork were to be found in the Tower's subterranean dungeons and Torture Chamber. The English captives who beat helpless fists upon the unyielding walls of their black and evil-smelling prison pits left behind no evidence of their frenzy on the solid Roman stonework. Immune to time and decay, also, seemed the Roman sewer through which the fluxing waters of the Thames flooded the terrible oubliette, relentlessly rising inch by inch, till the doomed man within struggled no more and the Roman sewer once again fulfilled its purpose.

Far, however, from the stench and laments of the captives dwelt the royal family. Narrow circular stairways within the thickness of the turrets led first to the Tower's main floor, where the soldiers of the garrison kept their unrelenting vigil. This floor was eternally dark, having only at rare intervals small round windows known as "loops," which were more for defense than light, for through them boiling oil and pitch could be flung down upon the heads of besiegers. By day as by night, therefore, lighted lanthorns hung from the ceiling, casting their glow in pale golden circles on the stone floor, but leaving the rest in crepuscular shadow. On the floor above this bristling camp, and reached only by means of the well-guarded turret stairways, dwelt the royal family.

One day in late June, William Rufus, the Conqueror's second son, stood just outside the royal apartments. His youthful form was prudently concealed behind the silken hangings that flanked the portal and his ear was closely pressed to a crevice in the paneled door. As he listened, a humorless smile played about his full, red lips and satisfaction animated the face shrewd beyond its years, for in the words that came to him through the tiny crevice he foresaw the furtherance of his most secret ambition.

Within the apartment the Conqueror and his wife held converse in carefully modulated tones. William had inherited his tall and splendid frame from his vigorous, if plebeian, Norse ancestors. Middle years and a gourmet's tastes had left their mark, yet still his movements held much of their youthful grace. Beneath his tight sleeve the strong muscles bulged, to rise and flex when anger swept his frame with the violence of a storm raging through his mighty Norman forests. Not yet was his strong and noble visage marred by the cruelties to which he became inured in after years; not yet had the attainment of power unleashed the immense forces of evil that he had kept locked well within him. Nor yet had the short ruddy curls receded from the noble brow, exposing the gigantic skull, the huge hairless dome which was to become a thing of horror to his luckless enemies.

For now, in his prime, the whole expression of his face was one of the keenest intelligence, iron strength of will, fearlessness and complete self-confidence. The proud, curved lips were full, set firmly in a massive jaw. His increasingly unpredictable moods dominated his dark eyes and if they were cold, it was that the turmoil of an orphaned and tragic youth had led him to mistrust both friend and enemy; had led him to read treason into the motives of those who longed to serve him and to repay only in coin the selfless loyalty and devotion sometimes directed toward him.

William had loved his wife, Matilda, from the moment he set eyes upon her at her father's Flemish court. The obstacles placed in the path of his marriage to the Flemish princess were many, the chief one being Matilda's scornful reply that she would rather not wed at all than wed a bastard. But William the Norman, William the Bastard of Falaise, was not one to relinquish a fixed purpose, however great the struggle.

The struggle that lay ahead to win Matilda was harder than had been the struggle to win his Norman dukedom; harder than would be the struggle in after years to win his English crown. Yet methodically and with infinite patience he set himself to overcome all opposition, even rigid canonical objections. The proud Flemish princess herself was won over by William's stern and forceful wooing, and if she could not bring to her marriage a love already irrevocably given to another, she had at last come to feel a deep attachment for the prince who with inflexible will had withstood temptations far exceeding those of a lesser man, and kept himself true to her.

"William," the Lady Matilda was saying (for in England the term "queen" had not yet come to mean the king's wife), "you must reconsider. To refuse bread to your first-born would be to place a curse upon us all."

"Then accursed we shall be," replied the Conqueror wrathfully, "for Robert will get no help from me."

For a moment there was a shocked silence.

"Such hatred between father and son is sinful and unnatural," Matilda ventured at last.

"Unnatural?" cried William. "And is it natural for my son to be so stirred by ambition that he demands to share my crown and my dominions with me while I live?"

The Lady shook her head.

"It is not ambition that caused him to demand his inheritance now," she replied. "It is the abject poverty in which you have kept him in an effort to insure a more filial devotion. None has cause to know better than you, William, how closely humiliation treads upon the heels of poverty."

The Conqueror's laugh was harsh. He felt neither regret nor grief at his son's plight.

"And Robert is such a weakling," he replied with scorn, "that he submits to both."

"He showed admirable boldness of spirit when he refused to continue as your hireling," protested Matilda.

"He showed only that he had squandered all he could borrow on parasites and harlots and that the usurers on the Continent have refused him any further loans," retorted William. "Like Absalom, he plans rebellion against his father; like Absalom, he shall perish. He refused, as you say, to remain my 'hireling,' and instead borrowed from every usurer in Normandy, Flanders and France, giving as collateral his expectant inheritance—the crown I all but gave my life to win. Shall I, too, become his dupe because he chances to be my first-born? Shall I share my crown and scepter with a profligate who has already pledged away half my kingdom and will likely lose the other half on a single throw of the dice?"

"That Robert is profligate, I will not deny," murmured Matilda. "That he squanders his time and his money, that he is raising a host of sons born out of wedlock, all that is true. But unwilling as I am to give tongue to the thought, William, it is equally true that had you been a kindlier father, Robert might have been a kindlier son."

"I ask no consideration from my sons," replied the Conqueror coldly, "and I give to them only that which they invoke. To Robert —nothing—save a desire never again to set eyes upon his face. William Rufus, whose pious filiality so artfully conceals his true ambition, I care little for. Richard, only, do I love; part for his likeness to you, Matilda; part for the unfeigned affection in which he holds me."

Matilda sighed, whilst outside the door the royal eavesdropper swore a sacrilegious oath.

"A son's misfortunes cannot that lightly be dismissed," the Lady murmured after a moment.

"He has brought his misfortunes upon himself," retorted William.

"Not all of them." His wife's tone expressed the pity of a lifetime she had secretly lavished upon her oldest son. "His physical deformities he was born with."

William, who in his wrath had been pacing the room, stopped short and stared keenly at his wife. He was oddly stirred by the sudden admission of what for almost eighteen years she had chosen to ignore.

"True," he admitted slowly.

"Yet from infancy he has learned to expect from you no compassion—no sympathy, only scorn," Matilda continued. "Legs as short and thick as Robert's are ill suited to horsemanship, yet with grim defiance he has learned to hold his seat—because you call him 'Shorthose.' A father's scornful tongue can be a cruel lash, William."

"What happened in his infancy and youth are passed," replied the king roughly. "Robert is now a man."

"Yet you keep him as dependent upon you as when he was a child," replied Matilda. "Robert is a king's son who is recompensed by his father for his military services with the wage of a lowly mercenary. You have enriched your followers, William, with wealth and grants of land, while you have kept your own son in a state of penury. To any young man, such a state is a source of constant humiliation. To the heir of a reigning king and duke, such a condition is intolerable."

William looked down meditatively at his wife for a moment with a strange glint in his inscrutable black eyes. When he spoke his voice was unusually smooth and pleasant.

"Robert is not my heir," he said.

The shock was so great that it brought the Lady to her feet.

"Not your heir!"

"No."

"But he is your first-born."

"Nevertheless, he is not my heir."

There was a long pause.

"Then who will inherit?"

"Richard."

"Richard? But he is not suited for kingship—he is too compassionate—too forbearing."

The Conqueror's impenetrable face softened into a faint smile.

"He is like you, Matilda," he said.

"But Richard will always be more scholar than statesman, more saint than scholar," cried Matilda. "How can he rule this race of rebellious outlaws who still boast that they are free, even though conquered? If they withhold their allegiance from you, William, whom they fear, they will in no way kneel to Richard, whom they fear not."

"Richard is just and wise," replied the Conqueror. "Therein lies the key."

He stood in the deep-embrasured window looking pensively northwards where in the distance sun-shot clouds dappled the dim green of the forest.

"I am England's jailer, not her king," he murmured, "for it is the conqueror's unhappy lot that he must hold by the sword that which he has won by the sword, or cease from conquest. But I start to know these English. With them, sometimes gentleness has a greater strength than force."

Matilda sat with furrowed brow, trying unsuccessfully to probe the profound depths of her husband's wisdom. But soon the thought of Robert returned to chase all else from her mind and she arose, moving over to stand beside him, whilst debating within herself how best to renew her attack on Robert's behalf.

But it was William who broke the silence. He turned and put one arm fondly about her, while with the other he lightly touched the hair from which the dark luster had all but fled, leaving it smooth and white as birch bark.

"You have been a good and dutiful wife to me, Matilda," he said, yet only for a fleeting second was there the slightest trace of tenderness in his voice. "You have at all times stood by my side, sharing my early struggles as you now share my glory. Bearing this in mind, I have watched you distribute at will the riches I have confided to your care; have even humored your caprice when the costly trinkets I bestowed upon you have disappeared with curious regularity from your person. These I have replaced without comment and without question, being fully aware that they, too, would soon find their way into Robert's hands; that they, too, would serve to pay my own soldiers whom he has seduced against me; that they, too, would be turned into weapons by Robert, who at this very moment plots to take up arms against me in Normandy and undermine my ducal throne."

Matilda shivered and withdrew from his embrace, fearfully searching, as she had innumerable times, the aloof, dark face beneath the ruddy curls.

"That which aids rebellion, Matilda, can no longer be humored as a mother's natural whim," continued William. "Therefore I place this stern injunction upon you; that you do not enrich my enemy with my wealth, nor supply him with the wherewithal with which to buy arms to be used against me. Disobey me, and by the Splendor of God, you shall pave your son's way to the darkest dungeon in my domain."

Matilda's face was pale as she struggled against the fear of him she had never learned to overcome.

"You seem to know many things, William, that I have sought to conceal from you," she admitted. "Therefore I question the fitness of your laying so harsh a command upon me, since you must also have guessed that, of all our sons, Robert is to me the most dear, in that he is the least fortunate."

But William's stern countenance was unrelenting.

"In treating with rebellion," he said, "I am not concerned with a mother's devotion."

He strode toward the door. Suddenly he turned.

"I will tolerate no enemies in my own household, Matilda," he said.

The door opened and closed, and he was gone.

The corridor seemed empty as William strode away, but as he disappeared down the turret stair to the floor below, the youthful eavesdropper stepped calmly from his place of concealment and made his way noiselessly in the opposite direction. Already his brain was at work with its devious scheming, foreseeing the direction his activities must take to secure for himself his father's diadem. There was nothing further to fear from Robert. Richard alone stood between him and his goal.

And from that day forward William Rufus bided his time. He only smiled his humorless smile—and waited—and watched.

That night Samson, the Negro eunuch who had served the Lady since childhood, slipped from his mistress' boudoir and glided with the stealth of a cat through the dark corridors of the Tower. He proceeded cautiously, keeping close to the wall. His gigantic form was naked, save for a loincloth into which was carefully tucked the brocade jewel case his mistress had bidden him carry to Robert "Shorthose" in Normandy. As he moved, his huge muscles contracted rhythmically and his bronze flesh glistened beneath its heavy coat of grease.

At the end of the corridor he paused, peering down the circular stair well that led to the floor below. He listened, cocking his head to one side, and for a moment the faint beam of a lanthorn fell upon him, illuminating his gleaming, crouching form; his dark face with its short beard, scant and curly; his thick lips; his flat nose, broadening at the cheeks.

As he listened there came from below the soft tread of a guard upon his rounds. Samson waited. The footsteps died away and he started warily down, hugging the circular wall with his shoulder and leaving behind a sloping line of grease. Step by step he descended, edging away from the lanthorn into the shadows, so that only the whites of his eyeballs and the pink soles of his naked feet were visible in the gloom. At the foot of the steps he took cover behind an angle of the wall, awaiting the next guard to make his rounds. Taken unawares, the surprised man crumpled soundlessly beneath the eunuch's heavy fist. Samson stooped, and gathering the inert form in his huge arms, deposited him out of sight behind an oaken upright. Then he turned and scanned the long, empty corridor ahead.

It seemed endless. The pale golden circles on the floor pyramided up to the lanthorns above them, but beyond that, in the distance, there were only vague blue shadows. The eunuch, as he stole forward, avoided these patches of light, thrusting forward his head in an effort to search the dusky shadows beyond. He was already halfway down the corridor when suddenly he stopped short and listened. Again the regular footbeats, approaching slowly. Samson glanced behind him. He had proceeded too far down the corridor to retrace his steps. He darted into a doorway, pressing his naked form back against the flat wooden surface. He waited.

The guard came on with measured tread. Samson could see his shadow first, creeping like a black specter over the stone floor. He drew back as far as possible, pressing his limbs against the door. As the guard came into view the eunuch slowly bent his knees ready to spring and his long fingers curved, as though already he could feel the throbbing of the man's bare throat beneath his thumbs. But the guard passed on, unaware of the tall, dark form blending so perfectly with the shadows.

Into the vast, tomblike spaces the footsteps faded. Only then did Samson breathe again, easing his aching lungs. His tense hands relaxed and dropped limply to his sides. For a moment he continued to lean back against the door, trembling violently. There would be other guards, many guards, more alert, more vigilant. Into his childish mind sprang the desire to flee up the steps from whence he had come; to hide until dawn; to fling himself down before his lady and admit that he was afraid.

But instead the faithful Samson stepped from his hiding place, and turning his back upon safety, sped on his way.

There was only the faintest sound as of a bee humming in the gloom and an arrow pierced his back. He bounded forward, but from out of nowhere Norman guards rushed down upon him, forming a human wall. He glanced behind him. There, too, they were crowding down the corridor and their excited voices were to him like sounds out of hell. He turned at bay, his back to the wall, fighting with all the courage and desperation of the jungle. His well-greased body eluded each attempt to grasp him as he twisted and turned, and his hammerlike fists cracked their jaws and sent them reeling backwards to lie unconscious on the stone floor.

But the arrow in his back was rapidly draining his strength. His brain clouded over and he sank slowly to the floor. Instantly they leaped in upon him. Snapping iron fetters on his wrists and ankles, they dragged him to a tiny dungeon within the thickness of the wall, a space scarcely large enough to hold a child. Somehow they crowded the all but lifeless form into the tiny chamber and forced the door shut, leaving him sagging against the cold wall, half reclining for lack of power to stand; half standing for lack of space to lie.

The following morning the miserable eunuch was brought before King William. The captain of the guard had omitted to search a prisoner already so scantily clothed. But not so the king. He directed the short search and showed no surprise when he was handed the familiar brocade jewel case. He did not question Samson as to the purpose of his attempted flight. Too often had the Lady utilized his almost feline ability to slip past sentries unheard and unseen. She had done so for the last time.

Almost fainting with terror, the faithful eunuch was half carried, half dragged to the fearful subterranean bowels of the keep. The anguished cries that rent the fetid air below were stopped by the unimaginable thickness of the walls. They rebounded against the reddened stonework, shattered the tombal silence of the adjoining vaults and faded at last into the distant blackness of the pits, leaving behind only the tremulous echoes of the eunuch's exhausted, whimpering sobs.

A few moments later an attendant stood at the door of the Lady's apartment.

"His King's Grace requests your presence, my lady," he said. "Will you be so kind as to follow me."

Matilda arose. It was not William's custom thus to summon her. She noted the lighted taper in the attendant's hand and felt a tremor pass through her frame. She fought down her fear and motioned the attendant to precede her.

With increasing apprehension she followed him down the narrow spiral stairway to the dungeons beneath the keep. The foulness of the air sickened her, for the immense solidity of the walls allowed for neither ventilation nor light. The dim taper in her escort's hand barely illuminated the low-browed passage with its ancient Roman stonework and curious red patches. Abruptly the attendant paused outside a nail-studded door of massive oak heavily banded with iron and the Lady glanced up at him with a frightened face. He knocked. The door was opened from within and the attendant stood aside to permit her to enter. Slowly, to hide her agony of suspense, she raised her voluminous skirts a few inches from the floor. Then she stepped across the threshold.

Inside the Torture Chamber William awaited her. He stood alone by the west wall, his back to the bare masonry, his face in the shadows. In the dimness of the Chamber Matilda was unaware of his presence. She saw only the crude wooden table in the center of the room lighted by a few flickering tapers. Upon the table was the brocade jewel case.

For a moment William remained motionless, watching the horror creep over her face as she sighted the case. Then slowly he emerged from the shadows and stood on the opposite side of the table looking down at her, an odd little smile curving the corners of his full, red lips.

There were others in the Chamber, the torturer and two or three assistants, but Matilda was conscious only of William and of his black eyes, inscrutable—merciless. She wanted desperately to ask where Samson was . . . what had become of him. But she could only stand there unable to speak or move, fascinated by William's unfathomable smile.

"My thanks for your prompt response to my summons," he said courteously.

Matilda raised her chin and in her mounting fear of him deliberately sought courage in the weakness in his armor. He was born a bastard; his mother was a laundress—the daughter of a tanner. William read her thoughts and his mouth tightened.

"Madame," he said, and his ice-capped words swept away her last shred of hope for Samson, "as you see, your messenger has been intercepted."

He waited for her to speak, but still Matilda was unable to move. As if under some strange compulsion, she could only stand there staring up at him, inept, speechless.

He turned and gestured to the wall behind him.

"Will you not look at him," he asked, "to gauge his future usefulness to Your Grace?"

Matilda's gaze traveled the gloom behind him, searching for Samson. William noted her difficulty. He lifted a taper from the table and with it moved to the far end of the Chamber. He raised his arm, letting the tiny beam of light fall full upon the prisoner.

The gigantic eunuch was crouched against the wall, naked still, save for his loincloth. His agonized sweat formed on his greased bronze skin tiny beads which rolled downwards slowly from time to time as his sobbing jolted them free. His arms were stretched above his head, fettered by the wrists to an iron ring in the wall. His eyes had been torn from their sockets and down his cheeks the scarlet rivulets mingled with his last tears, slid down the tendrils of his scant beard, then dripped with silent regularity to the floor.

"I have said that I will tolerate no enemies in my own household, madame," William was saying.

But Matilda did not hear him. She heard only Samson whimpering there against the bloodstained wall; thought only of the lifetime he had spent watching over her faithfully, vigilantly, with an almost canine devotion. Suddenly his spent sobbing became unendurable. She turned frantically to the torturer.

"Unfetter him!" she ordered.

The torturer glanced at the king. William made no motion. Only by the most subtle change of expression on the Conqueror's countenance did the torturer divine his will. He moved over and unshackled the prisoner.

Samson's arms dropped heavily to his sides, but he made no effort to rise. He lolled back against the wall, his childlike mind lost in the abysmal depths of his suffering, leaving it in complete darkness.

"Come, Samson," Matilda said gently.

Samson did not hear her. Matilda stood looking down at him helplessly, angered by William's unconcern; irked by the hushed curiosity of the torturer and his assistants. Then without a further word she stooped, and taking the sobbing eunuch by the hand, led him gently through the door and up the turret steps.

Letwold, in the meantime, blithely unaware of the tragic happenings at the Tower whither he was bound, lazed in a willow grove by the river, not two miles from the city gates. Pillowed by the fragrant turf, he lingered blissfully in the ethereal world between sleep and wakefulness, loath to dispel the magic moment and return to reality.

The condition of his clothing, the same rags in which he had confronted Hereward Leofricsson but a few short weeks before, was now indescribable, it being Letwold's firm belief that, upon the king's highway, filth made for security. His dark hair hung in long matted strands and to its disorder were added mementos of the many spots that had cushioned his head on the long journey south. A scraggy beard half hid the hollows of his cheeks. His garments all but fell away from his naked sides, exposing the white flesh. His feet were bound in rags. Only his neck and chest were well concealed from view, as though even the summer air brought no warmth to his lean frame.

He stirred, reluctantly opening his eyes to let a sleepy gaze pass over the low bushes to a small clearing directly before him. Sunlight broke through the willow's delicate foliage, dappling the rich turf below with patches of light and dark. In the center of the clearing stood an ancient statue of the Roman goddess Britannia. Scattered at her feet were fragments of her arms and trident.

Letwold contemplated her idly for a moment. She was gazing loftily ahead, condescending to notice neither the guest who shared her grove nor the interposition of the willow's breeze-swept foliage. Only the perpetual flutter of the sun sequins on the river engaged her rapt attention.

"Do you not deign, proud lady," he asked, "to look upon one so lowly as I?"

He waited as though expecting some reply. But Britannia, the proud Roman goddess, unaware that through the strange whimsey of Fate she would come to symbolize the Unity of Empire on British coinage, continued to ignore the humble Briton.

"You think the lowborn merit no consideration?" asked Letwold. "In that there's nothing new, since half the world contends that it is so. Yet Harold Godwinsson, noblest of the earl-born, was wont to defend the lowly serf, saying, 'The humblest of men are ofttimes touched with greatness.' "

For a few moments he lay quite still, while his hand stole beneath his rags and he fingered the amulet concealed there. Then, arising from his rough couch, he shook himself free of his thoughts. In the neighboring bushes he retrieved a large unsavory-looking bundle that he had carefully concealed the previous night, and shouldering it, started down the riverbank and disappeared.

When he returned the change was indeed startling. His tanned skin was washed clean of the hoarded soil of months, and now shone with cleanliness. His hair was short-cropped and neatly combed; his beard snugly shaven. His rags had vanished and were replaced by a wool tunic of Candale green, which was gathered at the neck and fastened with a simple clasp of white metal. His legs were clad in light brown hose; his feet neatly encased in black pumps, in which he had cut a cross at the toes for comfort and carefully blacked with soot. Upon his back was slung an ancient ghittern, fastened about his shoulders by means of a leather strap. In every detail he had now assumed the respectable demeanor of the wandering minstrel.

A pathway through the trees brought him out on to the highroad. For a moment he stood looking toward Westminster, making out the familiar lines and recalling once again the joyful day on which his master had been crowned there. Two years and more had passed since Harold Godwinsson fell at Hastings, yet to Letwold the memory of his pensive countenance was still fresh. It was as though a door had just closed upon Harold's back and he would return anon. Thoughtfully Letwold fingered the halfpenny in his pocket, passing his finger tip over its uneven surface. Then, stemming the inner river's rise, he turned quickly away, and with solemn and resolute mien, headed east toward the city of London.

He could see it in the distance, walled and towered, heavy storm clouds almost obscuring its conical Saxon steeples. Letwold knew the road well. At the crossing where the cowpaths met still stood the ancient monument erected to one Charing. Who was Charing? What deed had earned him so great an honor? What was his fate? But already the man, his fate and his deed were sunk in the dim and unrecorded history of the past and all that remained was the crumbling monument where the cowpaths met still called, though none could say why, Charing Cross.

He turned off on to the Strand, a dusty country lane on the river-bank leading straight to the Ludgate. It was deeply rutted and so full of pits and sloughs that it appeared to drop away into space from time to time, then climb again from out of nowhere and amble on. Spring and winter travelers were hampered by these sharp declivities, for when the path was flooded they were forced to swim across or strike out northwards across the meadows seeking higher ground.

But here a strange quiet prevailed. The pleasure boats, which of yore lent charm to the river, now were gone. The fields and meadows stood empty, untilled, idle. Where once the tinkle of the sheep bell and the lowing of cattle fell upon the air, there was now only silence. Anxiously he viewed the long perspective of the Strand for signs of another living creature. The road was empty. It was as though a sudden death had overtaken man and beast, leaving him utterly alone.

He hurried on, past the small enclosed plot where Norse gods still presided over moldering pagan graves; past the once prosperous Roman villa that lay rotting by the water's edge. With gaping sides it stood open to the morning light, its spacious rooms, once centrally heated by a hypocaust, now swept by wind and rain; its sunken bath crumbling away. The sagging lintels harbored only multicolored webs and within the abandoned rooms brown leaves of autumns past lay in small, damp heaps. Only the tessellated floors endured. In the brilliant mosaic the chariot race was run; the sun god roamed the skies and Orpheus still played his flute, surrounded by enraptured animals and birds in flaming plumage.

Beyond the villa, a crumbling wall sheltered an unkempt mound where some Roman dignitary slept beneath alien sod, clutching between his teeth a coin in fee to Charon the ferryman of the Styx. Encircling the mound were the remnants of a ghost hedge, placed there to prevent his restless spirit from roaming. Despite the oppressive heat, Letwold shivered. Beneath the threat of an approaching storm the countryside had assumed a sudden gloom. He cast a hasty glance behind him at the gray river, the gray meadows, the lonely gray mound, then increased his speed to a trot, hastily invoking the patron saint of travelers and crossing himself fervently to ward off the pagan devils.

It was with a deep sense of relief that he traversed the little wooden bridge across the Fleet and approached the Ludgate, but as he did so he became aware of the close scrutiny of two Norman guards who stood just within the portal awaiting him. He answered their suspicious glances with a pleasant nod, as though he saw nothing strange in their standing at the gate of Britain's capital, guarding it with their Norman crossbows. But his pleasant nod did not dissipate their mistrust. The first sentry motioned him to stop, while the second one sauntered around him, carefully examining the ghittern on his back.

"Whither are you bound?" the first sentry asked. His tone was surly and his English hesitant.

"I am bound for nowhere, friend," replied Letwold blithely. "I have arrived."

"So?" said the Norman, scanning Letwold's amiable countenance. "Then from whence do you come?"

Letwold gestured back toward the empty Strand.

"As you see," he replied, "I come from Westminster, where I have just crossed the river from the south."

But the Norman was aware that there was no bridge at Westminster. His eyes instantly dropped to Letwold's shoes. They were dry.

Letwold appeared not to notice the crushing silence. He, too, looked down at his feet and his hollow face displayed an almost childlike pride in the condition of his footwear.

"A kindly fellow, seeing that I wished to cross the river and he about to ford, bade me seat myself upon his spindle-shanked nag," he continued easily. He turned and pleasantly included the second sentry in his conversation. "This, sirs, I did with great reluctance, not wishing to trust my neck to the feeble efforts of a starveling beast whose very species was in question, yet desiring to spare my brogues, for in my profession clothing, 'tis thought, proves prowess. This last I disclaim, since a minstrel must needs travel from town to town——"

The sentry cut him short.

"Where do you hail from?"

"From the southern shires, may it please you," replied Letwold, "where the happy peace of King William lies like a benediction upon the land—as it appears to on this fair city."

The sentry glanced at his confrere. Then he nodded.

"Pass," he said briefly.

Letwold gave him a grateful smile.

"Gran'merci," he said. Then he turned and sauntered away from them down the cobbled street.

The city appeared to be as deserted as the countryside surrounding it. Only the swine roamed the streets hunting scraps of refuse, invading even the sacred precincts of St. Paul's. But the human population, holding dear the lives their conquerors held so cheap, found momentary refuge in the dark confines of their shuttered homes.

Letwold's footsteps echoed oddly through the narrow streets. Desiring to avert suspicion, he ambled along slowly, following the ancient river wall. Just before reaching the fortress, however, he turned off at the bridge leading to South Wark. In the center of the bridge he paused, leaning over the side and gazing down into the muddy waters with the deep contemplation of a Londoner of pre-Christian days, who murmured his pagan prayer before dropping a coin into the water in offering to the river god. But the cautious Letwold was not concerned with the spirit of the mighty river. He waited only long enough to allay the suspicions of any watchful Norman, then he raised his head and for the first time beheld the Tower.

He was startled by the formidableness of its appearance. The massive quadrangular structure was built of hard white stone quarried in Normandy and brought by barge up the Thames to London. The third floor, still unfinished, was begirt with scaffolding, and from barges moored all along the riverbank foreign laborers were busily unloading the great white blocks and hoisting them in a cradle or lift to the scaffolding above, from whence they were borne across a short bridgelike structure to their destination.

From the angle at which he stood Letwold could see the south and west faces and the impregnability of the fortress dismayed him. Even if he could effect an entrance and succeed in getting a moment's speech with the earl, how could Waltheof flee such a prison? Certainly there was no chance of descent from the second-floor windows with their heavy prisonlike bars. And the floor below, aside from one tall window in the south face, had only loops too small to permit the passage of a man.

There was something about the structure, something inexplicably odd. Letwold pondered. Suddenly it came to him. The Conqueror's fortress had no portal!

Bewilderment creased his brow. Such a development was unexpected. He looked again, making a careful, though unrewarding search of the west and south faces. Then he shook his head.

"Since the east is bounded by marshlands," he said to himself, "only the north remains."

He retraced his steps across the bridge and climbed the low hill leading to the Tower, but his search of the north face left him as puzzled as before.

"One must needs grow wings to enter such a fortress," he muttered.

He looked up at the sky. The storm which had been brewing all day would break at any minute. The heat had become intense.

"I shall play my ghittern for the amusement of the sentries pacing with such tedium back and forth within their low stockade. Then they can do no less than invite me into their hall when the storm breaks." So saying, he slipped his ghittern from his back and started up a sentimental ballad which he had learned from some foreign minstrel.

He had not been playing for more than a few minutes when he became aware of a man standing at one of the deep-embrasured windows of the upper floor, listening with deep absorption. The gloom of the imminent storm in no way dulled the fire of the ruddy curls and even from a distance there was that about him which was at once arresting and awe-inspiring. After a few moments the man called to the sentries below, and stretching a hand through the bars, gave a signal. Immediately the postern opened and a youthful guard advanced toward Letwold.

"You are invited to enter," he said.

Letwold's smile was suitably obsequious.

"That will I gladly do, my friend," he replied amiably, "if only to see how it is accomplished."

The young sentry laughed at the Briton's compliment to Norman ingenuity and led the way through the stockade and down toward the river.

"It may be your pleasure to play for the king," he confided genially.

Letwold winked.

"The pleasure will be doubled if the purse is heavy," he replied.

Again the sentry laughed, amused by the minstrel's simple wit.

They had come now to the Tower's south face overlooking the Thames. The sentry looked up and called in Norman French to the lookout above. The sill of the tall central window started slowly to descend. It stretched out like a concertina till it reached the ground and Letwold perceived to his undisguised amazement that they stood before a flight of wooden steps supported by stout chains.

Letwold's companion smiled.

" 'Tis simple," he said modestly.

" 'Tis clever," rejoined Letwold, though to himself he added, "so clever that when things grow too hot within this hornet's nest, how do I depart?"

They climbed the steps to the slender portal and passed down a long, narrow passage hewn straight through the fifteen-foot wall. Letwold's astonishment grew as he noted that, because of the narrow impregnability of this passage, the Tower's sole portal could be defended if necessary by a single man. Truly, the Conqueror had overlooked nothing.

As they stepped from the passage and the heavy door slammed behind them, the storm outside broke with shattering suddenness, but within the capacious interior of this chill sepulcher its blasts were scarcely audible.

"It must indeed be a fearsome lord these Normans kneel to," reflected Letwold, "to entomb himself in a den of solid stone. For myself, I shall deliver my message and get gone with all speed, though, since Waltheof must devise for himself a means of flight, I fear 'tis no less than a command to suicide I must relay to the captive earl."

And accompanied by these gloomy thoughts, Letwold followed the sentry through the same corridor wherein the eunuch Samson had been trapped the previous night, and up the turret steps.

Chapter Six

ESCAPE

THE Banquet Hall into which Letwold was ushered was one of unexpected luxury. Coming from the tomblike atmosphere of the floor below with its naked stone walls and floors, the sudden change was startling. The massive walls were hung with exquisite tapestries, whose motifs of fragile human forms were set against a background of foliage worked with the most delicate artistry. Crimson velvets draped the tall windows, concealing the deep embrasures and the prisonlike bars. The gold-fringed valances were taut, displaying with sharp clarity the Two Lions of Normandy emblazoned with gold thread upon the center of each. Priceless carpets from the east covered the cold stone floor. At either end of the Hall huge fireplaces were surmounted by mantels of hand-hewn marble, whose virgin whiteness was despoiled only by the rubescent reflection of the leaping flames, for despite the heat of the waxing summer without, the Hall was eternally chill.

Tables ranging the full length of the Hall were covered with embroidered linens, and the elongated glimmers from numerous silver candelabra fired the gem-studded drinking cups to riotous colors. Seated on either side of the tables at their evening meal were many who had fought with the Conqueror at Hastings and had since claimed their guerdon, men of Norman name, but English title, William FitzOsbern, now Earl of Hereford; Roger de Montgomery, Earl of Shrewsbury; old Galitier Giffard, Earl of Buckingham and a host of others.

Letwold looked about him in amazement. The wealth of the entire world seemed assembled in this one apartment. Then slowly, through the mist of surprise, he became aware of the fixed regard of the man with the ruddy curls, the listener at the window. He was seated at the head of the table in a chair raised upon a dais. Two golden lions adorned the breast of his green velvet tunic and the jeweled chain about his neck was second in splendor only to the one Letwold wore about his own.

The Briton was gripped by the awe-inspiring aspect of this man's presence. There was about him something at once noble and fearful; something that bespoke immeasurable strength untempered by weakness. His was the proud, majestic mien of one who, by his own greatness and courage, had risen from the dregs of humiliation to scale the pinnacle of power. Yet his own strength had in some ways disimpassioned him, had enabled him to overcome all inner conflict and dip his hands in the blood of his fellow men; had enabled him to recognize no means as being too unscrupulous or too unprincipled to gain his ends and had at last left him disillusioned, fixing upon friend and enemy alike the mistrusting, aloof regard wherein still brooded the long loneliness of his childhood.

It was this regard that was now fixed upon Letwold, chilling him with the sudden realization that this was the man who had left Harold Godwinsson dead on the blood-soaked hill at Senlac! This was the man who with his own hand had slain the gentle Gurth! Anger and hate rushed in upon the loyal heart of the serf, yet, beneath the compelling eye of the Conqueror, his aplomb dissolved and vanished, his impertinence ebbed.

Letwold, the serf, trembled before William, the king.

The king gestured to him to play. Obediently Letwold slipped his ghittern from his back, and influenced by the melancholy tempest of his soul, the tune he instinctively selected was plaintive and sad. The king stopped eating and leaned back in his chair, his cheek resting on his hand. Though unaccompanied by words, William recognized in the melody its tale of heroism, and the pathos in the homespun art of the player stirred the royal listener to such profound depths as heretofore only the superb minstrelsy of the dead Taillefer had been capable of reaching.

At the end of the melody he beckoned to Letwold, who advanced and fell on his knees before the Conqueror.

"Has your song no words?" asked William, speaking English slowly and with the greatest difficulty.

"Sir king," replied Letwold, "where would one find words to match so sad an air?"

"Has it also no name?"

"May it please Your Grace," replied Letwold, "the melody is

Welsh. It is called the 'Air of the Rhuddlan Marsh' and is a lament of the Cambrian people for their fathers, who fell to a man in a futile defense of their homeland."

The king's dark brows met in a frown. The minstrel's words displeased him, recalling as they did a similar tragedy.

"We would welcome ballads of a happier nature," he said with the sudden sternness his courtiers had learned to expect. "We Normans love not melancholy."

Letwold rose to his feet and bowed as he backed away, recalling with a start what the magnetic power of the king's presence had all but chased from his mind—the message to Earl Waltheof.

" 'The men of the north are united; the time is now,' " he repeated to himself, and with a gay little love song on his lips, he moved cautiously down the hall among the guests.

It was not long before he espied the captive earl. He sat moodily plucking the meat off a quail and ignoring with despondent indifference all attempts at conversation on the part of the two Normans who flanked him. In his middle thirties, he was of immense stature, was reputedly possessed of the strength of three ordinary men, and in odd contrast to the dark, close-cropped Normans, his long wavy hair fell about his shoulders like a cloak of shining metal.

Legend had it that the Fairy Bear, from whom the earl was descended, had captured a Norwegian princess and carried her off to his domain among the glaciers and icebound oceans of the north. Since then the sons of this fairy race had all borne the marks of their ancestry. Fur-fringed were their long ears, slack when relaxed, pointed when alert; Fur-fringed were the backs of their strong, square hands, and beneath their conventional apparel men said that their bodies were clothed in a coat of silky fur. White, the Fairy Bear had been. White from birth had been the locks of Waltheof's father, the great Siward who vanquished Macbeth; white from birth had been the locks of Waltheof's brother who fell at Dunsinane. The locks of Waltheof himself were the lustrous, gleaming white of the polar regions, of the storm-swept floes, of the white gyrfalcon's plume, and quick with the breathless radiance of a snow star glistening in a young girl's hair.

Letwold recognized him instantly, but dared not move too rapidly in his direction. Instead, he paused behind each guest in turn, murmuring a word to each, stooping to sing softly into the ear of each, being careful to make his pauses longer as he drew nearer to Waltheof.

At last he stood directly behind the earl, who still appeared to be so immersed in gloom that even Letwold's gayest melody failed to rouse him. Suddenly the minstrel lowered his voice and commenced the stirring ballad of the Battle of Maldon. He stooped, singing close to the earl's ear the words that had so deep a meaning to every Englishman; the words with which the English leader, foreseeing annihilation at the hands of the pagan invaders, inspired his men to stand and perish gloriously on the field at Maldon. Softly, clearly, Letwold repeated the immortal words:

> *"The will must be firmer; the mind must be keener.*
> *The heart must be bolder, as our might lesseneth——"*

To the surrounding Normans, who were for the most part ignorant of the idiom of the subjugated people, the words held no particular meaning. But upon the despondent English earl they had a startling effect. While he neither moved, nor spoke, nor otherwise gave a sign, Letwold noted that his long, furry ears were pointing warily aloft.

Having thus gained the earl's attention, the minstrel continued his song, but now, in place of the familiar words, new ones were neatly substituted and Hereward Leofricsson's message was delivered with faithful accuracy.

At the end of the ballad he leaned toward the earl.

"I misdoubt not," he said aloud, "my lord is English."

The buzz of conversation ceased abruptly and suspicious Norman eyes were turned curiously in their direction. But the minstrel smiled amiably and with disarming servility.

"A penny for my singing, lord—or perhaps a halfpenny?"

Waltheof perceived the hidden purpose behind the minstrel's request, yet prolonged captivity had left him penniless. He hesitated, then leaned across the table toward a Norman knight, whose unassuming clothes and demeanor stood in odd contrast to the richness of his surroundings.

"Sir Herlwin," said the earl, "could I impose——"

But Sir Herlwin had anticipated the earl's request and had already drawn his purse and tossed it across the table toward Waltheof.

"My lord," he replied with such simple courtesy and grace as Letwold had never thought to meet in any Norman, "the minstrel's singing has pleased us all. Pray undertake his recompense on all our parts."

Waltheof accepted the purse, from which he extracted a few coins and then returned it, with a word of thanks, to its owner. The minstrel in the meantime had been fumbling with his ghittern and now stood humbly awaiting his fee. The earl signaled him to approach. As he dropped the money into the minstrel's outstretched hand, he felt the sharp angle of a coin being pressed upwards into his own palm. His fingers closed about it, and though he dared not glance at it, he knew that it could be none other than Hereward Leofricsson's token. He immediately returned his attention to the quail, methodically stripping the meat from the carcass until, with a careless gesture, he could carefully slip the halfpenny into the secure confines of his empty pouch.

Letwold saw no more of the earl. When he passed by an hour or so later, Waltheof had already obtained the king's permission to withdraw and his seat was empty. It was, therefore, with considerable relief that the minstrel once again obeyed the king's signal to approach. As he did so, William held in his hand a purse, not too small, not too large, which he cast on the floor before the Briton.

"Take this gratuity," he said in his hesitant English, "and in your wanderings say to those you meet that you have entertained your king. Say that your singing pleased him—that he was moved by the ancient ballads of your people."

With that he dismissed the minstrel, who lost no time in retrieving the purse and seeking the exit.

"I will say only that I found nothing to love in yonder man," Letwold muttered fiercely to himself, "but much to fear."

A few moments later he was given exit through the slender portal and, with many a simple pleasantry to hide his relief, made his descent down the chain-bound steps and out through the postern gate to the street. The savage storm was spent and the air was clear and fresh. As Letwold disappeared into the night, a horseman, accompanied by a dozen men-at-arms, rode at top speed up to the Tower and demanded instant audience with the king.

The captain at the portal above demanded to know the name and rank of the horseman.

"Sir Guy de Lussac, lord of the castle of Cruc Maur," came the harsh reply.

Instantly the steps were lowered and after but a moment's waiting the horseman was received by the king in his privy chamber.

The king looked at Guy questioningly.

" 'Tis not two months since you fretted to quit our court and return to your demesne in the fenlands," he said. "What is it now brings you back in such hot haste it cannot cool till the morrow?"

"Sire," replied Guy, making his obeisance, "I have come to bring you some news. Oger of Bayeux has been slain."

"Oger! Slain!"

"Aye, Your King's Grace."

"When?"

"About a month ago, sire. Apparently an immense English force descended upon Bourne Castle. The garrison was wiped out."

"Were any of the outlaws apprehended?"

"Unfortunately, no, and all inquiries concerning their identities have proved fruitless."

"How large was the rebel force?"

"In an effort to approximate its size," replied Guy, "my captain minutely examined the ground about the castle the morning after the event occurred. He swore to me by all the saints that it was the weirdest case he has ever encountered. The only footprints he discovered seemed always to be those of the same two men, and they, sire, headed for the marsh and seemed to sink therein."

"And why did you wait so long to report the matter?"

"Because, sire, due to the unusual circumstances I myself have been engaged in questioning the English," Guy replied. "But they are a stubborn lot and do not readily divulge what they know. It was only after much persuasion that they succeeded in recalling one single detail."

"What was that?"

Guy shrugged.

"That on the night in question the demons of the marsh were unusually restless. They called and babbled all night long, boasting loudly and repeatedly of their deed."

"You must improve your methods of persuasion," observed William dryly.

Guy was imperturbable.

"I did," he said.

William turned away. The egotism of this man never failed to irk him. He moved slowly down the room, his hands clasped behind his back.

"And what did your improved methods uncover?"

"That Hereward Leofricsson has recently returned to England."

William swung around.

"Ah-h——"

He resumed his pacing, but now his splendid form seemed suddenly flooded with energy. He had known that sooner or later he would come to grips with Hereward Leofricsson; sooner or later these months of sluggish peace would end, months during which England had lain supine, sullen, leaderless, inactive. Earl Waltheof had been lost to them. He dared not so much as request his release. And now, when the land was smoldering with rebellion, wanting only a leader capable of creating unity, Hereward Leofricsson appeared. It was no coincidence. William had known he would someday return to end this space of idle waiting that had hampered his own plans and progress, leaving him unfree to pursue his further aims.

Guy broke in upon his reverie.

"Sire," he said, "my men are nervous. Assuredly a like descent will be made upon my demesne in due course. It would appear wise to strengthen the garrison beforehand."

"When do you plan to return?"

"At sunrise, sire."

"You shall be accompanied by a large body of men-at-arms who will be garrisoned with you until the need has passed," replied the king.

Guy bowed.

"Then I shall detain you no longer, sire, save to offer you my profound thanks."

He picked up his cloak from the chair and threw it carelessly over his arm. The gesture was quite natural, yet as William watched him a frown creased his brow. There was something about Guy's manner that warned the king, that alerted all his senses; something that told him that the real purpose of Guy's hasty visit had not yet been disclosed.

"His Hastings guerdon was never paid in full," reflected William. "If that is what he has come to claim, it is indeed an ill-chosen moment. My coffers are low, my patents of nobility exhausted." He appraised the slight form, the crafty countenance, lined and creased like ancient parchment. "The wily Guy bears in mind that a king must needs sell his favors dear. By concealing from me its true magnitude, he calculates to purchase it at a minimum cost."

Guy had now bowed himself to the portal and was about to turn and open the door. Suddenly he paused, as though upon the moment a thought had occurred to him.

He looked up with careful indifference.

"There is a small matter," he said, "scarcely worthy of Your Grace's consideration."

He waited for the king to speak, but the king said nothing.

"My neighbor, Sir Toustin de St. Denys, has a sister, sire—the lady Althya."

"Yes?"

"I feel the inclination to wed her."

The king appeared to be examining his buskins.

"The lady is, I seem to recall, the orphaned daughter of Turgis de St. Denys, who so strangely vanished a month back."

"She is, sire," Guy replied. "Your Grace will also recall that a few days after his disappearance Turgis' body was washed up on the beach. I myself examined it and found signs of violence which indicated that the English were responsible for this terrible crime."

"Then you must be aware that Turgis' death leaves the lady's brother, Toustin, in the position of her legal guardian," William said. "Have you discussed the matter with him?"

There was a moment's angry silence.

"Yes, sire," Guy admitted reluctantly.

The king did not question him further. He moved over to the fireplace and stretched his hands before the blaze. There was something here that he could not fathom, something whose significance eluded him. Toustin de St. Denys had petitioned him to inquire into the strange circumstances of his father's death, for which he claimed that de Lussac was responsible and presented his sister, Althya, as witness of the fact. William, however, already overburdened with his own complex affairs, had found it convenient to point out that it was merely the girl's word against Sir Guy's; that not only was there no apparent motive for the crime on de Lussac's part, but there was not the slightest shred of real evidence that he had committed it. Sullen and scowling, Toustin had requested leave to return with his sister to the fenlands.

Now this new request greatly interested the king, aroused his curiosity. If Sir Guy really *had* murdered Turgis, why did he now want to marry Turgis' daughter? Vengeance? Vengeance for what? "In any case," reflected William, "it is understandable that the lady has rejected his suit. So Guy has come to beg my intercession which, if he can procure gratis, will enable him to still claim his Hastings guerdon later. Well, if he wants the girl, he shall have her—but at my price."

He turned and faced Sir Guy.

"The matter can perhaps be satisfactorily arranged," he said, "though it might be difficult—and costly."

"Costly?"

"In view of the existing circumstances there will, of course, be certain compensatory considerations to the lady's brother."

Guy hesitated, mindful that the king's generosity in this case would lighten his own purse. Yet there was no way in which the king's assistance could be dispensed with, for only the king could accomplish what both Toustin and Althya herself had refused to countenance. Recalling the circumstances of his brief but fruitless courtship brought to mind the memory of Althya's scorn. A sudden rage filled him.

"Regardless of the considerations, sire," he said between his teeth, "this is to me a matter of the greatest magnitude."

The Conqueror's eyes snapped, and too late Guy realized his mistake. So the king was toting up the score! Despite his dissembling, this favor would be debited against the sum total of his guerdon.

The Conqueror's next words confirmed his suspicion.

"Recalling your services at Hastings," he said smoothly, "I was prepared for a claim of a somewhat different nature."

But Guy was not one to be so lightly maneuvered into the complete dissolution of a debt. He was prepared to fix the price of the favor at only one half the guerdon.

"Perchance there might be some small matter at a future date," he replied, struggling to conceal the malevolence in his voice. Then he added to make the matter clear, "—since Your King's Grace is always so generous."

But the king was still not finished. The matter of the guerdon would be concluded now, before he undertook the first step that would unite Althya de St. Denys with Guy de Lussac.

"As I recall her dowry is uncommonly generous," he observed.

So now the king was paying off the remainder of his debt with the maiden's dowry!

Guy's eyes blazed. For a moment he considered abandoning his plan to wed the girl, save that caution warned him to weigh carefully the prospects of an implacable king's future generosity as against the maiden's present wealth.

"I believe it is adequate," he conceded.

The cards being on the table, the king smiled graciously.

"I shall summon Sir Toustin from the fenlands immediately," he said, "and the matter shall be arranged as you desire."

"Can I count upon it, sire?" asked Guy.

"The girl shall be yours," replied the king. "You have my word upon it." So saying, he bade Guy a curt good night and departed down the chill corridors to his bedchamber.

But the king's step was heavy. The dimness of the corridor hid his troubled frown and the thick walls muted the sound of his sigh.

"It is regrettable," he murmured, "that even such a one as Guy should thus be deprived of his well-earned guerdon. Yet if all my just debts were justly paid, there would be little left with which to hold my kingdom." He paused, his hand on the latch of his chamber door. "Sometimes Majesty and Justice so ill accord that, without Tyranny, it were futile to be king."

He, on the other hand, who had fought and lost, smiled as he made his descent down the turret stairs to the floor below where he would be sheltered for the night.

"If the cost has been high," he muttered, scarcely moving his lipless mouth, "it will be worth it in the end. Aside from my plans for the wench, it is true that she is immensely wealthy and the king, who can unscrupulously outbargain me in the question of my guerdon, will nevertheless hold it a point of honor to keep his given word."

Earl Waltheof, in the meantime, tossed restlessly upon his couch, struggling with his fevered thoughts and haunted by the minstrel's words, words now seared as with a branding iron upon his brain. "The men of the north are united. The time is now."

The meaning of the message was clear. Hereward Leofricsson had somehow wrought order out of disorder, had somehow succeeded in uniting the unruly northerners into a workable military machine. No other man could have accomplished such a feat, for no other living Englishman possessed the natural generalship of Hereward Leofricsson. This had been evident when he first left England and joined the famed Vaeringer Guards of the Greek emperors where he soon carved out for himself a military career of extraordinary luminosity, becoming, in a few short years, a general whose exploits set him amongst the foremost strategists of his day and whose fame flashed like a comet across the Eastern orbit. In time he had come to be called "the Wake" and indeed his name was well earned, for such were his unwearying patience, his consummate skill and alertness that never once was he caught unprepared; never once was a contingency unanticipated. Aye, he was well nicknamed "the Wake."

Earl Waltheof was acutely aware that he himself could not bring to the cause a like military ability, yet he knew himself to be possessed of another qualification which was equally indispensable. Without him, the north would not fight, for not only had he been born and raised among these unbridled Northumbrians, but his father had been their chosen earl. Siward, Earl of Northumberland, had been beloved by them because he defended his rugged earldom against all hostile forces with a tenacity for which he was renowned, each hedge as though it were a fortress; each inch of ground as though it were a field of battle. "Digera," they surnamed him, meaning "the Strong," for he could smite a rock of granite in twain with his bare fist. His gigantic stature, his immeasurable strength and his personal prowess served to weld his people to him, whilst his ancestry on the non-human side, coupled with his romantic exploits, had made him the favorite hero of the Northumbrian scalds. Many a savage crime had been mingled with his glowing exploits, yet when he died his wild men mourned him in their wild way, and mindful that, bowed beneath the weight of years, he had at last come to kneel contrite before the Cross, they forsook their Viking tradition and laid him to sleep within the four walls of the church he himself had reared to the glory of God. The memory of Earl Siward still stirred the fighting blood of the men of the north; Waltheof Siwardsson's presence, now that the signal for revolt was sounding throughout Northumberland, was indispensable to Hereward the Wake.

Waltheof leaped to his feet and strode in agitation about his chamber.

Two years before, caught in the maelstrom of the dark and hopeless days after Hastings, he had accepted William's bounty as the sole alternative, submitting to the Conqueror because he judged England lost and her people hopelessly enslaved. In exchange for his fealty William had allowed him to retain nominal possession of his earldom and demesnes, at the same time inviting the earl, in a way

which made refusal impossible, to be his honored guest at court, free
to come and go as he chose. Such was the example of beneficence
William set before English eyes. But as the Conqueror's grip on England became more secure he was able to dispense with subterfuge.
Waltheof's position emerged as that of a political prisoner—a hostage
securing the good behavior of the Northumbrian people. Two weeks
ago he had been transferred to the Tower. Since then he had never
left the floor on which he dwelt.

Waltheof ceased his agitated striding and stepped to the barred
window, extending the cupped palm in which two small objects re-
posed. A high-drifting moon bathed the tall white fortress on the
riverbank in its calm brilliance and as its light crept down the window casing it enabled the earl to minutely examine the halfpennies.
They matched perfectly.

The earl wavered, weighing well the consequences. The odds were
against him, for he was unfamiliar with the Tower's ramifications,
and detection in the midst of attempted flight would draw down
upon his insurgent head the terrible force of a vengeance untempered
by mercy. His wracked bones would whiten on the floor of the
dungeons below. But to succeed? His Viking spirit soared. To succeed would mean freedom; to don his armor and fall in battle, his
wounds in front; to sleep eternally in a lofty barrow close to the sky
on some windy headland, swept by the ocean's spray and lulled for
ever by the deep, familiar murmurings of the ocean's depths.

Waltheof wavered no longer. With a bound he reached the door.
Noiselessly he opened it and stepped out into the corridor.

He by-passed the first turret, for he surmised correctly that it led
to the Torture Chamber. At the next stairway he hesitated, then
started slowly down, hugging the inner wall. He paused halfway to
lean forward and peer around the thick stone column of the circular
stair well.

A long corridor stretched before him. Moonlight fell slantwise
through the loops, merging with the yellow glow of the lanthorns
to cause a curious, eerie light. But at the foot of the stairs, immovable
as a statue and seemingly grafted to the spot, stood a young sentry,
his casque polished with such industry that the earl could see his own
reflection in it.

Waltheof waited, conscious of the footsteps that re-echoed below
like the mighty smiting of Thor's hammer. To attempt to penetrate
the corridors would be folly, for the guards were apparently as

vigilant by night as by day. Instead, Waltheof fixed his hopes upon a subterranean passage, the low brow of which was barely visible from where he stood.

He waited. His muscles ached and his lips grew parched, but still the sentry stood there, springing partially to life only to exchange an occasional word with his confreres who passed by from time to time. Two hours dragged by. The earl, concealed still behind the column, had begun to think of returning to his chamber, when suddenly instinct warned him that the sentry below had moved. Bracing himself, he leaned forward and peered around the column. The sentry was out of sight. He stood just beyond the outer wall of the stair well, talking to a comrade. Waltheof could barely hear their muffled laughter. The earl's heart thumped against his ribs. His eyes measured off the distance to the passage. He broke from concealment and reached the foot of the steps. An instant later he was lost in the security of the friendly gloom below.

But the sentry, having ceased his conversation with his comrade, turned abruptly to return to his station, chuckling to himself. Suddenly the chuckle died upon his lips. Slowly he approached the short flight of steps leading to the subterranean passage. Fear and bewilderment darkened his face as he stood quite still, endeavoring to penetrate the obscurity that cloaked it. True, he had actually seen nothing, save that as he turned the quick flash as of a knight's shining shield caught in the moonlight had hung for an instant in the darkness. Nothing more than that, and it had vanished with the suddenness of a floating specter.

Once again he took up his position, standing as before with his back to the stairway. But instead of abating, his sense of uneasiness increased and he turned from time to time to peer fearfully down into the gloom. Were his nerves, taut after the experience of last night, playing tricks? Should he summon the captain? Yet if it was difficult to explain to himself just what it was he had seen, would it not be doubly difficult to answer the captain's questions? How would he explain his absence from his post? Yet the dungeon was his responsibility. The king himself had warned that above all else no Englishman must ever guess what lay below. It would be more prudent to say nothing until he had made his investigation, then, if he saw anything suspicious, a single cry would bring a hundred men to his side.

Having thus made his decision, he crossed himself fervently, and raising his arm, unhooked a lanthorn that hung just within his reach.

In the meantime Waltheof, unaware of the perturbation one glimpse of his long white hair was causing the hesitant sentry, sped on his way, driven on by a hope that lent speed to his heels. At the foot of the stairs he cast an eager glance around. No windows! No doors! One single aperture in the interminable stone—a low, thickset archway. Waltheof leaped through it, then drew up abruptly.

He found himself in what appeared to be an immense subterranean dungeon. It was unlit, save that a ray of light escaped somehow from the floor above to fall slantwise through the arch, vaguely illuminating the adjacent wall and floor. The remainder was veiled in impenetrable obscurity, from out of which he sensed rather than heard the faint, persistent washing of water against a stone surface. Waltheof edged slowly forward across the rough floor, following the sounds, ignoring the sharp cemented boulders that cut through his thin pumps. As he drew nearer to it, he fell to his knees, pressing forward anxiously, feeling his way with trembling hands. A small patch of evenly laid brickwork set in a circular pattern brought him to a ledge, from whence his exploring hand fell away into space. He leaned over the ledge, dangling his arm into the void. His fingers found the water.

Waltheof sank back on his heels, laughing bitterly. The laughter thrown back at him from out of the well hung mockingly upon the thick, dank air, re-echoing through his throbbing brain as he arose and started a systematic search of the dungeon walls, groping with his outstretched hands for some opening. The search proved fruitless. The Conqueror's dungeons were not built to aid escape.

Dispirited, he started back toward the stairs. With his foot on the bottom step he stopped. Raising his head, he perceived to his horror the reflected light from a swaying lanthorn creeping down the walls. Icy sweat chilled him. He backed away, then turned and ran halfway across the dungeon floor.

He stopped running with a sudden jerk, turning slowly to face the beam of light that glided across the wall before dropping soundlessly to the floor. But the man who turned was a cowering, terrible sight, gripped by one of the rare but violent paroxysms of cringing fear that had been his unhappy heritage, the unconquerable fear that from childhood had been the malignant secret of his innermost being.

His face was now a hideous, livid mask that worked spasmodically as he fought to breathe. His widening eyes were riveted upon the light that had somehow become a creeping yellow mass gliding relentlessly forward, threatening to submerge him. He tried to cry out, but no sound came. Desperately he fought to check the abject, primeval terror that grafted him to the spot, but he could only stand there, slowly raising his palsied hands to ward off the formless yellow mass that still came on, spilling itself out over the floor like an unstemmable flood, hypnotizing him by its stealthy progress.

Waltheof was lost!

Suddenly from behind him a hand reached out. It took a slow but firm grip on Waltheof's shoulder. He could feel the long, clawlike nails bite into his flesh as with almost fanatic strength it drew him backwards. The earl's back hit the bars of a rounded iron cage, but still the hand did not relinquish its grip. The sentry was almost at the threshold now. Swiftly and with inescapable force the hand steered Waltheof, till the cage stood between the earl and the sentry, then it exerted pressure on the earl's shoulder, forcing him to crouch.

None too soon. The sentry stood in the archway raising his lanthorn above his head and swinging it in all directions to cover each bare well, each empty corner. He advanced toward the well, lowering his light into the cylindrical pit to gaze intently down. Then he straightened up and looked toward the cage.

"Is someone here?" he demanded.

"I am here," came the sarcastic reply from the cage.

The sentry laughed with surly insolence and continued for a moment to cast the beams from his lanthorn into the far corners of the dungeon.

The prisoner in the cage chuckled.

"Your comrades would laugh," he said, "to see with what diligence you search an all but empty vault."

In angry spite the sentry focused the light full upon the cage. The prisoner within turned his face abruptly away, for his eyes, accustomed to eternal darkness, were troubled by the light. Instinctively Waltheof, crouching behind him, raised his head to glimpse the profile of his deliverer.

His long hair hung wild and matted, a silvery profusion wherein a few dark strands still lingered. His face was streaked with grime; his nails were like the talons of a hawk, yet the hands gripping the bars of the cage were arrestingly youthful, almost those of a boy. He wore neither shoes nor hose and the tattered tunic which appeared to be his sole garment was knotted raggedly about his thin thighs and shoulders. But even in this unkempt state there was no mistaking the profile. Waltheof was staggered by the shock.

This caged creature was a Godwinsson!

The sentry kept his lanthorn focused upon the cage.

"Did you not see someone come down those steps?" he demanded.

Waltheof did not stir, confident that in so far as a Godwinsson could shield him, he would do so.

The Godwinsson laughed.

"If someone were here for me to see," he replied, "would you not see him also? No, my friend, there is no place here wherein even a specter could find concealment."

The sentry turned away abruptly. Satisfied, he hastened to return to his post, sweeping the light from the dungeon as he went. Without a further word he mounted the stairs, leaving the earl and the Godwinsson once again in total darkness.

Waltheof addressed the Godwinsson in a low voice.

"You must be the youngest of the brothers," he said. "You must be Ulfnoth."

"Aye," replied the prisoner. "And you?"

"Waltheof Siwardsson," the earl replied. He hesitated, debating as to how much of his uncontrollable fear the Godwinsson had been able to observe. Not much, he judged, for only his silhouette could have been visible against the approaching light. "You have done me a great service," he added at last.

"Speak not of it," replied the other, "but rather waste no time in seeking your freedom by some other route. There is no exit here."

"Tell me first where to find the keys to this cage," the earl replied, "and if you are willing, we shall try together."

"To have keys," murmured the Godwinsson, "a cage must first have a door."

It took Waltheof a moment to grasp the full significance of the Godwinsson's words. A cage without a door!

"Come," urged the Godwinsson, "bethink you of your own escape, since you seem disposed to take the chance. Is the guard posted near by?"

"Aye, at the head of the stairs."

"Then conceal yourself," said the Godwinsson with the placidity and cunning of the long-immured. "I will summon him. There is something he fears. He will come. When he does, you will know what to do."

The earl concealed himself in the shadows of the archway, listening as the sentry rushed down the steps in answer to the Godwinsson's cry. As the man sped past him, Waltheof sprang, enveloping the hapless guard in a grip that held him inert against his massive chest. The sentry formed his lips to cry out, but before he could fill his lungs with air a massive white-furred arm shot upwards, catching the man's chin in the crook at the elbow. There was a low gurgle—a sharp crack—and the man sagged limply in the earl's arms, his knees buckling helplessly. The earl released him. He dropped with a soft thud to the floor, dead of a broken neck. The earl stooped, and lifting him easily in his arms, carried him over and dropped him into the well.

The Godwinsson had followed Waltheof's movements in the darkness with increasing interest and curiosity, unable to reconcile this present coolheadedness with this same man's strange conduct of a short while ago. Unaware, however, of the Godwinsson's acute interest, Waltheof found his way back to the cage, where he sought the Godwinsson's hand.

"Do not despair," he said. "If all goes well, I shall return to repay the debt I owe you."

Ulfnoth clasped the outstretched hand.

"God speed you," he said.

"God save you," replied Waltheof. Then he turned and sped from the dungeon.

But as he safely vaulted the last few steps to the floor on which he dwelt, he was crushed by the bitterness of his failure. Even his words of encouragement to Ulfnoth seemed suddenly imbued with all the gloomy aspects of a hollow promise. Others would fight. Others would free England from the Norman yoke, but while they did so he, Earl Waltheof Siwardsson, would continue to subsist upon the Conqueror's bounty, dependent upon him for each morsel of bread, each cup of wine. He would live here weaponless, penniless, deprived of everything save his own useless life. For him there was no escape! In this fortress he was as trapped as the Godwinsson in his doorless cage!

But at the head of the stairs he drew up abruptly, his feet in a small pool of rain water. He stood looking down at them, working his toes inside his light shoes, letting the water seep through the seams, feeling its coolness against his flesh. He raised his head.

The stairway continued on, leading to the unfinished third floor.

The storm had ripped away part of the temporary barricade and with it the protective covering, and Waltheof perceived up beyond the rubble-strewn steps a small patch of night sky encircled by the blackness of the stair well.

The sky! Freedom!

He vaulted up the steps, coming out on the scaffolding leading to the river. He bounded across the short bridge, shedding his garments as he ran. In the east the first gray glimmerings of dawn were already robbing the moon of her brilliance. Waltheof hesitated only for a moment, gazing down into the writhing waters of the Thames well over fifty feet below. Suddenly he threw back his head with a low laugh, thrusting out his furry chest and filling his lungs with the clear, crisp air. Then he plunged in and headed east toward the marshes, swimming under water close to the reedy banks, leaving only an occasional air bubble on the restless black waters to show his progress.

Chapter Seven

THE REBELS TAKE YORK

OF THE once great castle the Conqueror built at York, hardly a trace now remains. The earthwork he selected for his purpose had all the indications of being a prehistoric barrow and indeed later excavations disclosed a rough cist wherein some Champion had, centuries before, been laid in crouched burial. Such a ready-made site, conveniently situated at the confluence of the rivers Foss and Ouse, could not escape the Conqueror's keen eye. Deep in the bowels of his burial mound the Champion slept on undisturbed, whilst above him the Conqueror raised his donjon, surrounding it by walls and towers and defending its land approaches by a moat spanned by a drawbridge.

Time has swept all the Conqueror's buildings, all save one decaying keep which through the ages stood watch whilst the rest crumbled into ivied mounds and half-obliterated ditches; whilst the moat dried up and the dark waters of the Foss alone gave life to the spot, washing, as they had for centuries, the outworks of the castle. Even the trained eye of the archaeologist can scarce make out the place where the Great Hall once stood; the chapel where the Conqueror worshiped, his hands stained with the blood of a hundred thousand souls; the armory where his soldiers hung their crossbows, or the grand staircase at whose head Hereward, fighting the fight for freedom, his fearful sword dripping with the blood of Normandy, found himself once again face to face with Althya. All is swept away now, the glory of the Norman; the futile struggle of the English; the castle that held them in thralldom, awing them with its might and filling their hearts with a bitterness that death alone could assuage. And of the descendants of those who laid down their lives in Freedom's cause, or of those who opposed them, who shall say which now is the Englishman, or which the Norman, for they are one.

It was a serene October night, some four months after Waltheof's escape from the Tower. Sir Toustin de St. Denys, newly appointed assistant governor of York Castle, awakened suddenly from a deep sleep with an odd sense of alertness. He lay tense for a moment, warily examining the darkness. When nothing stirred, he breathed again, and arising cautiously from his bed, threw a fur robe about his thin linen shift and stepped to the window.

Below, all was well. Upon the castle walls the sentries paced the rampart walks with their usual equanimity, pausing at each embrasure to scan the surrounding countryside. The quiet waters of the moat reflected an angle of the donjon, a monstrous black mass relieved only by narrow slit-shaped windows behind which flickered the torches. Reflected thus in the water, they looked like so many red, blinking eyes in the monster's bulk, eyes which bespoke the grave need of ceaseless vigilance by the Norman conquerors. The gatehouse, too, showed nothing irregular. The heavy oaken doors were securely locked and barred, portcullis down, drawbridge raised. Beyond the moat slumbered the great city of York, from whose English inhabitants there was certainly little to be feared. Already they had assumed the eternal demeanor of a conquered people, obsequious, servile, grateful for a kindly word or smile. It was well. It was as it should be.

Sir Toustin found himself reassured by such overwhelming evidence of Norman supremacy. Whatever unaccountable fears he had experienced a few moments before were quite dispelled by the scene before him. In the heavens the half-moon was partially concealed by an opaque veil that promised rain. An owl hooted shrilly in the distance. Grazing peacefully in the wastelands beyond the castle's outer wall were a few cattle whose English owner had neglected to corral them. In the morning they would set the poor fellow a merry chase.

Sir Toustin yawned and returned to his bed, sinking back luxuriously among the pillows. Assistant governor of York! So singular an honor was rarely bestowed upon one so young as he, he reflected contentedly. If he was not cheered by the prospect of wintering in this raw northern climate, it was at least gratifying to know that he found such favor with the king. He could almost forgive William for his former negligence in the matter of his father's death, for which Toustin did not doubt he was now trying to atone. Only the unhappy fact of Althya's recent betrothal to Guy de Lussac loomed

like a cirrus cloud in the blue sky of his contentment, though there,
too, the king had certainly been most gracious, taking it upon himself to look out for the girl's welfare and personally selecting her
future husband.

Here Toustin frowned into the darkness. He loved his sister and
would not willingly see her wed to a man she feared and hated. Aside
from their own suspicions concerning de Lussac, he was surely a
sorry prospect for any young girl, especially for one as self-willed
and spirited as Althya. When she had announced her determination
to accompany Toustin to York, he had readily fallen in with the
plan. For the moment at least, she was spared the unpleasantness of
de Lussac's visits, though in the end, despite her stubborn resistance,
she would undoubtedly be forced to wed the man. The king's wish—
his stern "command," Toustin admitted uncomfortably to himself
—could not be ignored.

With a sigh, the new assistant governor turned his thoughts to
happier channels. The plump, dark beauty in the city across the moat
—did she really think her high birth entitled her to privileges denied
the tavern girl? Well, for the Englishry, it didn't. She would find
that out. Tomorrow he would handle the matter with a firmer hand.
Willing or no, he would give orders to have her taken and smuggled
into the castle at nightfall along with the other wenches. He would
teach her that the Normans were the masters now. He would teach
her—and here his thoughts sped on until, comforted by the prospects
of so earthy an Elysium, Sir Toustin drifted off into a deep and pleasant slumber.

An hour later he leaped to his feet with an oath. In the center of
the room he paused to listen, tense and motionless. All was silent, yet
the sense of imminent peril persisted. He sprang to the window. The
rampart walks were deserted. The sentries had vanished. Then he
saw them, sprawled in the courtyard where they had been flung,
their throats cut before they had found time to breathe a last Pater
Noster. Others lay in the wastelands beyond the wall, among the
carcasses of the strayed cattle—no, not the carcasses—the empty
hides! Sacré Dieu! Could it have been the English he had watched
"grazing," penetrating to the very foot of the castle walls without
arousing his own suspicions or those of the luckless sentries? He
could see their rope scaling-ladders swinging idly from the curtain
walls.

As Toustin sprang into action, a watchman's voice broke in upon the stillness, giving the alarm. For a second only the man cried out, then he was abruptly silenced. Time for armor there was none. Sir Toustin grasped his sword, and clad only in his night shift, threw open the door of his chamber and dashed out.

A moment later the sounds of battle raging in the Hall below filled the castle; the desperate, warning cries of the Normans; wild joyous shouts from the attackers. Above it all the tocsin sounded, harsh and hollow. Men scrambled from their beds, reaching out on all sides for their weapons, and the corridors swarmed with half-clothed, half-armed men. The governor, Sir Herlwin FitzHugh, sallied forth, sword in hand, his lean face still surmounted by a wool cap, his lean form clad in a nightshirt.

"Down the back stairs, men, and surprise them from the rear," he shouted. "Six of you help me hold the stairs!"

Wheeling, he sped on down the corridor, whilst the men quickly dispersed. Sir Toustin hesitated, then elected to follow the governor. He was vaguely aware that his sister's door opened abruptly. For an instant he saw Althya standing white-faced upon the threshold, listening with horror to the sounds of slaughter below, then he sped on.

Meanwhile in the Hall the fighting was savage and bloody, with the English venting all their consuming hatred on the defenders of the castle. The manner of their assault had precluded the use of armor, and the English were clad only in faded, ragged garments. Their faces and arms, stained with berry juice, were as black as the hides that had concealed them, and those who lacked swords fought with long woodsmen's knives or implements of husbandry. As the defenders fell back, the English surged grimly forward, trampling underfoot the bodies of the Norman wounded, heeding neither their curses nor their prayers. Their leaders in the foreground, by some miracle still unscathed, fought with skill and cold precision; Hereward the Wake and Waltheof Siwardsson, shoulder to shoulder, striking down all who had the folly to present themselves.

With the arrival of the governor's reinforcements the defenders had taken new heart. But only for a moment. The English superiority of numbers was soon apparent. Backed against a wall, the Normans fought bravely, but with every Englishman they felled, ten leaped in to take his place and many a Norman was left all but limbless by the short English axes. Sir Herlwin, pausing momentarily at the head of the stairs up which a few wounded were struggling vainly to crawl, was appalled at the carnage. "A moi, mes hommes!" he cried to those behind him, "Ha! Rou!" to those below, and thereupon, undeterred by the sight of the swarming enemy, he bounded down the stairs.

"God's blood!" exclaimed Waltheof, recognizing him instantly. "Sir Herlwin! My friend of the Tower!"

But the governor had no time to waste on greetings. He was met at the bottom of the stairs by a solid wall of English. Hereward, confronted by so comic a figure as that of Sir Herlwin, cap on head, his spare form clad in a nightgown whose many pleats and folds implied an obesity which his skinny calves denied, seemed convulsed with merriment. But Sir Herlwin, an expert swordsman, swept all merriment from his face. The swordplay that ensued lasted for several bitter minutes before the governor slowly gave ground, parrying all the while with desperate courage, edging backwards step by step, his eyes never leaving his opponent. The knights who flanked him had already given way beneath the crushing blows of Waltheof and Eadric the Wild. As they fell, Toustin de St. Denys took his place on Sir Herlwin's right, whilst the governor's son, a lad of sixteen, stood upon his left. Side by side the three Normans fought, giving way grudgingly as the English pushed them back, till already half the staircase lay below them.

Above the noise of battle Hereward addressed the governor.

"We hold the castle," he said pleasantly, parrying still. "I will give the order to cease fighting at your pleasure."

Sir Herlwin, unaware that his own cheek was bleeding and that the blood from numerous wounds mottled his white shift, took advantage of the moment of parley to glance behind him. Two men alone were left upon the landing. Beyond them, several women cowered behind the slight form of the lady Althya. Somehow they must be saved. At the hands of such an undisciplined mob no indignity would be spared them.

"Back!" he cried suddenly. "Back! To the tower!"

This only brought the English surging angrily forward. Before their onslaught the Normans again gave ground. Unexpectedly Sir Herlwin lunged so that the point of his sword ripped Hereward's shoulder, but with an adroit movement the Wake brushed aside the blade. There was a sharp crack. The governor's sword splintered, falling with a clatter to the stairs, and Sir Herlwin was left gripping only the useless hilt.

The Wake laughed and with an insolent gesture pricked Sir Herl-win under the chin, tilting back his head.

" 'Twould serve me better to save you for ransom than to run you through," he said. Then he turned his attention to Sir Toustin.

But Toustin was no match for Hereward. Already his right fore-arm was pierced through. The blood flowed freely downward into his palm so that his sword hilt slipped as he strove to grip it. Just as they reached the top step Hereward, with a skilled thrust, pierced him through the armpit. Toustin reeled, but by an effort kept his balance. Leaning against the balustrade for support, he again raised his sword to protect himself. Hereward sprang toward him, and Toustin, chilled by the Wake's sudden, fierce laughter and dazed by his wound, stood grafted to the spot unable to move.

At that moment, with the speed and fury of a tigress, Althya leaped between them and threw herself upon Hereward, clenching her fists and reigning blows upon his face and chest with all her strength.

"Can't you see he's dying, you black-faced savage?" she stormed between rage and grief. "If you strike him again I'll kill you—I'll kill you—I'll kill you——"

Hereward, veteran of a thousand campaigns, found himself, in the heat of battle, confronted by a situation new to him, the verbal and physical onslaught of an opponent's female relative. For a moment he was too startled to do more than study the crown of his unknown assailant's head, which bobbed and oscillated somewhere below his chin line, then he glanced helplessly at Toustin, who, though suffer-ing from his several wounds, was obviously in no way near death. Already he was rallying himself to continue the fight and replied to Hereward's unspoken question with a crooked smile which clearly expressed his embarrassment at his sister's extraordinary intervention.

"We are orphans," he murmured apologetically. Then, in an effort to further excuse his sister's frailties, he added, "We have only each other."

Hereward, meanwhile, still at a loss, returned his attention to the girl. By now, being somewhat exhausted, she was delivering her blows with less vigor and he was able for the first time to catch a glimpse of her face. The discovery he made bereft him of the power to move or speak. With a gasp of amazement, his arm dropped to his side. He lost all awareness of the fighting going on around him, was unaware even of her last feeble blows. He stood as though paralyzed, gazing down into the angry, upraised face of Althya.

Earl Waltheof at his shoulder prodded him rudely.

"What ails you, Hereward?" he queried. "Dost sleep at such a time?"

Hereward didn't hear him. The two Normans on the landing above, observing his apathy, prepared to attack. But at that moment the end came. Sir Herlwin's son, who had withstood a full quarter hour of savage fighting at his father's side, received a knife in the breast aimed at him from the Hall. He fell forward against the balustrade, then, half slipping, half toppling, crashed head over heels over the balustrade to the floor below. Sir Herlwin chanced to see the lad fall, and he, fearing that the enraged mob would hack the boy to pieces whilst he lived, determined to capitulate at once in an effort to save him.

"Hold!" he cried. "Hold!"

Like an automaton Hereward raised his arm, signaling to his men to cease fighting. Still his eyes never left the girl's face.

"Hold!" again cried Sir Herlwin. "I shall confer with your leader concerning terms!"

At that Hereward raised his head.

"We make no terms," he snapped. "The castle is already ours. We will accept the submission of its defenders."

Sir Herlwin glanced anxiously down at the prostrate form of his son. The governor's face was pale, though not for himself, for Sir Herlwin FitzHugh was a brave man.

"Shall the wounded be treated?" he demanded.

"Aye."

"And the women? What of them?"

"We do not war upon women," replied Hereward. "The men will be held for ransom."

He turned back to Althya, but she was no longer there. Looking up, he caught sight of her white-clad form disappearing rapidly down the dim corridor. The door of her apartment opened and closed and she was gone.

About noon of that same day, in the tower of the castle's square donjon keep, three men sat in council. The chamber was small, its thick stone walls naked, its floor devoid of rushes. The narrow slit windows faced north, overlooking the castle bailey where the dead, both English and Norman, were being piled in heaps awaiting final disposal. Beyond the moat lay the ancient city of York, girdled still by walls and battlements built by the Roman. Through the circuitous streets thronged a surging, writhing mass of people, some of whom were still too dazed by the unexpectedness of their liberation to do more than gaze rapturously up at the English banner above the keep which had already replaced the Two Lions of Normandy; others were giving vent to their joy with hoarse cheers, shouts and yells which, borne by the wind to the tiny chamber in the tower, went unnoticed by the three men who held council there.

Hereward, his face now cleansed of berry juice, his tall form clad in an immaculate tunic and chausses provided by the ingenious Lightfoot, leaned forward and traced a line with his forefinger upon a rough chart spread out upon the table.

"I estimate that it should be no more than a two-day ride to our prearranged meeting place," he said. "Allowing one day for the consummation of my business with Asbiorn and two days to return, I should be back at York before a week is out."

Eadric the Wild looked up, his cynical gaze roving over Hereward's face. His character was clearly written in the lines of his forehead; a man both savage and brave, both ruthless and staunch. He leaned back against his chair. Slowly his hands gripped the ivory and silver weapons at his waist; slowly he crossed long muscled legs, whilst the cold green eyes beneath their rubicund lids never wavered in their faintly hostile scrutiny.

"Hereward Leofricsson," he said, "I do not question your ability to negotiate favorably with Asbiorn. But most emphatically do I question the wisdom of your binding us to a contract whose terms we cannot fulfill."

"You refer, of course, to our empty purses."

"Precisely," replied Eadric. "When we agreed to engage the services of the pirate Asbiorn, it was on the assumption that we would be able to pay for those services with the proceeds of the castle coffers."

"Aye," murmured Earl Waltheof, shaking his pale head regretfully. "There was lamentably little in the governor's strongbox. 'Twas a sore disappointment."

"We all know," continued Eadric, "that those who deal with Asbiorn must be prepared to pay in gold for what they buy."

Hereward shrugged.

"That suits me well enough," he said.

Eadric lowered his head like a bull about to charge.

"It would suit me, too—if it could be done," he retorted.

"It is a question only of *how* it can be done."

"You play with words," cried Eadric angrily, "since the answer is the same in the end—it cannot!"

Hereward leaned back in his chair, immersed in troubled thought. It was Waltheof who broke the silence.

"Hereward," he said, "perhaps there is still a chance of obtaining armaments from other quarters. What of those who a short while back were so eager to help us?"

"They prevaricate, growing daily less and less disposed to declare themselves," Hereward replied. "Malcolm of Scotland would welcome us as fugitives, but active aid he fears to give. Flanders pleads that she herself is too involved at home to afford us assistance, the result, no doubt, of Baldwin's increasing fear of William. France wisely prefers to have the Norman occupied here in England, rather than engaged in the business of conquest near her own borders."

"But there are others," insisted Eadric. "What of Olaf of Norway, who swore an oath of amity toward England? What of Swen of Denmark? He was a kinsman of Harold Godwinsson."

"They are both immobilized by fear and caution," replied Hereward. "If things go well with us, then we can count upon them for some help later. But first we must show that we are at least able to hold our own against the Conqueror."

"That will be no mean task," grunted Waltheof.

"With Asbiorn's help, it can be accomplished."

"But, God, man," burst out Eadric, "the hazards of our undertaking are already great enough. Let us not add to them by entering into a pact whose terms are obviously beyond our power to fulfill. Already we have performed the impossible. We have built an army out of stragglers from all parts of England. We have armed them as best we could. We have disciplined them, trained them. Our sacrifices have been great, even to the point of relinquishing patrimonies we could have clung to by submission, in order to help wrest England from the Norman—inch by inch if need be. Care, time and patience have built a rebel force that stands ready to sweep through England, freeing the shires one by one and gathering an army as we go. Shall we risk all this by deliberately contracting to pay a monumental sum we do not possess to a man so vengeful he will seek to destroy us if we do not pay it?"

"Of what use is an army without arms?" asked Hereward. "The money to buy them must somehow be obtained. As for Asbiorn, while we would all prefer an ally of less unsavory repute, where is such a one to be found? Only such as he, whose ship is his home, would dare incur the Conqueror's enmity. He has no territory to be invaded. At sea he would be hard to catch."

"I still say he is the wrong man," insisted Eadric. "He has been known to plunder, even to massacre, those whom he was engaged to help."

"Like all his breed, his code is 'an eye for an eye,' " replied Hereward. "Where he has plundered and massacred those who employed him, it was in retaliation for some actual or intended double-dealing. He is known to be possessed of a certain rugged honesty. Where he has been fairly treated, he has never failed in his commitments. We would be foolish, hampered as we are by an urgent need of men and arms, to inquire further into the moral shortcomings of the only man who is willing to supply them."

"In any case," interposed Waltheof complacently, "there is no hurry. Let us postpone a decision until later."

Hereward shook his head.

"The decision must be made now," he replied. "Today."

Eadric gave a short, fierce laugh.

"And what makes us so pressed for time?" he queried. "Is it not still our intention to sit here at York until spring?"

"Yes, but it is scarcely likely that the Conqueror will wait until then to attack us," replied Hereward. "It would be more in his nature to be knocking on the gates of York before a month is out."

"Tsch!" scoffed Eadric.

Earl Waltheof leaned forward, raising the thick white eyebrows which fringed his eyes like a gigantic forest.

"You think he will act with such alacrity!" he gasped.

"With the fall of his northernmost citadel, the whole of Northumberland is lost to him," Hereward replied. "It is a loss he will spare neither lives nor energy to recover."

"Natheless," snapped Eadric, "he will not attempt the march so soon."

"His strategy seems obvious. He must crush us before we grow too strong."

"I am willing to concede the logic of that," retorted Eadric, "but already the last week of October has brought unseasonable storms and light flurries of snow. By the time the news reaches William, winter will have set in. Even the so-called Conqueror would hardly dare lead an army from London to York without considering the many hazards of such an ill-timed undertaking; the roughness of the country through which he would have to march; rivers swollen by the winter's rain; ice and sleet; lack of provisions; even the possible mutinous temper of his troops under such adverse conditions. And certainly only a madman would brave such perils to besiege a walled city which for centuries has successfully withstood military attack."

"Eadric is right, Hereward," said Waltheof hopefully. "William might well hesitate to embark upon an enterprise which would not only be impractical, but all but impossible to carry out. What would he gain by leaving his men to sicken in drafty tents outside the city walls all winter?"

"He would gain much." Hereward arose and strode about the room, his thumbs hooked in his belt. "To pen us up all winter would achieve a twofold purpose—to prevent our enlisting foreign aid and to starve us into submission by spring."

A shadow crossed Eadric's rugged features.

"Before I kneel to the Norman I'll stand upon the city walls and slit my throat with my own dagger!"

"Such a display, though highly commendable, would benefit us little."

"But, Hereward," said Earl Waltheof, his fur-fringed ears erect, "if William should succeed in penning us up, what then? We have neither sufficient arms, nor sufficient men to raise a siege."

"Asbiorn has both."

Eadric the Wild emitted an exasperated grunt, then lapsed into a sullen silence.

"How many men could he provide?" asked Waltheof.

"Five thousand."

"William's army will be fully as large."

"William's army will be larger, but we will have the advantage of surprise."

"Of surprise?" repeated Waltheof. "Have you a plan, Hereward?"

Hereward paused in his striding.

"Aye, I have a plan," he replied. "A plan which has taken months to formulate, months to perfect; a plan which, with adequate outside help, stands as good a chance of success as any I have ever witnessed in military combat."

Swiftly he returned to the map spread out upon the table, concentrating his attention on the area directly outside the ancient battlements of the city, whilst in low tones he proceeded to unfold his plan. As he did so, Eadric the Wild came slowly to life. His green eyes swung upwards, fixing themselves with renewed interest upon Hereward's face. When the Wake ceased speaking, his habitual combativeness and hostility had vanished and were replaced by a somewhat grudging admiration.

"Hereward," he said, "a prettier plan I have never heard. It therefore grieves me to be the one to point out its solitary flaw."

"That Asbiorn Estrithsson is no dispenser of charity?"

"Exactly. He will expect to get paid."

"And paid he shall be," replied Hereward. "Half in advance, half upon the completion of his mission."

Eadric made no effort to disguise the sarcasm in his voice.

"What manner of payment will it be?"

"He will be paid in gold."

"Ha!" Eadric's face flushed. His truculence quickly returned. "That's what I thought! Now we're back where we started with little to show for our time. And where, may it please you, shall we look for this gold? On the moors? Hidden in the fells? In the stomachs of the fish we catch?"

"Eadric's question is well put, Hereward," said Waltheof. "Asbiorn will demand no less than forty thousand marks. Where is such wealth to be found?"

They waited for Hereward's answer, but instead of replying he turned suddenly and crossed to the window where he seemed to become instantly absorbed in what was passing in the bailey below. Before the central door stood a small cart, roughly constructed of withes and drawn by a pair of oxen. The driver lolled near by, waiting indifferently for his vehicle to receive its full capacity of Norman corpses, whilst a Norman priest, having gained permission to accompany the deceased on this pilgrimage to their common grave, raised his kirtle and climbed aboard. The driver pricked the oxen and the beasts started forward. Hereward's eyes followed the cart as it rumbled off across the bailey, out through the postern gate, and started the trek to the hills. He observed the most minute detail of its passage, the careless jolt of the cart as a wheel leaped over a boulder, the rhythmic swinging of a lifeless hand, yet he did so without any awareness of having observed them.

"Where is such wealth to be found?"

The answer to Waltheof's question was simple, yet so inextricably intertwined with Althya's presence here at York that Hereward was reluctant to supply it. Since their unexpected meeting on the stairs some ten hours before, he had found it impossible to focus his attention upon even the most crucial decision. All morning, whilst engaged in the business of preparing the city for defense, appraising walls and battlements, or inspecting engines devised to repel attack, Hereward had been lost in abstraction. He was conscious of being filled with a fresh and exciting vigor which did not result from the successful completion of the first step in their plan to liberate England. It stemmed from the simple fact of Althya's nearness.

Looking back over the morning's work, Hereward was disturbed to realize how little he had accomplished in his efforts to rouse himself from reverie. Somehow a close inspection of his chief engineer's new and revolutionary ballista had revealed, not the gut skein with its ingenious trigger for lobbing over the walls a javelin, a boulder, or even a dead horse, but the bright form of Althya, clad in her night shift, springing down the castle stairs. Or, peering into the trough to gauge the size of the smooth round boulder which the new machine could hurl through the air upon a besieging enemy, it was the crown of Althya's head that he seemed once more to be gazing down upon, whilst upon his chest he could almost feel the small fists pommeling him wildly, fists which could scarcely harm a sparrow, let alone perform her threat to kill a man. And Hereward knew now, beyond a doubt, that he loved her.

"Where is such wealth to be found?"

True, the castle coffers had not provided it. Sir Herlwin FitzHugh could pay a ransom, but only a modest one, for he was not a rich man. But Toustin de St. Denys? News from the fenlands had included word of Turgis' decease. That left Toustin a rich man— forty thousand marks, Althya had told him that night by the campfire. Forty thousand marks—the exact sum required to pay off Asbiorn. By plunging their hands into Toustin's bursting coffers they could, in exchange for his life and liberty, obtain the outside aid without which they could scarcely hope to achieve their goal. Yet how could he permit Toustin to become the sacrificial lamb? How could he permit Toustin to be led to slaughter? How could he

permit Toustin to be mulcted? Toustin was Althya's brother!
Hereward swore fiercely.

Already he had let half the day drag by without seeing her because the recollection of her savage onslaught on the stairs proved
an almost maternal devotion to her brother. How would she view the
levying of such an unheard-of ransom, and one which would surely
reduce Toustin to a state bordering on pauperage? She could never
be made to see it as it really was, an unfortunate circumstance of war
of which he was compelled to take advantage. Why, therefore, since
his information had come to him through Althya, would he not be
justified in ignoring what he knew and in ransoming Toustin, like
Sir Herlwin, for five hundred marks?

Yet even as Hereward wrestled with himself, his real duty stood
forth with unwelcome clarity. The liberation of England from the
Norman scourge must come before all else, even before his love for
Althya. As the leader of the English he could not permit his love for
a girl to dominate his actions. He must not hesitate to wring the
necessary forty thousand marks from Toustin, for by failing to do so
he would be placing in jeopardy the very lives of these men who had
linked their fate to his and sacrificed all to follow him; brave men
who were defying the Conqueror in his hour of triumph; matching
his military might with little more than their own desperate valor;
facing tremendous odds unflinchingly to free England from her
bondage, yet knowing that if they failed they could expect no
quarter from the Conqueror. They would become fruit for the gallows tree and rot thereon.

He turned abruptly to find both his companions watching him intently; Waltheof with a perplexed frown, Eadric merging curiosity
with his usual incivility. Hereward crossed to the door and addressed
the sentry outside.

"Have Sir Herlwin and Sir Toustin brought to me here at once,"
he ordered curtly.

Eadric's curiosity instantly turned to scorn.

"If it's their ransoms you have in mind, Hereward," he cried, "then
dismiss all thought of Asbiorn. I doubt if between them you could
force those swine to disgorge a paltry five hundred marks."

"Eadric is our salamander," observed Waltheof lightly. "The fires
in his cranium could roast an ox."

Eadric the Wild sprang up, his green eyes narrowing dangerously.

"By the face of Mary!" he cried. "Two years of glutting himself on the Conqueror's food and wine have left the earl's tongue suspiciously jaundiced."

"Enough," interposed Hereward. "Waltheof's words were spoken with neither malice nor motive. Let us forget them."

Slowly Eadric resumed his seat, tilting back his chair and sprawling out his long legs before him. He lowered his head till his chin was sunk upon his breast, but his smoldering eyes rested with reflective distrust upon the earl's countenance.

Hereward, divining the direction of Eadric's thoughts, found himself troubled by his own. A strange man was this Waltheof, whose inmost nature was concealed behind a likable exterior. What, Hereward asked himself, did they actually know of him? If the magic of his name had roused the north to battle fever, it was because that name was Siwardsson; it was because these were his father's people, not his own. Waltheof was in England when Harold Godwinsson summoned all men against Hardraada at Stamford Bridge, yet Waltheof had been absent from the field. Why? Why, also, when all England flocked to Harold's banner at Hastings, had he failed to present himself? There was something about the earl that Hereward could not define; something elusive, something hidden deep within him. Hereward determined to be wary of this Waltheof. He must——

His reflections were broken in upon by the sentry, who returned ushering in Sir Herlwin FitzHugh and Toustin de St. Denys. The former seemed to have aged considerably in the past few hours. His graying hair was unkempt, his eyes like dark pools in his gaunt and pallid face, and though it was past the noon hour he was attired still in his bloodstained nightshirt, over which he had hastily flung a cloak. Hereward, seated once again at the table, was quick to guess the cause of the governor's ravaged appearance.

"How fares your son, Sir Herlwin?" he inquired.

The governor shook his head sorrowfully.

"It is hard to say, sir," he replied. "He has not yet regained consciousness."

"Has the infirmarer attended him?"

"Aye, he has bled him twice and has been most kind."

"Do not hesitate to call upon us at need, Sir Herlwin," Hereward told him. "In the meantime, though this is not the moment I would choose for a discussion of your ransom, the matter is not one which will await our pleasure."

"What figure do you propose?"

"Five hundred marks."

Sir Herlwin flinched.

"Minus one gold piece," interpolated Waltheof, "which you advanced me to pay a certain minstrel at the Tower."

"With what I now possess and what I can borrow, perhaps it can be raised," Sir Herlwin replied. "But if I succeed in doing so, how shall I ransom my son? I myself shall not leave here without him."

Hereward reflected a moment.

"If he lives, the ransom shall cover you both," he replied.

The governor bowed.

"That is fairly spoken, sir," he murmured, then, as a faint flicker of interest animated his eyes, he added, "are you he, sir, whom they call 'the Wake'?"

"I am," answered Hereward abruptly, turning to Toustin. His gaze wandered somewhat hesitantly over the boyish countenance with its transparent skin; over the artless, limpid eyes, over the short straw-colored hair, and finally came to rest on the exquisite jeweled ring-brooch which secured his cloak at the shoulder. "I am glad to see, Sir Toustin, that your wounds do not incommode you," he said.

Toustin laughed pleasantly.

"Indeed, Sir Wake," he replied, "slight though they proved to be, my sister tends them with grave concern."

"I can well believe it," replied Hereward dryly. He paused. Toustin's manner was casual and conveyed the impression that Althya had, for reasons of her own, withheld from her brother the knowledge that Hereward was known to her. "Your ransom, Sir Toustin," he continued, making an effort to dismiss Althya from his thoughts, "has been set at forty thousand gold marks."

Toustin emitted an uncertain half laugh.

"This is some pleasantry," he hazarded.

"It is no pleasantry."

Toustin flushed angrily. His hand flew to his weaponless waist.

"Pardex!" he burst out. "Such a demand is an outrage!"

"Scarcely so," replied Hereward. "We English have been unlawfully deprived of everything that is lawfully ours, our national heritage, our personal fortunes. If, in order to regain them, we resort to such methods as a kindly Providence suggests, we are only doing what you yourselves would do in our place."

"And did Providence suggest that the worth of an assistant governor is eighty times that of a governor?"

"Sir," replied the Wake, "in setting the price of a man's ransom, we do not evalue his worth. We evalue his ability to pay."

"And what leads you to the ridiculous assumption that I can pay this mammoth sum?"

"Do you, upon your honor, deny it?"

Toustin stood irresolute. He glanced helplessly at FitzHugh. The governor returned an indifferent shrug.

"If you have it, you must pay it," said Sir Herlwin.

Toustin turned back angrily to Hereward.

"But this rapacity—" he cried, "this unheard-of, churlish greed—it will all but ruin me!"

"Such a consideration can scarcely be expected to perturb us," replied the Wake coldly.

Toustin was abashed at his own naïveté.

"No," he admitted with sudden, though sullen acquiesence, "I suppose not. But since I cannot possibly arrange for so large a sum upon such short notice, will you be good enough to instruct my emissary to ride to the manor of Sir Guy de Lussac in the fenlands——"

"Let us not waste time there," snapped Hereward. "I have some knowledge of de Lussac and, even if he had it, he is not a man to risk his money for a friend."

"Sir Guy is more than a friend," explained Toustin. "He is affianced to my sister, Althya."

"The devil!" ejaculated Hereward.

"So under the circumstances, he cannot refuse his help."

"His help?" Hereward's thoughts were obviously elsewhere.

"Aye, in the matter of raising the money for my ransom."

"Oh!" With an effort Hereward returned to the business at hand. "You will select your own emissaries," he continued curtly, "but choose them for speed. If they are not back within two weeks, the ransom will be doubled."

"You play a shrewd game," observed the governor.

"The stakes are high," replied the Wake.

Ten minutes later, astride his favorite mare, Hereward was already on his way to keep his rendezvous with Asbiorn, having received from Eadric a benedictory smile accompanied by an approving handclasp, and from Waltheof an offer to ride with him through the maze of winding city streets as far as the gate, and set him on his way. Behind his master, Martin Lightfoot trotted at an easy pace, indifferent to the panoramic limitations set by the mare's generous rump, but rather finding its graceless undulations conducive to judicious meditation.

"The gods must indeed be convulsed with ribald laughter to see with what energy we struggle here below against our fates," he mused. "Were I, for instance, to say to my lord, 'Lord, your most herculean effort cannot deviate by one iota the predestined course of England's fate,' he would think me heretic to the cause, or mad, or both. Wherefore I do most wisely hold my tongue. Or were I to say, 'Abandon this contest with the Bastard now, lord, for all the sacrifices you will be called upon to make can avail us nothing without the concurrence of the gods, who have but to will the end to be, for it to be,' my lord would only mournfully shake his head and pronounce me addled. Yet to me these truths are clear, for I have long ago resolved that we can no more expect our puny efforts to change the course of England's ultimate destiny than we can arrest the alternation of day and night, the cycle of the seasons, the pulsation of the tides. Still, I shall not do my lord the disservice of acquainting him with these sagacious observations, for were he also to perceive therein the futility of all human effort, he would surely suffer more from enlightenment than he would gain. Wherefore I do, once more, most wisely hold my tongue."

Hereward, on the other hand, found little in his thoughts to cause him any part of the personal satisfaction that was Lightfoot's happy lot. Indeed, his meditations were fraught with gloom, being centered upon Toustin's revelations with regard to Althya. The news of her betrothal had made him change his mind about seeing her before he left, and the things he had planned to say to her, the things he had rehearsed all morning, had therefore gone unsaid.

Why was Althya betrothed to Guy de Lussac? Hereward asked himself. Surely such a marriage could offer only misery. How would he treat a wife, this man who found pleasure in breaking the backs of sheep and cattle and leaving them to slowly die; or who, upon the slightest provocation, carried off a helpless fenman to his dungeons, from whence the luckless fellow was released only after such torments as Guy personally devised had so shattered his mind that thereafter he could only babble and weep in pitiful dementia. Toustin seemed like a nice enough young man, not at all the kind to force his sister into a marriage against her will. It did not seem at all likely that he would have permitted this betrothal unless his sister desired it. Was it possible that Althya herself had made the choice?

"What ails you, Hereward?" asked Waltheof suddenly. "Has something gone amiss?"

Hereward shook his head.

"Yet you look almost as though we had lost the city, not won it." He paused, watching Hereward intently for a moment. "Ah, well," he continued, when it became apparent that no reply was forthcoming, "if 'tis something you would rather not discuss, why, I'm not the man would force you against your will."

They rode on for a while in silence. The narrow thoroughfares through which they passed were made the more hazardous by low gables and overhanging pentices, but Waltheof, ducking and bobbing with the ease of one who had spent a lifetime roaming these labyrinthine streets, soon found the silence wearisome.

"Did it not strike you as odd that the Bastard should elevate this youth, Toustin, to a position of such responsibility as that of assistant governor?" he asked.

"Aye."

"Being somewhat acquainted with William's devious machinations, I calculate it was in quittance of some favor for which the Conqueror assuredly received more than he has given."

"Aye."

"Nevertheless, Sir Toustin is not devoid of courage. He put up a spirited fight this morning for one who is such an inferior swordsman."

"Aye."

"It was a lucky chance you did not kill him right before his sister's eyes."

"Aye."

"Doubly lucky, since dead men pay no ransom."

"Aye."

"One might say, 'Slight though he is in form, he is still a fat prize.' "

"Aye."

"I calculate that besides paying off Asbiorn, his ransom will provide arms for most of us who lack them."

"Aye."

"Then, of course, there is the governor."

"Aye, the governor."

"Fate played us an ill turn when she made him a poor man."

"Aye."

"Nevertheless, his five hundred will help."

"Aye."

"And the men-at-arms who are not exchangeable. 'Twere better to hang them, than feed them."

"Aye."

Waltheof threw Hereward a quizzical sidelong glance.

"My friend," he said slowly, "reluctant though I am to admit it, I grow weary of your 'ayes.' "

Again they lapsed into silence, but Waltheof's spirits were too high for him to remain thus long. He pointed to a tall church spire visible beyond the city wall.

"My father built that church," he said, "and in it was baptized when he renounced the old gods and embraced Christianity. In it, also, he was laid to rest when his battle days were over."

"Are you Christian, Waltheof?" asked Hereward suddenly.

Waltheof frowned.

"I cannot say," he replied. "Like your man Lightfoot, I acknowledge more than one god. In battle I lean toward Thor and call upon him to vanquish my enemies. If 'tis scald-craft I desire, or wisdom in debate, I appeal to Odin. When these two fail me, I invite the favors of the so-called True God in the assumption that whomsoever cares for my adherence most will serve me best."

Hereward gave a dry laugh.

"You profess to a strange religion," he observed.

" 'Tis not unusual in these parts where the Nordic strain predominates," explained Waltheof. "My father embraced Christianity late in life and spent his latter years in prayer and penance, yet when, after fourscore years of outwitting death upon the battlefield, he lay dying in his bed, he rejected the pious death—arms crossed upon breast and eyes reverently closed. 'Shame upon me,' he cried, 'to have missed death in so many battles only to die in bed like a sick cow.' With that he arose and summoned his attendants to clothe him in his shirt of mail, to gird on his sword, to place his helmet on his head and shield on his arm and thus, standing, supported on either side by a stalwart son of Odin, he met his Maker in full harness. 'Twas scarcely a Christian death, yet Earl Siward was held by all to be a good Christian."

"Indeed," murmured Hereward, "he was such a man as we should all strive to be."

Waltheof turned upon Hereward. The earl's pale face was flushed a shocking scarlet and an unnatural vehemence was mingled with his bitterness.

"Some of us are controlled by superhuman forces against which there is no striving," he cried passionately.

Hereward made no reply. He scrutinized the earl's countenance, conscious, as he did so, of a recurrence of the vague and unwarranted mistrust of Waltheof that had disturbed him earlier; a mistrust which he felt certain was also germinating in Eadric's mind. And these disquieting thoughts persisted when, upon reaching the city gate and thanking the earl courteously for his guidance, he set his mare's head to eastward and rode away, drawing singular comfort, in the midst of his perplexities, from the rhythmic footfalls of the faithful Lightfoot close behind him.

Chapter Eight

THE SEA-KING

A THICK fog hung low above the broad estuary of the Humber, muting the cries of the sea birds and obscuring the vast wastes of heather and sand that girt the lonely coast. Under cover of this fog screen a strange craft had anchored a half mile offshore and now swung easily on the bosom of the swells. No gilded dragon head adorned the prow of this pirate craft. Instead, she was black from stem to stern, the more easily to penetrate unobserved the narrowing river reaches, or moor in the shadow of some river islet. She was a one-masted snekke, or warship, built for speed, having eighty rowers' benches and a square, black sail. Her gunwales were hung with protective overlapping shields and above her, wet with fog and hanging limply from the masthead, was the feared Raven banner of her viking master.

Aboard this privateer an unusual calm prevailed. Her warriors had deserted their benches and now idled in the stern, their oars stowed neatly away. Her sail was lowered, her steering oar pulled up and made secure to starboard. Only the fog wraiths moved about her deck, languorous, spectral forms. Born of their own motion, they hovered briefly on the air, then, by virtue of their ceaseless convolutions, dissolved into the vast, opaque infinity from whence they had come.

Amidships, within the narrow confines of the center gangway, a splendid ship-tent had been erected and here Asbiorn Estrithsson, master of the snekke, sat alone. He was a man of immense girth and heavy features, whose thick grey hair fell in matted strands almost to the waist. From his bull-like neck hung an ivory war horn, used in battle for rallying his men. About his soiled but lavish tunic of scarlet silk brocade he wore a wide jeweled belt, from which hung a sword of curious workmanship, drawn by Asbiorn himself from a grave mound and inscribed with a potent charm. His brawny, naked arms were ridged with purple battle scars and braceleted almost to the elbow. A barbed spear had claimed his right eye in bloody warfare off the Jutland coast and Asbiorn exposed the empty socket with his customary swaggering arrogance. His other eye was preternaturally keen and of a restless nature, keeping under close scrutiny the people and objects that came within its orbit.

At the moment, however, the eye had abandoned its ceaseless roving. It had lost interest in the luxurious furnishings of the tent, in the rosy-tongued lanthorn, in the table with its platter of dried salted meats. Instead, the whole expression on Asbiorn's countenance was one of uncontrollable fear, an emotion altogether new to this sea-king who claimed to be as brave as the Thunderer and almost as strong. He sat hunched back in his chair, both hands clutching a goblet brimming with mead-ale which he held upon his lap. From time to time a tremor passed through his frame, palsying his hands, spilling the ale and spreading its dark stain over his tunic. Apparently unaware of this, however, he continued to stare at the embossed forms upon the goblet as though they hypnotized him; as though, being tortured by what he saw, he still lacked the power to withdraw his gaze.

"By the serpents of Hel!" he muttered. "You cannot frighten me. Though you unleash a thousand demons to fill my dreams; though you haunt me nightly, goading me with your pious words till once again I obey the urge to crush your shaven skull with my bare fist, still you cannot frighten me. I do not fear the approach of night! I do not loiter when the world retires, deferring the moment when I, too, must seek my couch, lest I find you already there, waiting to share it with me. Nor do I arise at dawn beforetimes, pale from a night's contest with your bloody-visaged fiends. Chimeras, all! Do your worst! You cannot frighten me!"

With a herculean effort he sought to replace the cup upon the table. His action was arrested in mid-air and instead, as though compelled by some superhuman power, he slowly raised it to the lanthorn's light and gazed up at it with unrestrained virulence.

Its gold was of a brilliant reddish yellow, embossed with the seated forms of the twelve Apostles, whilst in the center the White Christ stood with arms outspread in benediction, a nimbus of pearls and rubies about his brow. The pagan Asbiorn knew nothing of the purpose for which the cup had been wrought, nor could he recall on which of his many coastal forays he had seized this trophy. St.

Cuthbert's Abbey at Lindisfarne? St. Columba's on remote Iona? He recalled only a lonely isle at sunrise as he and his men stole noiselessly ashore; recalled how they had converged upon the tiny stone chapel within which the monks were piously chanting; how they had burst in upon them, surprising them at Mass, and how, to the horror of the holy men, Asbiorn himself had snatched the goblet from the altar and drained it of its contents, red wine which the monks held to be no longer wine, but the blood of one of their gods.

Only the abbot had dared confront Asbiorn, had dared denounce his piracy and his sacrilege, but a single blow from the viking's massive fist had crushed his skull like an eagle's egg, so that he fell at the altar steps never again to rise. At this the brother monks were paralyzed with a sheeplike fear. They made no protest when he ridiculed their faith and their holy rites; made no motion to stay him when he leaped upon their altar in defiance of their gods; made no effort to hinder his men from swarming through the tiny chapel, looting as they went. And when at last, having purloined all the treasures of the Holy Isle, the invaders hauled up anchor and sailed away, Asbiorn himself carried off the sacred goblet to serve him as a drinking horn.

The blood of one of their gods! Ha!

That was eleven long years ago. Yet ofttimes at sea, when the sail caught no breeze and his exhausted warriors drowsed at the oars, Asbiorn would sit hunched in his chair, remembering; deliberately shunning the society of his men; whiling away the interminable hours with no companionship other than that of the White Christ upon this sacred goblet brimming with mead-ale.

It was on such a day that he first detected the singular change that had come over the gentle countenance of the White Christ, becoming, in some inexplicable manner and for protracted intervals, that of the long-murdered abbot. For months after he first made this observation, Asbiorn continued to be incredulous, unconvincible. He began to spend his days watching the cup, watching this curious metamorphosis occur with ever-increasing frequency, till at length the White Christ returned no more. In his place upon the goblet, permanent, immutable, stood the black-garbed, shaven-headed abbot.

It was then that the sea-king first began to be afraid!

In a lifetime of pillage and piracy many a man had died at Asbiorn's hands, hands long hardened to sacrilege and steeped in the blood of monks. Why, therefore, could he not forget this single, distant crime? Why had the monkish companion of his days started to menace his

nights, sharing his couch, invading his dreams? Why, in these nocturnal visitations, had the solemn piety gradually faded from the
abbot's face, changing instead to an expression of unspeakable evil?
All night long this apparition kept up a torrent of blasphemous
volubility, a flow of frenzied words without interruption, foul,
demoniacal, urging Asbiorn to the committal of some action as yet
obscure, yet whose sinister seedlings were already germinating deep
within the viking's subconscious being. Each night, with harrowing
repetition, Asbiorn strove to silence him by crushing the glistening,
shaven crown, by shattering it with his fist. Each night the abbot
crumpled at the altar steps, a tiny scarlet stream issuing from the
gaping skull, faster, faster, a river of blood!

It was not surprising that the activity of his nights began to sap
Asbiorn's energy and vigor. He awakened at dawn exhausted, his
clothing cold and damp, his tent ringing with the abbot's blasphemy,
with his hideous curses and abuse, till Asbiorn felt sure his warriors
must hear him. By day the sea-king idled, yielding to a lassitude he
could not dispel. Unremittingly and against his will he was drawn to
the goblet, unable any longer to resist its fascination; lacking the self-
mastery, the supreme volition to tear his gaze from the hated face.

The need to hide his secret from his warriors tormented him now
beyond endurance. His one eye constantly searched their faces in an
effort to read their thoughts, to discover how much they knew, how
much they guessed. But if his crew remarked anything of the unnatural fascination the goblet held for their master, their faces gave
no sign. Asbiorn determined to outwit them. He would watch them
now more closely. The first man to suspect the truth would die
speedily, before he could confide his suspicions to his mates. He
would kill him in such a way as to imply dissension among his men.
Jealousy, perhaps. The sea-king smiled cunningly. Who would suspect Asbiorn Estrithsson himself of murdering one of his own crew?
No one—no one——

At that moment Asbiorn was roused by a sudden surge of activity
on deck. With an effort he wrenched his gaze from the goblet and
listened. Voices came to him clearly now; footsteps outside his tent.
Quickly and with infinite care he composed his features, artfully
concealing his growing madness beneath his customary swaggering
insolence.

He had only a moment to wait. The curtain of his tent was thrust
aside. A tall form stooped, stepped across the threshold, then,

straightening to its full height, stood revealed in the rosy glow of the lanthorn.

Slowly Asbiorn arose from his chair to receive his guest, at the same time exerting every effort to control his heavy, spasmodic breathing. His thick lips were still unnaturally white and drawn back tightly against his teeth as though he had just ceased from an exhaustive labor. At that moment it was instinctive with him to conceal his countenance and this he did by taking a step forward so that the illumination of the lanthorn fell upon his back, leaving his face in shadow.

"It is a great honor you do my humble galley," he said courteously. "I bid you welcome, Hereward the Wake."

Hereward bowed.

"My thanks, Asbiorn Estrithsson," he replied, "though, but for the timely amends of a capricious Fortune, I might have been hard put to keep our tryst. For four days I have pursued a vain search for your vessel from shore to shore, whilst she has kept you carefully shrouded in this unseasonable fog. Then, just as I had begun to despair, the lady herself steered me directly to you."

"We were of course aware of your difficulty," replied Asbiorn, "yet feared to send a 'halloa' across the water lest it arouse the suspicions of the Norman watch."

"—or disturb their slumbers," added the Wake amiably.

By now the sea-king had quite regained his composure. He gestured to a chair, and reseating himself, clapped his hands for refreshment for his guest. His keen eye had already noted that Hereward's attire was somewhat unconventional for a chieftain engaged in the performance of an important mission. He was clad in the humble garb of a fisherman; a blue, sun-faded tunic reaching to the thigh, its long pointed hood thrown back across his shoulders. Ill-mated cloth hosen half covered his calves, the one red, the other green, whilst his feet were encased in wooden clogs. He was unarmed, except for a sheath knife in his belt. The long yellow hair was dusty with travel and damp with fog. His face was somewhat drawn, evincing extreme fatigue, but despite this his lips were parted in a careless, half-humorous smile.

"Did you come alone?" Asbiorn inquired.

"Not all the way," answered Hereward, "but when I neared the coast it seemed advisable. Men in twos and threes are always stopped and questioned, but a single man is seldom suspect." His smile deepened as he glanced down at his outlandish costume. "My humble occupation permitted the unimpeded search for your vessel," he added. "Even the Normans could not quarrel with the need of a fisherman to fish."

They paused in their conversation as an attendant entered with biscuits, salted meat and ale, but when he had withdrawn Asbiorn leaned across the table and spoke in low tones.

"Rumor has it that you have taken York."

"Then Rumor travels fast. It is but six days since the city fell to us."

"Mjollnir!" exclaimed the sea-king. "You are to be congratulated. Such a stronghold would have been fully garrisoned and must have required a considerable force to storm."

"Storm?" Hereward laughed softly at the memory of the grazing cattle. "Indeed," he said, "while it would delight me to describe for you some brilliant and classic example of military skill, I am constrained to the admission that our measures were highly unorthodox."

"What matters?" shrugged Asbiorn. "Every commander knows that the back door also leads to the castle Hall." He paused expectantly, then, perceiving his guest's disinclination to pursue the subject further, reluctantly abandoned it. "But now to our business," he said. "Your emissary spoke in guarded terms, being careful to let fall no hint of your ultimate aims. Nevertheless, upon reflection it seems evident that your action at York is not intended to begin and end as an isolated local incident, but rather as the rallying point of a nationwide movement, a declaration, in fact, of active hostility. Permit me to say, my friend, that the very boldness of your action proves your consummate skill and generalship. It can hardly fail to rekindle in your despairing countrymen the smoldering flame of patriotism and to attract the allegiance of volunteers from all parts of the kingdom."

"You overestimate our ambitions," replied the Wake warily. "It is true that almost daily we welcome some partisan who has traveled far to join us, but for every one who succeeds in reaching our camp, ten are caught and hanged. Eadric the Wild was more fortunate than most. Since the beginning he has been William's most formidable opponent on the borderland of Wales. He steadily defied the Conqueror, refusing all inducements to submission, time and again beating back the Normans from the districts he controlled. When at last he was taken prisoner, he escaped on the very eve of his hanging and found a way to lead his small band across England to join us."

"One hears much of his perverseness."

"Aye, he is perverse, but he is also steadfast, courageous and loyal," replied Hereward. "He has been of inestimable assistance in the formulation of our future plans, which, as you have already doubtless gathered, are the reason for my visit."

"And in the promotion of which you desire to enlist my aid," added Asbiorn. "My answer to that—my willingness to help you or my refusal—will have to depend upon two things; the nature and extent of your requirements and your ability to pay for them."

"My requirements are two hundred and fifty ships of arms and food; five thousand mounted men for the space of thirty days."

"That would suggest an operation of considerable proportions," calculated Asbiorn. "Can you suggest its probable location?"

"Its location will be Yorkshire."

"So far north!" Asbiorn stroked his beard, combing it with his fingers as was his custom when engaged in deep meditation. "Hereward Leofricsson," he said at length, "have you ever asked yourself why, after subduing the south, William failed to make a determined effort to do likewise in the north? Have you ever asked yourself why he has so far not found it expedient to penetrate the wildernesses beyond York, and, by the erection of castles and fortresses, to confirm what is now a purely nominal dominion over Northumberland? Or, to put it more bluntly, why was a man like the Conqueror satisfied with only half a kingdom when a whole one was to be had for the taking?"

"The answer to that is to be found in the open and acknowledged hostility of the men of Northumberland who have known how to take advantage of their inaccessibility, and in the likelihood that William himself is not yet in a position to risk decisive action in unfamiliar enemy territory."

"Precisely, my friend," said Asbiorn. "And all this, being apparent to you, has suggested the north as the logical springboard from which to launch your campaign against William. You have even selected a battleground, which obviously will offer advantages to you which it will deny to William. All that remains is to find some bait for the setting of your trap which will induce the Conqueror to come north to meet you. But in your calculations you have overlooked the fact that William is both wise and prudent. He will not make the gross and irreparable error of facing you on a battleground of your own choosing, and no bait can lure him into your trap, however skillfully contrived."

"Nevertheless," replied the Wake calmly, "the success of our enterprise depends entirely upon our ability to do so."

Asbiorn leaned across the table, exposing each cunning line of his countenance to the lamplight.

"It would be interesting to know by what stratagem you propose to effect so fortuitous a circumstance," he prompted.

His guest evaded a direct answer.

"Our final decision with regard to tactics must await certain future developments," he replied.

"Do you, Hereward Leofricsson, believe it can be done?"

"I have good reason to believe so."

"And if you should fail?"

"Then we, and not you, are the losers, since in any case I pledge myself to the payment of your fee."

Asbiorn relaxed.

"Fair enough," he granted, "fair enough!"

"There is one point, however, which I should like to stress immediately," continued Hereward, "since it must be given primary consideration in the calculation of your costs. Your men must be recruited in Iceland, Greenland and northern Norway."

Asbiorn raised an interested eyebrow.

"It is difficult to see what you gain by such an arrangement since you must be aware that so difficult an undertaking will incur additional costs," he replied. "But, since the stipulation is yours to make, and my fee will be raised accordingly, I shall not quarrel with it. The arena, then, is Yorkshire. Inland, or near the coast?"

"Inland."

"And the civilian population has been prepared?"

"Northumberland is loyal to the House of Siward and Siward's son, Waltheof, is one of us."

"What form will the engagement take?"

"Roughly, all-out battle in open field."

"A surprise attack," Asbiorn estimated shrewdly. "Such an action will entail considerable losses."

"Losses are to be expected."

"Widows must be recompensed; a legal price paid for every loss of limb, for every wound, large and small." Asbiorn looked dubious and slowly shook his head. "Everything considered, your demands are both intricate and arduous. The shiploads of food and arms, the lengthy, unseasonable voyage for the recruiting of the men you specify, the fleet required for their transportation—all these conspire to create a task of the most complex nature. Indeed," Asbiorn's battle-scarred hands were eloquently rejective, "it is an assignment that is little to my liking. You must find your help elsewhere."

Hereward's face gave no hint of the extreme mental anguish produced by the sea-king's answer. The ruin of his hopes was like a dagger thrust in the pit of the stomach. All the strength ebbed slowly from his body and hopelessness overwhelmed him, leaving his lips dry and his palms clammy. It took every ounce of self-control to master the expression of his face. He braced himself with the single thought that Asbiorn's reply might not be final. This possibility seemed to be borne out by the sea-king himself, for he sat watching his guest closely, his keen eye engaged in the dual function of detecting any evidence of dismay in his guest's demeanor whilst at the same time boring through to Hereward's brain in an effort to appraise the extreme limit of the English coffers.

It was with an outward display of unruffled calm that Hereward relieved the painful tension of his whole being by physical action. Stretching forth his hand, he drew Asbiorn's goblet toward him and proceeded to examine it with a pretense of casual interest. He did not see the almost jealous absorption with which the old sea-king followed his action; he did not see the swift and sudden fear that took possession of Asbiorn's rugged face, nor the unbridled working of the thick lips behind their heavy beard. When at length, with a word of genuine admiration, he looked up, he was in time to catch the strained, covert expression with which the sea-king pursued his nomadic search of Hereward's features.

So engrossed, however, was the Wake in his own immediate problem of winning Asbiorn's support that he was only vaguely aware of this subtle change. Instinct warned him that something had rudely interrupted the normal continuity of his host's thoughts and prompted him to relinquish the goblet without demur into the hand that Asbiorn had stretched forth to reclaim it. In silence and with mild surprise he watched the deliberation with which Asbiorn, instead of replacing it upon the table, set it down in his lap, nursing it gently, clasping it tightly in both hands.

It was Asbiorn who spoke first. Apparently he had quite forgotten his previous rejection of Hereward's proposal.

"What will you pay me?" he asked suddenly.

"What is your price?"

"You cannot pay me my price."

"Then what will you take?"

"One hundred thousand marks, payable in gold; half beforehand, half upon the completion of the mission."

Hereward thought fast. The demand was preposterous and clearly proved one thing; the sea-king was aware of the acute need of the English and was determined to push his advantage to the fullest. Only by a swift bold stroke could Hereward checkmate him, for any show of weakness now would arm Asbiorn with a weapon against which there would be no competing. The gamble was great, the chance of success slender, but there was no other way. He must take the risk. With a short, scornful laugh the Wake arose to depart.

His hand was already on the curtain of the tent before the sea-king recalled him.

"Come, come, Hereward Leofricsson," he said soothingly, "do not let your rashness outweigh your caution. Where would you go were you to depart from here? Back to your cohorts to tell them you could not reason with me? That I demand a sum you could never lay your hands upon? No, my friend. Do not hasten so into the chill arms of Defeat." His voice grew soft, caressive. "You may have your men. You may have your ships."

Hereward faced him.

"On what terms?" he demanded.

"Terms?" For the moment Asbiorn waved them negligently aside. "It must be a source of embarrassment to you, Hereward Leofricsson, that in the end you must deal with me, for I am aware that a man of your repute approaches a man in my profession only where the need is great. You came here prepared to pay a pirate's price for a pirate's services. Why? Because you could not obtain the required help in more legitimate quarters—say in France or Flanders. You found that though they gave you their sympathy, they withheld their aid." He spat in vigorous contempt. "Their fears rob them of their manhood!"

"Come," interrupted Hereward, "our little game needs only an ending. Let us hasten it lest the fog lift and deprive us of our cover."

The old warrior appraised Hereward shrewdly. He seemed to be laughing silently to himself.

"It is haste you want? Then I shall be brief. I accept your forty thousand marks."

Hereward started. There was only one way in which the wily Asbiorn could have learned of Toustin's capture and the exact price of his ransom.

"Your foragers did the emissary no harm, I trust?"

"None at all," Asbiorn replied reassuringly. "They detained him only long enough to learn his mission, then courteously set him on the right road. His return to York will be the speedier for their personal interest in the successful completion of his task." Asbiorn smiled blandly. "Why not? The gold is, I presume, destined for me."

A moment later, the terms of their pact formally agreed upon, Hereward drew from his pockets a piece of charcoal and a square of white cloth upon which he proceeded to draw a careful map of the city of York, its Roman walls, its bars and posterns, its castle situated on the narrow tongue of land at whose tip converged the rivers Foss and Ouse. He took particular care to outline a stretch of land bordered on the south by the city walls, and on the north and northwest by almost impenetrable forest.

"By now, if the emissaries have done their work well, William has learned of the fall of York," Hereward was saying. "Already he is sending out spies to discover our future plans and is deliberating upon the most effective measures of combating us. He has two alternatives; to refrain from action until he has laid the groundwork for all-out warfare in the north, or to strike at once in the hope of catching us unprepared and annihilating us."

"And the success of your plan depends upon his adopting the latter course?"

"It is expected that our actions will force him to such a decision," Hereward replied. "But let us follow his probable line of reasoning step by step. The loss of his northernmost citadel will remind him how far he is from subduing Northumberland, how imperative is the campaign he has so long postponed and to which will now be added the task of seeking out an embryo rebel force whose survival should normally depend upon its mobility, the ease with which, in the face of gathering opposition, it can scatter and retreat."

"Continue," murmured Asbiorn.

"While William is thus deliberating his spies should return to him with the news that the English rebels, too flushed with the success of their initial venture for a cautious appraisal of their position, are collected within the narrow confines of the walled city of York. A rebel force deprived of its mobility! A rebel force wintering in a walled town that invites siege! Sitting ducks, William will say. Within a few weeks his army should be moving rapidly north, whilst his scouts, watching the city for any signs of suspicious military preparations on our part, report to him from time to time. But, save for the usual carousing customarily enjoyed by a victorious army, there will be no undue activity. Sitting ducks, indeed. Under cover of night William will surround the city, trapping us in our own bailiwick. The rest is simple. He has but to besiege us and wait until our food gives out and our empty bellies scream their surrender."

"Perhaps you are not acquainted with William's prescribed policy in the handling of rebels," suggested Asbiorn. "Or perhaps you do not set much value upon your lives."

"On the contrary, being left with little else, we love them dearly."

"Yet as I see it, in setting a trap for William, you trap yourselves," observed Asbiorn. "But since this is your battle, I will say no more. How long do you estimate it will take William to march north?"

"A month at most," replied Hereward. "By Christmas we should be surrounded and besieged." He indicated the narrow neck of land between city and forest which he had taken care to clarify upon his map. "This stretch of land was the determining factor in the selection of York for our purpose. Owing to the peculiar topography of the region, rivers, forest and city walls, William will be compelled to assemble the greater part of his host in this plain. There is no other location available to him. This will be particularly favorable to us since in battle the Conqueror has always depended chiefly upon his cavalry and this area is too small for it to be used to full advantage."

"And what do you calculate will be the strength of the army he will bring against you?"

"It is difficult to say with any accuracy. Already he is hard put to hold his far-flung outposts in subjection. I would estimate, however, that his army would comprise some ten thousand men."

Asbiorn scrutinized Hereward obliquely.

"Against which I am to bring my five thousand?"

"Dysentery and exposure will considerably reduce William's army during the winter months. He should lose no less than three thousand men. These in all probability he will not replace, believing such a measure to be unnecessary."

"Upon what will he base such a conclusion?"

"He has spies planted in Denmark, Flanders and France, waiting to report any unusual military activity. When none is reported he will conclude that by moving quickly he has succeeded in isolating us from the outside world, thus cutting us off from any possible help. Such a conclusion is purposely aimed at."

"By my beard!" exclaimed the sea-king, exhibiting for the first time a certain eagerness. "I see now why the recruiting must be done in Iceland and Greenland. Proceed with the plan."

"In the meantime we English, some two thousand of us, will be trapped within the city. All winter we shall barrage William's encampment with missiles; barrels of flaming tar, rocks, plague-breeding refuse. Toward spring these attacks will slacken, then cease entirely. William will conclude that our inertia is caused by starvation."

"Indeed," murmured Asbiorn, "with two thousand mouths to feed I guarantee that by spring you won't be far from it."

"It is hoped that William will make the same miscalculation," replied Hereward, "for rather than feed in the winter and starve in spring, we shall starve in winter to feed in the spring. The Normans, however, will await the momentary surrender of a starving rebel force. Being overconfident, they will also be less prudent, less vigilant."

"I perceive the emergence of a pattern," murmured Asbiorn.

"Upon a given day you, having sailed your longships up the Humber, will disembark at Stamford Bridge. Without delay you will engage William from the rear, whilst we, acting in concert, surprise him in a frontal attack. Being unprepared, the Normans will be unarmed. They will be compelled to defend themselves berserk, whilst we will be mail-clad."

"Mjollnir!" exclaimed the sea-king suddenly. "My former doubts are turned to confidence. The very insolence and cunning with which the scene has been set will betray him." He leaned forward, following on the map the nine miles from Stamford Bridge to York, calculating the time required to cover the distance on horseback. Minutely he inspected the prospective battleground, the hills and forest in the background. "Mjollnir!" he exclaimed again. "It is an admirable plan!"

A short while later, having reached agreement on all points, Hereward arose to depart.

"Five days hence you can dispatch your lieutenant to pick up half the gold agreed upon," he said. "The first week in April I shall await your attack to strike simultaneously. Until then, bear well in mind the particulars of the plan. Our success depends upon your strict adherence to them."

"Dispel your qualms," replied the sea-king. "You have my word upon it, which, despite my other failings, is as good a bond as any man's. Farewell, Hereward Leofricsson."

"Farewell, Asbiorn Estrithsson."

Hereward turned away. He stretched out his hand and raised the curtain of the tent, then paused suddenly and glanced back.

Inconceivable though it was, Asbiorn had apparently already dismissed his visitor from his thoughts. He sat quite still with bent head, his attention fixed upon the goblet which he gripped in both hands. Slowly, with the reluctance of one driven against his will, he raised the cup for closer scrutiny, holding the embossed figure of the White Christ uppermost, staring down at it, tipping the goblet so that the mead-ale spilled over unnoticed to form a dark pool on his scarlet tunic.

It was strange that Hereward could afterwards recall the impression of the moment; the wisps of drifting fog whose smell filled his nostrils; the sea-king's curious absorption, imponderable, remote; the deep, almost pregnant silence of the tent; the vague and nameless stirring of uneasiness within himself. But at the time none of these things penetrated his conscious mind. He was aware only of intense relief at his mission accomplished as he bent his tall form and stepped out into the night.

Chapter Nine

THE MEETING

THE thick fog that had shrouded Asbiorn's pirate snekke rolled inland, gripping the forest south of York and the ancient Roman road that cut through it. But the three travelers making their way slowly southward were indifferent to the nebulous world about them, a world peopled only by the ghostly shapes of trees and boulders that sentried the cobbled road.

Sir Herlwin FitzHugh, his head sunk upon his breast, mused upon his departed son whom he had been compelled to leave behind, interred in the alien sod of York. Sir Toustin de St. Denys looked straight ahead, but saw nothing. His face was flushed with fever, his lips compressed by the pain of the sword wound inflicted by the Wake beneath his left armpit whose increasing agonies set his whole body on fire. To this physical discomfort was added the memory of his lost fortune, a loss which sat hard upon him. Between them rode Althya, whose brooding face was almost completely hidden by her fur hood. She had scarcely uttered a word since daybreak when they had been given their freedom at the city gates.

"Sister," said Toustin sourly, "your present moodiness palls upon me. You at least should smile, leaving the gloom to me. The Conqueror's uncommon generosity in elevating me to the assistant governorship of York has stripped me of almost all I possessed, whereas the other half of his whimsical arrangement—your betrothal to Guy de Lussac—at least assures you of a suitable marriage."

Althya's face emerged for a moment from her hood, and minus the radiance of her hair, any stranger would have been instantly struck by the resemblance between brother and sister. They had the same profile, regular and finely chiseled; the same delicacy of bone structure. Yet there was about Althya's face a firmness that was noticeably lacking in her brother's, a stubborn turn of chin and lips which at times caused Toustin no small amount of uneasiness.

"I have already said I shall not wed de Lussac."

"Indeed!" snapped Toustin. "Well, my girl, you'll find it isn't easy to oppose the king's will once he has set his mind to something."

"My mind is also set. De Lussac does not please me."

"That phrase, Sister, grows monotonous. I have heard it too often of late. 'He does not please me.' Nom de dieu! Why don't you point out the man who does please you and let me approach the king and see what can be done."

Althya remained silent.

"You see?" cried Toustin, appealing to Sir Herlwin. "She has nothing to say concerning a preference. It is the same every time I question her on the matter. I'd swear the girl has set her fancy on some obscure young strutling she dare not name."

"No doubt," murmured Sir Herlwin absently.

"And anyway," continued Toustin, "you can't fight the king, so you may as well submit gracefully. Guy is counted a good enough match. This business of conquest has brought him a measure of prestige and a fair demesne, and he unquestionably holds the king's favor."

"Nevertheless," said Althya firmly, "I intend to wed the man of my choice, or remain unwed."

" 'Intend,' you say?" cried Toustin. "That word, Sister, was never meant to be employed by women. You are seventeen, an age when most girls would be eager enough to find a husband." His voice softened suddenly. "Dear Althya, I would do anything to make you happy, even to the point of incurring William's displeasure. Yet, much as it would grieve me to see you wed to a man you can't abide, I confess that at the moment I fail to see how it can be avoided."

They lapsed again into silence. But presently Toustin's brow creased in a puzzled frown.

"There is one thing," he said, "that I would give much to know."

"What is that?"

"How was this 'Wake' able to so accurately gauge the extent of my fortune?"

Althya's voice was listless. "Is it possible that you have not already guessed?"

"Guessed?"

"That he was the nameless fenman who helped me slip clear of de Lussac last spring. I told him."

Toustin's jaw dropped. "By the Virgin!" he gasped. "So that's it! Ha, my dear, your fine Englishman was quick to turn a chivalrous act to his own advantage."

Althya made no reply, and glancing at her, Toustin perceived that she was once again wrapped in her own thoughts. Her lips were set in a straight, angry line and he silently speculated as to what was going on in her mind and against whom her wrath was directed.

By the following morning a light wind had arisen to dispel the fog and by noon the air was clear, so that even from a distance they were cheered by the sight of the river which separated English from Norman-held territory. Upon reaching it, however, they found to their dismay that the rebels had already destroyed the bridge that spanned it and now only the jagged ends hung down into the water from either bank. The water itself was high, swollen by autumnal rains. It rushed past them with a force that seemed capable of carrying away both horse and rider and the Normans drew rein on the bank and gazed gloomily down upon it.

"My dear Toustin," said Sir Herlwin at last, "I think we would do well to rest our mounts for a few hours before setting them against so strong a current."

Althya glanced quickly at her brother. During the two days on the road she knew his fever had steadily mounted until now a heavy sweat beaded his brow and his slight frame was shaken with chills. Though he had not opened his lips in complaint, she had secretly observed the way he kept slipping one hand beneath his cloak as the pain of his sword wound increased and she guessed the effort it was now costing him to rouse himself sufficiently to reply to the governor.

"Let us make the crossing at once, Sir Herlwin," he said. "I myself shall not rest until the river lies between ourselves and those cursed English."

Althya leaned over and laid a hand upon his arm.

"Toustin," she said, "you know it would be suicide for you to attempt the crossing in that icy water."

"We cannot fly across, Sister," he answered fretfully.

Sir Herlwin, who for the most part had been too concerned with his own grief to pay much heed to his companions, now turned a searching eye upon Toustin and was shocked at what he saw.

"Your wound, lad?" he inquired after a moment's scrutiny.

"Aye."

"There is no question, then, but that your sister is right." He looked thoughtfully down at the rushing water, then turned and scanned the green forest wall that hemmed them in. "Perhaps if I ride up the riverbank a way I might locate a ford. You stay here with your sister, Toustin. I shall not be long."

He spurred his horse and soon vanished among the trees, though for several minutes they could hear his mount breaking through the heavy underbrush along the bank. Somewhere afar off a wolf howled, long and fearsome. A moment later the cry was answered from near by and their horses raised timid ears and snorted. Althya glanced uneasily at her brother. He sat with head bent and eyes closed, his breath coming in short, hard gasps which frightened her. She dismounted and unhitched the wineskin from his saddle. "Drink, Toustin," she said. He roused himself and drank eagerly, looking down to thank her, not with words, but with a gentle smile that in no way resembled the irascible Toustin of the past two days.

It was at that moment that she became aware of the motionless figure of a man standing watching them just within the shadow of the trees. He was too far off for his face to be distinguishable, but she could still make out the tall form, legs spread wide, thumbs hooked in belt. She recognized him instantly by the familiar stance and an angry flush crept up her cheeks. She knew that Toustin, too, had seen him, for he was feeling covertly for a weapon, but the man, with a short dry laugh, sauntered slowly toward them.

"Leave your weapon be, Sir Toustin," he advised. "Since you cannot outmatch me, you had best quell your eagerness to fight me."

"Pardex!" exclaimed Toustin, a sudden energy flooding his body. "This is indeed a contemptible trick, Hereward the Wake, to release us only to recapture us."

"I intend no such thing," replied Hereward, bowing courteously to Althya. "I myself have been absent from York and was not aware that you had been liberated. The presence of strangers in the forest so close to our military headquarters was something that called for investigation. Your ransom has been duly paid, I take it?"

"Aye, never fear," answered Toustin sourly. "Your fellow brigand, he whom you so aptly call 'the Wild,' counted out every coin, then, being of a suspicious nature, weighed it carefully before allowing us to depart."

"Such caution was commendable."

"It was insulting, sir," retorted Toustin, then, with a groan, he crumpled suddenly and slipped from his horse to the ground.

Hereward turned quickly to Althya.

"What ails him?" he inquired.

She dropped to the ground and took Toustin's head in her lap, then she looked up. Her face was white.

"Hereward Leofricsson," she replied icily, "do not think you deceive me by your play of innocence. You are perfectly well aware it is your sword wound that ails him."

He stared back at her, his customarily well-schooled features expressing complete astonishment at her words.

"My sword wound!" He moved slowly forward and stooped to examine Toustin's face. "Devil take me! The lad's in a bad way. What induced you to leave York while he was in this condition?"

"Your lieutenant did not offer us any choice."

"Still, if Toustin had explained that his wound was infecting and had requested permission to remain until——"

" 'Requested'? Of those rebel ruffians! Possibly he preferred the discomforts of the journey to their prolonged companionship."

"Those 'rebel ruffians,' " Hereward answered dryly, "may not be clothed to please a lady's eye, but many of them boast nobler blood than that which flows in the veins of any Norman. As for your brother, he made an unwise choice. He's now in a raging fever and without the proper care he won't last out the night."

"We shall find him the proper care once we have crossed the river and are out of so-called English territory."

"And how do you expect to cross? Sir Herlwin won't find a ford, you know."

"Are you going to pretend there isn't one?"

"There isn't—upon my honor."

"I naturally have little regard for your honor."

"Nor is there a homestead for miles around."

"Then," she flared, "you might have told that to the governor and spared him the time and exertion of a futile search."

"I might—had I not thought that the lady Althya would have as little regard for my veracity as she has for my honor and would insist upon him looking anyway."

She arose and planted herself squarely before him.

"Hereward Leofricsson," she said, making an effort to keep her voice level, "I am not afraid to remain here alone if you find yourself pressed for time and wish to continue your journey."

If he heard her words he paid them no heed. His gaze had drifted past her and now rested thoughtfully upon Toustin.

"It is quite true," he was saying, "that there is no way of getting him across the river without giving him a chill fit to kill him. As I have said, there is no ford, there are no homesteads. The only possible shelter of sorts in this vicinity is an old watchtower on a bluff overlooking the river, and since I have had considerable experience in the handling of wounded men, I suggest that you let me take him there and see what I can do for him."

"Why?"

His gaze returned and rested upon her face. "Because," he said with quiet deliberation, "I sold him his life and I'd like him to have what he paid for."

She was quick to sense some mental reservation, some underlying motive behind his words and she began to speculate as to what it could be. His face revealed nothing, offered no clue. His manner was impersonal. What he said might be the truth, but she did not for a moment believe it to be the entire truth. What did he stand to gain if he could save Toustin's life? Why should he feel any especial concern for Toustin? Under this Englishman's generalship hundreds of Normans had been killed in the taking of York Castle. Why, therefore, should it matter to him if one more Norman lived or died? Could it be that Toustin was right after all—that Hereward Leofricsson deliberately planned to recapture and reransom him, squeezing from him the last remnants of his fortune? If that were so, it would of course profit him to save Toustin's life. That no doubt explained his solicitude.

Yet if she obeyed her natural impulse to reject his offer, what of Toustin? What could she herself, or even Sir Herlwin, do for him here in this desolate, hostile region? The English rebel leader, on the other hand, was clever and resourceful. She had seen him in action. Whilst it irked her to be obliged once again to accept his help, she nevertheless realized that time was pressing and that if there was a way to save Toustin here was the man to find it. They could take up the question of ransom later.

"And the governor?" she asked.

"I will have Lightfoot wait for him here. They can follow us as soon as Sir Herlwin returns."

Her acquiescence came slowly, grudgingly. "Very well."

Hereward turned, and placing two fingers to his lips, gave a low, strange cry. His summons was instantly answered by the sound of running footfalls on the soft earth and in a moment Martin Lightfoot appeared with Hereward's mare in tow. He drew up and waited with an air of modest expectation for Althya to acknowledge him, and when it became evident that she did not intend to do so, he turned an unruffled countenance toward his master.

"Son," said Hereward, "wait here for FitzHugh, then follow us to the bluff with the horses."

"Aye, lord."

Hereward slipped a saddlebag from the mare's neck, then, lifting the unconscious Toustin gently in his arms and motioning Althya to follow, he set off through the forest. He took the opposite direction from that which Sir Herlwin had taken, turning east along the river-bank and pressing on through the heavy underbrush until they came at length to a primitive stone tower looking south across the river from the summit of the bluff and designed to offer a full view of the rolling hills beyond.

It stood round and squat, completely overgrown with ivy, its doorless entrance a gaping mouth in the green façade. Inside, the vague light revealed walls of massive boulders enclosing a tiny central area and, to one side, an ancient stairway whose steps were worn by the impress of countless feet down through the centuries. The vagrant river winds had caught up the leaves and swept them together in one vast heap near the far wall and upon this rough couch Hereward gently laid Toustin. In a moment he had a fire burning and by its light he swiftly proceeded to divest the unconscious Norman of his clothing.

As he started to remove the bandages Althya observed an abrupt change of expression on Hereward's face. Soon she understood, for the stench of the wound began to pervade the air and when at length he exposed the gangrenous flesh she was sickened by the sight and drew back. Hereward, however, made no comment. With deft and experienced hands he performed what surgery he could, carefully dressing the wound with unguents taken from his saddlebag, then he replaced Toustin's garments and cushioned the Norman's head upon his own cloak. For a moment they sat in silence, listening to the irregular breathing and to the low hiss that accompanied each rise and fall of the chest, then Hereward leaned over and gathered Althya's hands in his own.

"Althya," he said, "I think you know already—there is little anyone can do now for Toustin."

She sat very still as a new awareness took possession of her. Toustin was momentarily forgotten. She was conscious only of this Englishman and of what, at his touch, had come to her in a flash of intuition—that he loved her. This rebel leader, who had all but killed her brother, then wittingly beggared him, was in love with her! The realization was so startling that at first it occupied her thoughts to the exclusion of all else. But only for a moment. Soon, as though repeated from a distance, his words began to penetrate her conscious mind, to paralyze her with their terrible meaning. A numbness crept through her limbs, draining her of all feeling so that she seemed in the grip of black Eternity, remembering no yesterdays, expecting no tomorrows. There was only the present with its strange nothingness, its terrible calm, its blessed apathy, and even when she spoke, she herself was startled by her own words and by the casual tone in which she spoke them.

"So Toustin is going to die." It was not a question. It was a cold statement of fact.

Hereward made no answer, and she returned her attention to Toustin. Her eyes dwelt with detached curiosity upon his face, studying the grayish pallor, the fine, almost imperceptible muscular twitchings that were visible about his lips and eyes. She had ofttimes observed such manifestations on the faces of dying men and the appearance of them now upon Toustin's countenance brought to her the terrifying impact of the first rush of fear and grief. What would she do without Toustin? They were bound by more than the mere ties of blood, for they had been motherless from earliest memory; made fatherless, too, for the most part by William's incessant wars. They had grown up interdependent, loving each other passionately, quarreling violently, yet each upholding the other before the world with a stubborn, fierce loyalty.

He had been a virgin knight at Hastings, proud of his armor, prouder still of his exploits. He had never tired of describing to her the details of the battle, magnifying his own part, exhibiting for her staunch admiration the scars of his trifling wounds. She had always secretly known that he was no warrior in the true sense of the word, for he displayed none of the physical or mental ruggedness characteristic of the born soldier. From childhood he had quailed at the sight of a toad or a snake, and in the dark she still stayed close to his side, not to seek reassurance for herself from his nearness, but that he should take confidence from hers. Yet he was not entirely without courage, the kind of courage that was born of a too cruel appraisal of his own weaknesses and of a gallant if apparently futile attempt to master them. And because she instinctively understood the torments of his morbidly sensitive nature, she had always striven to ease them with an excess of tenderness and love.

But now he was going to die, and this Englishman was responsible —this Englishman had killed him. She looked up suddenly at Hereward. Her eyes were tearless, hard and bright.

"You're in love with me, aren't you?" she said.

Quickly his glance met hers and she found herself wondering if, in the face of her undisguised hostility, he would have the courage to admit the truth.

"Yes," he said. "I am."

"Then, by heaven, you are cruel to those you love!"

"I did not know he was your brother when I struck him."

"No, but when you learned it later, you dealt the more harshly with him because of it."

"In warfare, honor requires that love be subordinate to duty."

"Or, to be more blunt, to forget you love a woman when it becomes inconvenient to remember." Her voice was deathly calm, her eyes empty. "That night in the fens I fell in love with you, too, but I was willing, for your sake, to resign the ties of my whole life—my father had he lived, my racial identity, even Toustin. I wanted only to belong to you, to share your poverty and your hardship, to wait upon your needs by day and lie in your arms at night, to be your wife and your mistress, to bear your sons."

A single stride and his arms were about her. He drew her to her feet and held her.

"Then, Althya, 'tis a great deal to ask when I have so little to offer you, but don't go back. Stay with me. We can be wed at York."

She stood quite still in his arms, unmoved by his nearness, wondering a little at the warmth of his kisses when she herself felt so apart from him, so aloof and indifferent that she could endure his embrace without protest. But he was quick to sense her unresponsiveness. For an instant he looked searchingly down at her, then his arms fell away and he stepped back a pace, his face taut and suddenly masklike.

"You forget," she said dully, "how rude a disenchanter proximity can sometimes be. At least it has been so for me, for at York I was able to see you as you really are, the leader of a handful of half-armed, half-fed rebels whom you have shrewdly induced to risk their necks to your personal financial gain. I am sorry for all those who have linked their lives to yours, sorry for the ragged men you lead and call an army, sorry for their futile struggles and for all their petty strivings, for the uselessness of their lives and for their wasted valor. They are doomed men, every one, through your misguided leadership, because the Conqueror will catch up with them—and with you, too, someday. And when I hear, Hereward Leofricsson, that you've been captured and strung to a tree as you deserve, I won't feel any regrets. I'll think of Toustin and I'll be glad."

She stopped speaking, but he said nothing, only stooped and busied himself with the fire. The flames leaped up and she perceived suddenly how much he had changed since she had seen him in the fens. Gone were the exuberant gaiety, the lightheartedness, the carefree manner. Now his face was grim, drawn by the strain of countless anxieties. The cheekbones were leaner than before, the jaw more resolute, the mouth set in so stern a line it could have been chiseled out of granite.

She was long to remember the expression of his face at that moment, to be haunted by what she read there and to wish she had uttered a single kindly word. But now she let the long moments drag by in silence until the sound of footsteps was heard without and the shadow of Sir Herlwin FitzHugh fell across the threshold.

Toustin died at the twilight hour when the gray day was dying, when the evening wind dirged the dying year and sent the summer's leaves drifting, brown and lifeless, to the ground.

Althya shrank from the thought of leaving him behind, alone in this vast solitude, so far removed from the friendly sound of human feet and human voices and where his frail body would soon be gripped in the ice fangs of the winter forest. She begged Sir Herlwin to let her take him with them to Lincoln for interment in Norman-consecrated ground, but this the governor steadfastly refused to do, for the marauding wolf packs seemed ever drawn by the scent of death. So Toustin was buried in the forest, his head upon a pillow of pine boughs gathered by Lightfoot, his cloak for a shroud, his sword belted knightlike about his girlish waist.

Before the three men lowered him into the hastily dug grave, Althya drew aside the cloak and kissed him tenderly on the forehead, murmuring her farewell in words so low they could not be overheard. Then she stood by, listening impassively to the muffled thuds as the earth was flung in upon him; watched the last patches of dark cloth vanish; watched the pit slowly fill, until only the narrow mound of fresh-turned earth marked the place where he lay. Through it all she maintained an air of drugged weariness. The unnatural brightness had faded from her eyes, leaving them lusterless. Her face was without expression. Hereward, watching her anxiously, was reminded of a fenland water lily, pale and tranquil.

The governor's prayer for the deceased was brief and to the point as befitted a soldier; a mention of his name and rank, a plea to the Almighty to receive his soul and grant it peace, a brief account of his merits; of his part in the Hastings battle, of the subsequent years in the Conqueror's service and of his recent elevation to the assistant governorship of York. "He was a good soldier," Sir Herlwin concluded, "who, of all the men in my command, seemed always to school himself to the sternest kind of courage——" And at these words, hearing Toustin's lifelong struggle thus rewarded, a sob broke from Althya's tightened lips, and burying her face in her hands, she turned and fled uphill to the tower. Impulsively Hereward started after her, then he turned back. "She is too proud," he thought, "to weep in my presence, and it is good for her to weep."

As the dusk deepened the men worked on, building a cairn of large boulders above the grave mound lest the wolves unearth the body in the night. But Hereward's hands moved slowly, for his thoughts winged always uphill to the tower where Althya would be sitting alone in the darkness.

She had a right to despise him, he reflected, to believe the things she had said, since he himself could offer no explanation for his actions. There was no anger in his heart against her, for she could not guess at the vital need of the English to bribe Asbiorn, or at his own desperate struggle with himself to fulfill his moral obligation to his men. He loved her none the less for the disesteem in which she held him, yet paradoxically he half wished he could cease to love her, so that his thoughts would not always be torn from the difficult task at hand to dwell unwearyingly upon her; so that he would not face battle less eagerly, or be less willing to die. And if today his wits and ready tongue had failed him when he most needed them, he would remedy matters in the morning. Before she left he would find a way to have a few moments alone with her——

"You had known her before York, had you not?" the governor's quiet voice broke in upon his reflections.

Hereward looked up. Instinctively he had always liked this Norman with the quiet eyes and kindly manner. Sir Herlwin was of little more than medium height, but was lean and wiry and possessed of a powerful sword arm which had as yet taken no cognizance of the heavy passage of the years or of the streaks of gray in the shorn black hair. By reputation he was a good commander, strict in the enforcement of discipline, but tolerant of human frailties, slow to anger and wise of judgment, qualities for which his men held him in high regard.

"And you," Hereward turned the subject without answering the question directly, "also renewed an acquaintance at York, though I neglected to inquire of Earl Waltheof what was meant by the gold piece he claimed to owe you."

"The incident in question occurred whilst we both abode at the Tower," Sir Herlwin explained. "Some unthinking minstrel solicited a fee of him and thus caused no little embarrassment to the earl, whose purse had long been empty." He paused, then continued sadly, "By strange coincidence the minstrel also chanced to be at York. It was he who threw the knife that killed my son. Alas! My son!"

"I trust, Sir Herlwin," said Hereward after a moment, "that our national enmity will not prevent you from accepting my condolences."

"On the contrary," replied the governor, "since I know they are sincerely spoken."

They continued working, forming a neat pyramid of the boulders collected by Lightfoot and deposited at the graveside. When the pile lacked but a stone, the governor took up the last one, set it in place and made it firm. Then he straightened up and faced the Englishman across the grave.

"Sir Wake," he said, "I have soldiered all my life and have come to admire nothing so much as a brave man, whatever his race. But it is the bravest who sometimes outwit themselves by overconfidence in their own prowess, or by posting themselves as a barrier between their countrymen and legalized oppression. You are in the way of committing both these follies—and in the end of being hunted down for a rebel or run out of your own land."

"Sir Norman," retorted Hereward promptly, "if it is your intention to urge submission I say, to be plain-spoken, cut short your words since they can only sound like so much rant to my English ears. Whatever the future holds for me, let it come. I shall make no peace with the Bastard—now or ever!"

The governor sighed.

"I cannot say your attitude confounds me," he replied. "You have seen your homeland overrun by Normans who part out your lands among themselves. You have seen your race crushed beneath the heels of men of hostile blood and hostile speech. But good and evil ofttimes work together in a common cause and the incursion of strangers ofttimes breeds a hardier race."

"Aye, man, for us—a hardy race of vassals!"

"Today, perhaps," allowed the governor, "but I own to twice your years and therefore possess perhaps one tithe more wisdom. You appear to exaggerate the deleterious effects of submission. In actual fact you personally would have much to gain thereby, for the king would undoubtedly receive you into his favor and in time you could persuade him to temper his rigorous measures toward your whole race. Thusly could you also serve your nation. And what have you to fear from such a course? This is not the first time England has been conquered and, as has happened before, England will rise again. Future generations will see a fusion of the races when the whole fabric of Norman usurpation will be swept away. Those born of our Norman blood, Sir Wake, will be born to your English soil. How, then, shall they call themselves, if not by the name of Englishmen?"

Hereward looked away to where the bluff loomed large and dark against the sky.

"Dream your dreams," he said, "and let all future generations look to themselves. For myself, I vow I shall never offer my sword hand in peace to the Bastard. I would as lief offer it in amity to the wolves."

They turned away from the grave and all three made their way uphill toward the tower, silent, because there was nothing left to be said between them. The autumn moon, though low in the sky, was shining brilliantly. The wind moaned above the wide river spaces and the dampness clinging to the ground intensified the odors of the forest. As they drew near the tower Hereward slowed his steps.

"She will wish to dry her eyes," he said. "Let us walk heavily to warn her of our coming."

It was dark inside the tower, and pausing on the threshold, Hereward sensed, rather than saw, its emptiness. He called softly, "Althya, Althya," though already he knew she was not there. Ignoring the governor's questioning glance, he turned and ran to the horses. One was missing. Swiftly he plunged into the forest, running a zigzag course through the trees, following the tracks in the moist earth where the moonlight fell upon them and where his sharp eyes discerned a faint discoloration which told of how, in her torment to be gone, she had spurred her mount till the blood ran.

Down where road and river met, he drew up. Fresh hoofprints were again clearly visible in the mud at his feet. His gaze shifted, passed over the cold, racing water to the opposite bank. There, too, the trail was plain, a row of black hollows in the mud. The road beyond stretched away south, the only road, the road to the Norman citadel of Lincoln. It lay white in the moonlight, and he could see it for miles, cut by the Romans through the very heart of the forest, cobble-paved, straight and long.

And it was empty.

Chapter Ten

ON THE ANCIENT WALLS

WITH incredible speed the Conqueror appeared before the gates of York, once again proving his magnificent ability to overcome all obstacles. He himself led his army north through blinding storms of snow and sleet; indifferent alike to cold, fatigue or hunger; enduring privation with the meanest of his men; killing horses with his own hand to feed them; lending his own mount to those no longer able to walk, only to heartlessly abandon those same men to the wolves when their sickness grew too great a burden; reaching York at last with only half his army to sight, beyond the snowy heath, the castle rising gray and formidable, and at its feet the city girdled by her ancient Roman walls and swept by icy winds that blew in from the sea across bleak Yorkshire moorlands.

Yet despite his haste, William had chosen to make an ally of patience, it having cost him much time and effort to circle around in order to avoid enemy outposts and thus appear unexpectedly from out of the northwest when the English, if they were looking for him at all, would be watching the southern roads. His plan was to strike suddenly, to bottle up the rebels within the city before they got wind of his approach and had time to scatter, and in this, according to his scouts, he was entirely successful. His army had surrounded the city in the dark of night and his camp was now set up on the open heath betwixt the city and the Galtres Forest to the north. Here the Norman pavilions were so skillfully arranged as to give the appearance of being twice their number, and his knights and men were ordered to circulate continuously and thus create the illusion that the Conqueror's army was twice its actual size.

But William was ever circumspect. It was not his way to engage in the hazards of battle if the fight could be won by threat or negotiation, and thus it came about that one day in early January three

Norman horsemen sped across the heath, unarmed and beneath a flag of truce, and headed straight for the city. As they drew near they could see, from the large number of mail-clad forms stationed at their posts, that the walls were fully manned, and by the time they drew rein before the north gate the officer on guard was already awaiting them in the tower above the portal, challenging them to state their business without delay.

"I come as King William's nuncius," replied the central horseman, "with orders to speak with your leader, Hereward Leofricsson."

"We recognize no king of yours, Sir Norman, wherefore his orders matter little to us," came the blunt reply. "If you desire to have speech with the lord Hereward, be so good as to identify yourself and I will acquaint him of your coming."

"I am Sir Guy de Lussac of Cruc Maur."

The officer disappeared and the Normans sat and waited, glancing about with affected unconcern, yet all the while furtively appraising walls and battlements in an effort to estimate the strength of the city's defenses.

De Lussac, impressed by what he saw, found himself beset by a rising curiosity concerning the rebel leader. He had heard, of course, that a Hereward Leofricsson, presumably the same, had preceded him as lord of Cruc Maur and every Norman was familiar with the Wake's military reputation. But it was only now that Sir Guy came to the startling realization of how little was actually known of the man himself. Owing to his long voluntary exile in the East, there was even some dissension as to his personal appearance. Some of the English described him as being fair-complexioned and of exceptional height, but the fenmen, who were in the best position to know, steadfastly clung to their assertion that he was short and dark. Well, reflected de Lussac as he drew himself up in the saddle, the best military minds were ofttimes to be found in men of small stature. In any case, it would be interesting to meet him face to face.

He was roused by the sound of hoofbeats coming from within the city and in a moment, to the accompaniment of various groans and creakings, the gates were thrown open, the portcullis raised, and a horseman rode out toward them. He was unattended by either knight or squire and, like the Normans, was unarmed, being clad in a blue tunic beneath a simple dark wool cloak. He was capless, so that his long yellow hair flew in the wind, and at the sight of him de Lussac gave a start and swore obscenely beneath his breath. The memory of their former meeting returned with a rush, making the Norman's small frame shake with anger, but if Hereward likewise recognized Sir Guy, his countenance gave no sign.

There was neither salute nor preamble to their parley.

"Are you Hereward Leofricsson, leader of the rebels?" demanded de Lussac.

"To be rebels," the Wake retorted, his voice cool and unhurried, "men must first have a lawful king or government, and having neither, we do not count ourselves to be such. For the rest, my name is indeed Hereward Leofricsson."

"Then your liege lord, William, King of England and Duke of Normandy, sends you this command," continued de Lussac. "That you instantly lay down your arms; that you receive him into his own city of York with all due honor; that you kneel in submission and take the oath of allegiance to him. In return, His King's Grace pledges himself to grant pardon to all and to receive you into his peace and favor. He further pledges himself to listen to the claims of each man among you who has forfeited lands or possessions by virtue of the Conquest. These are the Conqueror's terms."

The Wake waited courteously for the Norman to finish speaking, but his reply came at once and without hesitation.

"We will make no terms with the invader," he said in ringing, final tones. "Nor will we ever submit to foreign rule."

Quickly de Lussac glanced up at the walls. He was aware that every eye was upon them and that every ear was straining to catch their words.

"In so arbitrarily voicing your own inclination, you are showing no concern for your men," he cried, raising his voice, "for a rejection of the king's present offer will doom them to annihilation. Is it fair that one man should impose his will upon so many? Is it fair to force them to fight and die upon these walls when they can live to return home, each to his own hearthside? Are they freemen —or serfs—to thus be denied the right to dissent? I call upon you, Hereward Leofricsson, to apprise them fairly of the king's proffered clemency, and to permit each man the choice of honorable submission."

At that a low, surly laugh was heard from the wall and a soldier leaned over and threw down a leather jerkin which glanced off de Lussac's shin and fell heavily to earth.

"Aye, we are freemen, and there is our free answer," he jeered.

"Take it with you. Say we have no submission for the tanner—only hides!"

De Lussac scowled at this reference to the Conqueror's dishonorable birth, for the father of his unwed mother had been a tanner by trade. Hereward likewise scowled and swung around in the saddle.

"Hold, above there," he ordered sharply. "These Normans are here under truce, for which all courtesy is due them. Let there be no more affronts. The man who threw that jerkin shall descend and retrieve it."

There was a hush upon the wall as the mail-clad offender detached himself from his fellows and prepared to obey. But as by a miracle the scowl had vanished from de Lussac's face. It was replaced by a covert, satisfied smile as he motioned to one of his companions to dismount and pick up the garment, then, without a further word or gesture, he turned his horse and sped back to the Norman camp.

The assault began within the week, the more savage and determined since de Lussac piously and with carefully feigned reluctance related the incident of the jerkin, embellishing it with a few details of his own invention to further incite William's wrath against the rebels. The proud Conqueror, he well knew, could endure no reference to his bastardy; nor could he stomach, nor ever forgive, an insult to his ancestry on the spindle side.

By the sullen light of a January dawn, after Mass had been said, King William marshaled his troops on the heath to the north of the city. From this side only could a land attack be launched, since to east and west the swift-running rivers of Foss and Ouse, and to the south and southeast the vast expanse of marshlands formed by their juncture, presented a formidable natural barrier. The nature of the assault precluded the use of the matchless Norman cavalry and only the king and his captains were mounted, the more swiftly to move from point to point and direct the storming of the walls. The rest were afoot, clad in ring mail and armed with kite-shaped shields, lances, swords and rope scaling-ladders. Behind them, ranged in serried lines, were the archers, slingers and crossbowmen whose function it was to remain stationed in the background, ready to let fly a protective barrage of arrows and heavy missiles above the heads of their comrades and pick off anything that moved upon the walls.

At a signal from the Conqueror the Normans started to advance cautiously across the heath, protected by movable wooden sheds cov-

ered with raw hides which were designed to shield the men from
the boiling tar and flaming arrows of the city's defenders. With
every step they scanned the walls and battlements through their
peepholes, expecting to see a sudden bustle of excitement at their
approach. Instead, a baffling silence reigned. No single human form
showed against the dull gray sky line; or sentry on his beat, or
watchman in his tower. All was quiet. The beleaguered city slept.

They were almost within the shadow of the walls when the English
sprang to life. In an instant every tower, every bulwark and embrasure bristled with mail-clad men. Spurning their encumbering
shields and defiant alike of slingstone and arrow, they stood, battle-
axe on shoulder, and hurled their javelins at the oncoming Normans.
From below, the English engineers sent up a black hail of rocks and
boulders which screamed through the air, landing on sheds and
smashing their roof beams, so that the men within were crushed or
forced out into the open to be felled by the deadly accuracy of the
English bowmen.

Beneath so murderous a barrage a section of the Norman van-
guard recoiled and wavered. Already the heath was strewn with the
mangled, writhing bodies of their comrades, whilst the English, high-
hearted by the carnage they had so speedily wrought, reveled in a
wild war cry, and gripping their gleaming battle-axes with both
hands, whirled them above their heads as though in eagerness to
cleave a human skull in twain with a single backstroke. The Normans wavered no longer. They turned in flight.

Then, swift as the hawk upon the heron, the Conqueror wheeled
and swooped upon his men.

"What have I here?" he cried in a voice that thundered above
them. "What shame lies hidden by your ring mail? Are you women
I lead and call an army? Am I shepherd to a flock of sheep? Turn
back, men! Turn back, I say! To the walls! Ha! Rou!"

The fleeing ranks halted and stood irresolute, but the Conqueror,
caring nothing for the men felled by the hoofs of his excited steed,
swept in among them, chiding, threatening, whilst with the terrible
side strokes of his iron mace he brought a dozen more to their knees.
"Are you stags to run before the English dogs?" he cried, his eye
flashing with the splendor of his wrath. "Turn and fight, men! To
fight is to vanquish! Ha! Rou!"

The old familiar battle cry, recalling as it did the exaltation of
many a hard-fought, hard-won battle, was a potent intoxicant.

Within them, the men felt their fierce Norse blood leap. Their hearts swelled; their spirits soared. "Ha! Rou! Ha! Rou!" they cried, and turning, rushed for the walls, throwing up their scaling-ladders, scarcely waiting for the hooks to bite into the masonry and take firm hold before swarming upward. Heedless they were, now, of the shafts that pierced their armor and stuck like quills in their flesh; heedless of their comrades dropping lifeless from the ropes above them; heedless alike of the jeering English and the forest of spears lowered over the parapet in a barbarous death trap. Upward they clambered, drunk with the love of battle, and as the Conqueror watched them his dark eyes shone. They were his countrymen; akin to him in blood and heritage; in the fierce, urgent impulses which decades ago had brought the red-haired Rou from out of the north on his pirate quest. The Conqueror knew these men as he knew his own heart and therefore he knew that no voice, nor hand, nor weapon could recall or stay them now.

And just as William's consummate generalship had ofttimes saved his hot-blooded warriors from their own folly, so it did now, before they reached the top and hurled themselves recklessly upon the English spears. Wheeling his horse, he signaled the Norman archers, who let fly a storm of arrows above the heads of their comrades, picking off everything that moved upon the walls.

Thrown into momentary confusion, the defenders fell back and the Normans, unimpeded, swarmed on and up. But the Wake watching from the walls, ordered his own archers to harass the Norman bowmen, returning shaft for shaft, whilst at the same time he roared to his engineers to shift their ballistas and discharge their missiles almost perpendicularly into the air so that they fell just outside the walls. This brought down a deadly hail of rocks directly upon the heads of the Normans swarming up the ladders, crushing their skulls and knocking them to the ground to be trampled by a thousand mailed feet.

In vain, now, for the enemy to fight their way up the ropes, for the English, pressing forward once more against the parapet, grimly slaughtered every Norman whose helm showed above it. Like a host of wild and savage paynims the English fought that day, swinging their axes aloft, bringing them down with such force that a single stroke sufficed to cleave in twain both head and helmet, to sever arms from shoulders, whole trunks from legs. Their own unyielding valor inspired them to superhuman effort. "Out! Out!" they cried with every mighty backstroke. "Holy Crosse! England! England!"

Caught midway on a ladder, de Lussac found himself confronted by a ruddy-faced Yorkshireman armed with a long billhook which he kept jabbing into the Norman's face in an effort to dislodge him. With his mailed hands de Lussac grasped the blade and grappled with his opponent until both lost their balance and hurtled down together to the mass of mangled human flesh below. The Yorkshireman's neck was broken in the fall, but swiftly de Lussac drew his dagger and plunged it again and again into the dead man's breast in an orgy of insensate rage that was part of battle madness.

So savagely had the onslaught raged along the summit of the walls that the furtive work of undermining them had been progressing unobserved. The Norman sappers, having succeeded in picking out a single boulder, were hastily inserting in its place a bundle of straw-bound faggots. This they set afire, igniting the wooden props and struts of the intermural structure, and soon a small portion of the wall collapsed, making a practicable breach. A cry of horrified warning went up as the English perceived their new danger, but too late! Already a horde of Normans were swooping down upon the smoking heap of rubble and loose stones, their bloody swords waving menacingly, their lips shouting their triumph, each man eager to be the first to storm across the ruins into the city.

But suddenly from the ramparts above, Earl Waltheof Siwardsson leaped down and stood within the breach, a fierce and formidable barrier. "Thor-aid!" he cried as the first Norman attempted to force his way through, and because the joy of battle filled him with immeasurable strength, he picked up the hapless Norman, and raising him aloft, crushed his bones before hurling him back to lie a sagging heap upon the ground at the feet of his comrades. Before so terrible a sight the Normans recoiled in awe. Even their captains wavered. A godless berserker, he seemed to them, with his long white hair streaming from his helm, his eyes red and crazed with the smell of blood and battle. In his frenzy he bit upon his shield, then his voice lifted above the hubbub in a war chant of unmistakable pagan origin. The Normans drew back, crossing themselves with superstitious fervor, then, in a simultaneous action, they turned and fled to another section of the field, leaving the earl alone and unharmed within the breach until it could be repaired.

Meanwhile, knee-deep in a level plain of corpses, Sir Herlwin Fitz-

Hugh was leading the attack against the city's north gate. His men, working beneath shields held by others above them, had at last succeeded in prizing up the portcullis by a few precious inches when suddenly the gate was thrown open from within and the English let loose a flight of arrows between the bars of the portcullis. Being prepared only for attacks from above, the Normans were caught off guard and without any frontal defenses. The foremost fell to earth with scarcely a groan, to die where they fell; the rest cursed roundly and gripped their weapons in expectation of a sortie. But the wary English intended no such thing. With a mighty crash the grille fell once again into place; the gate slammed shut; the heavy bolts were shot home.

King William, ever alert, spurred his horse and swept up angrily to Sir Herlwin, who was clutching a wounded shoulder.

"Haste is what we have need of, Sir Knight, if we are to enter the city by nightfall," he cried, then, turning, "ho, there, let us have up the ram. By the Splendor of God! The grille that cannot be prized up can be battered down!"

The dead were roughly thrust aside and piled in heaps as a giant battering-ram was run up and set before the portcullis. Her stout oaken beam was shod with an iron cap and slung by chains from a massive frame. Beneath the Conqueror's lightning directions the engineers sprang into action, drawing back the ram, then dashing it forward mightily against the bars of the portcullis. With dripping bodies and panting breath they labored until the bars had separated sufficiently to permit the passage of a man, and even the head of the iron-shod ram could penetrate far enough to begin the work of battering in the stout oak gate beyond.

"A few more blows and the work is done," the Conqueror cried jubilantly. "Pardex! I would as lief enter the city through the portcullis as beneath it. Shatter the gate tonight, men, and tomorrow each of you shall claim his knighthood!"

The engineers raised a loud "Ha! Rou!" and redoubled their efforts. Fortune was theirs that day, bright and beckoning. A few more blows and—— Then suddenly, "Back! back!" William, with his swift, uncanny instinct for danger, wheeled his horse and sped away, but the engineers scarce had time to glance upwards before a cauldron of boiling pitch was heaved up over the wall and emptied in a black torrent upon their heads. With tortured cries they dropped the ram and fell to earth, some already scalded to death; some writhing in such helpless agony that William, in a moment of rare compassion, dispatched them with his own hand.

To a low hillock slightly removed from the throng of battle the Conqueror retired, and here, astride his war horse, he surveyed the field. There was no hope now to retrieve the day. The sun had almost completed its slow descent of the sky, yet still above the city the English ensign showed. The Norman attacks were weakening; the scaling-ladders had long since vanished from the battlements, slashed to bits at the top by the English axes. The gray masonry of the ancient walls was red from foot to summit with Norman blood, and like a ghastly moat begirding them was the oozing, scarlet heap of hacked and contorted bodies; the stirless dead; the dying, maimed and maddened with pain, shrieking, cursing, praying, sobbing. In the air above, the kites circled with sharp and greedy eye, patient, confident, their pinions as tireless as their vigil.

Suddenly the Conqueror set spurs to his horse and galloped back alone to his pavilion. Here he stood, brooding and silent, as his squires divested him of helmet and hauberk, removed his sword belt from his waist and wiped clean his mace. Then he sent forth and summoned his captains from the field.

"Retire your troops and halt the assault," he ordered, when they were assembled before him. "Strengthen the cordon about the city. Invest it so tightly that not even the most desperate man among them will attempt flight. There must be no loophole through which they can call for help or otherwise communicate with the outside world. The city shall fall without a further blow. My lords, I intend to starve the English into submission!"

The barons glanced uneasily at one another, and each knew what was in his neighbor's thoughts. It was FitzOsbern who dared give it voice.

"Such a siege as you propose, sire," he said, "could take considerable time, and the winter has yet many months to go. Under such difficult conditions we must look to lose countless men from exposure and sickness, and this without any certainty that siege is the answer to our need. How long, therefore—I crave Your Grace's pardon—do you plan to put it to the test?"

"How long?" The Conqueror ceased his striding and turned. As though by chance his glance fell upon the leather jerkin hanging by the pavilion's entrance and instantly his dark eyes quickened, his voice became low with bitterness and wrath. "How long? Until they lower yonder ensign and hoist a white one in its place. Until they cringe, begging pity and pardon. Until their food gives out. Until fasting shrivels the stomach of each man within him like the shriveled kernel of a dry nut. Until they have eaten their last dog—their last rat—and under the stress of hunger, disdain not their own kind. How long? How long can men live without food . . . ?"

The barons fell silent, for there was not a man amongst them who had not himself, at some time, undergone siege; not one but could still recall its grim horrors and know with certainty what the English were about to face. Some were moved to pity for a gallant enemy. Some were indifferent.

De Lussac was the only one who smiled.

Chapter Eleven

THE CONQUEROR'S VENGEANCE

S PRING came slowly for the hungry men within the besieged city, yet despite their hardships there were few who thought to complain.

It had been a winter of unusual severity, with heavy snow and bitter winds that swept down from the north so that the narrow cobbled streets were sheathed in ice and the birds lay frozen upon every roof and sill. From the battlements the English could clearly see the encircling Norman host, a tight-knit cordon broken only to the southeast where the boggy Foss Isle and its adjacent stretch of swampland formed an impassable barrier. To the north, in the shadow of the Galtres Forest, lay the Norman encampment; row upon row of tents for the common soldiers, the gaudy pavilions of the barons, and, upon the summit of a gentle rise, the pavilion royal, its silken pennons stiff with ice, the Standard of the Two Lions planted firmly in the ground before it.

Everywhere about the camp footprints crisscrossed through the snow, converging always upon the glowing braziers where the men gathered to warm themselves and pass the time, drinking, dicing, praying, according to their inclination, or listening to the songs of their minstrels; bawdy songs which sent coarse laughter echoing across the heath; songs of Roncesvalles and Val-ès-dunes; songs of their Norman homeland that silenced them and set them to gazing pensively into the flames, forgetful now of individual loneliness and of the comrades who daily fell victims to fevers, coughs or frozen limbs and quit their ranks for ever.

But within the city the men faced each new day with solemn mien and their only songs were the loud protests of their empty bellies. In the pens, it is true, the hogs and cattle still called end-lessly and the granaries were amply stocked with grain, but these supplies were distributed daily in meager quantities, for the Wake was strictly adhering to his plan of starving in winter to feed in the spring. Through these long months of waiting he had sought to keep the minds and hands of his men ever busy, setting them the tasks of reinforcing battered gates, repairing walls and generally strengthening their defenses; and when this was done, of readying ring mail, swords and helms for the expected spring engagement. And so, despite the ceaseless torments of hunger, the men were high-hearted, for an inherent scorn of slavery made them prefer any fate to the villeinage that would be their lot under William Bastard.

Yet it was remarked by some of the more discerning that of late Hereward Leofricsson's countenance seemed never to be devoid of its moody frown. They remarked that he ofttimes sat alone during the long evenings spent around the fire in the castle Hall, gazing ahead of him, lost in abstraction. One man swore, corroborated by another, that, by the Face of the Virgin, he had heard Hereward sigh, though this was generally discounted as being altogether too unlike Hereward. To all queries the Wake replied that nothing was amiss, yet few believed him. At length among themselves his men began to speculate as to who it was had so taken Hereward's fancy that he behaved at times like a man in love, which again was not at all like Hereward.

So winter passed and spring came and the lean men within the beleaguered citadel began to dine more heartily; the bedimmed eye regained its luster, the enfeebled arm its strength. By the first day of April all was in readiness for Asbiorn's scheduled attack. Long before dawn every man capable of fighting was up and armed and had joined the assembled ranks at the appointed place near the north gate. Men there were from every shire of England, clad in quilted tunics beneath their ring mail, shield on arm, some clinging still to the ancient broadsword, some carrying javelins, hatchets, clubs, but all armed with the terrible two-handed battle-axe which the Normans had cause to remember and to fear.

There was an air of suppressed excitement as the Wake once again outlined the details of the plan, adding a few final instructions. No warning sounds must alert the enemy, he reminded them; no hubbub of voices to indicate a sortie, no laughter, no rattling of weapons, no clang of shields and armor. The Normans must continue to regard York as a doomed city and its defenders as a handful of famine-racked men. Only then could the surprise be complete and the plan successful.

From the rampart walk of the east wall Hereward watched for the first sign of Asbiorn's approaching host, for the first telltale cloud of dust, the glint of armor, the clatter of horsemen. Morning passed. Noon came and went. The afternoon wore slowly to its close. Dusk set in, but no sign was there of Asbiorn. At last, with orders to reassemble the next morning at daybreak, Hereward dismissed his men.

The following week was one of unendurable suspense, with each dawn a little less hopeful than the last, each dusk a little more despairing. As the second week progressed, anxiety began to show upon the sleepless faces of the men. What if Asbiorn did not come at all? What if he had deliberately abandoned them? There would, of course, be no exit for them from this self-devised trap, save to sally forth in one last vain, if glorious, onslaught. And because they sternly faced the possibility that they were doomed men, their thoughts strayed ever back to home and loved ones, dwelling upon them with such intense absorption that they could now recall a detail, a lineament, a gesture, that they had never caught before, as though memory were more discerning than the eye.

And Hereward thought of Althya; and Lightfoot of the fens; and Letwold of his poor witless son; and Waltheof of his lost earldom; and Eadric of his young wife, raped and killed by the Normans; and one and all thought upon father, mother, wife, sweetheart, a newborn child, a sky-lit meadow, an oft-trot road; and to all came the same intolerable yearning to submit to any terms in order to behold them one last time. But such tender thoughts, being of a demoralizing nature, had to be rudely brushed aside. And each man swore that if die he must, he would die as he had lived—free, defying the invader, cursing the Bastard whose greed and personal ambition had orphaned his children and robbed every Englishman of homeland, hearthside and liberty.

As the second week of waiting drew to a close Hereward summoned Eadric the Wild and Earl Waltheof to a meeting in the tower room of the square donjon keep where they habitually held council.

"It is imperative," he told them, "that, before determining what further action to take, we get news of Asbiorn and learn for certain whether he has violated his agreement with us, or is merely late in the keeping of it."

"God's beard, man!" exclaimed Eadric. "How can such a thing be done? There is no way in which a scout can pass the Bastard's cordon—short of flying over it, or burrowing under it."

"Aye," solemnly agreed Waltheof, "by day a thousand pairs of eyes keep watch of our walls and of the narrow no man's land beyond. By night the guard is doubled and flares light up every yard of the way. No, my friend Hereward, there is no escape from here, and any fool attempting it is like to get himself trussed up like a fowl and lobbed back over the walls by a ballista. 'Tis a painful death, I am told, but William has found that the sight of the broken body ofttimes discourages further attempts at flight and hastens capitulation. What is more, he has never been known to overlook a single avenue of escape and if you think you now perceive one, then reverses must have snarled your wits."

"What I have in mind," said Hereward, "can scarcely be regarded as an avenue—merely a tiny vent."

"Then," cried Eadric, "point it out, and though the odds be against me all the way, I vow to attempt it."

Hereward glanced quickly at the earl, who appeared to be totally absorbed in an inspection of his dagger's blade and made no motion to volunteer. The Wake frowned. How often during the past months he had paused in the task at hand to search among his men for the white-haired Waltheof. Yet what, he would ask himself, was he seeking? What did he hope, or fear, to find? Certainly this man had proven himself brave beyond description when the Normans mined their walls, standing with inconceivable grandeur in the breach. And what courage was required of him to flee the Conqueror's Tower! Indeed, this Siwardsson must be a valiant-hearted man and certainly none had shown himself to be more loyal to the cause.

"The mission," he said, looking squarely at the earl, "is particularly suited to Waltheof's talents."

Waltheof looked up sharply and Hereward was able, for one rare instant, to gaze full into the depths of those strange, lutescent eyes. There was in them now no trace of evasiveness, no dismay, no irresolution. Only a mild surprise.

"In what way," he inquired, smiling, "do I outrival other men?"

Hereward arose. "Come, I will show you."

He led his companions over to the east window and pointed down below to the river Foss. From there his finger moved in a northeasterly direction, following the river's course, passing directly between the two Normans posted on either bank to link up the Conqueror's cordon, and continuing on until it reached the Galtres Forest some short distance beyond.

"From the city wall to the forest," he said, "is some four hundred yards."

"But even at night no man could swim them," snapped Eadric. "The flares would search him out and he'd get a hundred arrows in his back."

"The waters of the Foss are deep," Hereward explained. "The Normans see only the surface."

"Devil take me!" Eadric exclaimed, whilst Waltheof, finally grasping the full import of these words, began the expansion of his gigantic chest as though already he were inhaling huge draughts of air.

"I could do it!" he said, his furry ears pointing aloft. "Have I not done it before? What then?"

"Having attained the forest," continued Hereward, "you will commence your search for Asbiorn at Stamford Bridge, following the Derwent to the Humber and the Humber, if need be, to the sea. If at Spurn Head there is still no sign of Asbiorn or his fleet, you will return here with all speed and so inform us."

"When do I leave?"

"At dusk."

That night, clad in a dark tunic, thin hide brogans and a dagger for defense, Earl Waltheof Siwardsson was lowered from the battlements to the riverbank outside the walls. There was a light drizzle which obscured the Normans standing at their posts a long arrow-flight away, yet with animallike instinct he could sense the exact location of each one of them. Cautiously he moved forward, sliding his feet over the uneven earth until he reached the river's edge. Here he stood a moment gazing down into the rushing torrent. He felt no fear. They were friendly waters. All waters were friendly to Waltheof Siwardsson. He inhaled deeply, filling his lungs with air, then he plunged noiselessly and vanished.

He knew when he was passing the Norman cordon, for the water above him was luminous with the reflection of the flares. He could see the writhing water plants which brushed his body as he passed, and the shoals of tiny fish scattering at his approach. But in a little while the light faded, leaving him in a tunnel of darkness, and only then did he become aware of the increasing agonies of his bursting lungs and the faintness which threatened to overcome him.

Instinct told him when he had reached the forest's fringe and he pulled himself out of the water and lay panting on the bank. In a little while he arose and shook himself like a shaggy white dog, then he crept down to the edge of the trees and peered out. Through the drizzle he could see the blurred outlines of the Norman camp, the pavilions, the soldiers' tents, a ballista standing naked in the background. But all was quiet. The complacent sentries paced back and forth, pausing to bank a fire or stand a moment gazing across the heath toward the aloof, dark city. Waltheof spat suddenly. "By Thor's hammer," he muttered, "your Norman corpses might yet prove to be the weal of ravens!" Then he turned and padded away silently and swiftly through the trees.

He reached Stamford Bridge the next morning, where, being recognized by his splendid stature and radiant white locks, he easily procured a horse. Turning south, he followed the Derwent to the confluence of the rivers, then sped east along the Humber bank, pausing here and there to inquire after Asbiorn. He had nothing to fear from Norman outposts, for throughout the winter the men set by William to guard the river had been systematically slaughtered, and likewise their replacements. The English had overlooked no detail in their plan to have Asbiorn's attack come with devastating suddenness, yet nowhere was there any sign of Asbiorn.

On sped the earl, along the dreary trackway in sight of the river, past the goblin-haunted barrows of Aber; past the Idol Temple of ancient heathenesse, fallen and forgotten behind its ditches; across the dreary marshes of Wik, across the sand bars into Cava Deira, the "hollow land of the Deiri," until he hit the Roman way from the Picts' wall; south, then, to Praetorium, moldering city of Antoninus, where he learned that an immense foreign fleet had, for two weeks past, lain at anchor off Spurn Head. Was it still there? Aye, they thought so. Eagerly the earl sped on down the narrowing tongue of land to Spurn Head, where, on the heights, with the Humber below and the ocean beyond, he drew rein. No fleet was anchored in the estuary, nor yet at sea, but far out, motionless, surely at anchor, lay a single craft. Earl Waltheof shaded his eyes. The intensity gathered in his gaze.

This was no ordinary vessel. She was a warship from out of the pirate north, built for speed—to chase or to flee. She was painted

black, with no gilding at her prow to betray her by sun or moonlight, nor any special markings to identify her should her master
choose to lower his ensign and sail the seas unrecognized. Now, apparently, something had occurred to dissipate his long passion for
secrecy, for in full daylight his banner flew from the masthead, and
the earl knew it well.

It was the black Raven banner of Asbiorn Estrithsson!

Earl Waltheof left his horse grazing and made his way down the
rugged cliffside to the beach. He had thought to swim out to the
snekke, but the sight of a fisherman's skiff drawn up out of reach
of the tides made him change his plan. He hauled it across the sands
into the water. A moment later he was pulling rapidly out toward
Asbiorn's vessel.

An evening hush had descended upon the sea and a soft haze
hung above it. In this intensified silence he became acutely aware,
as he neared the snekke, that nowhere was there any sign of life. The
warriors' shields were gone from the gunwales; the rowers' benches
were empty; the deck deserted. Waltheof frowned in bewilderment.
This was a costly vessel and was apparently undamaged. Why, therefore, had she been abandoned by her crew? And why, if such action
were forced upon them, had they, contrary to custom, left their
master's banner still flying from the masthead? As he came within
the ship's shadow he noticed a rope ladder hanging down, trailing
idly in the water, and toward it he directed his course. "Halloa,
above there!" he called. He waited for a reply, but only his own
voice came back to him through the stillness, so, having made fast
the skiff, he laid a hand upon his dagger and climbed aboard.

The yellow radiance of evening illumined the deserted deck, lending it a false air of slumberous calm. A damaged hauberk lay upon
a bench; beside it, a sword, shattered beyond repair. In the center
gangway sprawled the huge black sail, carelessly lowered and left
where it fell. Beyond it stood a luxurious ship-tent fashioned out of
rare white bearskins, its silken tassels stirring in the listless breeze,
its curtains tightly drawn. How he knew, Waltheof could not tell,
but he knew it was not empty. He was acutely aware that someone
—something—waited in there for him. He stood a moment, listening
to the creaking of the ship's lumber as she rode the swells, to the
wash against her prow, to the hollow tapping of the breeze upon
the bearskins, then he moved slowly toward the tent, raised the
curtain, and entered.

Asbiorn Estrithsson, the mighty sea-king, sat alone, his head tilted slightly to one side, his eye fixed hypnotically upon the doorway. His face was pallid and wore a ravaged, hunted look. His long white locks fell about him in wild confusion. All day the sun had beaten down upon the bearskins so that now the heat of the tent was oppressive, yet despite this Asbiorn was enveloped in a long fur robe and the air was heavy with the stench of his unwashed body. He neither moved nor spoke, and as Waltheof stood there he was conscious of a sense of vague uneasiness he could not define.

"You are Asbiorn Estrithsson?"

The sea-king made no reply, yet his fixed gaze did not falter. He appeared to be in a state of drugged weariness.

"I come as Hereward Leofricsson's bode," the earl continued, "having been sent by him to learn why you failed to appear at the trysting two weeks past. Since that time we have daily awaited your attack. Daily we have donned our mail at dawn, only to lay it aside unused at dusk. Daily fourteen hundred men have needed to be fed until now even our last reserves are all but exhausted. The city is surrounded, as you have doubtless surmised, and there is no way for these men to escape. If you fail us now, they will all die—either by famine or by the Bastard's pitiless methods. What, Hereward Leofricsson demands to know, has held you back? When will you keep the trysting?"

Something in Waltheof's words seemed at last to penetrate the sea-king's slumbering awareness. He stirred uneasily, shivered, and drew his fur robe more tightly about him. "I have no men to keep a trysting," he replied.

"Then what are you doing here off the English coast? Did you not assemble an army as you engaged to do?"

"Aye—aye——" Asbiorn was now beginning to collect his scattered thoughts. "I spent the winter recruiting men in Iceland, Greenland and Norway. Five thousand men I had—and of the best—warriors so wild they disdained to sleep beneath a roof, or drain the bowl on the sheltered hearth; mariners who defied the hurricane by running over the oars while they were in motion; marksmen who could throw three javelins to the masthead and catch them alternately without missing. A fleet of galleys I amassed to transport these men, each one fully laden with arms and supplies. At last, when the proper time had come around, I set sail for England to keep the trysting."

"Then where is this fleet? Where are these men?"

"Gone! Deserted!" Asbiorn replied dully. "I tell you, there was a curse upon the expedition from the first. The men felt it. They knew! They began to behave strangely a few days out, spending their time huddled in the prow, whispering—whispering. Men are like wolves. They follow the strongest in the pack. There was one among them—an Icelander—who was their leader. But he wanted more than that. He wanted what was mine. He wanted to be their ship-king, to occupy my place, my tent. Soon, to align the men against me, he began to tell them lies. Lies! About me! The men listened to him, believed everything he said." There was a sudden fixed intentness in Asbiorn's gaze. His face assumed an expression of singular cunning. "One morning he was gone."

"Gone? In mid-ocean?"

Asbiorn leaned forward, challenging. "What do you find so strange in that? He was our steersman. There had been a squall the previous night and the men concluded that he fell overboard while he was raising and making fast the steering oar."

"Sound reasoning, no doubt," allowed Waltheof. "But how could the loss of a single man affect so formidable an undertaking?"

"At first the men attached no importance to it. It was only later, after many such losses had occurred, that they thought to question it." Now Asbiorn's breath was coming fast. He seemed to be under the stress of intense excitement. "I knew what they were thinking—that these losses had not been accidents at all, that someone—someone among themselves—was responsible. They began to regard each other with suspicion, each man mistrustful of his former friend. They began to lie awake at night, fearful of sleep. There was no more fraternizing in the prow. No more gossiping. The men were cowed. Ha! Their tongues had been effectively silenced—and I was master of the snekke once again!"

Waltheof frowned, at a loss to understand the sea-king's triumphant exaltation. It was as though he had fought a battle single-handed against his entire crew, and won.

"How many men did you lose?"

"Ten—twelve—fifteen——"

"All from your own galley?"

"Aye, that was why the men were afraid. They said there was evil aboard, that we should abandon the snekke—set her adrift—sink her! I refused to countenance any such unreasonable demand, so when the wind changed and we had to take to the oars, the men turned sullen, rowing so sluggishly that they retarded the entire fleet. It was only yesterday at sunset that we finally sighted Spurn Head and dropped anchor for the night." Asbiorn paused and took a long breath. "Now I have answered your question. Now you know why I could not keep the trysting."

Waltheof regarded the sea-king with puzzled curiosity. He was lying, but why? Why, when all the land from Praetorium to the Head was agog with the news of a vast viking fleet having lain at anchor for two weeks past, did he claim to have anchored only yesterday? What did he have in mind to conceal? The earl reflected a moment and determined to proceed with the utmost caution.

"And yet, having come so far, the fleet deserted just short of the disembarkation point?"

The simple question caused Asbiorn's manner to change abruptly. He became querulous, wary, evasive.

"What captain can answer for his men's actions?" he cried. "I can only tell you what I think. Bearing in mind the Wake's severe admonition regarding secrecy, I had carefully withheld from my men all details of the projected engagement, but seeing us off the coast of England, they were likely rath in guessing something of the truth. Perhaps they feared to face so formidable a foe as the Bastard. Perhaps they feared to face me and admit their cowardice. However it may be, all was quiet last night, with nothing untoward occurring to indicate their intentions. At the usual hour they brought me my supper and left me. When I awoke this morning, they were gone. The crew—the fleet—sailed away in the night."

They sat for a moment in silence, while the sea-king's eye shrewdly hunted his companion's face, striving to appraise the earl and to discover whether behind that affable exterior was harbored any vestige of suspicion or doubt.

Waltheof, on the other hand, had been careful to suppress any outward manifestation of his feelings throughout the discussion. As he listened to the story, he had been conscious of the odd impression that much that was pertinent had been slurred over or deliberately left unsaid. Now he sensed something vaguely threatening in the sea-king's manner, something sinister in the way he sat there, tense, hunched over, as though beneath his cloak he were holding some object which he guarded with febrile jealousy. Doggedly the earl reined in his fancy. He must escape the exhausting heat and smell of the tent. He must sleep. He must have time to think things over, to piece together the broken threads of the story.

"I shall remain aboard tonight," he said, arising. "Time enough tomorrow to discuss what action we must take, since if we are becalmed, so also is the fleet. But this is a speedy vessel. She is said to outrun any ship on the seas. Could we not, at the first favorable wind, hoist sail between us, overtake the fleet and persuade the men to return?"

He waited, expecting the sea-king's eager acquiescence, but Asbiorn's thoughts were already elsewhere. He appeared to have suddenly lost all interest in the complex problems of fleets and battles and men. "Aye—aye——" he replied at last, and Waltheof, detecting a note of irritation in his voice, turned and left him.

Night was closing in about the deck. In the distance he could see the Head, shadowy in the dusk. The tide was ebbing. Its gentle swells broke against the prow. The earl stood for a moment in the central gangway, glancing about, then he turned and made his way noiselessly behind the tent to the stern where he carefully inspected the steering oar. It was lashed in place and was, as he had somehow suspected, thoroughly dried through by long days of exposure to the sun. The earl frowned, puzzled, and returned to the gangway where he quenched his thirst at the water cask and helped himself to a handful of dried salted meats from the ship's locker. Then he crossed to the crumpled sail and threw himself down upon it, lying on his back and gazing up at the sky, wondering, turning things over in his mind, struggling with the obscure complexities of the sea-king's story.

That most of it was true, Waltheof did not doubt, but Asbiorn was lying when he claimed to have dropped anchor off the Head only last night. No ship could steer its course without its steering oar, and this one was dry. It had not been in the sea for weeks. That proved the truth of what had been told him at Praetorium, that the fleet had indeed been anchored in these waters some fifteen days or more. Why did Asbiorn deny it? And how had he spent these two lost weeks? From the extreme pallor of his skin, he was a man who had long shunned the sunshine, but why did he keep to his tent? How did he pass the time? There was something odd in his manner, as though at times he was quite out of touch with reality. His men would have observed it, of course, but could there be a connecting

link between that and the fleet's desertion? And what was he concealing beneath his fur robe? One of his many treasures? It would
indeed be interesting to know what it was, what he had come to
value most after so long and successful a life of piracy——

Above, the stars glimmered. The sky was a deep night-blue. The
ship rocked gently on the swells. The wash against the prow made a
soft swishing noise. Waltheof closed his eyes and listened to its murmuring. Soon his large furry hand relaxed its grip upon the meats
and they fell, uneaten, to the deck. A loud snore like the contented
grunting of a bear broke the quiet. Waltheof slept.

He was awakened by a noise, a strangling human cry. He leaped
up and glanced hurriedly around. The dawn was about to break and
in the graying light he could see a bloody trail running across the
deck from the ship-tent. Upon the gunwale was the crimson imprint
of a hand. Leaning overboard, the earl searched the opaque green
waters, but if a man was thrashing out his life somewhere below
there, the sea held its secret well.

Back in the empty ship-tent Earl Waltheof found everything as it
had been yesterday. The pallet had not been slept in. Its skins lay in
orderly piles, its cushions unrumpled. The burned-out lamp stood in
its place upon the table. The fur robe hung over the empty chair.
Then he caught sight of what he was unconsciously seeking, on the
floor at his feet, rocking gently back and forth to the motions of the
vessel. The earl stooped and picked it up.

He saw now that it was a goblet of purest gold. The lower half
had been defaced, crushed in as with an angry heel. The upper half
was unmarred and as Waltheof gazed upon it he was struck by the
peculiarly lifelike expression on the face of the White Christ. Pious
and loving hands had fashioned this goblet, hands whose consummate artistry had been able to impart to the image something of the
infinite goodness, the omnipotence, the divine compassion of the
Godhead. The lips were beardless, the brow high and serene, and
about it circled a flanging nimbus of rubies and pearls.

The earl was puzzled by his discovery. He lowered himself into
the sea-king's chair and gazed thoughtfully down at the cup reposing in his two large palms. Despite its beauty of workmanship, it
could have no exceptional monetary value. Why, therefore, did the
sea-king prize it above his other, greater treasures? Why had he
seemed to be hiding it? What was the heathen Asbiorn doing with a
sacred Christian goblet?

And Earl Waltheof pondered these questions long and hard, but found no answers thereto. And the ship rocked, and the dawn came up, and the sea was still.

Back at York, Hereward summoned his men to a meeting in the castle bailey and there, with the travel-stained Waltheof by his side, he told them of the sea-king's death and the ruin of their hopes.

"There is little choice for us now," he concluded, "save to determine, each man for himself, whether he will crave mercy of the Bastard, or arm himself and go forth one last time to battle, slaughtering if slaughtered, but thinning the Norman ranks before he falls. Let each man consider the issue and thereafter stand forth and freely speak his mind, without hindrance or censure, according to our ancient English code."

But the men needed no deliberation. Their answer came at once and with a great shout. "We will fight! We will fight!" they cried. "We would scorn to crave pity of the Bastard and kneel to him in submission!" And Hereward, seeing his band of starving men so English-hearted still, found himself wordless before them, and turning suddenly, he strode away, through the castle and up the narrow winding stair to the solitude of the tower room that had served them as council chamber. Here, driven by agitation, he paced and circled the tiny room, now bitterly chastising himself for having so periled the lives of his men, even in such a cause; now searching desperately for a stratagem whereby he might yet save them. And thus Eadric, coming to seek him, found him later and for the first time in their colleagueship the wild man's wildness was gone and his voice was almost gentle.

"Do not upbraid yourself, Hereward," he said, "nor think yourself to blame for our evil case. If you took the sponsorship for this plan, so did we all wholeheartedly embrace it once we had attained a full comprehension of it. Had it succeeded, William would now be our prisoner or dead, his army destroyed, and every remaining Norman in the land scurrying for ship and home. But having lost, there is still something we can do; for by our example we can at least show other Englishmen how to fight and die for England; we can perhaps, by the very valor with which we go forth to die, so inspire those who survive us that they will rally and unite to shoulder the burthen of our incompleted task. And for your comfort, my friend, let me advise you that these words are not my own. This is the gist of the talk in the bailey below."

"They are brave men," Hereward murmured, "and their lives are in my hands. It is for me to find a way to get them out of York."

Eadric stared in astonishment. "Are you mad!" he cried. "There are fourteen hundred of us left in this trap—a trap which only Waltheof has a means of quitting."

"Natheless," said Hereward, "there has to be a way to freedom. We have but to find it."

Thereafter the Wake scarcely spoke a word to any man, and none dared address him. His face was grim, his eyes sleepless, his cheeks hollow, yet there was something in the set of his jaw that made the men hope on. By night and by day he strode through the castle and through the city streets, back and forth, from battlement to gate, from tower to river, and always somewhere close at hand, the shadow of his master's shadow, hovered Lightfoot, ever silent, ever watchful.

A way had to be found to do the impossible, to get fourteen hundred men out of the besieged city; to spirit them away; to so effect their escape that the Bastard, for all his watchfulness, would suspect nothing lest he dispatch his cavalry over the countryside to round them up and slaughter them. Waltheof's method of slipping through the cordon could be employed by none but Waltheof. What, then, of the rest? There had to be a way to save them, to lead them to freedom and safety. But how? How?

And somehow in his restless wanderings Hereward always found himself back again in the little tower room, and always he was drawn to the window which looked out over the marshy lands beyond the Foss Isle to the southeast. He knew full well that there could be no escape in that direction, for, unlike his native fens, this morass had no causeways, no sunken paths, no reed-ronds, no shining meres or gleaming waterways, no marsh birds, no emerald surface. It was a vast expanse of bottomless black mud, of stagnant slime which no human had ever crossed, nor ever could. This he learned from Waltheof, who declared emphatically that no man had ever attempted to cross the marsh. Down through the centuries when danger threatened, and so long as their food held out, the citizens of York had always relied upon their impregnable walls for security. They had never been able to use the marsh as a place of refuge. It would be impossible, the earl said, for even an experienced fenman like the Wake to make a crossing where there were no waterways for navigation and not a yard of solid footing. And certainly any attempt to get a host of fourteen hundred men across would end in a hideous death for them all in the fathomless slime.

So Hereward abandoned all hope of finding a route to freedom across the marsh, yet still, against his conscious will, the hope remained. Perhaps it was by habit that his thoughts turned involuntarily in that direction. Perhaps it was because to him a fenny tract had always signified home—freedom—escape. Or perhaps it was that the seed of a plan was already germinating in his brain, though he himself was as yet unaware of it. But always, by night and by day, he would find himself back in the tower room at the window, gazing out across the marsh. And always the thought was there, insisting, nagging, like a persistent person plucking at his sleeve.

The marsh! The marsh!

Then one day as he stood there it chanced that a storm moved inland from the sea. A towering mass of black clouds shadowed all the land and on the fringe of the nearby forest the wind gusts bore savagely down upon the trees, hurling back their branches and leaving great gaps in the dense green forest wall. A driving rain narrowed the vista until the encircling Normans looked like phantom watchmen at their posts. Beyond the outworks of the castle the river Foss, already swollen by the spring melting of the Galtres snows, was overflowing its banks so that the boggy Foss Isle lay partially inundated. The flood had not yet extended to the desolate stretch of marshland beyond, but the rain had water-soaked its muddy levels and continued to beat down with such force that it set tiny fountains to playing all over it.

And as Hereward watched, a plan took shape, emerging at last perfected, crystal-clear. His face was locked and rigid, he scarce dared breathe, but his spirit soared like an eagle in skyward flight. Aye, that was it—that was it! That was the way!

Breaking loose from the grip of his own ascendant thoughts, he bounded to the door and down the stairs to the Hall where the men were collected against the storm. They looked up at the sound of his speeding feet and a silence fell upon them, and when he paused upon the bottom step and addressed them his voice rang with his old energy and vigor.

"Men," he cried, "we are quitting York. By sundown tomorrow I want you to have built fifty rafts, each to hold thirty men and each equipped with blown-up bladders or cattle hides to float them in shallow water. For the timber, strip the houses—the castle—the rampart walks, but have the rafts ready by sundown. On the first moonless night we will evacuate the city."

The men said nothing, only gazed doubtfully at Hereward, then at each other, and filed out into the storm to do as they were bid. Earl Waltheof was troubled as he watched them go. Eadric looked questioningly into Hereward's sleepless face and wondered mightily, but for once forbore to give voice to his usual remonstrances and objections. Only Lightfoot smiled, happy to see the anguish lifted from his master's countenance and confident in his master's ingenuity, however difficult the case.

That night, assisted by a team of carefully selected fenmen, Hereward tested out his plan, damming up the river Foss immediately below the Foss Isle and thus deflecting the waters to overrun the marsh. But the Wake was too wary to permit total inundation to act as a forewarning to the Normans, for should they suspect his design they would extend their cordon to circumvent the entire marshy area. He therefore removed the dam shortly before dawn and waited anxiously to learn the result of his night's work. By the time the sun came up he was satisfied that his plan was practicable.

Several nights passed before the weather was right for the attempt, but at last at the end of a gloomy day the cloud banks hung low in a windless sky. There was no moon. Not a star was to be seen. Under cover of an intense and impenetrable blackness Hereward worked at damming up the Foss, instructing his men meanwhile to lift the rafts over the wall, carry them to the river and set them in the water.

It wanted but a few hours to dawn before Hereward was satisfied that the marsh was sufficiently flooded for them to hazard the crossing. At a signal from him, his fenmen loaded their rafts with the required number of men and set out, quanting noiselessly through the swamp, seeing the distant margin only in the mirror of their memories and having only their uncanny fenmen's instinct to guide them to it. Not a ripple was heard; not a plash; not a word was spoken. When at last they reached the edge of the swamp they were well behind the Norman cordon, with only a mile or so of heath lying between them and the woodlands. Thither they hastened, carrying their rafts to conceal them in the shrubs and thus leaving behind no evidence of their flight. The Wake himself was the last to quit the city and it was almost sunup before he, too, had crossed the heath and reached the shelter of the woods. Here he paused a moment on the brink of free-

dom to glance back at their erstwhile prison, to where already the
uppermost battlements were becoming faintly discernible in the graying light.

The city was empty, yet it would be some days before even the
vigilant Conqueror came to suspect it. The marsh was draining. The
Foss flowed on its normal course, for he had removed the dam before
he left. Behind the loops could be seen the flickering cresset lights.
Peat reek curled from a dozen roofs. Above the castle the English
ensign stirred in the first morning breeze. And for the first time since
the siege began the Wake's tired face relaxed into a smile, and he
turned and plunged swiftly into the thickets.

Incensed at being defeated even in victory, William scoured the
countryside for the straggling survivors. Those unlucky enough to
be captured were blinded and maimed in William's presence, then
let loose in the open country to die by their own hand or be devoured by the wolves. But even with the punishment of those who
had taken an active part in the city's defense, his wrath had not ex-
pended itself. His vengeance was yet to come, was yet to fall upon
the innocent.

To forestall any possible chance of future rebellion in the north,
William ruthlessly and wantonly harried the whole of Northumberland, traveling himself through the wildest and most inaccessible
regions to see that his will was done; systematically burning every
house, burning the stores of precious corn and other foods, butcher-
ing the livestock and slaying without mercy those who raised their
scythes to protect their families, their homes or their goods. Those
who were not slain eventually died of hunger, subsisting till the last
upon the flesh of cats and dogs, driven in their extremity to devour
even their dead countrymen until, when these, too, were exhausted,
they laid themselves down and quietly died in the knowledge that
their bodies would at best rot where they lay, since not one among
those who were left had the strength to cover them with a handful
of soil.

Northumberland was now a wilderness; the fields untilled, the
highways untrodden, the crumbling towns uninhabited save by the
wild beasts who hunted through the ruins, while those whose only
crime had been to defend their own hearthstones from the invader
lay beneath the open sky, their bones whitening on the blackened
soil.

Chapter Twelve

BELSAR'S HILL

KING WILLIAM was hunting in the forest north of London where, in ages past, the druids cut the mistletoe with a moonsickle of gold. At some fifty yards behind him rode his retinue, outdistanced by the more swiftly mounted king; before him ran the hounds, excited by the chase, leaping forward with sharp yelps as the weary stag slackened his pace and the scent grew stronger. For an instant William's straining eyes glimpsed the flying antlers and he spurred his horse, sweeping up a steep escarpment and through a colonnade of silver-shafted birches, across a heathy plateau scattered with pixie mounds and fern and bilberries, then down into the deepening shadows of a ravinelike cleft.

A sudden turn and the Conqueror was all but pitched over his horse's head as the beast, speeding downhill, pulled up abruptly. For the moment the hounds were lost in the gloom ahead, but William knew they had stopped running, for their excited yelps rebounded deafeningly on all sides. As his eyes began to penetrate the obscurity he found himself in a basinlike hollow hemmed in all around by a heavy growth of yews, whose boughs reached out to interlace in matted density, and whose trunks, with their moldering bark and fibrous offshoots, stood like a host of grisly satyrs in the dim transmitted light. A stagnant pool lay straight ahead, ringed in now by the noisy hounds. In the center of the pool, at bay, stood the quarry, a snow-white hart, his mighty antlers snapping the branches above him as he strove to fight off his attackers.

Never before had the Conqueror, a passionate huntsman, glimpsed the rare albino deer, and here, with the black waters below and the black yews above, he felt within him a thrill of unparalleled wonder. "Jesu!" he breathed, and without pausing to forethink, without even comprehending his own action, he lowered his bow, placed his horn to his lips and recalled the hounds. The hart stood a moment, nostrils dilating, watching the hounds reluctantly fall back, then with a leap he gained the summit of the ridge behind him and vanished swiftly into the gloom.

A silky voice sounded behind the king. "Wherefore, sire, did you spare the hart?"

The king turned to find Sir Guy de Lussac at his side and involuntarily he frowned.

"Already," he admitted, with studied cordiality, "I can almost regret it. 'Twas a stag royal, magnificently crowned, and having no less than seven summers."

"So I was privileged to observe, sire," replied de Lussac, "but there will be many who doubt the story you will tell. Indeed, were I not here to attest the truth of the case, your own courtiers might well smile behind their hands and say—again, 'The king cannot run the deer to soil.' "

" 'Again'?"

De Lussac glanced obliquely at the Conqueror. "Know you not they say it now? 'The king cannot run the deer to soil—the king cannot catch the Wake.' "

If de Lussac expected an explosion of wrath, he was disappointed. There was only scorn in the king's voice. "Say they so?" he murmured.

"Aye, that and more." Now Sir Guy chose his words cautiously, craftily. "It is a matter of much discussion that the English were able to make good their escape from York. True enough, scores of them were taken, and their sword hands severed so they could never fight again. But what, sire, of the rest? Whither have they fled? Do they not live to fight again? And what of their scheming and plotful leader, Hereward the Wake?"

The king turned and gazed coldly down at his companion, a strange glint in his unrevealing eyes.

"Sir Guy," he said, "I have known it is not your oft-expressed love for me keeps you here in London where the June sun beats hot, when at your own Cruc Maur the sea winds blow fresh and cool. Your motives are your own—I seek not to unravel them. Perhaps you have fears for your person while the Wake is abroad. Perhaps you fear for your lands and chattels, counting them less your own while he is alive to claim them. What is it you want, then—to see him caught and hanged? Wherefore it will gratify you to know that I have acquainted myself of his whereabouts. Within the month the deer shall be run to soil."

So saying, the king spurred his horse, and without so much as a nod at the oncoming horsemen, he sped alone through the forest and back to London and the Tower.

But that evening, after they had supped, the Conqueror summoned to his privy chamber several of his captains, among whom were Fitz-Osbern, Roger de Montgomery, Galitier Giffard and de Lussac.

"My lords," he said, "the Wake has not fled England as some of you supposed. I have learned that the survivors of York headed south to a prearranged trysting in the fens, where already Hereward Leofricsson has started the reorganization of his army and the formulation of new plans."

There was a gasp of astonishment at such audacity on the part of the English rebel leader.

"Sire," said FitzOsbern, "if that be so, permit me to counsel instant action. The fall of York has had a strange and contrariwise effect upon the English, for instead of sinking them in the blackest despair, it has rekindled hope among them. They begin now to smile, to whisper that what the Godwinsson could not do, the Leofricsson may; that the Wake may even yet outwit the Conqueror."

"Action in this case," snapped de Lussac, "is more easily counseled than taken. The fens are some seventy miles long and half as broad, and he who thinks to catch the Wake in his own bailiwick is like to learn of a few new tricks and stratagems—to his sorrow."

"Is it your counsel, then, Sir Guy," demanded the king with a faint tinge of raillery, "that we leave him free to roam the fens at will?"

"Nay, nay, sire," cried de Lussac, "but this time let us plot with care; this time let us have him so tightly in the bag he cannot wriggle out."

"Seventy miles makes a big bag," quoth Giffard.

"And what of this trysting place, sire?" asked FitzOsbern. "Have you been able to learn its exact location?"

"It is the Isle of Ely, a monastery in the southern fens, whose monks, being English, think it no treason to welcome the rebel horde. As to its approaches, two causeways traverse the morass to connect with the isle, but being of Roman origin and consequently of extreme antiquity, it were wise not to count too heavily upon them for safe passage."

"It were wise for still another reason, Your Grace," de Lussac pointed out, "for if any such causeways existed, the Wake will have had them cut and sunk in the bog long since."

"Have you thought to use the fleet, sire?" asked Giffard. "Could it not penetrate the inland waterways and land troops on the isle?"

"We know nothing of these waterways," the Conqueror replied, "and would therefore be compelled to depend upon the fenmen to pilot our vessels through the shallow waters. Such a procedure would be hazardous, for these fenmen are fanatically loyal to Hereward Leofricsson and we could never be sure that the hand that was pocketing our gold was not at the same time fixing to trap us in the bog."

"Pardi!" exclaimed Montgomery. "So, having driven the lion to bay, we still cannot lay hands upon his hide!"

A slight smile curved the Conqueror's lips.

"Patience, bold Roger," he chided. "Let us not dispute the results till the chase is run." He arose suddenly and looked at his captains, each in turn. The smile was gone now. His face was hard, his lips set in the firm lines which his courtiers had learned to both dread and respect. "You will prepare yourselves to set out for the fens within the week," he said. "It is my intention to bring the collected forces of my kingdom to bear upon the isle immediately, before the summer wanes. Whatever the difficulties, it is my intention to find a way to cross over into Ely; to make the Wake my prisoner, and to hang his men."

"Hang his men!" De Lussac's voice was sharp. "Sire, is it not your intention, then, to also hang the Wake?"

The Conqueror reflected a moment, and sighed, and moved toward the door.

"Indeed," he answered slowly, "there is little I so much admire as a truly brave man. Would that he were Norman. What could I not do with such a captain!"

So saying, he turned, and still immersed in thought, strode off down the corridor, leaving his captains staring at one another and marveling at his last words, for they could make nothing of them.

But not so de Lussac. As he looked after the receding figure of the Conqueror, his eyes clouded over with the sudden comprehension of that which he had not dreamed could ever come to pass. For a moment his new-found knowledge left him speechless, then, as the royal footfalls faded into the distance, he murmured angrily, "Have

a care, mighty King, when you start to love your enemy. On just
such reefs has many a ship of state been wrecked."

And so it chanced that a week or so later, Martin Lightfoot, having borrowed a boat from the monks, was fishing some few miles
west of Ely with his friend, Letwold. It was early evening and in the
soft sunlight the waters of the mere lay mirror-smooth. From every
sallow and alder carr came the ventriloquial song of the warbler and
the scream of the jay. The grebes and the coots swam out from the
reeds and dove for food. A swallow midge hawked above the floating peat and every bank was lush with meadowsweet and hemp
agrimony, with sundew, cinquefoil and gold and purple loosestrifes.
In the air above, the wild fowl wheeled and cried; on the mere below, all was silent, save for a light splash as Lightfoot made his cast,
then slowly drew his line toward him.

Letwold, dreaming in the prow, turned quickly as a giant rudd
broke the surface of the water and the tightening line told that he
had been hooked. With tense and eager face, Lightfoot fought to
keep him in the open, skillfully drawing him away from the reed bed
for which he instinctively headed and among whose roots he could
entangle the line and gain his freedom. But Lightfoot, aware of the
danger, worked patiently, playing the line, drawing the struggling
fish nearer and nearer the boat until at last, slipping the net beneath
him, he scooped him up and threw him, thrashing and gasping, in
the bottom of the boat.

Letwold watched his companion, amused at his complete absorption with his task, amused at the way the long pink tongue trembled
with excitement as he viewed his prize, and the look of ecstatic pleasure on the dark face.

"Martin, my friend," he said at length, "you have caught enough
fish today for ten dinners. Let us start back to Ely now, while the
sun still lights the spire which is our only guidepost. I do not hanker
for a night in the open fen. Besides, they will be supping at the isle
and I fear that even now we may have missed the nightly repast."

Lightfoot looked up, startled, like a man awakening from a deep
sleep. His eyes swept the sky, then the fringes of the mere where the
shadows thrown by the reeds upon the water were fast lengthening.

"You are right, good Letwold," he replied, "it grows late. But
grieve not the loss of your meal, for whatever it is they eat, we can
better it. Tonight we shall sup on rudd, you and I, and every man

and monk upon the isle shall stand around and envy us our supper."

"Is it then considered such a goodly fish?"

"Aye, and well worth the fight to land one," replied Lightfoot, starting to stow his tackle. "But let me caution you against praising it in the presence of the monks. I would not offend the good brothers, for they take great pains to serve us royally of everything on hoof and wing. But marry! My palate tires of forest fare. I tell you, Letwold, since embracing the outlaw life I have eaten so much venison that my stomach starts to leap like a stag at the sound of the hunting horn."

Letwold smiled, so that the flesh grew taut about his hollow cheeks, and by habit he raised a hand to straighten the clothpiece at his throat.

" 'Tis well," he said, "for now the stomach befits the legs."

A few moments later Lightfoot had left the mere behind and was poling swiftly up a waterway in the direction of Ely. Already the sun had sunk out of sight, but its amber afterglow gilded the church spire that was to guide them home. All along the shore, in their jungle of reeds and sedges, the birds noised furtively. A vole rustled in the hovers, then dropped pelletlike into the water, leaving widening circles where it had disappeared. From the copse of a nearby isle came the strange, chilling laughter of a green woodpecker. A flock of feeding wild fowl arose at the boat's approach and with a loud, protesting clangor made off across the marsh.

Lightfoot was glad that Letwold showed no inclination to talk. He loved this aloneness. He loved the stillness of earth and sky and water. He loved the way a familiar willow or alder scrub would change its shape in the dusk and become instead a thing of dread, a thing to chill the heart of the unknowing. That would happen tonight, for they would not be home before nightfall. Already over to the east a dark veil was being drawn over the earth's tired face. To the north, only the shining tip of the church spire stood out against the darkling sky. To the south, to the far horizon, the undulating sea of reeds lay gray in the fading light, and beyond that——

Lightfoot stopped poling suddenly and shaded his eyes. Beyond that—Holy Virgin!—beyond that rose a dozen or more spiraling white columns, uncannily like smoke from the cookfires of a host of fighting men!

"What is it, Martin?" asked Letwold lazily from the prow.

"Stand up, my friend, and tell me what you see. If we both see alike, then 'tis no phantasm."

Obligingly Letwold arose and peered above the reeds, gazing off across the fen and following the direction in which the bony finger pointed.

"Pish!" he said. " 'Tis merely fog."

"Choke on your 'pish,' man. Look again!"

And suddenly the gleam of armored men in motion showed clearly across the fen, then the faint, but unmistakable, neighing of a horse and a hammering as of an armorer at his anvil.

"In truth," said Letwold, "I see it all now plain enough, yet though 'tis all quite plain, I can make nothing of it."

"Nor I," agreed Lightfoot, "the more urgent, then, to tell it to my lord."

It was quite dark when they reached the monastery, which they were enabled to do that night only because Hereward had thought to hang a lanthorn upon a tall pole and plant it on the shore. Lightfoot wasted no time in seeking his master, who, having heard him out, straightway took him to an office where Waltheof and Eadric the Wild sat together playing a stormy game of chess.

"The Bastard in the fenlands!" exclaimed Waltheof in amazement, after Lightfoot had repeated his story. "What can he be thinking of? Does he hope to find causeways left everywhere intact for his convenience?"

Hereward paced up and down, his thumbs in his belt. "Where were our scouts, that they failed to report his coming? They were good men—and wary, yet not one succeeded in getting word through to us. Why? In any case, we know enough of William to be certain he is not the man to make a move without first conceiving some workable plan of action. The fact that he has ventured into the fenlands at all is proof that he has some such plan in mind."

"Said!" agreed Eadric. "Said, indeed!"

"That being so," the Wake continued, "we would do well to waste no time in learning just what that plan is, for only by so doing can we successfully forestall it."

"From where we sit," muttered Waltheof, "reading the Bastard's mind will be no small matter."

"We would divine his intentions soon enough if one of us could find a way to penetrate his camp and observe his activities."

"Are you crazed!" Waltheof stared at Hereward in amazement. "Penetrate the Bastard's camp! Then let any such dolt go shriven, for his folly will be worth his life!"

At that Eadric the Wild sprang up, and with an oath swept the chessmen from the table. "What would you have us do, lord earl? Sit here like eels in a sett while the Bastard takes his own time to come and hang us?" He tilted back his head and his green eyes were filled with scorn. " 'Waltheof the Berserker'? The 'nithing' were nearer the truth!"

The insult brought a flush to Waltheof's pale face. "Beware, Eadric," he warned. "Beware!"

"Be damned!" Eadric retorted. "And sleep easy, brave earl, for I will go to the Norman camp. I will go—while you stay here and play the lion by knocking down any underling who shows a yellow streak."

"Enough!" interposed Hereward sternly, then to Eadric, "Hold your anger, man. We are not all possessed of your fine recklessness. And when it comes to visiting the Bastard in his den, you, being outborn to this district, are hardly the man for it. If flight led you to the fenside you would be finished for sure, in that if the Normans didn't get you, the bog would." He turned to Lightfoot. "Tomorrow at dawn you will saddle me a horse and have a barge in readiness to ferry me across to Erith. From thence I shall circle about and approach the Norman camp from the south, making as if I am fresh from London town."

Lightfoot made no reply, only turned away his face so that his master could not read his thoughts. And that night he went supperless to bed, leaving his hard-won rudd forsook and forgotten in the bottom of the boat.

The sun was high by the time Hereward stepped off the barge the next day at Erith, pulled his horse ashore and bade farewell to Lightfoot and the bargeman. Some slight change had been wrought in his appearance by Martin, for his yellow hair was now brown and even his skin was several shades darker. Nevertheless, it was with considerable apprehension that Lightfoot watched his lord's broad back recede into the distance, and straightway he began to mutter to himself, dwelling upon all the risks and hazards involved in this new undertaking; and he heaved, and sighed, and beheld fearsome visions all the way back to Ely.

But with Hereward it was otherwise. He rode, for the moment at least, with cheerful abandon, experiencing a sudden sense of release from the restraintful atmosphere of the isle; feeling once again the lure of the long forest road, the joy of a horse between his knees and he knew not what ahead of him. Swiftly he sped on southwards, through light and shadow, by howe and heath, until he crossed the Ouse and met the Ermine Street just below Godmanchester.

Here, as he turned east along the Roman way leading to Cambridge, his thoughts sobered abruptly and he began to think of how he would go about gaining access to the Norman camp. At least four Norman knights knew him by sight. De Lussac would remember him, likewise the two men who had also been present at the parley at York, and if ever he chanced to come face to face with Sir Herlwin FitzHugh, it would not be a little brown berry juice would prevent recognition. No, it needed something more, something which would, at the same time, account for the presence of an Englishman in the Norman camp.

It was then, just as he was turning the matter over in his mind, that he became aware of a crazy clatter up ahead and, upon rounding a bend, saw at some short distance away a potter striding along beside his nag. It was from the beast that the din emanated, for she was all decked out in crocks and panshins and other potter's wares, and carried besides a pannier on either flank which was likewise filled.

Hereward swore, reflecting somewhat wryly upon the vagaries of Chance and wishing that this time she had chosen to serve him better, then, with a hasty glance to make sure there was no one else in sight, he spurred his horse and came up alongside the potter.

"Brave churl," he said, "what will you take for your nag?"

The potter looked up in astonishment. He was a large and burly man, garbed in a ragged tunic of green cloth and equally ragged black hosen. His brogues were down at heel and out at toe and upon his head was perched a pointed, grease-rimmed cap adorned with a bedrabbled widgeon's plume. He had to think hard before the import of Hereward's words penetrated his slow intelligence, but when at last it did, he firmly and resolutely shook his head.

"My horse is not for sale," he replied, "for then how should I carry my pots?"

"I mean to have those, too—and your apparel, if, indeed, it has not already fallen from your back before we conclude our bargain."

The potter laughed, showing a set of strong white teeth through his dense beard. "And what of me?" he asked merrily. "There is a bit of woman in the next town whom I hanker to wed. Would you have me court her baresark?"

"That would depend upon whether she be maid or matron," replied Hereward, with a wink. "But since the question troubles you, you shall have my tunic, which I'll warrant is handsomer than yours, and my fine gelding to replace your nag."

Still the potter looked doubtful. "Such a shuffle would suit me well enough," he said, "were it not for the sheriff. When he sees a clod like me so finely mounted, he will think I stole the brute and clap me in jail."

"Clap you in jail! With a solid gold piece in your moneybag to prove you a man of means!"

"Ah, that is different."

Whereupon there, in the middle of the highway, they disrobed and exchanged clothes, with the Wake holding back only his dagger, hidden away out of sight. And when the potter beheld Hereward in his own castoff attire, he was completely overcome with mirth.

"Sweet heaven!" he chortled. "Those rags of mine were well got rid of. And though, strange sir, I like you well enough and would not willingly take you for a witless man, yet witless you must be to make such a bargain."

"I am fresh come from the Holy Land," quoth Hereward solemnly, "where for my sins I vowed to forswear all wealth and worldly goods." He stood off and regarded his new nag with a horsemen's practiced eye, finding her so ill-proportioned and of such exceeding ugliness that, for all his freshly averred piety, a barracks oath escaped him. "A horse, you call it? This monstrous creature, a horse? Dog's meat, say I, though he must be a spiritless cur who would content himself with such a dinner. Has it a name?"

" 'Tis a girl horse," the reprimand was gently made, "as sweet and loving a creature as ever trod the highway. And so that beauty shall in some measure attend her, I have named her Swallow, which is a beauteous name. Added to all this, you will find her possessed of only one shortcoming."

"She cannot walk without I help her."

"On the contrary," declared the potter. "At times she is uncannily fleet of foot—too much so for mortal man. Which is why you must never set spur to her, for at its touch she will away at fantastic speed, her nose to the wind and the wind in her mane, and before you know what she is about, she will have slipped right out from under you and will have left you squatting in mid-air."

"I'll wager," retorted Hereward, "that if Swallow and I ever attain to that much speed, I'll be running and she'll be astride my back."

"Ho! ho!" roared the potter. "You will see!"

With that he leaped on Hereward's horse. And so well pleased was he at the change in his fortunes that he laughed up at the sky as he galloped away, leaving Hereward to mount Mare Swallow and jog slowly on, to the rustic music of his pots.

He sighted the Norman encampment late that afternoon, on the southernmost fringe of the fen, spreading out on all sides over the grassy rampires of an ancient British earthwork known from earliest times as Belsar's Hill. Even from a distance it was apparent to the Wake's well-trained military eye that the Conqueror had in mind an operation of stupendous magnitude, intended, no doubt, to sweep the fens clean of the rebel English. The Norman host seemed numberless, and included warriors from every corner of Europe as betokened by the floating banners of the close-serried pavilions; and on all sides, girdling this impressive cantonment, the Bastard's outposts kept watch, guarding more against unauthorized ingress than egress, since there was little to fear from desertion while the odds were favorable. Those who fought for the Conqueror did so for the moment voluntarily—each man looking to secure his own share of the loot of England once her people were properly enslaved and shackled.

Hereward swore long and mightily, and his hand sought the weapons at his waist that were not there. But soon the sight of the sentry box at the entrance to the camp recalled to him that he must at all times play the meek and servile potter, whereupon he wiped the scowl from his face, dismounted, and leading Swallow by the bridle, approached the Normans humbly and afoot.

"Pots!" he cried. "Pots! Fine posnets and crocks!"

The sentries stood in the middle of the road and cast him a belligerent eye, for a long-haired Englishman amongst the short-cropped Normans was at all times to be regarded with suspicion.

"Villain," said one of them, as Hereward drew close, "what are you doing here?"

"Good sirs, fine sirs," replied Hereward, bowing low and trying to reduce his height by a foot, "I go on the assumption that wherever there are men there are kitchens, wherever there are kitchens there are chefs, wherever there are chefs there are broken crocks—which I can replace and thereby earn myself a few silver pennies. 'Tis logic."

" 'Tis fast talk, too—for a potter."

"Sir, the man who trades mostly with women must learn to talk fast, if he would talk at all."

"Well enough." The sentry moved over to Mare Swallow and peered into her panniers, removing a few crocks from the top to see what lay below. Satisfied, he turned back to Hereward. "See that you keep out of mischief," he warned. "The kitchens are to the left."

Hereward bowed. "My thanks, gentle sir," he said humbly, and taking Swallow by the bridle, he passed by the sentries into the Norman camp.

He moved at a leisurely pace along the narrow thoroughfares left between the rows of tents, glancing to right and to left with affected unconcern, but making mental note of everything he saw. He had stopped crying his wares, the more easily to escape attention, although until he was safely out of sight of the sentries he diligently followed their instructions to keep to the left. But soon, or so it seemed, he lost his way, and instead of coming out near the kitchens, he wandered slowly through the camp streets, scrutinizing, searching, observing.

It wanted still an hour or so till nightfall and the whole camp was astir; knights on horseback, whose faces were as prideful as the devices broidered on their bosoms; common soldiers afoot; silk-clad pages and leather-clad squires, the latter bearing their lords' armor to be repaired or their lords' horse to be shod. Wherever a tent flap was raised Hereward glanced inside and saw therein dark shapes industriously engaged in some warlike task. On all sides campaign preparations were in progress, and so engrossed was each man in the business at hand that few thought to glance twice at the lowly potter who had lost his way. Once a young dandy threw him a quick, suspicious look, as though struck by something familiar in the Englishman's appearance, but Hereward, instead of averting his gaze, gaped stupidly back at him with open mouth and vacant eyes, and the Norman shrugged as though mistaken, and passed on.

In a little while he saw ahead of him a group of stately pavilions, in the center of which was one more splendid than the rest; its curtains drawn, the banner of the Two Lions planted in the earth before it. It was not the first time he had beheld this standard, yet still he paused, recalling the long days at York when he had looked out across the heath and first learned to hate the vaunted symbol of Norman military might and despotic power. But this portion of the encampment was blocked off by a solid ring of sentries clad in ring mail and armed with sword, spear and crossbow, and Hereward passed on his way, unnoticed in the crowd.

But soon, having wandered far and wide, he came at last to the fringe of the encampment where there were no tents, no camp streets, no crowds to make him inconspicuous. He knew that if his suspicions were correct he would find what he was seeking down here by the fen, yet still he dared not venture out into the open where a solitary figure, and an English one, must at once attract attention. The Norman outsentries were everywhere visible, their lonely forms silhouetted in chainlike formation against the sky. He paused, therefore, just within the shadow of the last tent, his hand on Swallow's bridle. For an instant his gaze lifted to the distant spire of Ely, within whose shadow men still were counted free, then it dropped to the fen bank some few hundred yards away.

Beyond a stretch of rough, open ground he could clearly make out a gang of men at work. From their hair he knew them to be English, and indeed, for all the Norman overseers wrapped long whips around their thighs, they still worked with the reluctance of men pressed into service against their will. In slow procession they filed back and forth, hoisting rocks and tree trunks on their backs and carrying them down to the marsh. Already a long stretch of causeway had been completed. It ran from the shore out into the fen, pointing straight at the heart of Ely.

So that was it! The Bastard was clever. He knew nothing of the fenlands, yet his reasoning had led him to deduce that while they could eliminate all trace of the surface causeway, there was no way to destroy the centuries-old foundation that lay beneath the bog. He had searched for, and found it; and now, instead of setting his own inexperienced men to fumble with the work, he was impressing men native to the district; he was utilizing wherever possible the highly specialized skills of Englishmen acquainted with the difficult technicalities of causeway construction, forcing them to lay a new surface upon the remains of the old, across which his Normans could march dry-shod to the isle. Hereward was awed by this exhibition of fixed purpose and unbending will no more than by the speed and efficiency with which the Conqueror labored. Ere the summer was out he would once again have forced the English to disband; would once again have forced them to scatter before him—unless a way could be found to prevent it.

And there was a way.

Hereward's keen eyes passed slowly over the scene before him, noting each detail and fixing it in his memory against his return; the English corpse dangling from a crossbeam, left, no doubt, as a warning to the recalcitrant; a willow coppice bordering the marsh; the rock pile; the stockaded enclosure wherein the English would be herded at nightfall. The corpse he recognized as one of his own scouts. He had been taken, then, and compelled to work for the Normans, and being loyal, had either attempted flight or tried to get a warning through to Ely. Poor Edwine! The Normans cared nothing for an English life——

"Rascal, what are you up to?"

The voice came from directly behind him and he turned to find a Norman knight eying him with cold suspicion.

"My lord, gentle lord," he replied, bowing almost to the ground, then standing hunched over with a dull, bewildered look, "since you are so gracious as to address one so lowly as I, do, I implore you, direct me to the kitchens where I hope to sell my pots. Mayhap the guards at the entrance were mistaken when they bade me come hither. 'Down by the lake,' I thought they said, but I see no lake, save that that vast quagmire yonder be considered a lake. But if lake it be——"

"A curse on your babble! Get moving—back the way you came," and forthwith the Norman turned and strode off toward his tent, leaving the poor potter to find his way alone.

The kitchens turned out to be a row of long, low tents wherein a host of chefs wrestled mightily with fleshhook and spit. They blasphemed in seven tongues when they saw him enter, a pannier on each arm, for they were in the process of serving the king's supper. But they soon forgot him, for, with perception mismated to his doltish aspect, he instantly sized up the situation and moved over to a corner where he sat, his pots about him, staring with openmouthed wonder at the dainties being readied for the king's repast. But later, after the chefs themselves had supped and had quaffed generously of French wine from the royal cellar, they turned cheerful enough, cuffing him only two or three times, and lightly at that, when he haggled over prices. They purchased a dozen or more pots, persuading him to accept, in part payment, a fat pheasant direct from the king's own table, even throwing in a horn of wine when he suggested that, it being an English pheasant, he was being put upon. And so amiable a churl did he prove to be that they let him sit by the fire while he devoured his bird, for, as he blandly pointed out, it had started to rain outside.

So there in the king's kitchen he sat, loitering; deliberately letting the hours pass, whilst outside the rain sweeping in from the wide marshes lent a chill to the already impenetrable night gloom. Soon, he knew, the thoroughfares would be empty. With good luck a man might then pass where he would unnoticed, if he kept to the shadowy fringes of the camp. He waited, therefore, revolving his plan in his mind, covering its last detail, until the proper hour was come; then he arose, and stowing the remains of his pheasant in one half-empty pannier, he thanked the chefs, bade them good night, and left them.

But once outside, he lost his stoop and shed his doltish air. Swiftly, with the decisive motions of a man who knew what he was about, he loaded the panniers on his mare and led her off, heading straight for the unilluminated tract between the camp and the outsentries some few hundred yards away and moving cautiously against the furtive chatter of his pots.

Down by the fen all was quiet. He could no longer see the landmarks he had noted earlier, so obscured were they by rain and darkness, but he knew just where the willow coppice lay and found his way there without difficulty. He set the panniers on the grass, then, taking a piece of rope from one of them, selected a spot from whence Swallow could not be observed from either causeway or shore and tied her to a tree, removing her bridle so that she could comfortably crop the tall grasses and making certain that she was well within reach of the spring that watered the coppice. Then he left her.

Now, noiseless as a shadow in the gloom, he moved toward the stockade wherein the English captive laborers lay sleeping. When he sighted its vague outlines a short distance away, he dropped to his stomach and waited, listening for the soft squishing of feet in the rain-soaked earth. Soon he heard them, approaching with measured beat, and a sentry's form loomed blurry as a marshland boggle through the rain. Hereward lay still, marking the speed with which he paced; the time it took him to round the bend and disappear; the duration of the interval between his departure and the appearance of his successor. Soon he had gauged his time exactly. In the brief interregnum that fell to him, he arose, and speeding toward the stockade, he leaped over and dropped down among the recumbent forms.

A few minutes later he was sleeping as soundly as the rest.

Chapter Thirteen

SWALLOW'S FLIGHT

THE addition of an extra man to their gang of slave laborers passed unnoticed by the Normans, nor did they immediately perceive the slowdown in the work or detect the many structural imperfections suddenly appearing in their causeway. For although the Wake's co-workers were not aware of his identity, they were proving themselves to be apt and willing pupils, quickly learning the many new tricks he taught them; how, instead of setting a boulder in its appointed place, to surreptitiously roll it off the causeway into the marsh where it would never be missed; how to set a pile upright in a reed-rond in such a way that it would appear to hold, yet would tilt and give way later, precipitating a part of the structure into the bog. The Wake himself worked industriously beneath the sharp eye of the foreman, yet somehow as the days passed there was made but little headway. After a full two weeks had been spent upon the causeway, so diligently had Hereward labored that they scarcely had a week's work to show for it.

In all this time he contrived, on moonless nights, to visit Swallow in her coppice. She soon grew to know him and showed her pleasure at his visits by softly rustling the grasses when she heard him approach, as though to guide him to her. And when at last she felt his outstretched hand, she would turn her head and nuzzle him, displaying toward him a distinctly feminine coyness which sat a little oddly on a creature of her massive girth. He would change her position to provide her with fresh pasturage, and when he came to leave her, he would know, for all the darkness, that she was standing there in an attitude of mournful reproach, peering in the direction of his receding footsteps. Then he would return and pat her reassuringly, smoothing his hand over her great head. "I shall be back, girl," he would whisper, after which promise she would finally suffer him to depart. Nor did she once neigh or whinny or otherwise make a sound to betray her presence. She seemed to know intuitively that absolute silence was required of her.

And so the days ran on, each one like the last; breakfasting at sunup on bread and broth; the long, dreary day on the causeway; returning at dusk to more bread and broth, to fall at last to earth and sleep exhausted beneath the great open sky. At times there would occur a brief intermission in this monotonous routine, for whenever the Conqueror came down to cast a dissatisfied eye over his project, the English were herded back to their stockade where they were made to sit cross-legged upon the ground. And although they themselves, for all their neck craning, never once caught a glimpse of the Conqueror, they were whipped regularly after every visit in retaliation for the royal wrath which their sloth had caused to fall upon the heads of their taskmasters.

Yet still, with every eventide, Hereward felt himself a little nearer his goal. For with the autumn would come savage gales and wild weather when the vast, miry levels would be inundated, and even the highest causeway lost beneath the floods; when low-hanging fogs distilled brown moisture that killed men off with chills and agues; when at last the fen lay manacled in ice; when even marshmen were lost in snowstorms which obscured all landmarks and the scud whirled up from the drifts and battled the wind. Even the Conqueror would find he could do little in the autumn and winter months ahead. If he were impeded now, he must perforce abandon his campaign for another year, by which time the English army would be reassembled and strengthened. Aye, there were ways to stop the Conqueror. One had but to find them. One had but to have faith in the turn of the tide; faith that a nation lay never so prostrate it would not pick itself up from the muck and strike a blow for its freedom.

And always on the horizon lay the isle, so near—so far, becoming at length a symbol of England's defiance. With every dawn the Normans watched it rise as though from out of the fen, wreathed in its aqueous rainbow veil; a vision, elusive and unattainable; an enchanted isle; now clearly discernible, now fading out of sight, lost again in the mystic vapors of the marsh.

"You sons of whores," the foreman would shout, "we are no nearer today than yesterday. Work! Work! Move along, you God-damned lazy hogs!" And he would lash out indiscriminately with his whip until, for all their pride, the stern-faced English flinched and the blood ran again from their scabious weals.

Then one day it chanced that Hereward was among a group of men sent down regularly to the forest at Madingley, some few miles south of the encampment, to cut and haul back lumber needed for the causeway piles. On these occasions the men were placed under heavy guard, the Normans on horseback, the English chained in pairs and each pair set upon a wagon. Despite the constraint of a "chain mate," the men were generally glad enough to be selected for the job; glad, for a few days, to exchange the hot sun of the causeway for the cool of the forest; glad to exchange their bread and broth for venison which each man roasted for himself at a campfire shared with his mate; and, for all they were chained to a tree at nightfall, glad to exchange their overcrowded stockade for a mossy couch, a bracken pillow and the smell of damp loam.

"To slip free of these chains," said Hereward's chain mate one evening as they dined, "might not be too difficult. A man might stand a fair chance of escape here in the forest."

Hereward chewed awhile, and glanced carelessly about. There was no one within earshot, for the other captives were similarly chained in pairs at widely spaced trees and the guards themselves were at some distance, occupied with their own meal.

"It would take more forest lore than you possess, Haco, to elude their dogs," he replied. "Besides, your Berkshire speech makes you a stranger hereabouts. Who would dare give you shelter? Where would you go?"

"To the isle, to fight for the Wake."

Hereward raised an eyebrow. His identity was still unsuspected by his co-workers, with whom he passed for a hard-working fenman, and since he labored always in his tunic no one guessed at the telltale scars that lay beneath it. "Easier said than done, lad," he replied. "But do many Berkshiremen feel as you do?"

"There are always those who cherish nothing so much as a whole skin. Still, many a man starts now to quit his home in the night and head for the fens."

"Is that how you came to be taken in these parts?"

"Aye, myself and some others. They were older and had seen battle. I think they were hanged. We were on our way to the muster. 'Tis said that although the Bastard cannot find a way to the isle, an

Englishman may do so. 'Tis said the fenmen are right willing to ferry a long-hair across if he be a good fighting man."

Hereward half smiled, for Haco was but a youth of eighteen years, whose arms were yet unmarred by battle scars.

"And do you count yourself a good fighting man?"

Haco hesitated. "Leastways," he replied, "I think I should not turn tail in battle. My father stood, and fell, at Hastings."

Hereward studied him thoughtfully. He was a handsome youth, tall, sinewy, ruddy-haired and ruddy-complexioned, with the proud eye of the Celt and the Celt's fierce and turbulent nature. His tunic was of black cloth, close-fitting to the form, and about his throat he wore a heavy golden torque inscribed with the ancient cognizance of his House.

"Sometimes, son," Hereward said gently, "there are other ways of fighting for a cause. It cannot always be the gleaming harness and the glory of battle."

Haco looked up and his eye quickened. "You mean the causeway?"

"Aye, for the project cumbered until autumn is a battle fought and won."

Haco considered this. "You may be right," he allowed. "Yet still, if I live I shall fight for the Wake. There is time, yet. He will fight on, however scanty his army, however many setbacks he encounters. He will never surrender. He will never kneel to the Bastard. And however things turn out in the end, whether for good or ill, victory or defeat, he will at least have stirred us from our lethargy and redeemed the honor of English manhood. His courage is our beacon. In him lies England's hope."

They ceased talking, for the sentry was approaching to stamp out their tiny campfire. Stoically, impersonally, he bent over, testing the chains that linked them ankle to ankle, and fettered them to the tree. Then he passed on.

Hereward lay back and pillowed his head upon the tree's gnarled and moss-grown roots. For a moment he thought back upon Haco's words, and sighed. "England's hope!" Such sentiments were unwelcome. They made a man feel grizzled and weighted with responsibility. And if he failed . . . ? He closed his eyes, finding comfort in the familiar forest noises, in the churring of the nightjar and the lilting, soaring wind song. Yet those, too, he would block out if he could, for they forged a chain of unwanted thought—the forest—the

Gronnaswald—a campfire—Althya. There were times when a man needed a fiery besom to sweep his mind clean of his thoughts; to sear it, to erase the picture of a girl sitting by a campfire, her face mud-spattered, clothes disheveled, hair in wild disarray—yet so inexpressibly dear to him withal.

It was strange, he reflected, the way certain moments that are past, return; flashing back unbidden upon the mirror of one's mind. So it was with that one hour in the Gronnaswald. Deliberately he shunned the memory of it, yet it was always there, hovering on the fringe of all conscious thought, waiting to harass him in an unguarded moment. He had loved her then, of course, but did not know it. And when Toustin died—— A curse upon Fate! If a man could but retrace his steps and undo one part of his actions, how changed would be the course of his life. It had grieved him near to madness to see her face so white and pinched—so hard. "And when I hear, Hereward Leofricsson, that you've been captured and strung to a tree as you deserve——"

He sat up abruptly. "Haco," he said, "have you a lass?"

"Aye."

"Tell me about her."

He expected the eager flow of words that such a question, especially among men cloistered at camp, generally called forth; a welcome torrent that would occupy his own thoughts to the exclusion of all else. But Haco lay still. Hereward waited, astonished, thinking perhaps he slept, so motionless was he. Then suddenly the youth turned his face. In the dusk his tawny eyes were yellow as a leopard's and he answered swift and direct, baring his heart with the tortured, surging passion of his race.

"I love her! She is a star, God's fairest creature. She will not wed me—penniless and dispossessed. She is Norman!"

Hereward said nothing, only lay back again and stared up at the boughs laced darkly against the blue night sky. To tell so much in so few words! The lad suffered. His love would fulfill his manhood and bring him to maturity, but little solace would he find now in the prospect. Little solace was there anywhere for the man who lay alone at night, haunted by a woman's face.

And the minutes passed until the silence between them was a chasm which neither wished to bridge, so alone was each in his love, so isolate, so lonely of heart.

And in a little while they slept.

A day or so later, the wood being cut and loaded on the wagons, they set out on the return trip to Belsar's Hill. The sun was hot, the sky a cloudless blue and the road north of Cambridge was thronged with knights and hired mercenaries on their way to join the Conqueror's army; with riders up from London bearing messages for the king, with baggage trains of armor, clothing, weapons and foodstuffs; oil from Spain, wine from Burgundy and cattle on the hoof from English grazing lands.

It was well past noon when they sighted the camp, which seemed to them to have grown appreciably during their few days' absence and surged, if possible, with more activity than before.

"Preparations for invasion seem to be progressing with alarming speed," said Haco, as they drew near. "Obviously the Bastard has in mind to catch this Wake fast and at all costs."

"Aye, for time is ever a conqueror's enemy—which William well knows."

"I wonder how fares the causeway? Its progress must make dreary watching for the men of Ely."

"There are stout hearts shut up within the isle, lad," Hereward replied. "And for men bent upon preserving the last fragments of their freedom there is always hope, even if they be armed only with their courage and a will to fight. 'Tis seldom that——"

He broke off. For standing there at the entrance, not three yards away from the wagons' route and directly facing it, was Guy de Lussac!

Hereward stared, and swore, and stared again. But there was no mistaking that silhouette; the stunted build, the narrow shoulders, the gigantic head. He was bowing with intended elegance to a girl on horseback who seemed just about to take her departure from the camp, for she was cloaked for travel and surrounded by a body of men-at-arms.

"What is it?" whispered Haco. "What is amiss?"

"Ahead there, at the entrance—that ghoul."

"With so many of them about, 'tis hard to know which ghoul you mean. Ah, yes, the manikin. But how can you know him? He is Norman."

"Suffice it that I do, lad, and he would give much to lay hands upon me."

"S'blood! What have you done?"

"S'blood!" echoed Hereward. " 'Tis now a question of what I am going to do if he sights me."

"In chains, my poor friend—what can you do?"

The wagon moved forward in line with the rest, nearer, nearer; horses clopping, wheels creaking, logs rumbling. Hereward tipped his pointed cap to one side, then bent over as though to relieve the weight of the chains at his ankles. From the corner of his eye he could follow everything that passed upon the road. De Lussac took the girl's hand and kissed it, apparently in farewell, then, as he stood addressing his final words to her, his attention strayed toward the wagons. Undoubtedly he enjoyed the sight of so many fettered English, for his eye reviewed each prisoner in turn, moving on dispassionately and with cold precision as the wagons passed before him, until finally Haco, sitting erect on his seat, came under his scrutiny. Hereward knew his turn was next. There was no preventing it. Yet at that moment, without knowing why, without conscious reason or motive, he raised his eyes to meet those of the girl.

And the girl was Althya.

Hereward could only stare. The sudden sight of her, and in so unexpected a place, overwhelmed him completely. For the second time in his varied career he found himself at a loss, and, as at York, she the cause. He heard her gasp of recognition, read the astonishment in her eyes and knew that the moment was come when he must pay wergild for the shedding of Toustin's blood. She had but to cry out—to speak his name—to warn de Lussac——

But Althya did none of these things. Instead, she turned hastily back to Sir Guy, and with an excited gesture of her arm, drew his attention from the wagons and directed it toward two marsh harriers engaged in a death struggle in the sky. She found much to exclaim about in the way the hawks jabbed and crossed each other, fought for height, trod the air, circled, climbed, and wheeled for the new attack. Her stream of chatter ran on, keeping de Lussac's interest fixed skywards until Hereward was safely past. A few moments later, when he glanced back over his shoulder, she was already speeding away from Belsar's Hill surrounded by her men-at-arms, whilst Sir Guy, all in happy ignorance of how great a prize had just slipped from his fingers, strutted back to camp and was soon lost among the tents.

For once Hereward made the journey through the Conqueror's camp oblivious to his surroundings, observing nothing that passed about him. His face wore a distant, preoccupied look. Even Haco's whispered congratulations went unheard as he reviewed the events of the last few moments. At first glance they seemed fantastic, devoid of all logic. Althya, for personal reasons, was his avowed enemy. She was Norman, and he here in the Norman camp working his own mischief. She had recognized him, there could be no doubt of that. Then why had she not denounced him? She had declared once that she would like to see him hang. Today her actions proved otherwise. The woman who wished a man dead did not deliberately save his life. But why had she done so? What had moved her to stand between himself and de Lussac's vengeance? What impulse had stirred her to behave in this strange, unaccountable manner?

Soon the wagon came to a halt down by the fen bank. Hereward climbed out and stood, still immersed in thought, while the guards dropped the fetters from his ankles, then he started to unload the tree trunks, hoisting them on his back and setting them down in neat, orderly rows by the stockpile. Such industry was suspect, and the guards watched him closely, but said nothing. When the wagon was empty he drove it off, unharnessed the horses and stabled them, then, because it was dusk and the other prisoners were filing into the stockade, he did likewise, accepting his bread and broth as he passed in, then sitting down upon the sward to eat it. In all this time not once was he fully aware of what he did. He worked automatically, with mechanical co-ordination of hands and feet, for his mind was totally absorbed with one simple, unbelievable, indisputable fact.

Althya loved him!

But the exuberant joy of his discovery was soon replaced by a black depression. "Penniless and dispossessed." Haco's words, but he must not forget them. At the moment, being wed to him would be like being wed to an outlaw, since that was what he surely was in the eyes of every Norman. Even if she had the courage to forsake her own people, what would be the consequences to her of marriage to him? What could he offer her? Indeed, upon the surface it would appear that, regardless of where her happiness lay, her security lay in marriage to de Lussac. But no, such a marriage was not to be thought of. She loved him! She must wed him—yet there was no denying that at present it would go hard on the woman who linked her life to his.

All night he wrestled with his problem, to which he still had found no solution when, at dawn the next morning, he went back to labor with the rest upon the causeway. The work, he instantly noted, had progressed too rapidly during his absence. He must find a way to set it back a pace. On the next moonless night, when he visited Swallow, he would come down here and do an hour's work, loosing a few piles to slip one section into the bog. That would suffice for the moment, for too much havoc would breed suspicion. "Penniless and dispossessed." Aye, and he must not forget it. He could wed Althya only when his work was done; only when he could reclaim that which was his; only when he could give her a roof and her children a heritage. Wed her now, he must not; for if someday he rode forth and failed to return, what would become of her, expatriated, outcast by her own people? He must beware lest, for the second time, he bring tragedy into her life. He must beware, too, lest he himself lose sight of these factors in the urgency of the moment.

But in the meantime what of de Lussac, to whom she was officially betrothed? He would not be put off indefinitely. The prospect of so lovely a bride would make him understandably impatient to have the nuptials performed. The wonder was that he had waited this long. Holy Mother of God! But had he? Perhaps they were already wed! Perhaps that was why she was here at camp—to visit him——

"You, there," bellowed the foreman. "Idle hands, eh? Basking in the sunshine—gazing off across the marsh. You scum! Villain! Pig's bladder! I could hang you for that. I could string you up by the thumbs and thrash every spark of life from your flea-bitten body!"

As he spoke his lash descended with savage fury, intended to cut Hereward across the eyes. But the Wake sprang back and the hide landed instead full upon his chest, its thin pliant tip twisting snake-like around one of the buttons on his tunic. With a jerk the foreman sought to release it, but it held tight, until, beneath the fury of his tugging, the ragged garment parted and its front came away with the whip. The foreman was overcome with malicious mirth at the sight of the Englishman's breastpiece dangling in the air like a trout from a line. Then his expression changed. For upon the bare chest now exposed to view he had caught sight of the scarlet imprint of a Saracen dart.

"Christ in heaven! What have we here?" he demanded in amazement. "A fighting man among our host of lowly laborers? The Conqueror mislikes spies in his camp. Who are you? Where did you come from? How did you get in?"

But the Englishman seemed confused by so many questions. He

was standing there rolling his head from side to side in a state of utter bewilderment.

"I do not conceive you, my noble lord," he answered. "I was examined for scars with the rest before being admitted to the camp. I am no fighting man. I came by my scar in the normal pursuit of my trade, for, my noble lord, I am a potter."

"O-là! So now it pleasures him to claim he is a potter." He advanced menacingly upon Hereward and stood before him, his eye level with that of the Englishman. "By Satan's hoof, you're something else besides. Roll up your sleeve, man. I'll soon tell if you have a profession other than that of potter."

Hereward glanced hastily about. There was no help for it, then. The foreman meant to have his way. They had only to see his arms, welted and ridged and scimitar-scarred, to suspect the truth. He raised his hands as though to comply with the other's orders, but instead his fist crashed full in the foreman's face, felling him with a mighty blow. The next minute the Wake was speeding down the causeway toward the shore.

By the time he reached the fen bank the foreman was back on his feet, shouting wildly to the guards to take the prisoner alive. Hereward started across the open ground near the stockade, but already a dozen Normans were converging upon him from that direction. He swung around. They were coming up on all sides. From over by the tents came the sounds of excited battle cries and the thudding of horses' hoofs. Again he changed his course and sped on, keeping to the open. But escape seemed hopeless. Even if he managed to elude the guards here, he could never cover that quarter mile between the camp and the outsentries before they were alerted. On horseback, perhaps—— Swallow! He had forgotten Swallow waiting in the willow coppice. Without even a backward glance he veered north and headed for the marsh.

The mare pricked up her ears when she heard his running footsteps. She pawed the grass and for the first time whinnied nervously.

"Come, girl," he urged, "you've got to show what you can do."

She seemed to understand. Quickly he slipped the rope and leaped upon her back, but by the time they quit the coppice the Normans were already there, blocking their path. With whoops and shouts they ran forward, reaching for the rope around Swallow's neck, but she reared and flung herself against them, sent them sprawling, and sped on.

Yet still the chase was all but lost, for the horns were sounding, alerting the outsentries. His only chance now was to head west along the open terrain of the fen bank, to try to get clear of them before they were mounted and waiting for him. But how to do it? How to withstand their deadly shafts? How to cover that desperate quarter mile?

He urged Swallow on, spurring her with his heel, and as he did so, the potter's admonition flashed across his mind. Again, with all his force, he set heels to her sides and this time she felt the drive. With a sudden lunge, she gathered speed, racing sure-footed over the rough ground, nose challenging the wind and nostrils flaring, galloping swift and free, stretching out her mighty forelegs till it seemed her belly must touch the ground. She was running now with a kind of savage rapture, like a thing possessed; like a giant, low-flighting bird, white above the green sward.

She passed the outsentries just as they mounted and they stopped to stare wide-eyed at the marvelous sight; a huge Englishman, tatters aflying, astride a huge mazy brute with flying feet. The mythical Sleipnir come down to earth, they swore, and when they heard no hoofbeats, they looked again, and indeed she moved so light and swift her hoofs scarce touched the ground at all. But in an instant they had sufficiently recovered from their astonishment to give chase, aiming their shafts at her as they rode. But there was no calculating her speed and her mazy running was more than the trained eye could cope with. As the distance widened between them, she remained unscathed by their arrow hail, though she left a wake of shafts stuck in the ground thick as quills in a hedgehog. She headed for a strip of woodland and vanished therein. Nor, though they pursued her for miles, did they succeed in setting eyes upon her again that day.

It was already sundown when Hereward came riding along the old Roman road leading north toward Bourne. His eyes were fixed searchingly upon the distance, and for once he gave no heed to the vast stretch of fenland through which the road passed. In the air above, the screaming of the wild fowl had ceased, for they had taken flight to their feeding grounds in the uplands. But their clangor was replaced by sweeter marsh music, for the wood doves cooed softly in the copses, abetting the night song of lark and warbler, and from the ronds came the silvery call notes of the bearded titmice, though they themselves kept shyly to the green twilight of the reed jungles. The meres lay calm, reflecting the last fading hues of the sunset sky, and, ignoring the hour, the herds of red cattle browsed knee-deep in sedge grass, solemnly exploring the fringes of the boggy lands.

Afar off, on the horizon, there came into view the great pile of Bourne Castle, looming dark and stern, and for an instant Hereward's gaze rested thoughtfully upon it. It was deserted now, haunted, so the Normans said, since those strange and unexplained happenings of the previous spring. But this, too, slipped from his ken and his eyes narrowed as suddenly, in the distance, he perceived what he was seeking. If Althya had been on her way home yesterday, this would be her route. The body of horsemen yonder were Norman men-at-arms, about the size, he judged, of her escort, and amongst them he glimpsed a tiny female form.

He leaned forward and whispered in Swallow's ear. "Come on, girl," he said.

The Normans turned angrily as the unsightly Englishman caught up with them. He appeared to be fleeing as from the Devil himself, for he clung to the rope about his nag's neck and kept turning his head to glance fearfully behind him. Rudely he brushed up against the men-at-arms in an effort to pass them by, even jostling the captain, who instantly grasped Mare Swallow by the rope and stopped her.

"Whither are you bound, rogue, in such a hurry?" he demanded.

"May it please your lordship," cried Hereward in tones of terror, "the countryside is alive with the king's men who search behind every shrub and hedge, behind each blade of grass——"

"Perchance it is you they seek, ruffian," snapped the captain suspiciously.

"Nay, gentle sir," replied Hereward, meekly dropping his eyes to where the captain's hand still held its grip on the mare's rope, "—for as you see, it is easy enough to lay hands upon me. What, indeed, could they want with an unhappy potter who had already been robbed of all his wares today—and his mare's saddle and bridle, too!"

The captain let go the rope, inspecting his hand with dainty distaste before whipping out a kerchief upon which to cleanse it.

"Then speak up, man," he said impatiently. "Whom do they seek?"

"May it please you, noble sir," replied Hereward, "they say on all sides 'tis the Wake they seek, that he is abroad today in these parts."

"The Wake!" exclaimed the captain with immediate interest. His eyes glistened. "And how would one know him?"

"Good sir," cried Hereward in astonishment, "you would know him anywhere, for his armor, they say, is so beset with jewels that he looks like a peacock in full plumage. And lucky indeed is he who makes the capture, for the price set upon the Wake's head has been raised by the king to thirty thousand gold marks by Tower weight."

The captain gasped, and likewise his men. Thirty thousand gold marks? The price of an earldom!

The captain wavered, but the men did not. As a body they wheeled about and sped back the way they had come. The captain's glance moved uncertainly from the lady in his charge to the receding backs of his men. Then his face paled. The long, sharp point of a knife thrust betwixt helmet and hauberk was pricking his throat and the hand that held it there was that of the potter.

"And now, sir," the potter was saying pleasantly, "you are my prisoner. Pray disarm and cast your weapons on the highway."

The captain, guessing the potter's identity, knew better than to argue.

"Thirty thousand gold marks!" he muttered as he divested himself of his arms. Then he added with a sneer, "You rate yourself high."

"Nay, man," laughed the Wake, "'tis the Bastard rates me high. And as for my capture, console yourself with the thought that it will better profit you to make it when the price is doubled."

By now the captain had dropped his arms upon the highway and sat sullenly awaiting further instructions.

"Come, come," said the Wake, "descend from your horse. The way back to Belsar's Hill is pleasanter afoot."

"But my lady——"

The Wake smiled. "It will be my pleasure, sir, to conduct her safely home."

Obediently the captain swung down from his mount, and as Hereward sent the animal racing off in a northerly direction, he, with a stiff little bow to Althya, turned sullenly south.

Hereward watched him until a safe distance lay between them, then he turned to Althya. She sat motionlessly upon her splendid Spanish horse, her long pelisse hanging in graceful folds about her. She eyed him steadily and disapprovingly as he descended from his mare and advanced toward her, frowning suddenly as she caught sight of the gaping hole in his tunic and the bare chest beneath with its dreadful scar.

But Hereward only laughed at her dismay.

"Forgive me, my lady," he said, "for appearing half clad before you, but the foreman at the camp purloined the rest of my tunic. Indeed, it gets so now that an Englishman thinks it folly to wear any tunic at all when he goes strolling, since he invariably loses half of it to some Norman on the way." Then suddenly he was serious. He took her hand and kissed it gently. "I owe you my thanks, Althya," he said, "for not exposing me at Belsar's Hill."

"You owe me nothing," she replied curtly, withdrawing her hand. "I do not forget that you incurred de Lussac's enmity on my account, or that you did me a similar service once."

He dropped his thumbs to his belt and stood regarding her, a little half-smile on his lips.

"Then it is indeed my good fortune," he said, "that you are so punctilious in the payment of your debts, else I would now be making food for the crows on the Bastard's gallows."

She shuddered. "Are you a madman," she burst out, "to take such risks? How dared you come to Belsar's Hill? How dared you take the chance of being recognized there? The camp is bristling with Normans who would give half their fortunes to lay hands upon you. De Lussac is not the only one who knows you by sight."

He listened patiently to her scolding, smiling still. "I regret," he said, "that my actions cause my lady such alarm."

"Do not delude yourself that I feel concern for your actions," she retorted, "—nor that I admire your bravery. You are merely a rash and headstrong man."

"Madam," he laughed, "if you Normans start to think of us now as men instead of cattle, then our lot has indeed improved." He swung himself on Swallow's back. "Come, I will take you home."

He led her off the old Roman road and across the fens by paths indiscernible save to the fenmen, his hand on her horse's bridle to keep him from straying off the path.

"Does your ladyship still reside at Orchard Isle?" he inquired presently.

"Why should I not?"

His reply was noncommittal. "I wondered," was all he said.

Yet still he knew well enough how to soothe her anger when he had a mind, talking to her in soft, melodic tones; telling her of the fens; of the fenmen's superstitions; of their quaint beliefs and fears and of the "fen steppers," whose giant forms, glimpsed through the writhing mists of eventide, vanished on sight. He told her of the rare white geese which were the fenman's wealth and pride; which he prudently lodged in his own house, or even his own bedchamber. By day, he said, they roamed the isles at will, looking from a distance like huge daisies in a meadow, save twice a year, when the fenman reaped his silver and the geese were raw with plucking.

"Is it true, as they say," she asked, "that you were born in yonder pile of stones?"

"Aye," he replied, "and a right ancient pile it is, too, built in the days before Christianity took its hold upon these parts. And because the quaking fen breeds fear in man, as well as love, a host of fearsome fenland gods were set to guard it, their likenesses being carved in stone above the windows. The dim shapes of these old-time gods still float in the background of every fenman's fancy. For when, at dusk, he barricades his windows and bars his doors against a benighted terror of the marsh he cannot name, his fears are in some way linked to the pitted, stone-faced deities who brood over the fens from the castle's ancient keep. Even the sudden spark of the will-o'-the-wisp as it hovers above the morass at night is shrouded in superstition, for if the unwary traveler seeking shelter for the night follows that tiny light, he never returns, and the fenman, hearing his agonized pleas for help echoing across the wastes, only crosses himself and draws his fur skins up above his head till the cries have ceased."

"And why do they hold the Gronnaswald in so much awe? Indeed, it affrights me now to recall that I have been there, with the fenmen themselves fearing to set foot therein."

Hereward laughed. "So you have informed yourself on these matters? Aye, the Gronnaswald. See how soft it lies now in the dusk, its foliage no longer green, but of a pearly blackness. Well, 'tis not the wolf and the boar or the other wild forest creatures the fenmen fear there."

"What is it, then?"

"A species of creature, not rightly man, perhaps, nor yet rightly animal, either. Wild-fowlers on the marsh have glimpsed them, peering out, half hidden by the foliage. But they are shy and gentle and vanish on sight. 'Tis thought they worship the moon, for on bright nights they are always by the fenside. And in the light breeze that stirs the slender reeds and rocks the stars embosomed on the meres, there linger still the inarticulate murmurings of these creatures who leave footprints on the marshy fringes of the forest."

She had been watching him closely as they rode, remarking his smallest gesture; the easy grace with which he sat the mare's bare back; the lean, muscular frame and vast breadth of shoulder; the reflective, searching eye; the hand that gripped her stallion's bridle and quieted the nervous beast with its touch.

"Hereward," she asked slowly, "are you still as determined upon this course as you were a year ago?"

His face grew suddenly stern, the jaw set in a way she remembered all too well.

"Hearing of William's ravages in the north does not incline me in his favor," he replied.

"With you he is prepared to be generous. At Belsar's Hill I heard him say you were a good enemy, but would make a better friend."

Hereward frowned. "I am certain of only one thing at this moment," he replied, "that William will never count me among his friends."

"He also said," she persisted, "that if you could be captured alive it might not be too difficult to persuade you to exchange your outlaw's life for an earldom."

"So?"

"That if ever you placed your hands between his own and swore to be his liegeman, then would he truly be England's king, for with your sanction the crown would fit more snugly on his brow."

"He must be given to making pretty speeches."

"William does not express such sentiments lightly," Althya replied. "It seems he admires you greatly."

"And I," quoth the Wake, "set more store by the admiration of my mare, Swallow."

"Yes," sighed Althya, "I believe you do. Yet William is a great man, and a great king."

"Great men do not wantonly murder and maim."

"Northumberland was his tragic mistake."

"And great kings do not wantonly tamper with the private lives of their subjects."

There was a moment of silence.

"You are referring, of course, to my betrothal to Guy de Lussac."

"Am I not right, then, in supposing it is the Bastard's doing?"

"Yes, it is his doing."

"And was it not in that connection that you went to Belsar's Hill?"

"Yes, he summoned me there at Guy's request. He commanded me to put an end to my shilly-shallying and set a date for the wedding."

"And has it been set?"

"Yes—for September."

"Do you want it so?"

"No."

Hereward made no comment. When he was not occupied with the treacherous pathway he sat gazing straight ahead into the gathering dusk. And when the moon arose, shedding its light upon the meres so that they lay like silver shields on the dusky wastes, when night brought a sudden hush so that the brittle reeds stood silent in the windless air, the rhythmic clip-clop of their horses' hoofs sounded strangely lost in the immense silence that surrounded them.

They reached Orchard Isle at last and Hereward leaped down from Mare Swallow and lifted Althya from her horse. As he did so her hood fell back and in the moonlight he could see that her cheeks were wet.

"Why are you crying, Althya?"

She did not answer, and he took her face between his two big brown hands and raised it.

"Is it because you love me?"

"Yes."

"Is that why you want me to submit to William?"

"Yes, for if you do not, it is hard to see how this thing will end. William will always fear for his crown while you are free. He will be driven to relentless efforts to take you. I am afraid. I could not bear it if you were caught."

"Would you wed me now, Althya, if I could ask you to?"

"Yes."

He sighed and drew her close to him.

"You know why I can't."

"I know why you think you can't."

"And am I wrong?"

"You are proud and stubborn."

His lips brushed her cheek. "Nay, my love, I am thinking of you. Have you ever considered what it would mean, being wed to me now? Have you ever thought how it would be, following me from place to place, hunted as I am hunted, having no home, sometimes no food, no clothes, no roof? Can you think of that, Althya, and say that any man is worth it?"

And she laid her cheek against his bare breast and kissed it and left a few tears thereon. "You are, my Hereward," she said.

At that he was silent and she thought she had won her point. Then slowly he shook his head.

"No," he said, "you might come to hate me in the end."

And he stooped and kissed her long, reluctant to go. Then, without a backward glance, he leaped upon his mare and took his way back in the direction of Ely.

But as he rode, haunted by the memory of her face in the moonlight and the tears on her cheeks, he was shocked to find himself exploring the possibilities of William's bribes and inducements, providing that she, too, were included in the bargain. Althya and his own fenland estates! A string of curses put an end to such wayward thoughts. He dug his heels into the mare's steaming flanks and sped like a fiend across the wastes.

Chapter Fourteen

FALL OF THE ISLE

JULY passed and August came and still the causeway was nowhere near completion. The Conqueror began to visit his project
daily and his dark countenance grew darker with every visit, for at
last he had begun to suspect the truth. The English were deliberately
obstructing the progress of the work. As his last doubts were swept
away a violent wrath possessed him. He gave orders to have the
laborers taken out and hanged, every one, then his deputies rode
down into the southern shires of Kent, Sussex and Surrey, where the
English were for the moment more thoroughly cowed and submis-
sive. They hunted down every man capable of construction work
and shipped them back to Belsar's Hill with promises of amnesty,
mayhap even wealth, if they would renounce their racial ties and
serve the Norman. For time was short, and the Conqueror was determined at all costs to complete the causeway and exterminate the
outlaws before the coming of winter.

The new laborers worked well and conscientiously—their wives
and children having been left at home under the surveillance of Normans specially appointed to the task. Beneath the summer sun, therefore, the work went forward, overcoming one by one the hazards
that confronted them till two miles of mud slimed by bitter salt
springs were spanned at last and meres were bridged that had once
lain concealed by flags and rushes.

By the end of August, when the reeds were dry and yellowing
in the sun, the Conqueror began to spend his days pacing up and
down the narrow way. Sometimes he would pause and stand gazing
out across the marsh to where the English were also at work upon
the opposite shore, strengthening their defenses, throwing up earth
rampires, and erecting timber and hide sows from behind which
they harassed the Conqueror's laborers with shafts and bolts. Wil-

liam had foreseen that it would be all but impossible to complete those last few yards of causeway, for the closer they drew to their objective, the thicker grew the arrow hail. But he had ordered the construction of a long portable bridge which could be thrust across that treacherous gap and over which his troops would stream in countless numbers to the other side.

When it wanted but a few more days to the completion of the work the Conqueror's impatience knew no bounds. His eyes began to shine once again with the hard, triumphant glitter that had lit them at Hastings and his soul lifted with the exaltation that only victory brought. His captains, FitzOsbern, Montgomery, Giffard and de Lussac, were carefully drilling their troops and there was about the camp an air of silent, eager tension. Not one man but lusted for battle now the hour drew nigh. Not one but knew his appointed task. Not one but already counted as his own the promised recompense of service to the Conqueror; a bag of gold, a strip of English land, a knighthood—for a few, an earldom.

Then one morning the sky was blackened by a vast flock of birds sweeping inland from the sea. They paused above the causeway and hovered in the air uttering harsh, wailing cries, then swooped down savagely upon the laborers, beating them with their wings, pecking them so viciously that some fell from the causeway and perished in the mud, while the rest threw down their tools and fled. The next day the birds returned, and every day thereafter, until at last the workmen, imbued with the superstitions of the age and fearful of the outlaws' wondrous magic, fell sick in a body and all the Conqueror's threats and all the foreman's lashings could not induce them to return to work.

And the causeway had wanted but fifty yards to its completion! Fifty yards was all it lacked!

One late afternoon Sir Guy de Lussac, having set out in search of the king, found him standing by the fenside, alone, gazing out moodily to where the isle slumbered beneath a somnolent sun. For a moment de Lussac remained respectfully in the background as though waiting for the king to acknowledge his presence, yet all the while slyly watching William's angry countenance from beneath lowered lids; observing with malicious precision how inexorably the span of years were leaving their traces on the ruddy head, dappling it with gray; how the broad and stately brow was higher than of yore, so high already as to give an aura of diabolic dreadful-

ness to the once lofty countenance; how the noble symmetry of form
was lost beneath increasing corpulence. When at length the Conqueror, sensing the other's scrutiny, turned in his direction, Guy
advanced and stood solicitously by his side in an attitude of meditation.

"Sire," he began with his usual obsequiousness, "a punier man than
you would never have attempted this gigantic task."

William made no reply. Whatever Guy had come to say would
not remain unsaid.

"My lord king and duke," continued the wily Guy, "there is far
less magic in these birds than our untutored laborers suppose—
merely a species of lapwing native to the fens. The need, then, is
not to waste good time denying the existence of such magic as
lends color to the laborers' dull lives, but in their eyes to counteract it by an even greater magic."

"I set no store by magic," retorted the Catholic William.

"Sire, it is not your sweat that builds the causeway."

The king turned slowly toward Guy, searching his face in an
effort to unveil the contrivings of his dark, sadistic brain.

"Come, de Lussac," he said at length, "state your meaning with
more precision."

Guy's mouth twisted into a confident smile. "There dwells not
far away a pythoness, sire, a sorceress—a witch, who sways simple
men such as these with her charms and spells. It is claimed that by
her incantations she can drive out the most obstinate devils. Her
presence alone would do much to embolden the quaking hearts of
our laborers, and a few of her tricks might well induce them to
recover their good health and return to work."

Guy had been watching the king's face closely to ascertain the
effect of his suggestion. It was instantly apparent to him that the
king was out of sympathy with it. He leaned, therefore, closer to
William and spoke in a low, conspiratorial voice.

"It will not be necessary for Your Grace to countenance this ex-
periment," he said, "—merely to refrain from forbidding it."

The king returned his reflective gaze to the horizon. The outlaws'
isle lay like a green oasis in a desert, and the silver spire of St.
Aethelthryth's minster gleamed against the azure sky as temptingly
as a fountain of limpid water to a parched traveler.

"I do not forbid it," he said shortly.

And Guy turned and left him.

Returning to his pavilion, de Lussac called for his horse, then, attired for travel, he rode forth alone from the camp. None guessed whither he was bound, and being as he was a man of secretive nature, he himself volunteered no hint as to his purposed destination. He set off toward Cambridge, turning east at the village, and after riding for three or four hours came, by the light of the rising moon, to a heath across which he slowly started to make his way.

As he rode his eyes carefully scanned the horizon. He had learned that the pythoness was always to be found hereabouts, yet nowhere was there any sign of a human habitation. Before him, clear to the sky, the heath lay smooth and pasturelike in the moonlight, without even a tree or shrub to disturb the bleak monotony. When in a little while he discerned a gentle rise against the flat horizon, he hastened toward it, but found it to be nothing more than an ancient earth mound girdled about by low, obelisk-shaped stones. In the center of the mound lay another stone, flat and altarlike. Upon it, something stirred.

De Lussac dismounted, and stepping over the stones, started toward the center of the mound. He moved swiftly, his feet swishing through the heather, his eyes fixed upon the central stone. As he drew near he saw, in the brilliant light that flooded it, that upon the slab lay a snow-white rooster. It was dead, yet it showed no signs of violence and its unstained feathers ruffled mournfully in the night wind. He laid a hand upon it. It was still warm. He glanced about for any sign of the pythoness, calling her by name. There was no reply. He stood awhile, oppressed by the silence and solitariness of the spot, made ill at ease by this relic of paganism on the wild, bare heath; then, suddenly eager to be quit of it, he regained his horse and rode slowly on.

He had not gone far when, from right beneath his horse's hoofs, a frightened hare leaped up. With a sharp cry it scampered away, the creature and its shadow forming a dark, elliptical, fleeting shape as it ran. The horse shied, and stumbled, coming down heavily on both knees. When at last he succeeded in struggling to his feet he limped painfully in one foreleg. De Lussac cursed. He had no wish to spend the rest of the night on this lonely heath, yet still he had proceeded too far to consider returning to Belsar's Hill now, without completing his self-assigned mission. He dismounted, therefore, and taking his horse by the bridle, plodded on afoot.

He noticed for the first time how cold it had turned. The wind sweeping the heather seemed to carry with it the sharp chill of autumn. De Lussac drew his cloak about him and began to wish that he had not been so impatient to set out upon this journey. He should have held his eagerness in check until the morrow. Yet the thought of the rooster returned to comfort him, for since the bird was still warm, it followed that the pythoness must be somewhere near at hand. Once again he turned and searched the flat horizon for any sign of a cabin or another living thing, but, save that now the earth mound lay far to the west of him, the vista remained the same; empty, desolate, deserted.

As he started to move forward once more a cloud crossed the face of the moon and the heath was for an instant plunged in darkness. When it passed and the light shone forth again Sir Guy was astonished to find a hooded female form walking along beside him. So startled was he by her sudden appearance that he could find no words with which to address her, so they walked on, side by side, in silence.

It was the woman who spoke first.

"Wherefore are you seeking old Jennet?" she inquired presently.

De Lussac halted. Instinctively his hand flew to his dagger's hilt. "How do you come by your knowledge?" he demanded.

She, too, halted and turned and faced him and he could see now that she was vastly aged and wizened, with grayish wisps of hair about her brow and sparse white hairs sprouting from her chin. When she spoke her voice broke and trembled with age, yet still her eyes had the power to hold him, being black and glittering and fixed upon his face with an intensity that seemed to penetrate his forehead and lay bare his thoughts.

"I have read your coming in bird song and eagle flight," she replied. "I have been expecting you. I am Jennet."

De Lussac glanced hastily about as though seeking a chasm in the ground out of which she might have sprung. Discovering none, he scowled, not so much at his own mystification as at the knowledge that she had succeeded in hoodwinking him. True, he had heard much of old Jennet's arcane powers, but he did not for a moment believe her sudden and inexplicable appearance to be the result of magic; nor did he believe she had, as she claimed, any foreknowledge of his coming, or that their meeting here was anything but accidental. For de Lussac, like the Conqueror, had little faith in witchcraft.

"Old woman," he said, "when a man's business brings him to this tenantless heath, 'tis not hard for you to guess whyfor he comes. That is not divination, 'tis cold logic."

She was in no way abashed by his scorn. Indeed, not only was her manner totally devoid of the deference the Normans had come to expect of the conquered people, but her black gaze was tinged with a vaguely hostile insolence.

"Norman," she replied, "I care nothing for your credence or your skepticism. You have come a long way this night to buy my services, and that not without some expectation of receiving value for your gold. What is it you want of me? To learn how I raise a tempest on a summer's eve? To see me make snow to fall from a blue sky, or, by the power of illusion, show you an army bivouacked on this empty heath?"

De Lussac sneered. "Rest easy, crafty one," he retorted. "I shall not tax your powers by demanding wonders quite beyond your ability to perform. 'Tis much less a thing I want of you—merely your presence at Belsar's Hill, a few of your noisiest incantations, and a well-practiced trick or two to embolden a gang of cowardly laborers and induce them to return to work."

She stood silent a moment, apparently turning the matter over in her mind.

"It will cost you sixty gold pieces to have me work for the Bastard against my own countrymen," she said at last.

"Sixty gold pieces!" De Lussac was staggered. "Pardi! How precious a thing is patriotism when it is up for sale!"

She smiled, and beyond her smile lay something malign and subtly triumphant. She stepped back a pace, as though in dismissal of him. "You can ride on now, Norman," she said. "Your horse is healed."

To his chagrin and bewilderment de Lussac found himself remounting at her bidding, and when he had done so, was astonished to find that his horse was in truth healed. He sat a moment gazing darkly down at her, frowning, struggling against his own nameless misgivings. He knew intuitively at that moment that he was embarked upon a perilous course, that it was a mistake to have any dealings with this woman, yet his colossal vanity forbade any retraction now.

"Be at Belsar's Hill by noon tomorrow," he ordered in a voice so loud it echoed across the silences.

"Aye," she said. "I will be there."

She was smiling still. De Lussac's wrath surged. Had she, then, perceived his indecision? Did she think him in awe of her? Well, she would find that Guy de Lussac was scarcely the man to be taken in by an old woman's crafty tricks. Swiftly he turned his horse's head toward Cambridge and rode away, but when a moment later he glanced back across the heath, the old woman was nowhere in sight, and all he could see was a black briar scrub standing where none had stood before.

De Lussac's defenses crumbled. He crossed himself and muttered a hasty Ave. Then, setting spurs to his horse, he took himself off with all possible speed.

The next day at noon the pythoness arrived at Belsar's Hill to find de Lussac awaiting her at the camp's entrance. He lost no time in apprising her of how matters stood with them, first leading her down to the marsh where, above the causeway, the birds still wheeled and cried; then pointing out the laborers, cowering and idle behind their stockade.

"Yonder men," he explained, "are persuaded that strong magic is being exercised against them by the outlaws. It will be your work to make a demonstration of countermagic spectacular enough to overcome their fears and convince them that your presence alone is sufficient to counteract any further magic that might be directed against them from the isle."

He paused, detecting in her eye a gleam of furtive, malicious humor.

"Norman," she said, "why would you have me beat about the bush, or essay to prove that black is white? Why do I not simply dispel the birds?"

De Lussac leaped. "Christi!" he exclaimed. "Could it be done?"

Seeing him so eager, she craftily demurred, seemingly balancing the chances of success against those of failure.

"Perhaps I could achieve it," she conceded at last, "but it would be immensely difficult—and exhausting."

"A curse upon your soul!" cried de Lussac. "What is it you want now? More money? You have yet to earn your first sixty pieces!"

"What is gold, Norman—when weighed against your liege's favor?"

De Lussac sucked in his lip. The old hag was shrewd. Indeed, what matter the cost, just so the birds were dispelled. He could recoup his losses later. How much it would benefit him in the king's eyes to bring about the completion of the causeway! And how materially it would profit him to be responsible for the consequent taking of the isle!

"I am agreed," he snapped. "Fulfill your boast, and I will triple your fee."

Thereupon he led her to a wooden tower that he had had constructed for her and she climbed the steps to the platform and straightway began her ritual, intoning her spells in a rasping, fanatical voice. The unearthly hubbub immediately attracted the attention of the entire camp, so that knights issued from their pavilions and the lesser soldiery from their tents, and all congregated upon the fen bank where they stood, hands on hips, watching the pythoness' performance in silent awe. Before long it began to be apparent to all that the birds were behaving strangely, and when, whether driven off by the din or by the power of her spells, they did indeed wheel about and vanish out over the sea, the witch was acclaimed by all and credited with unsurpassing magic.

Even de Lussac's former misgivings were rapidly waning and he so far forgot the habits of a lifetime as to voluntarily, and with good grace, hand over the promised fee. He further persuaded her, for a like sum, to remain at hand during the forthcoming invasion and use her magic to help the Normans overcome the stubborn resistance of the English.

Under such favorable conditions it was little wonder that the work progressed steadily, with the laborers working behind shields to protect them from the shafts and bolts of the English on the opposite shore, and old Jennet in her tower above them, chanting her incantations, loudly summoning the spirits of the air and earth and underworld to assist her in her task. Within the brief space of a few days the Conqueror saw his causeway brought to completion. His army could now walk dry-shod to the isle, saving only for the narrow, muddy gap to be spanned at the last moment by his portable bridge.

The following dawn found the Normans massed upon the fen bank for the attack, with the knights not a little mortified at having to leave their steeds behind them and, contrary to the most sacred custom of Norman knighthood, walk into battle on their own two feet. Nevertheless, such were the king's stern orders and in this his wisdom was grudgingly acknowledged, for no destrier could be trusted under fire on that narrow way. By only the splendor of his mail and his accouterments, therefore, did the knight now differ from the lowly footman as the martial host stood in the dawning light listening to the Conqueror's final words.

"Dispel all thoughts," cried William, "that this will be an easy contest, for it is well known that the English fight for something dearer to them than their lives—they fight for England. Let your strokes be heavy and your onslaught fearless; steel your hearts to show no mercy, smiting down the fleeing coward no less than the hero who stands to fight; stay neither to take spoil nor captives, saving only the Wake whom you will recognize by his stalwart build and the yellow locks streaming from his helm. And know that for you there can be no flight, for this route is too narrow to permit of two directions, and leads therefore only to the isle. But the sinewed arms that vanquished the mighty Harold shall not tremble now before a band of half-armed, homeless rebels; and when the battle is won let each man come before me and claim his guerdon, and he shall have it promptly and forthwith."

At this both knights and men cheered lustily, for the latter part of his speech was well to their liking, and long ere the cheers had died away a knight was seen to detach himself from the ranks and Sir Guy de Lussac approached the Conqueror and dropped on one knee before him.

"A boon, Your King's Grace," he pleaded. "If I have served you well, then to me the honor of leading the attack against the isle and of thus being the first to set foot thereon."

The Conqueror hesitated. The skeptical de Lussac was fast becoming gullible as a child where his witch was concerned, and now had even gone so far as to have her tower set upon wheels so that he could take her with him into battle.

"Sir Guy," he said, "you are growing overconfident in the powers of your baldame. And how will Mother Church regard our lapse of faith in the Almighty, that at dawn Mass we beseech Him for victory, then employ a witch to insure it?"

"Sire," replied the crafty Guy, lowering his voice, "let us but take the isle and capture the Wake. Time enough then to discuss amends to Mother Church. Time enough then to burn the witch to the glory of God and the redemption of our souls."

And the Conqueror, all disapproving, nodded nevertheless, for

whether by the agency of God or of the devil, the isle must fall to
him that day.

"Let be, then," he said. "The honor of leading the ranks is yours,
since you have surely earned it."

Thereupon the Conqueror wound his horn and the Norman host
sprang into action, with de Lussac leading the advance and march-
ing rapidly off down the causeway. Beside him rode the witch, her
tower propelled by a score of willing hands; behind him, an endless
column of men already sweating beneath the excessive weight of
their armor, but cheerful and supremely confident in old Jennet's
ability to protect them from all harm. In the silent air the muffled
tramp of their feet swelled until it resounded across the marsh like
the rolling of countless drums, until the entire length of causeway
was jammed with troops, those in the foreranks carrying the portable
bridge, those behind treading hard upon their comrades' heels, pressing eagerly on, shouting, yelling, chanting loud the Song of Rou, and,
for sheer joy, rattling their naked blades in the air as their hearts
thrilled to the prospect of blood and battle. Above it all rose the
crazy, barbaric singsong of old Jennet's incantations, and she shook
her fist at the isle, and cursed the English, and dared them to defy
her.

The Conqueror, coming up at some short distance behind, was
struck by the ominous quiet of the opposite shore. Here was no
resemblance to the Wake's surprise strategy at York, for everywhere the English were visible in hundreds, mail-clad, and taking
sport in leisurely picking off the close-packed Normans with shafts
from their longbows. But they seemed, somehow, to be waiting;
deporting themselves more like an audience assembled for a grand
spectacle than like men preparing to wage a desperate fight. William's uncanny danger sense made him check his stride and frown
apprehensively.

"Splendeur Dex!" he muttered to a young knight by his side.
"What is it now? Something is amiss. Hasten forward to de Lussac.
Bid him mark well the lack of preparedness for battle. Bid him
beware lest this is some new stratagem of the Wake!"

The foremost ranks were pressing closer now. Beneath a hail of
arrows the bridge was thrust across the muddy gap and made firm.
De Lussac, his face alight with exaltation, turned impatiently at the
arrival of the king's messenger and scarce gave ear at all to his
words. When he finally gleaned something of their import, he

laughed, and with a jerk of the head indicated the witch in her tower, to whose unintelligible gibberish he apparently attributed any apathy on the part of the English. An instant later, loud-breathing, chiding the sluggards, applauding the brave, he had whirled about and was gone.

"On, men," he roared. "On, for Normandy! Across to the isle! Ha! Rou!"

So saying, and flourishing his sword, he bounded forward—the first upon the bridge. A hundred arrows pockmarked his shield, a dozen rocks clattered at his feet, his chausses were suddenly red with blood which coursed down his legs and filled his shoes, but he felt no hurt. "A Lussac! A Lussac!" he cried jubilantly.

Then he froze.

Upon the shore, directly before him, stood the Wake, whirling about his head a firebrand which he cast with careful aim into the reeds that flanked the Norman end of the bridge. A column of smoke, and the whole reed bed burst into flame, igniting the bridge and enveloping it in dark billows of smoke. De Lussac fell back, and turned, but already the flames were snaking rapidly through the reeds that fringed the causeway, belching up into fiery pillars which turned the narrow thoroughfare into a furnace; setting the tips of the wooden piles ablaze, licking the legs of the cowering men, igniting their garments and filling the air with the smell of singed hair and the sickening odor of burning flesh. De Lussac stood rigid, his eyes filling with horror; recalling—too late—something of the Conqueror's warning.

Yet still, long years of battle training came to his aid and desperately he strove to save his troops.

"Turn about, men," he thundered. "Pass the word! Retreat in good order!"

But his voice was quite drowned out by the frenzied shrieking of the witch and there was no way to halt the men. Already they had swung around in panic and were stampeding back the way they had come, shoving and jostling, hewing down those who stood in their path, trampling the fallen underfoot, hurling friends and brothers from the causeway into the oozing fen where each man fought to gain solid footing for himself on the sinking bodies of his comrades.

All reason had suddenly deserted the Conqueror's disciplined troops. In the space of a few minutes they had turned into a horde of screaming, cursing, fear-crazed madmen fighting savagely for their own skins; battling each other for a place upon the causeway; heedless of the hail of blows from behind; heedless of the English shafts winging blindly through the smoke; heedless even of garments aflame beneath their armor until, overcome at last, they fell, their charred bodies enshrouded in red-hot ring mail. When the tower blazed up and capsized into the fen the witch crawled out over the burning beams, shrieking pitifully for help. But de Lussac paused only long enough to curse the old hag for a she-devil before plunging, clawing and snarling like the rest, into the struggling mass that was fighting its way back to the mainland.

And back on the fen bank the Conqueror stood, with smothered rage and gloomy eye, watching the destruction of his army. Between billows of smoke he caught sight of the plunging multitude on the causeway; of the thousands wallowing in the slime below where their last struggles were being mercifully speeded by the weight of their armor. He watched the survivors stagger back, sobbing, babbling; some rolling in agony upon the sward in a vain effort to cool their burns; others stumbling on, dazed and wide-eyed, to wander aimlessly through the camp streets. He watched the brave FitzOsbern stagger beneath the weight of a bleeding youth and the aging Giffard weeping with chagrin, his white hair and eyebrows singed to a stubble. He saw de Lussac, by some miracle still alive, come reeling up the fen bank toward him; then Montgomery, his helmet gone, his chausses burned away, his face a scarlet mask of scorched flesh.

And to the proud Conqueror the sight of his routed army was too galling to be long endured. With raging heart he turned and strode away and hid his anguish from the world in the dark solitude of his own pavilion.

A few days later, when the dying had died and the living were on the mend, the Conqueror summoned his captains to council.

"My lords," he began, "we have suffered much in an effort to take the isle and have sacrificed many men; nor shall their lives have been spent in vain. For the moment the English will likely feel safe from further attack. After so disastrous a rout they will expect us to fall back—to lick our wounds a while. Need I say, my lords, that nothing could be further from my intent."

He paused expectantly, but no cheers greeted his speech. Indeed, it was evident that his captains had not yet recovered from their despond and were in a mood to mislike any plan he might put forth.

"One thing is clear," he resumed, "that until a new year brings forth new reeds, the Wake can set no new fire to impede our passage. Our way, then, lies open to the isle. Two days is all we can afford for preparation. On the third day from now we will attack."

"But, sire," said FitzOsbern in dismay, "our forces are disorganized and vastly shrunk in numbers. They are unarmed and more—unnerved. It will take weeks to refit and rally them."

"FitzOsbern," replied the Conqueror, "however depleted our armaments may be, they still outmatch the enemy by a hundred to the man. The English cannot stand against such disparity of numbers. And have you forgot, old soldier that you are, that to rally warriors one needs only sound the battle horn?"

"The battle horn, sire, is of slight avail against broken mail and shattered weapons."

"Then, my lord, for what each man lacks in arms, let him equate in valor!"

FitzOsbern sank slowly to his seat and the Conqueror's dark, calculating gaze passed quickly over the upraised faces of the rest.

"If we pause now," he continued softly, "and take our ease at camp for a week or a month, what of the English meanwhile? What will they be doing? Will they sit and wait for us to repair each tiny rent in our armor and polish it till our own happy reflections smile back at us? Nay, indeed! Even now they may be fleeing their stronghold, and if that be so, now is the time to press hard upon their heels. Now is the time to wherret them like blood-dogs!"

"Well and truly," cried de Lussac, springing to his feet, "but what if such is not the case? What if some new trap awaits us on the other side?"

"Then to you, my lord of Lussac," replied the Conqueror soothingly, "and in view of such unexampled services as you have rendered me of late, I grant permission to remain behind with the wounded and the maimed."

There was a light ripple of laughter at this, for it was known that de Lussac could ill endure even the most covert reference to his witch. Now he flushed and glared about him, but ere he could form a reply the curtain of the pavilion was raised and the captain of the king's bodyguard entered. Behind him, between two guards, unarmed, calm and smiling, stood Earl Waltheof Siwardsson.

The laughter died abruptly as the knights turned, breathless and hushed, to stare at the Englishman. Only the Conqueror showed no surprise. Without demur or hesitation, he motioned the guards to release their prisoner and withdraw.

"Waltheof Siwardsson," he said in his laborious English, "your visit falls opportunely, for, as you see, we are in council. Whatever you have come to say can be said before those present."

Waltheof took his time to straighten his attire as, unhurriedly, his glance passed over the startled faces of the Norman knights, noting the muscles tensed to spring and the speed with which each hand flew to its dagger hilt. Then, smiling still, he passed slowly among them and advanced toward the king.

"If, as I think," he said, "this is some new attack upon the isle you are plotting, then desist. The eagle has flown the eyrie."

"So? Whither has he flown?"

"To a stronghold whose approaches might well defy even the ingenuity of the Conqueror," Waltheof replied, "—to the forest of the Gronnaswald."

"And is it to apprise me of this that you peril your safety and enter my camp?"

Slowly Waltheof shook his head so that his radiant locks sparkled like hoarfrost in the taper light.

"Nay, Sir Conqueror," he replied. "The prodigal returns. I am come freely and alone to submit to you. I am come to make my peace with you and take you for my king."

There was a smothered gasp of astonishment at these words and the knights glanced quickly at the Conqueror. But if the submission of so consequential a foe had brought to the king's proud soul any rush of gratification or triumph, it was in no way reflected upon his inscrutable countenance.

"Then you are welcome back among us, Waltheof Siwardsson," he said with grave and formal courtesy. "Indeed, much did we mourn your absence from the court. Much did we grieve you after your hasty departure from the Tower."

"A departure I have oft regretted, sire."

"Regrets can happily be banished, my lord earl, once the action which caused them has been amended."

So saying, the Conqueror extended his two hands, palms cupped together, toward the Englishman, but for yet another moment the latter chose not to perceive them.

"One thing more," he was saying carelessly, "I have a few young sons, both legitimate and natural, scattered here and there—one of whom even fights with the Wake. I wish to be assured of eventual amnesty for all of them as they fall to you."

"You have my word upon it," said William.

Thereupon Earl Waltheof Siwardsson dropped to his knees, and placing his sword hand in token of submission between those of the Conqueror, he swore allegiance to him and became his man.

But that evening as King William supped in state, with Earl Waltheof in the seat of honor at his right and FitzOsbern, Earl of Hereford, on his left, the latter leaned over and whispered in the king's ear.

"Sire," he said, "the Siwardsson's submission is indeed a happy augury. Mayhap now, seeing in what high honor the Conqueror can hold a gallant foe, the Wake will see the wisdom of his countryman's action and emulate it."

The Conqueror turned his keen gaze upon the English earl who sat absorbed in the rare wines and culinary masterpieces which comprised the royal supper. A year of hardship had lost him nothing of his strangely compelling aspect and had gained him wide fame for the feats of strength and daring which already were being recorded in song by the wandering gleemen. In glorious and extravagant terms they sang of him; a worthy descendant of the Fairy Bear; a true son of the gallant Siward; a warrior gifted with incomparable courage and a fearlessness that knew no bounds. The Conqueror frowned. True, all of it, and yet—and yet——

He turned back to FitzOsbern. "Treat him well," he said, "but trust him not."

FitzOsbern stared. "You think, sire, he comes to spy?"

"Nay, he has not the spirit."

"Then what?"

"Bien-aimé," replied the Conqueror, "the valiant do not abandon their just cause. Rather do they die for it. This Waltheof is mutable as the wind and blows in as many directions. He has remained feal neither to himself nor to his own country. How long, think you, he will remain feal to me?"

And FitzOsbern, seeing how disdainfully the proud lips curled, knew that by submission Waltheof Siwardsson had not earned for himself the Conqueror's love, but rather the full measure of the Conqueror's scorn.

Chapter Fifteen

THE OUTLAWS' CAVE

THE evening sunlight fell aslant the trees, tinging the faded turf of the forest floor with arabesques of delicate gold. Above, the interlacing boughs of the giant oaks formed spacious scarlet canopies, beneath which their mighty trunks stood like purple columns in the hazy shadow. Here and there a tiny pool of rain water lay black against the turf's dull green, whilst upon the quiet air fell the muted vespers of a wood dove that had not yet marked the near approach of dusk.

Sir Herlwin FitzHugh stood motionless upon the bank of the brook where he had paused to drink, his reverie undisturbed by the endless glinting of the water, by the threatened frost upon the night wind or the autumn smell of rotting, rain-soaked leaves. At his feet, cupped in a small clayey hollow, lay a single spoor. It pointed toward the brook, indicating that his quarry had leaped across the water, though there was no evidence of it having reached the other side. Sir Herlwin knew it would be useless to search the surrounding area. The creature would have vanished as completely as if it had never been here, save for the single imprint left behind. Inexplicable though it seemed, that was the unvarying routine.

From the first there had been so little to go upon. Ofttimes, while hunting on the fringes of the forest to the southeast of Lincoln, of whose castle he now was governor, he had glimpsed through the thick foliage a curious animal, swift as lightning, shy as a deer. For some reason this creature seemed drawn to the fringes of the forest where it would linger, peering out curiously upon the world, though itself never more than half seen in the crepuscular gloom. It would turn and flee upon sight, vanishing without a trace, though its plaintive sighs, borne back upon the wind, were almost human. Almost human, too, was its spoor, about the size of a child's foot and similar

in shape, save that the toes were longer and seemed almost as pre-
hensile as the fingers of a human hand. Herlwin had found the first
one only after weeks of searching. Since then there had been others,
but these he had invariably found many miles apart, and always
singly.

The townspeople of Lincoln were shocked when the governor
evinced curiosity concerning the great forest which they, by tradition and custom, shunned. It was known, they said, to be inhabited,
but no man in his wits would seek to learn by what, or by whom.
Certainly no Lincolnshireman would guide him, for no Lincolnshireman had ever set foot therein, or ever would, so wreathed was it in
superstition, so steeped in legends of the long-dead past. To all this
Sir Herlwin listened with interest, but was in no way discouraged
thereby. And one day, with the king in London and comparative
peace settled on the land, he rode out to the edge of the forest, and
giving his horse into the hands of his groom, dismissed him.

That was three weeks ago. Since then he had spent his days gauging
his position by the direction of the sun and the scent of the sea, and
in a quest that now gave every indication of proving fruitless. Yet
the very perverseness of the quarry sustained Herlwin's curiosity
even when hope flagged, and now he stooped to examine with renewed interest the imprint left in the small clay hollow.

So engrossed was he in his discovery that he failed to notice the
sudden cracking of a twig beneath a stealthy foot.

The man creeping up behind him was dressed in an odd assortment
of clothes. His tunic was worn and shabby, barely concealing the
bronze chest beneath, and his ancient leather jerkin hung open in
front. His hose showed numerous rents and reached only to the calf,
leaving bare an expanse of leg toughened by sun and wind. A sword
wound, only lately closed, reached from his right ear almost to his
chest, whilst about his neck on a piece of string hung a little wooden
cross crudely whittled by hand. His hair was of a paler gold than was
usual even among the English. He could scarce have seen seventeen
summers, for an almost invisible down coated rosy cheeks that no
blade had ever shorn, yet the haze-blue eyes fixed upon Herlwin's
Norman clothing gleamed with a fierce and passionate hate.

Closer and closer he crept, then suddenly he sprang.

Herlwin threw himself backwards, trying to pin the youth beneath
him, but the Englishman was strong as a young ox. He twisted, and
together they went down, hitting the mossy bank hard. Over and

over they went, twisting and turning, arising and crashing into tree trunks, churning up the leaves and moss of the forest floor. Then suddenly Herlwin broke free, but only to go crashing down the slippery bank into the brook. The Englishman leaped down upon him and with their arms locked about each other they fell down into the churning waters.

They arose in unison. The beads of sweat were pouring from Sir Herlwin's brow and the graying hair clung damply to his head. His breath came in loud, hoarse gusts. Huge cords stood out on his throat and his legs could scarcely hold him. But the English youth was fighting fiercely. The sword wound at his throat had reopened and from it the blood poured freely, covering his own hide jerkin and smearing Herlwin's garments with its dark stain. But he was the younger man, and he fought with the dogged fury of the oppressed.

They were in mid-stream and Sir Herlwin's legs were already buckling beneath him when suddenly the Englishman slipped on a wet rock and fell. In an instant Herlwin grasped his knife from his belt and was upon him before he had time to rise. But the youth just lay there with lowered lips. The water that swirled about his rosy cheeks was dyed scarlet from a deep gash on his head, and the only other thing that stirred about him was the crude little wooden cross, bobbing to and fro to the eddies of the water.

Sir Herlwin paused, his blade in mid-air. This was the enemy, an Englishman. Yet he did not strike.

But the water was cool and refreshing and after a moment the youth opened up his eyes and his gaze shifted from Herlwin's face to the blade, motionless still in mid-air.

It was not fear Herlwin saw on the face of the Englishman at that moment. It was the fierce resignation of one who had always known that someday he would die this way, fighting the invader; fighting for his freedom and for the freedom of a land dear to him beyond his ability to measure. Then quickly his expression changed as he caught Herlwin's indecision, noted the compassion in Herlwin's soft brown eyes. Surprise came and went, and with it went the fierce resignation and suddenly, passionately, and above all else, the youth wanted only to live.

And Herlwin let him live.

With the Norman's help the Englishman arose and together they scrambled up the bank. For a moment they stood regarding one another uncertainly, then Herlwin drew his kerchief from his tunic and bound the youth's head.

"How are you called, lad?" he asked.

"Siward. And you?"

"Herlwin FitzHugh, knight, governor of Lincoln."

Again they lapsed into silence, then reluctantly the Englishman's eyes sought those of the Norman.

"I am fairly at a loss," he admitted unhappily. "You have just given me my life, yet I am bound to take you captive."

Sir Herlwin laughed. "Do not try it, lad," he advised grimly. "You are weak from loss of blood. A second encounter between us might not end as happily as the first."

"As to that," replied the Englishman, "we are not so much alone as you may think. I could summon aid fast enough had I a mind to."

"Aid? Are you then one of a band of outlaws?"

"Aye—so called."

"And though I spared your life, you still intend to take me for ransom? Pardé! I begin to think less highly of English honor!"

Siward flushed angrily. "Nay, Sir Norman, you misjudge me. 'Tis not a ransom I have in mind, but the security of my comrades. Were I to free you now to return to Lincoln, you would soon enough be heading back this way—and with an army at your back to slaughter us or rout us from our refuge."

"I shall not deny it," replied the governor slowly. "It would be my duty, as you can see."

"Aye, but it is equally my duty to prevent it."

Sir Herlwin's hand dropped swiftly to his dagger hilt. "If you can, lad," he said. "If you can."

But Siward made no motion to attack him. Instead, he placed two fingers to his mouth and blew a shrill signal. Sir Herlwin glanced hurriedly about, amazed at the speed with which running footfalls answered the call. Within a few minutes men began to converge upon them from all sides. They uttered various exclamations of anger and astonishment at the sight of a Norman in their midst and advanced menacingly upon him.

"Nay, nay, have done!" cried Siward, glaring at his comrades. "No one shall harm him! Hands off!" He turned to Herlwin. " 'Tis the aid I spoke of," he explained apologetically. "Come, I will take you to our leader."

He led Herlwin through the darkening forest by many circuitous paths till at length they came to the mouth of a huge cavern. Its entrance was very narrow, large enough for only one man to pass through at a time, but it opened into a huge vault whose roof, either because of its height or the thickness of the gloom, was indistinguishable in the light of the torch which Siward had taken from the entrance. Through the vault he led the Norman, then down a natural winding passage through the rock, alongside of which ran a stream of very cold water. The water bubbled ceaselessly, for within it, Siward explained, dwelt the Spirit of the Rill, whose voice ran on, sometimes scolding, sometimes coaxing, rising to tones of anger, then again soft and soothing, but never still.

At last, moving cautiously by a slippery ridge of rock running alongside the stream, they came to an immense rocky chamber. The vaulted dome above was pitted and scarred by the water which had dripped for centuries over its surface, leaving it seamed and glistening with moisture. The drip, drip resounding through the cave made it seem lonely and far removed from the outside world. The rocky floor beneath was strewn with boulders which had dropped from above, smoothed into strange and grotesque shapes by the ageless dripping of the water.

The cave was lighted by torches and in its center burned a huge campfire about which the camp cooks bustled, stirring caldrons of soup or turning spits upon which were roasting haunches of venison, pheasants and whole kids. The vast space was thronged with outlaws. They turned startled faces toward the entrance as the Norman emerged from the gloom, halting in their tracks and falling abruptly silent. Only one man stirred, and he, taller than the rest, sighted the Norman over the heads of his comrades. Swiftly he moved forward, pushing his way through the crowd, and once again Sir Herlwin FitzHugh found himself face to face with Hereward the Wake.

Sir Herlwin, recalling the friendly circumstances of their last meeting, smiled in recognition. But the Wake gave him no greeting. He turned instead to the youth and spoke in cold, stern tones.

"What is this, Siward? A Norman in our headquarters? Why?"

"Sir," Siward replied, "I will tell you. I found myself in a perplexity where to do right by this man I could not, and to do wrong against him I would not, so I am come to place both the man and the matter in your hands."

As Siward plunged into the story of his encounter with the Norman, Hereward turned and strode about the cave, moving restlessly back and forth. He glanced up swiftly as the conclusion was reached, then he returned and stood before the governor, gazing thoughtfully down upon him.

"Sir Herlwin," he said, "what was your purpose in coming to this forest?"

"You must know," Sir Herlwin replied, "how much the people of Lincoln hold it in awe. I was of course interested in their quaint superstitions and the legends with which they surround it. But I was interested in something more, a curious spoor which I discovered on the fringes of the forest and which I could not identify."

"And when you finally ventured to track this creature, were you aware then that you were entering the Gronnaswald?"

Sir Herlwin started. "The Gronnaswald! But the Gronnaswald reportedly lies in the fens."

"It does not end in the fens," the Wake replied. "It extends north almost to Lincoln, a fact of which we ourselves were unaware until we took refuge here and explored it for the first time. We found it to be surrounded on all sides by fen, saving only for the narrow neck of land to the north by which you entered it."

"Pardé!" exclaimed the governor. "Such knowledge would be handy to the Conqueror!"

"Which is why, now that you have chanced to come into possession of it, you are a menace to our safety. Your continued existence would be a threat to us."

"Aye," admitted Sir Herlwin with a rueful smile, "I commence now to see the hazards of my position."

"Yet still," continued the Wake, "it would seem iniquitous to repay your act of mercy by hanging you. I suggest, therefore, that for the moment we set all enmity aside—as we have before, you and I— that you give me your word to attempt no escape and that you come and sup with us the while. Tomorrow we shall again ponder this matter."

"Your proposal, Sir Wake, is a right fair one," the governor answered. "I accept its conditions and bind myself, upon my knightly honor, to abide thereby."

With that the Wake led Sir Herlwin to the far end of the cave where tables were set out for dining and here, with all courtesy, he seated his guest between himself and Eadric the Wild. Upon a signal a basin of water and a freshly laundered napkin were brought and presented to the governor by a boy of some eight or ten years. He was an undersized child with a wistful, sensitive face and as the governor washed his hands he found himself oddly disturbed by the expression of mistrust and fear with which the boy regarded him. "Rest at ease, lad," he whispered reassuringly. "I shall not harm you." But the boy shrank back and swiftly turned away his face and then it was that Sir Herlwin perceived he lacked an ear. Apparently it had only lately been removed, for the wound was not yet fully healed.

"The lad has learned young to mislike Normans," he remarked to the Wake, when the boy had passed on.

"And with good reason, as you have seen."

"That mutilation! What fiend would mutilate a child?"

"Can you not guess?"

"De Lussac!"

"The same," replied Hereward. "The boy's name is Wulf Letwoldsson. A few weeks back, before we brought him to the safety of the forest, Sir Guy came upon the boy one evening heading for home with some six or eight codlings in a small stone jar and straightway accused him of fishing his channels. When Wulf stood silent before him, neither revealing his name nor pleading pardon, de Lussac ordered his ears cut off to teach him his manners. It was only when the first ear was gone and the boy wept noiselessly that Sir Guy realized the truth. Wulf was born a deaf mute."

"A sad little tale," murmured the governor, then he added with attempted casualness, though with a searching, oblique glance, "it is little wonder that the lady Althya cannot bring herself to wed Sir Guy. Had you heard the news? It seems that the wedding scheduled for this past September was once again postponed by her on the grounds of ill-health. They are not expected to wed now until spring."

"Aye," replied the Wake with equal casualness. "I had heard it."

At that moment the cooks approached, bearing before them the roasts which were served as they were cooked, upon their spits. These, together with a slice of trencher bread, they presented to each man in turn, beginning with their guest so that he might select for himself the choicest cuts. At the same time bowls of steaming soup were passed, and flagons of water fresh from the rill.

As they dined the governor availed himself of the rare opportunity to closely inspect these rebels, noting how resolute and stern were their faces, how lean and sinewed their frames. It was clear that they were all possessed of one common character, an abiding passion for

freedom. Despite the shabbiness of their attire, they deported themselves with dignity and quiet assurance. Many men were there whom
the governor had seen at York, but if they in turn recognized him,
they gave no sign, returning his interested glances with mild hostility
which clearly bespoke their resentment at the presence of a Norman
in their midst. Save for the efforts of Hereward, therefore, the meal-
time passed by in sober silence. But later, when it was ended and they
were gathered around the campfire, the stern faces of the Wake's
men relaxed and their manner became almost cordial, as though they
found themselves regretting the grim necessity for hanging their
quiet-eyed guest upon the morrow.

"Tell us, Sir Norman," said a young knight, "tell us about this man
who calls himself our king."

And Herlwin told them of William's solitary infancy and youth;
of how, born to an age when only the strong survived, he had learned
to compass by subtle diplomacy and craft that which he lacked the
strength to otherwise achieve. And they listened in silence, for Herlwin had a way of telling, a way of making William come alive to
them, as though he were there now, standing afar off in the shadows,
blocking up the entrance of the cave. Then gently Herlwin implied
that William would gladly accept the allegiance of these outlaws if
they would but kneel to him and submit. More than gladly—generously.

"Aye," scoffed young Siward, "endow us with riches today, which
tomorrow he would find a means of retracting."

"Or," added Lightfoot, who possessed a store of curious knowledge, "like the druids of old, borrow wealth on earth to be repaid in
heaven."

And Herlwin, seeing the course their minds ran, let the matter rest,
asking them concerning the animal that had caused his present venture.

"There are many such," the Wake told him, "though what it is, we
also have been unable to ascertain. Some prehistoric creature, perhaps, more like a lost race of men—who can say? Wulf alone has seen
them, appears even to have held converse with them, though by what
means it would indeed be interesting to know. Howbeit, we live in
amity with them, for the English holly befriends us all and is as much
another man's shelter as our own."

At this Herlwin urged them once more.

"Such need not be the case," he told them gently, "for your own hearths await each one of you. What can you hope to gain by with-holding your allegiance to a king to whom you must eventually bow? Freedom? You have no freedom now, for this forest is a cage wherein you are trapped."

At this these gaunt-faced men sat without stirring and Herlwin feared he had offended them. But at last the Wake arose and stood, his yellow locks red in the firelight. He put out a foot and stirred the lingering embers, and a little cloud of feathery white ashes arose, and again subsided. Then the Wake spoke.

"Freedom," he said, "is like the sap running in a tree. It sends forth buds that blossom and bear fruit, when the time is ripe."

Then Herlwin urged them no more, but in turn listened while they told him why they risked life and limb in England's cause; why they preferred the hard life of the forest to the bribes of the Conqueror; why they would live out their lives as outlaws rather than bow their necks beneath the yoke of the Norman. And then it was that Herl-win mentioned Waltheof.

"I knew the earl well," he said, "for before the king commissioned me to York we both abode at the Tower."

"And doubtless he abides there again," quoth the fiery Eadric, rat-tling his ivory weapons, "surrounded by luxury, but with an empty scabbard."

Herlwin looked surprised. "Then," he replied, "isolated as you have been from the outside world, the news of his death has not yet reached you?"

There was a heavy silence as glances were furtively directed toward young Siward. Then, too late, the truth flashed upon Herl-win. This youth was Siward Waltheofsson!

It was the Wake who broke the silence.

"Though his name has become one that is never mentioned among us," he said, "we would count it a kindness if you would acquaint us with the manner of his passing."

Herlwin turned questioningly toward Siward, but he sat gazing stonily into the flames, whose shadows leaped up and danced upon his face. His rosy cheeks were pallid and his young lips were pressed together in a stern, hard line.

Herlwin addressed himself to the others.

"That will I gladly do, for you will see that it is a tale worth hear-ing, accompanied as it was by a manifestation. It was his misfortune," he began, "to become involved in a revolt led by two Norman barons

against the king. The revolt was discovered and the barons exiled. But
with Earl Waltheof it was otherwise, for the king had apparently
never been convinced of the sincerity of his allegiance. He was con-
demned to death and taken to Winchester, where his fellow countrymen caused such a clamor on his behalf that it was thought wise to
carry out the execution without further delay, lest the English storm
the prison and release him by force. Thereupon one morning before
dawn, while the citizens were yet abed, they awakened him.

" 'Follow us,' they said, 'for your time has come.' "

"He arose, attiring himself in the robes of honor that his rank entitled him to wear, and followed them through the graying streets
and out beyond the city gates to the summit of a hill. Here, divesting
himself of his princely raiment, he bestowed it upon the humblest
soldier present. Then he knelt down to say his morning orisons.

" 'Hasten,' said the headsman, 'that I may fulfill my orders.' "

" 'Wait yet,' replied the earl, 'one little moment. Let me at least
say the Lord's prayer for me and for you.'

"The headsman nodded and the earl, kneeling still, recited the
prayer till he came to the words 'Lead us not into temptation.' With
that a sob broke his voice, causing him to halt, for the words doubtless minded him of many things. As he struggled to regain his composure the executioner became impatient, and drawing his sword,
severed the earl's head from his body with a single stroke. The head
rolled for a space upon the sward, its lips still moving as if in prayer.
Then, to the terror of the men who had already turned to flee, it
ended in a loud and steadfast voice, 'But deliver us from evil.
Amen.' "

When he had finished, Herlwin turned to Siward Waltheofsson.
The youth's face was still stony, bereft of feeling, graven as an image.

"He died bravely," said Herlwin gently, then something made him
add, "he died like an Englishman."

At that Siward Waltheofsson arose, and covering his face with his
cloak, went out alone into the night to seek solace from his hurt at
the broad and sheltering bosom of the forest.

It was somewhere after midnight when Sir Herlwin, sleeping in
the cave with the rest, was awakened by the sound of stealthy footsteps on the stone floor. Thinking perhaps some vengeful Englishman
came to put a dagger through his heart whilst the others slept, he
furtively opened an eye, but saw instead, in the dim light of the

campfire's last embers, the Wake standing in deep converse with two men. The first of these the governor immediately recognized as one of the outlaws, but the second wore the tight-fitting garb of the fen-men and was too aged to be a fighter. The governor judged him instead to be an outside scout or spy, for his white hair clung damply to his brow and his chest heaved mightily, as though he had run far and long to bring the rebel leader a message of grave urgency.

The Wake listened with bent head to the old man's tale, then, crossing to his couch of skins, he reached up and lifted down his sword from the wall above it. His face was grim as he buckled it about his waist, at the same time moving swiftly among the men, awakening them by a tap upon the shoulder. They arose without surprise or query, as though this summons in the night was no rarity to them, then, after arming themselves with longbows and swords and donning light ring mail for defense, they filed noiselessly out of the cave, leaving the rest to their slumbers.

The next day the governor found the camp all but empty of fight-ing men. Save for young Siward, who lay quietly abed to heal his reopened wound, the only men left behind were those of humbler pursuits, cooks, wheelwrights, armorers, and serfs who had fled bond-age beneath a Norman overlord; each man going about his appointed task, yet each one keeping a wary eye upon the Norman captive.

Siward had warned him that for his own safety he must keep to the vicinity of the cave. There were men posted everywhere in the forest, the youth explained, who would suspect his motives were he to stray too far. The governor spent the day, therefore, moving rest-lessly about, strolling over to the improvised workshop of Outy the Cobbler, where he paused awhile to watch the old man fashion shoes for the outlaws from tanned deer hide. Over at the smithy he stood breathless in the doorway, for a more splendid sight he had never be-fore witnessed than the smith, Cynwric Hir, toiling over his anvil. Seven foot tall he stood in his shoes, and a mane of jet-black hair fell to his shoulders. He had discarded his jerkin, exposing to view the massive throat; the magnificently proportioned upper trunk, deep-chested and dusky; the vast muscles writhing like knotted whip-cord beneath the naked, steaming flesh. He glanced up as the shadow of the governor fell across his floor, but to the Englishman the spon-taneous camaraderie with the enemy that had sprung up the previous night by the campfire's glow seemed, by cold daylight, to have been nothing more than an inexpiable moment of moon madness, and without so much as a nod of recognition he sturdily returned his attention to his work.

The governor moved on, slowly, aimlessly. The day had been raw and bleak, with heavy, slate-colored clouds sweeping so low they were clawed by the treetops as they passed. The autumn winds rode roughly through the forest, whipping up the rain water that had lain stagnant in the bottoms, buffeting the half-stripped trees and scattering leaves in all directions. Gone, suddenly, were the gemlike, ruby tones of yesterday when the forest had stood bright in sunshine. Today all was gray; the tree trunks with their clinging lichens, the gloomy thickets, the moss and bracken underfoot, withered now, and made spongy by the moisture-laden air. The robins had ceased to sing and perched with chill eye and ruffled feathers, taking solemn cognizance of the world's disleafing. Such days, the governor reflected, made a man disconsolate; made a man shun solitude and seek the companionship of other men.

It was then that he detected the cheering sound of music coming from some short distance to the south of him, now drowned in the momentary plunging of the forest, now emerging clearly as the wind lulled. Following the sound, he came at length to a small clearing in which, upon a fallen tree, sat one of the outlaws. The governor did not immediately recognize him, for his face was hidden, bent above that of the boy Wulf, who sat beside him and whom he was painstakingly teaching to play the ghittern. The boy held the instrument lovingly in his square, serf-like hands, and though he played in no especially gifted manner, the wonder was that he played at all and seemed in some mysterious way to derive much pleasure therefrom, for the haunted expression the governor had previously noted upon his face was replaced now by a look of quiet joy.

Sir Herlwin listened till the end was reached, then he advanced toward the pair.

"How," he inquired of the man, "can he play, when he cannot hear?"

The man looked up, smiling, his face aglow with pride in his pupil's achievement. "'Tis all in the touch," he replied readily. "The lad has an uncanny sense of——"

Sir Herlwin heard no more, for at the sight of the Englishman's upraised face he gasped in recognition. How well he knew this man! He had seen him a year ago—at York. He could never forget his face; the hollow cheeks, the silken black beard, the brilliant eyes.

This man had thrown the knife that killed his son!

Sir Herlwin swung around and strode swiftly away, his heart hammering in his breast, his brain in a turmoil. The grief that time had narcotized now fomented anew, rekindled with cruel poignancy by a single glimpse of the slayer's face. Even the memory of his son's countenance was again frighteningly fresh and clear, as though the lad had stood before him but five minutes since. How lithe and straight of form; at sixteen years taller than his father by half a head. And how fearlessly he had flung himself into battle when the castle was attacked, facing the enemy with quivering eagerness, crashing sword edge through helmet and bone. From whence derived this feverish warrior's blood, this lust to fight, this intoxicating battle joy? Surely it was the stirring of some lingering cells of wild Norse blood from his viking forebears. Yet a right gallant knight he would have become when life had tamed and mellowed him, a knight of which a father could be proud. To have lost such a son! And to what end had he given his young life? Alas, to what end——

It was almost dark now; the sad, premature dusk of an autumn evening. Sir Herlwin had long since wandered from the trail, striding on through narrow glades of gorse and withered bracken. At moments when the wind abated he was vaguely conscious of a rhythmic swishing behind him, as though someone followed at his heels, but who it was he neither cared nor sought to learn, so immersed was he in memories of his son.

Then from some twenty yards ahead of him came the sharp twang of a bowstring as an arrow hissed through the air and stuck, quivering, in the earth at his feet.

"Stand where you are, Norman!"

Sir Herlwin stopped short and looked up to see two sentries advancing toward him, longbows raised, shafts pointed at his heart. They were eying him with suspicion and open hostility and only then did he realize how far he had strayed from camp and what the Wake must inevitably think when he could give no plausible explanation for his action. But suddenly from behind a hand fell lightly upon his forearm and Martin Lightfoot drew up beside him. He glanced only briefly at the Norman, a vague, aloof smile twisting his monstrous mouth. Upon his back he carried a heavy pile of nets.

"Nay, let be, Thomas," he said to one of the sentries. "You see well enough the Norman is with me. My lord will not return this nightfall so we are going eeling, he and I."

"You, Martin, are a free man and may go where you will," Thomas replied with heat, "but it is otherwise where the Norman is concerned. We have our orders——"

"Aye, likely enough," interrupted Lightfoot, "and I have mine—directly from the Wake."

With that, and heedless of the sentries' bitter protests, he pushed between them, drawing Sir Herlwin after him. "My lord confided you to my care," was all he said, and thereafter strode on in silence, slowing his pace to that of the Norman, moving with his strange, lumbering gait and seeming not to notice the chilling blasts that whipped through his faded tunic. It was only now, feeling the cold tears on his cheeks, that the governor realized with much humiliation that before the sentries accosted him he had been weeping. But this Lightfoot appeared steadfastly not to see, casting never a further glance at his companion, gazing straight ahead into the deepening gloom.

They came at length to the fenside. The wind had blown away most of the clouds and a few pale stars were visible. Lightfoot hauled a skerry out from among the reeds and after flinging into it his pile of nets and motioning the governor to enter, he himself stepped aboard and shoved off. He quanted slowly down the ea, his lank form bent as though he leaned upon the wind, his head cocked, his wolf-like face upraised, listening to the wild honking of the geese winging out of sight above a ragged bank of cloud.

The governor, despite his warm wool cloak, was numb with cold by the time they reached the tiny islet for which Lightfoot was heading, but to the lean and silent Englishman the bitter sea wind was the friend of his childhood and youth and was to him as much a part of home as the smell of the weed burner's fire and the bleat of the snipe. He took his time in setting out his nets, spreading them tight across the river to form an obstacle to the eels swarming toward the sea. Carefully he tested the weights resting on the river bed, checked the wooden blocks bobbing on the water's surface and calculated the position of his pods. When at length he was satisfied that he had left no passage open by which the eels could continue their seaward journey, he shoved over to the islet and moored the boat. From beneath one seat he drew forth a cloth bundle and a rug of fox pelts, then he led the way to a sheltered spot overlooking the river and protected from the wind by a grove of beeches.

"Take it," he said, handing the rug to the governor. "You will need it. It gets chill by dawn."

It was only then that the governor realized Lightfoot intended spending the night in the open fen. He was appalled at the prospect, thinking ruefully of the warm, bright cave; of the steaming roasts and the comfortable talk of the men. But Lightfoot was oblivious to the governor's consternation. He had opened up the bundle and had set out a loaf of bread and a skin of ale. He drew his dagger, and after wiping it on the turf, he cut himself a thick slice of bread, then, plunging the knife into the loaf, he pushed both toward the Norman. Sir Herlwin glanced at the weapon in surprise, then back at Lightfoot. But already the taciturn Englishman was immersed in his own thoughts, his long back propped comfortably against a tree, his jaws grinding with unconscious rhythm. As usual his eyes were hidden by elflocks and there was no way of gauging either the direction of his gaze or the degree, if any, of his vigilance. But the awkward, sprawling frame showed no trace of tension and the bony hands rested tranquilly on the bony knees.

The governor caught his breath. Such an opportunity was surely provided by the Almighty. They were here alone—just the two of them, separated only by the narrow distance of a few feet. What mattered a man's knightly word when he stood to be hanged upon the morrow? What mattered an oath given under duress? A man would be a fool to forgo the chance to save his own neck. He had only to take up the dagger, to fall upon this unsuspecting Englishman and stab him to the heart, then he could take the skerry through the open channels to the other side—to safety.

Wryly the governor complimented himself upon the logic of his arguments, meanwhile cutting himself a thick slice of bread. Ha! The Wake had judged him well. Come what may, he would adhere rigidly to his knightly code. Slowly, reluctantly, he replaced the dagger in the loaf and pushed them back across the narrow space to his companion.

"A witting fool deserves his fate!" he muttered half aloud.

They sat in silence. In the copse behind them the withered leaves rustled softly and the beech mast tapped at twig and branch as it fell. A night bird glided in on silent, widespread wings and circled overhead, but in a moment it was gone, its dark shape dissolving into the deeper gloom of the night. From afar off came a cry, shrill and lone and sad, reverberating among the meres and yellowing reed beds as though some accursed spirit of the marsh was abroad, wandering through the dusk. And all the while Lightfoot neither moved nor spoke, but sat with sleeping limbs, his head cocked in an attitude of listening.

"What secrets does the whispering fen divulge to you, Martin?" inquired the governor presently.

Lightfoot stirred, and the semblance of a smile flickered about his grotesque mouth.

"Nay, Sir Norman," he replied, "I leave such listening to the god Heimdall who sits at heaven's end and hears all things; the wool growing on the sheep, the seedlings springing in the earth, the salmon leaping in the falls."

Sir Herlwin raised his brows at the other's irreligion. "Have you no monks at camp to teach you better?" he asked.

"Aye, indeed," said Lightfoot, "one of whom has but lately schooled me in the Christian faith, to which I do now adhere in all extremities. But though a man may wish his soul washed clean in baptism, he still looks to the older faith for the poesy that delights his heart. Else whyfor does the plowman, though Christianized, still chant to the earth goddess as he plows his field? And who, gazing up at the round bowl of the sky, could bring himself to disaffirm that the gods created it from the giant Ymir's skull? Or that the way from earth to heaven is by the Bifröst Bridge, which we are wont to call 'the rainbow'? Why should we deny that Freyja weeps her golden tears for her lost Odr, or that the sighing of the wind is but the echo of her love-longing? Such legends are part of our tradition. We love them with a rough and simple joy."

"But when you were newly baptized, were you not admonished to sat aside these pagan fantasies?"

"Aye," Lightfoot admitted, "but death and devastation cause a man to think. And I have thought. And I have thought that nothing that has lived ever truly dies, and that though we older English may become in time an all but vanished race, we will leave behind us some traces of our primitive national life. They will linger everywhere; in the same plowman's chant and in the song of the blacksmith at his forge; in the memory of our lay deities who gave their names to weald or tree or hollow; on the ancient battlegrounds where our heroes died in a ghastly ring of corpses; in the days of the week; in the half-forgotten legends that cling to the gray stones of a cairn.

And I have thought that though a man's body may be shackled, his fancy rides free, and when those who come after us cluster through the long eventide round the glowing wood ashes of the hearth, they will recall these scattered fragments of our spiritual vision. Thus shall our orphan sons reach into the past to find us, for our folklore, which clothes our earliest beliefs in so noble a poetry, shall live when we are gone."

"You talk," said Herlwin, "like a man preparing to take his farewell. Does the lord Hereward plan, then, to quit the fight—to quit England?"

Lightfoot did not reply immediately, only raised his strange, wolf-like face as though to interrogate the sky; and a wind blast caught up his raven locks and flung them back against his brow and for a fleeting instant his eyes were wild, the eyes of a wild thing in the forest.

"A man's destiny," he said, "is writ at birth, when he is harnessed to the passions and principles which impel him onward to meet it face to face. Ofttimes I wish it need not be so. Ofttimes I wish my lord could outroot the love that is native to his heart—that he would be content to quit the fight, to live out his life in the East amassing a golden treasure of Cuftish coins. But yet he sets the freedom of England above the safety of life or limb, and so it will always be. He can no more change his nature than a sheep can fly or a crow crop grass."

Sir Herlwin fell silent, overcome by a sudden unreasoning sadness. And he thought again about his lost son and about those others, English and Norman, who were yet to die. And he was assailed once again by his old doubts as to the justice of the Conquest and of the right of any man to crush a nation by force of arms and rob it of its birthright. "God forgive us!" he began. "Such crimes have we Normans committed against England as can never be amended——" Then he stopped, shocked not so much by the ugly truth of his own words as by the fact that he, a Norman, had been the one to give them voice.

The next morning Lightfoot hauled up his nets and they headed back, reaching camp just as the outlaws thundered up the trail leading to the cave. It was immediately apparent to Sir Herlwin that they had been in heavy conflict with the Normans, for there was scarcely a man among them who did not bear upon his person signs of battle. The Wake himself had several slashes on his sword arm which, however, he ignored as he shouted orders to his men and helped lift down the more severely wounded from the horses to which they had been strapped.

Lightfoot dropped his sack of eels to lend a hand and in a little while the governor, too, stepped forward, helping to lift the men down and carry them into the cave, divesting them of ring mail and sword belt, then, all unbidden, fetching water and cloths with which to tend their wounds. Those to whom he ministered eyed him strangely, but being utterly spent with pain and battle, they suffered him to bind their bleeding limbs, to ease their fevers with compresses and hold to their lips hot herb draughts which soothed them so they slept.

"We thank you for your aid, Norman," Hereward told him as they supped.

"I must admit to some curiosity concerning your venture," came the reply. "I cannot help but speculate as to what news the messenger could have brought that caused you to ride out so hurriedly in the night."

" 'Tis ever the same story," the Wake told him, "patriots seeking to join our forces. The new men you see among us today are from the west. They had crossed the entire breadth of England and were almost within sight of the fens when they were apprehended and taken to Stamford. There they were imprisoned in the castle pending the Bastard's order of death by hanging."

"I know the castle well," said the governor, "it being situated directly on the route from London to Lincoln. But since it is built of stone and is at all times heavily garrisoned, and since the prisoners would have been incarcerated in the dungeons, it is hard to see how you were able to force an entrance and liberate them."

"We have our ways," the Wake replied, "as you should know, though in this instance I think I shall decline to explain that which to the Stamford garrison remains inexplicable." He smiled faintly. " 'Twas a neat trick, though, and the astonishment of the sentries was admirable to witness, for when first they sighted us we had already completed the task of liberation and were fighting our way out, not in."

"The wonder is that once within the castle you were able to get out at all. In the actual hand-to-hand fighting you must have been outnumbered three to one."

" 'He who would count himself a man,' " quoted the Wake, " 'must learn to hold his own against two foes and even against three; only from four may he flee without shame.' "

"Indeed," said Sir Herlwin, "it is generally agreed that where you English are concerned, we Normans are better acquainted with your fronts than your backs. But while it is true that there are many new faces here among you tonight, there seem to be a few I seek for in vain."

"Aye. We had our losses."

Hereward waited, expecting the governor to take advantage of this information, to use it as a lever wherewith to open once again the argument for capitulation. When the Norman failed to do so, the Englishman affected to chide him for being remiss, mocking him in friendly, bantering tones.

"By the hoof of Satan! What is this new attitude? You sit there, Sir Norman, silent as Vitharr himself. Do you thus easily relinquish a task once begun? Have you forgot all your fine arguments? Is the case not the same today as it was yesterday? If not, wherein has it changed? Come, take heart. You might yet convince us. Tell again why we would be wise to capitulate. Tell why it is now we should make our peace with the Bastard, now—while we have so much to gain!"

There was a long silence as the Norman, sorely troubled, searched about for a reply. "What would you have me say?" he asked at length. "I have a duty to my king."

The Wake turned in astonishment. The words had been spoken without predeliberation, without any conscious awareness of revealing a trend of thought which, if questioned, the Norman would steadfastly deny. Sir Herlwin was an honorable man; a man whose lifelong loyalties, Hereward now suspected, had suddenly come into conflict with a profound sense of justice. For an instant the Wake's keen blue glance swept the other's countenance, then swiftly he turned the conversation to other channels and thereafter the subject was never again referred to.

A week passed and nothing further was said about hanging the Norman. The men from the west, to whose nostrils still clung the stench of the Stamford dungeons, regarded him with open enmity at first, but even they soon learned to accept his presence among them. The governor could only suppose that for reasons of their own the English had decided to hold him prisoner indefinitely. He was surprised to find that the prospect did not actively disturb him, for he was now aware that he had come to feel a strong and enduring sympathy for these stern-faced men from whom all had been taken, save courage; men who wore their ragged clothes with dignity and set no store by wealth. It was only to Letwold, the mild-mannered slayer of his son, that Sir Herlwin could never bring himself to speak. Whenever their glances chanced to meet, the Norman turned his face away, and the other, comprehending, fell silent in his presence and fidgeted with the clothpiece at his throat.

And then one day the governor received a summons from the Wake.

"Sir Herlwin," said the English leader, "we have debated among ourselves the question of what best to do with you and we are agreed that there will be no danger to ourselves in setting you free."

"Free? Sainte Vierge! Free?"

"Nay, do not stand so amazed. You will not betray us. As a formality we shall require of you two assurances before you go; that you make no mention of having dwelt here among us, or divulge the secret of our forest. That is all."

"Sir Wake," Herlwin began, "I would thank you——"

"There is no need. As you yourself have said, you have a duty to your king. Now you will likewise have a duty to us. It is for you to find a way to reconcile the two. And furthermore, and for your peace of mind, let me add that you need have no hesitation in accepting your life at our hands, for, since you gave us a life when you spared young Siward, we shall in no wise look to you for an acquitment hereof should any of us meet again under reversed circumstances."

And thereupon, and in token of friendship, the Wake extended his sword hand to the Norman after the fashion of the English, and the Norman clasped it warmly.

" 'Tis odd," he murmured, shaking his head, "that, being free to go, I still would bide with you a little longer."

Thus it was that November passed and still Herlwin lingered with the outlaws in the forest, sharing their life, learning English customs and English ways. From Lightfoot, with his abounding passion for the strange and unfamiliar, he heard many a tale of the remote past when Britain was not yet an isle, but merely the arm of a great continent. And he heard how later, when the sea had broken through and formed a channel to the east, scattered tribes of men came to hunt and fish along the shores of the newborn isle; and domesticated the dog and the sheep and the ox; and regarded nature's seasonal changes as supernatural; and believed each tree and rock and pool to be the abode of some special spirit, which they feared and therefore worshiped.

And Lightfoot explained why many of the grave mounds of the ancient Britons were round; for to them the earth was the True Mother, and they laid their dead to rest in circular pits in crouched positions, as a babe in his mother's womb. And he told the Norman of the successive invading hordes from across the seas who beat back the island people to the mountains of the west and stayed to produce a new insular race; and how to discern in every Englishman certain specific racial characteristics and thus determine whether he be descended from the Norwegian or the Pict; from the Angle, the Saxon or the Jute; from the Celt or the "Black Strangers" who in their lustrous black hair and swinging gait bore the unmistakable mark of their ancestry.

And to all these things the Norman listened, and asked more questions, and pondered much, intending always to leave upon the morrow. And still he stayed. But when at length winter crept through the forest, when the last crumpled leaf had dropped silently from its naked bough, when a gray fog drifted through the hollows, leaving the tree trunks black and glistening, when the wind moaned above crystalline ponds and the frost lay in dazzling flakes on the forest floor, they led him back the way he had come and set him on the road to Lincoln. And as Herlwin rode away his heart was strangely sad, strangely moved by the odd finality in their parting.

Impulsively he reined in his horse and turned.

They stood as he had left them, gaunt and stern, their backs to the sunless forest, their faded garments whipped by the icy wind. They raised their hands in farewell when they saw him turn, and stood quite still; and vividly, and for all time, the picture of them standing there was imprinted on Herlwin's memory; the wind, and the sunless forest, and the men.

Then once more he turned his horse toward Lincoln, and rode away.

Chapter Sixteen

THE AMBUSH

SPRING came early in the year of 1071. By the middle of April the trees were in full leaf, their tender yellow-greens in brilliant array against the dark conifers. The lilac was in bloom. The summer birds had returned to their old haunts and were filling the woods with song, yet the Conqueror, heading north toward London, found little to delight him in the excited stirrings of the reawakened world, but rode instead with downcast gaze, his jaw set, his brow furrowed.

He would be glad, he reflected, to get back to London and the comparative quiet of the Tower. These past four months of setting things to rights in Normandy had called for continuous and intensive effort, and now the long ritual of the Easter feast at Winchester had wearied him. Yet even here in England there was but slight assurance of peace, for conditions had deteriorated in his absence. FitzOsbern, in whose hands he had left the realm, was surely showing signs of senescence and would have to be watched. The meanest soldier knew that any resurgence of activity on the part of the Wake and his men called for alertness, for instant and decisive action, instead of which FitzOsbern had left the outlaws to roam at will over Lincolnshire while he took his ease at the Tower, engaging in nothing more strenuous than evolving messages to Normandy urging the king's return.

And now he was here. Yet before he could set head on pillow tonight he would be called upon to answer Matilda's anxious questions. What could he tell her? That, but for the intervention of the Almighty, her first-born would now be a parricide? That Robert Shorthose and his wild companions had plotted to assassinate him and set the ducal crown on Robert's head, and, being discovered, had fled Normandy to France? That this smoldering hate between father and son yearned for its vent? Matilda would weep to hear it, but no matter. The day had passed when he concerned himself with her tears.

The Conqueror looked up as his horse clattered across the wooden bridge leading to the Ludgate. He forced a smile when the sentries threw wide their gates and bowed low in respectful greeting, but the instant he had passed them by the smile faded abruptly. Soon the narrow cobbled streets reverberated with the hoofbeats of his retinue and the people came forth from their houses to gape, ever drawn by the pomp and pageantry of royalty. The Londoners might be silent and sullen, William reflected, but they were honest. They showed no joy at their sovereign's return.

A few moments later he was at the Tower, being greeted by Fitz-Osbern and making his way up the circular steps to the second floor. As he reached the top he glimpsed Matilda among the men and women hurriedly assembled there to greet him, her face white with fears for her son. But the extreme pallor was caused by more than that, and William knew it. It sprang from the mysterious, deep-rooted, persistent pain that was gnawing her body and wasting her strength. And at that moment he knew, too, suddenly and intuitively, that their years together were drawing swiftly to a close. They would end in a rift for which there was no healing because of her fateful love for their ill-formed, ill-starred first-born.

But yet there was a defenselessness about her as she stood there, mute, her dark eyes fixed upon him brilliant with disease. He knew her so well that he could follow her every thought; what she wanted to know, why she feared to hear it. Had she heard rumors, then? Already she had been weeping. Ah! Could she but have loved the husband more, and the son less——

He forgot the crowd as he advanced toward her and with much ceremony bent and kissed her hand.

"Madam," he said, "things go better in Normandy than reports would have it seem. Your son is well and asks especially to be commended to you with all filial affection."

He could see the tension drain from her face as she continued to stand there looking up at him, half smiling now. Then abruptly he turned away. Motioning FitzOsbern to follow, he strode toward his privy chamber, entered and closed the door, then he set himself to wrestle with the problems of his kingdom and had soon immersed himself therein.

"My lord earl," he said presently, "pray acquaint me with fuller details of this new activity on the part of the rebels."

"Things continue much the same, sire," FitzOsbern replied. "They are still concentrating their efforts on the area surrounding Lincoln. For some thirty miles along the highway leading north through Lincoln to York, the Wake and his men are ranging in small, fast-moving bands. With lightning speed they strike at our vital supply columns intended to replenish the now dwindling resources of these two key cities, ambushing the patrols, slaughtering the armed escorts, setting fire to the supplies they themselves have no use for, then vanishing without a trace."

"And what measures have you taken against them?"

"I have doubled the armed escorts, sire, on all convoys."

"Such a move must have occasioned great satisfaction to the English. Being sportsmen at heart, they would welcome increased hazards where the quarry was doubled."

It was more the king's tone than his words that brought a flush to FitzOsbern's countenance.

"Sire," he replied, "perhaps you have not yet had time to comprehend the many complex aspects of the situation. This is a new kind of warfare. It is baffling in the extreme to a military machine accustomed to fighting in open field and in formation. The rebels are swift, mobile and resourceful. They are as elusive as the will-o'-the-wisps of their own marshlands. They know each inch of territory around Lincoln, each cleft and gully, each swamp and thicket of the vast and continuous forest that fringes the highway. Furthermore, they welcome pursuit—from which no Norman ever returns."

"To what extent has York been affected?"

"The city is virtually isolated, sire, with supplies reaching it only sporadically and by difficult roundabout routes."

"And Lincoln?"

FitzOsbern hesitated. "We have had no riders through from Lincoln, sire, in over a week."

The king sat a moment, his huge head sunk upon his breast.

"The governor there, Sir Herlwin FitzHugh, was formerly governor of York. In that he is familiar with the whole of the afflicted area did you think to consult him concerning his views? Did you ever seek his advice? Nay, I can see you did not. But it might have been useful to learn just what conclusions he has reached concerning the rebels' eventual aims."

"Aims, sire? What possible aims could these disorganized raids cover? It would seem clear that their only purpose is the gratification of a rankling malice and the acquisition of valuable loot."

"How many men do you calculate to be in the rebel force?"

"There is no way of even roughly estimating their strength, sire. It is generally believed, however, that countless scores of men have succeeded in slipping through to them from all parts of England and that their ranks have swelled considerably in recent months."

"And does the Wake suffer losses on these forays?"

"Of that we have no proof, for no English dead are ever left about for us to identify or count. But on one such occasion a young Norman soldier survived the attack, having fallen from his horse into the bushes by the wayside. Under questioning he repeatedly affirmed that our men killed several of the enemy before they themselves were wiped out."

The king sprang up and strode briskly about the room, his dark eyes bright, hands clasping and unclasping behind his back.

"And do you actually believe, my poor friend, that a general as competent and experienced as the Wake would risk the loss of a single life to no good end? Do you believe such a man interested in mere booty? Do you believe that he would expend his precious manpower in worthless forays? Nay, FitzOsbern! These raids are too well planned, too systematic not to form part of a larger pattern— and already that pattern starts to take shape. York, our northern-most stronghold, is isolated and therefore all but neutralized. Lincoln is next in line to feel the squeeze, and when it does a fog will slowly settle over the entire northeast area. The English will have driven us back, FitzOsbern, will have recovered all—and more—of the territory they lost when they lost York. What, then, do you suppose lies be-hind this carefully planned and carefully executed strategy?"

FitzOsbern looked startled, incredulous. It had never occurred to him to search beneath the surface for a master stroke of planning. Even now as he regarded the facts in a new light it seemed improb-able that, lacking money and arms, and having only a limited, hastily assembled, ill-clad army, the Wake would attempt once again to set himself against the Conqueror.

"My liege," he began, "how could Hereward Leofricsson presume to undertake a war of attrition? Even if he did succeed in placing at his back the broad territories of Northumberland and Lincoln-shire——"

He was interrupted by a hurried knock upon the door and the seneschal entered, ushering in a rider. The latter, from his dripping face and state of near collapse, must have thrown himself off his horse but a moment before. He fell speechlessly to his knees before the king. With fingers stiffened by the reins he struggled to open the leather wallet at his waist, then, successful at last, he drew forth his dispatch and placed it in the royal hands.

"Where are you from?" asked the king.

"From Lincoln, Your Grace," the man gasped, "—from Sir Herlwin FitzHugh."

The Conqueror motioned FitzOsbern to refresh the rider with a cup of red wine from the flagon and bade the seneschal send in his scribe. Then he turned his attention to the dispatch. He took his time examining the outside of the rolled parchment, turning it over in his hands, noting that it was soiled and smeared with blood, indicating that at some time during the ride it had been removed from its wallet; noting, too, and with considerable interest, that the seal had already been broken. Who had dared tamper with the king's dispatch?

He looked up as his scribe came hurrying into the room and silently handed him the parchment, then he sat back, following every word of the lengthy formal address, listening patiently until the text was reached.

" 'Herlwin FitzHugh, knight,' " the scribe read, " 'herewith humbly requests to be relieved of his present duties as governor of the City and Castle of Lincoln.' "

"Continue," snapped William, as the scribe halted.

"That is all, Your King's Grace."

The Conqueror frowned. He had expected the dispatch to contain words of warning, a prediction of imminent attack, an urgent appeal for reinforcements and supplies. But this seemingly simple request was unexpected. It puzzled him. Herlwin was an old soldier, loyal and disciplined. In nearly forty years of military service he had never been known to either shirk his duty or turn his back upon danger. Why did he appear to do so now? What lay behind this enigmatical and unexplained request?

"Tell me," he said to the rider, "did you receive this dispatch directly from the governor?"

"Aye, Your Grace, he placed it in my hands himself."

"And was the seal intact at the time?"

"It was, Your Grace."

"Then how did it come to be broken?"

"My lord king," replied the man, now somewhat revived by the wine, "I will tell you exactly what transpired. When the governor charged me with this mission, he also provided me with an escort of fifty armed men, instructing us to ride at top speed and never to halt until we came within sight of London town. This we engaged to do, but at some ten miles south of Lincoln, Your Grace, we were set upon by a band of rebels."

"How large was this rebel band?"

"I judged it to approximate two hundred men."

"Did you put up a fight?"

"That we did, my king, but to small avail. They had us neatly in a trap."

"Were any of your companions killed?"

"Aye, Your Grace, perhaps thirty."

"And the rest?"

"Taken captive—though they did not stay so long. Straightway the English threw up ropes and strung them to a tree—hanged them all!"

"And you?"

The rider shook his head in bewilderment. "Your Grace, I comprehend nothing of what followed. The rope was already around my neck when the rebel leader espied the wallet containing the dispatch."

"Then it was he who broke the seal?"

"Aye, it was he. He called for one of his men—a fighting monk I judged him to be—who read him the message as you have just heard it. That action, sire, for some strange reason saved my life. The rope was taken from my neck, the dispatch was replaced in the wallet and I was set once again upon my way."

"A truly strange tale," murmured the king.

He moved slowly over to the deep-embrasured window, and drawing aside the drape, gazed out across the darkening city. An interesting tale, too, he thought. Unimportant though it appeared to be, his curiosity was aroused.

Why had the rebels made an exception in this case? What stake had they in this? They had foreseen benefits to themselves by having the message reach him. Why? So that he would act upon it? Was it possible that Sir Herlwin's removal would somehow serve their ends by clearing the way for a full-scale attack upon Lincoln? Surely not, for they would know that even if FitzHugh were removed another equally competent governor would be installed in his place. Lincoln was a walled and fortified city; it was heavily garrisoned and Herlwin's presence—or the presence of any one man—could make but little difference to its defense. Yet somewhere there was a connecting link between this message and the rebels' future plans; a link, though, that was never to be found here in London, but up in the north where lay the present field of action.

The Conqueror turned with sudden decision.

"FitzOsbern," he said, "give the order below. I want to have assembled every available fighting man to form an escort. Tomorrow at dawn I set out for Lincoln!"

Old Godrith the Forester lolled in the fork of a giant oak, his face upturned to the spring sunlight. His white, wispy hair stirred in the breeze; his eyes were closed and he was smiling; a happy smile, it was, yet still a little sad, for he was reminiscing—looking back over a long, good life.

He had no way of knowing how old he was, but he clearly recalled the terrible famine which they said was all of seventy years ago. He recalled the struggle between Cnut the Dane and Aethelred for the English crown; and Edmund Ironside's strange, some said unnatural, death. He recalled the coronation of the Confessor and every detail of the glorious career of Harold the Earl; Harold, who fought the Confessor's wars and safeguarded his honor and his realm; who was exiled by him and reinstated by him and was king after him; king, not by right of birth, but by the free choice of a free people. Harold was the people's king.

Aye, much had happened in his lifetime. He had seen England pass through many a storm, yet always came the day when the sun shone forth again. So it would be now, if every able-bodied Englishman did his share. He himself, for all his years, was doing a young man's job, or so the Wake said; keeping his ear cocked and his eyes open; guiding impassioned, stout-limbed youngsters to the muster. Indeed, his humble cottage seemed to have become the focal point from whence all new patriots were spirited across the fens to the Gronnaswald. That, and more if he were able, would he do for England and the Wake. Did Hereward Leofricsson think old Godrith had forgotten how he avenged Hugh when the Normans tortured and murdered him and hung him up in chains? How he attacked

Bourne Castle almost singlehanded? And slew the Normans? And climbed to the roof to bring Hugh home for Christian burial? Could it be only two springs ago that Hugh was living, fishing, hunting, loving? Now all that was left of him was the lonely barrow in the fen—and his young girl-child, Edgitha.

Godrith roused himself at the thought of his granddaughter and hailed his companion, who sat above him among the upper branches.

"Letwold," he said, "have you spoken yet to Edgitha?"

"Aye, that I have," Letwold replied, "and would wed her to-morrow if she would have me. But she wavers, answering never a yes nor a no."

"Then make haste, man, and get the matter settled," said Godrith. "Edgitha is prime ripe for the altar. Ofttimes I see her sigh at her work, like a girl whose thoughts dwell upon love."

"If that be so, Father Godrith, 'tis not for me she pines."

Godrith made no answer, only closed his eyes again and returned to his musing. For sure, he knew well enough where her young heart was set, which was why he would like to see her wed before the summer was out. He knew well enough it was Hereward Leofricsson the girl loved. 'Twas not strange, perhaps, for a maiden to love her lord and wish to bed with him. But for a husband, a wise lass looked among her own kind. This Letwold was a widower and a steady man. He would be good to her. Besides, the lord Hereward had thoughts only for the Norman lady who lived on Orchard Isle, and although she was known to be otherwise betrothed, it was said they did find ways to meet upon occasion. Well, why not? A man might fight hard, but he still had time for love.

"Hist!"

Godrith glanced up, and obeying Letwold's excited gesture, hoisted himself out of his comfortable perch and clambered upwards. Near the top where the branches thinned he faced south and shaded his eyes, and saw, atop a distant elm and against a clear blue sky, the familiar snow-white banner.

"Aye," he agreed, " 'tis the signal all right. But look! Another! And still another! Holy Etheldreda! What can it mean? This noble con-voy must stretch all the way from here to London! Well enough, Letwold lad, hoist away. Three signals from us too then, to warn them to come heavy-armed and in fullest strength."

A short while later the Wake and his men swept through the forest and drew rein by the oak, Hereward in the lead astride Mare

Swallow. His company comprised some five hundred men clad for battle in ring mail and helmet, some armed with the stout English longbow, some with shield, sword and battle-axe; but each man alike tanned and lean and toughened by discipline and the stern forest life.

"Ho, there, Godrith!" cried Hereward. "Three banners! What means it? Does the whole Norman army come upon us?"

Godrith left his comfortable perch and dropped to one of the lower branches.

"Gentle lord," he replied, "you may indeed be close to the truth. It seems 'tis a rare big fish you are to grapple with today."

"From whence came the signal?"

"From the wych-elm, lord. They come up from the south."

"And there is no mistaking? You are certain of that?"

"It is three right enough, lord, as Letwold here will testify."

At that moment Eadric the Wild, who had drawn up alongside the Wake, leaned over and addressed him in undertones.

"Hereward," he said, "better, perhaps, to let this convoy pass unmolested. Apparently it is of unprecedented size and strength. We would be vastly outnumbered and stand to lose more than we would gain."

"If size and strength are going to affright us," the Wake replied, "then let us retire promptly to the seclusion of our forest and leave our highways to the Norman. For half a year we have plotted this operation. For three months past we have rigidly adhered to our plan of disrupting the mechanics of the Conquest by harrying all Norman traffic and thereby paralyzing transportation. Shall all this now go to waste because the monster drags a longer tail than usual? And how shall it be in the future if once they see they can deter us by a show of numbers?"

Eadric's gaze thoughtfully explored the long vistas beneath the aged oaks.

"I do not dispute your reasoning," he replied, "for I assuredly think as you do in this. Yet if from sheer doggedness we throw our men into a hopeless fray and lose them thereby, and if you and I, to whom all England looks for leadership, are likewise butchered, where stands our project then?"

"If, Eadric? . . . and 'if' there were a way?"

The green eyes quickened and returned abruptly from their roaming. "Ah, then——"

"Then let us cease debating, man, and act!" And forthwith the

Wake spurred Swallow and galloped off, followed by Eadric and his men.

Up the Roman road they sped, along the cobbled highway through the great primeval forest of oak and ash and beech and elm which then sprawled over most of Lincolnshire and into shires beyond. In some spots it thinned to pleasant passages lighted by brilliant shafts of sunlight; in others it was dark and awesome, with vine-choked trees gray with caterpillars' kells and dense undergrowths running down to the very cobbles. Never a Norman did they meet upon the way, since with good reason they had come to shun this highway. But here and there a hungry English serf, hauling wood for his Norman master, smiled at the Wake and his men and furtively greeted them, and beneath his breath besought Heaven's blessing on them, and success on their present venture.

They came at length to a river which cut directly across the highway. Its waters were broad and deep and swift. It was spanned by an ancient bridge of timber planks which were supported at either end and at midstream by uprights of whole tree trunks. Everywhere along the riverbank willow shrubs abounded and clustered thickly about the land approaches to the bridge.

It was here the Wake drew rein.

"Men," he cried, "we have little time and much to do. Peter—Will, you were clinchers by trade. Take six men and remove the nails fastening the planks to the uprights. Tom, do you take what men you need and see that these planks are not disturbed, but secured back in place by rope in such a way that they can be freed by a single slash of the knife. The work must be done with the utmost care. All debris must be cleared away and the mischief concealed. Under no circumstances must the bridge appear to be tampered with."

He paused a moment as the men in question sped away to do his bidding, then slowly he looked around him at the host of resolute, expectant faces.

"I want six volunteers to demolish the bridge," he continued. "These men will be required to post themselves by the uprights in pairs, two on this side, two in the center, two on the opposite bank, ready to slash the ropes and heave the planks into the river at the first sound of my battle horn. Give a moment's thought here, men, before you declare yourselves willing. You will be caught in the middle of the Norman cavalcade and may not escape."

Again he paused as, silently, six men spurred their mounts and moved forward.

"So be it!" said the Wake. "The four who are posted on the riverbanks will be adequately concealed by the willows. The two in midstream must lash themselves to the planks above to avoid detection. Our best marksmen shall be stationed in the trees near the river to cover you and help you effect your escape. Good luck and God keep you! As for the rest, the longbowmen stay by me. Eadric, do you take the others and distribute them as required along the highway. All right, men, you know what you have to do. Set to, then—and may the day be ours!"

A half hour later the work was complete. The outlaws had withdrawn to their appointed posts and quiet had once again descended upon the highway. The squirrels reappeared and poked furred faces through the foliage to inspect the crouching, mail-clad forms below. The birds recommenced their singing. A light breeze played in the treetops. All was at peace, as though for days no wayfarer had trod the cobbled way through the ancient forest that lay sleeping sweetly in the sun.

But presently the quiet was broken by a distant, muffled beat, the rapid clip-clop of horses' hoofs. The sound increased in volume until it rang out sharp and clear, and three Norman scouts came into view, riding abreast. They spoke no word among themselves, but proceeded warily, glancing to left and to right, scrutinizing every bush and tree, peering into the tangled thickets and essaying to probe the patches of deep forest gloom. But there was little there to arouse their suspicions and they rode on, sharp-eyed and erect, crossed the bridge and clattered up the road.

But scarcely had they passed out of sight than from southwards came a low, distant rumble. To the waiting English the sound was immediately recognizable as the pounding of multitudinous iron-shod hoofs. They listened, grimly estimating the convoy to comprise well over a thousand heavy-armed horsemen. As they came closer the earth began to throb as though deep within it a great heart had been set in motion. Louder grew the din and soon into full sight, making thunder on the cobbles, came the Norman cavalcade.

Immediately in the fore rode a knight whose arresting presence alone would have proclaimed him to be a personage of consequence. His armor was of simple and unadorned ring mail, but beneath it showed a tunic of orange silk heavily embroidered with pearls and

silver thread. The nosepiece of his helm was in place, partially concealing his visage, yet the deep lines about chin and mouth evidenced
the inborn habits of self-counsel and constancy of purpose; and
if an increasing corpulence had lost him much of the regal grace he
must have possessed in his youth, it was more than compensated by
the stern and compelling majesty of the flashing eye. He was flanked
by a pair of bodyguards on either side, armed cap-a-pie. Behind him
rode a formidable array of knights and men-at-arms whose rear
ranks stretched so far they were as yet lost in the distance.

The mighty column thundered onward to the bridge and the
nobleman in the lead started across, accompanied by his bodyguards.
His escort followed, breaking rank to file in pairs across the narrow
viaduct, reaching the safety of the other side in a seemingly endless
stream and moving on up the highway until they grew indistinct
in the distance. Still the English did not stir, only waited, motionless.
The passing Normans clearly had no suspicion of the outlaws' presence, no slightest sense of apprehension. They chatted noisily as they
rode by, casting never a glance at the dense forest wall. Then suddenly, sharp and loud, the battle horn sounded above the hubbub.
A barrage of arrows leveled at the entrance to the bridge felled a
dozen or more riders and their mounts, and thereupon the melee
of rolling, struggling bodies formed a physical barrier to all forward
motion, forcing the cavalcade to halt. Those horsemen who had
already embarked upon the crossing spurred forward in alarm and
for one fleeting instant the bridge was empty.

Then suddenly it was gone!

At first the Normans were too astonished to do anything but gape.
Those who had just reached the other side swung around in time to
see a pair of outlaws leap from the willow shrubs at their feet, plunge
into the water and swim rapidly away. They stared unbelievingly
at the bridgeless river, at the uprights standing there naked and
forlorn, at the loose planks floating crazily away on the flood, then
on to the other side where their own comrades, caught in the deadly
cross fire of English shafts, were being massacred with cool, experienced precision. A Norman knight, more valiant than the rest,
sought to go to their aid. "A moi!" he cried, and spurring his horse,
plunged straightway into the river. Others followed, and soon the
water was thronged with horsemen. But this had already been anticipated by the Wake, who had posted bowmen at strategic points
along the riverbank. Shrewdly they bided their time until the Nor-

mans reached the rapid current at mid-river, then they let fly an iron hail upon the tight-massed throng. The horses plunged madly, screaming in fear and pain, pitching their riders into the water, where, weighted down by their armor, they instantly sank out of sight. Only the agonized, fear-crazed beasts remained, and they, struggling vainly to escape from the crimson water, were borne swiftly down-river toward the sea.

Meanwhile the slaughter on the other side was terrible. The unexpectedness of the attack had momentarily unmanned the trapped Normans, turning the hitherto orderly ranks into a terrified, surging horde. They battled each other to find shelter for themselves behind their less exposed comrades. Soon the narrow space was filled with moans of the dying, the curses of the wounded, the screams of horses and the wild stomping of hoofs on the bloody cobbles. A few, from very habit, and midst a stream of senseless blasphemy, whipped out their swords and cast uncertainly about for the enemy, but long ere they could locate a single crouching form behind the dense foliage or in the overhanging branches above, they were brought down by a dozen shafts. Some broke away and darted for the river, only to find their escape cut off by a solid wall of twisted bodies which they attempted frantically but vainly to scale; others just sat in wild-eyed fascination, watching, as though they themselves were spectators having no part in this macabre performance.

But the Norman ranks were steadily thinning. Already the road was a ghastly quagmire of bodies crushed beneath iron-shod hoofs, and nowhere was there dry footspace for the living. But yet, revitalized by desperation, the Normans were slowly taking heart. "Ha! Rou!" The shrill cry of a frightened youth was heard with startled wonder and repeated by a dozen throats. "Ha! Rou! Ha! Rou!"—a miracle of sound having power to recall to mind other desperate, hard-fought battles and many a glorious victory. Painfully the scattered remnants of the Norman host began to draw together, to align themselves into some semblance of battle formation. But the Wake allowed them no time to re-form their shattered array. Above the din his voice rang out, "Axes, charge!" and for the first time the Normans caught a brief glimpse of their attackers. Springing from concealment, and with arms sinewed by ceaseless battle and toil, the English swung their two-handed axes above their heads and brought them crashing down to cleave in two the skulls of the Norman mounts. Their riders leaped aside and turned to flee, wading desperately through the muck. But afoot they were no match for the tall islanders who quickly overtook them, and, with the passionless skill of practiced veterans, severed head from trunk at a single blow. The slaughter was quickly over. A moment later, in obedience to a signal from their leader, the outlaws regained their horses, swept down the road and vanished.

The Conqueror did indeed reach Lincoln that night as planned, but with only half his men.

Chapter Seventeen

THE WEDDING

IT WAS shortly before noon of the following day when, beneath an ominous sky and with a savage wind at their backs, the Wake and his men swept through the Gronnaswald and drew rein before the cave. Leaping from Swallow's back, Hereward paused a moment to pat her steaming flank. "Good girl," he said, "good Swallow!" She turned and nuzzled him affectionately, as though to delay the inevitable moment when he must leave her, so he smiled at her wiles and loitered a moment, then, throwing the reins to a waiting groom, he strode swiftly away and followed his men into the cave.

He found the vast space already bustling with activity as the weary men unharnessed and hung their armor in place. There was much talk and laughter as they bathed in the cold waters of the rill and donned fresh clothing, for all were eager to forget the grim butchery of the Normans. In a little while they were seated about the dining board where mead-ale and hot food were set out, eating with hearty appetites, was-haeling merrily, talking of everything save yesterday's encounter—which was the one thing uppermost in every man's mind.

The Wake, clad in a freshly laundered blue linen tunic, listened thoughtfully as he dined. It was a routine which seldom varied, this overloud talk, this boisterous laughter; then later and for days to come the marked preference for solitude, the irritability, the long gloomy silences. Ofttimes at night the men fought and refought their individual struggles with some Norman, killing him again in their dreams. But of this no one spoke. They maintained a dogged pretense of indifference to all the slaughterings, to all the bloody yesterdays. It was the only way. For these were by nature peaceable men; men with no real love of warfare; men whose only goal was to return to the little plot of earth they called home, to be reunited to their wives and children, to regain their common freedom.

He became aware that someone stood beside him and looked up to find Martin Lightfoot patiently waiting for him to finish his repast; Martin, whose curious reserve forbade any show of joy at his master's safe return from these forays, yet who always found reasons to hover near at hand for days thereafter.

"What is it, son?" Hereward inquired.

"Lord," said Martin, "there is a man here, a prisoner, a Norman. He insists upon having word with you."

The Wake frowned. "Christ's beard! How did this new one find his way among us?"

"Nay, lord, be not alarmed. This man did not stumble upon our eyrie. He was brought here by Godrith the Forester, who found him yesterday in the fens near to death—to which state he is considerably closer today. He claims to have some information of great importance, but which he will impart to none but you."

The Wake arose. "Here is something that interests me," he said, "a dying Norman with a grudge! Take me to him."

He followed Lightfoot through the cave to a small natural alcove in the rock. At its entrance Martin paused an instant to reach down a torch from the wall, which, upon entering the chamber, he raised high above his head to illuminate a rough couch of animal pelts occupying the center of the floor.

Upon it, stretched out on his side, his back turned against them, lay a man of undoubted Norman origin. He appeared to be asleep, for his eyes were closed and the beads of sweat trickled unheeded down his face. Save for brogues and green chausses he was completely naked, revealing a frame which, though deficient in height, was muscled and wiry. His black hair was close-cropped to the head in front, at the back shaven from crown to nape after the fashion of the Normans. His arms were unmistakably those of a professional soldier, though now the wrists were braceleted in iron manacles whose severed chains hung loose. Hereward stooped and gently raised a linen cloth which lay across his back and saw beneath, and despite the heavy unguents, that the flesh was cruelly torn as though from repeated lashings with a spiked rawhide whip.

By now the man had opened his eyes and turned his head slightly in an effort to glimpse his visitors. He said nothing, however, but lay in expectant stillness, following each slightest movement of the Englishmen from the corner of his eye. Hereward motioned Lightfoot to hold the torch a little closer, then, stepping across the couch, he stooped and with the corner of a pelt wiped the sweat from the Norman's brow.

"I am Hereward Leofricsson," he said. "What is it you want to tell me?"

The Norman did not reply immediately, but took his time exploring the other's countenance in a minute appraisal. Satisfied at length that this must indeed be the rebel leader, he raised himself with pain from the couch and braced himself upon an elbow.

"Sir Wake," he began, in accents difficult to comprehend, "I have some information which, if you were a moneyed man, it would cost you much to know. As it is, the only payment I demand is that you keep me here in the safety of your forest until such time as you can provide me with passage on a ship sailing back to Normandy."

"You will first have to unbosom yourself," the Wake replied, "and let me determine if this information is worth the price."

The Norman considered this, then shrewdly shook his head. "My lord, only a dullard would agree to let another man's judgment stand betwixt him and a hanging, which is the fate you reputedly hold in store for all Normans who fall into your hands. Yet I had no course but to come to you since my recent master, Sir Guy de Lussac, was contriving for me an equally dismal death, a death which I only managed to evade because one of my comrades left a tool near by with which I could sever my manacles and flee. Wherefore it should at once be apparent to you that in my case it must be a straight bargain or nothing—your bounty for my knowledge. But be assured, Sir Wake, that you will not find yourself the loser in this compact, for," and here a slow, sly smile crossed his face, "my news concerns the lady Althya."

"The lady Althya?"

"Aye, in whom it is said the lord Hereward has more than a passing interest."

There was a moment's silence. Only the accustomed eyes of Martin Lightfoot could detect the imperceptible tightening of the muscles about Hereward's mouth, but to the Norman his face revealed nothing. "How did you come by such an unlikely tale?" he inquired.

"My lord, such gossip is current in Norman circles. The lady's men-at-arms assert that she has recently acquired the habit of absenting herself from Orchard Isle for hours at a stretch, and since she rides without an escort it is presumed that she does not go far, but has a heart interest in the neighborhood. Furthermore, her captain declares that it was the Wake who intercepted her party on the road back from Belsar's Hill this summer past, and after dispersing her retinue, himself escorted the lady Althya home across the fens —an act, he adds, concerning which the lady's plaints and imprecations were noticeably mild."

"This captain's tongue is busier than a woman's! But come, man, get on with the tale. I accede to the terms!"

"Well, Sir Wake, if all these rumors be true it follows that you will be interested to learn of Sir Guy's new plans with regard to her. It seems that, having wearied of the lady's repeated postponements of a wedding to which the king has long since given his consent, he plans to abduct her this very afternoon."

"The devil he does!"

"Nor is that all, for Sir Guy has made singular preparations for the reception of his bride at the castle, including new iron bars for the window of the tower chamber."

"What signifies that?"

"What signifies that! Does the lord Hereward, then, know nothing of Sir Guy's enmity for the lady's father, Turgis de St. Denys? Does he know nothing of Turgis' fate? Does he know nothing of Sir Guy's first wife, who was murdered in this same room in a most diabolical manner? It is common knowledge at Cruc Maur that a similar fate is in store for Sir Guy's new bride. Ofttimes in his cups he vows that, once in possession of her dowry, he will execute his long-planned vengeance with the same precision as if her father had lived to witness it."

Hereward's large hands closed upon the Norman's shoulders in a grip that made the little body squirm. "Where is the ceremony scheduled to take place?"

"I do not know—I do not know! As my lord can see, I quit the castle somewhat hurriedly."

The Wake sprang up. "Safeguard him against my return," he shouted to Lightfoot, and vanished.

Back in the cave he found the men still loitering about the dining board, talking merrily and bursting into snatches of song. They fell abruptly silent as Hereward reappeared, buckling his sword belt, so recently removed, back around his waist. Beneath the bronzed skin his face was pale with wrath held well in check, and realizing that something was seriously amiss, the men scarce breathed, but sat in muted curiosity waiting for him to speak.

"Men," he cried, "I have a score to settle and am in sore need of the help of a dozen champions. This being a private matter, it follows that you are all exempted from the obligation to fight, wherefore I put it to you squarely—who will volunteer?"

A tumult of eager assents greeted his words and the men leaped up from their benches and crowded around him. Eadric was the first to spring to his side. The wild man laid a tight grip on Hereward's forearm and his green eyes were fierce and probing.

"If you have a score, share it!" he demanded. "Do not take the risk of attempting to settle it without proper deliberation or adequate support."

"Eadric, man, there is no time for speeching," the Wake returned shortly. "In your good hands do I leave the selection of the required men. Choose them for swordsmanship, but longbows may be needed. Have them repair singly or in pairs to Godrith's cottage, where I shall look for them anon." With that, and despite their remonstrances, he turned and sped from the cave, leaving them staring after him in troubled wonder.

A few moments later Hereward was taking off across the fens on Swallow's back. It seemed more the hour of nightfall than that of midday, for the black storm clouds hung low and their sullen light cut off all the distances. The wind was increasing. It buffeted the sedges and new-grown reeds, flinging them back upon their withered undergrowths, and on the isles the fruit blossoms fell like flurries of snow to the sodden turf. The meres lay black, their waters churning as though impelled by the ocean's thundering tide, whilst from the air above them the birds had fled, save for a lone sea gull being tossed helplessly inland upon the blast.

As Hereward neared Orchard Isle he slackened his pace till he could dimly make out a sentry's metal casque afar off through the gloom. This would no doubt indicate that the second sentry was likewise at his customary post overlooking the southern fen, for during their meetings Althya had told him much concerning her home. He swung about, therefore, in a half circle, approaching the isle hidden from all watchful eyes by the willow grove. At the fen bank he dismounted, and bidding Swallow stand fast, he continued on afoot, moving cautiously beneath the drooping boughs.

In a little while he sighted the stone and timber manor standing, incomplete still, among the apple trees. As he drew near he halted an instant in the shadow of a lilac bush to survey the domain. The sentry now stood a short way off to the left, his back barely visible through the heavy foliage. The house had a deserted look, its portal closed, its windows shuttered against the approaching storm. Only the courtyard, as yet no more than a treeless, unpaved space before the door, gave him the answer he was seeking. It evidenced that a body of horsemen had loitered here a short while since, for the hoofprints of their mounts were still fresh in the moist earth. Hereward swore volubly. For all his haste, then, he had come too late! De Lussac and his men had been, and gone!

He slipped from cover and sped across the court. Finding the portal shut fast, he prized up the latch of a window shutter with his dagger and squeezed through the narrow aperture. He found himself in the main hall, a spacious chamber whose roof beams were of handsomely carved oak, and whose walls were likewise paneled. At its far end a fireplace was recessed in the thickness of the wall; to its left, an ornamental archway led to an outer chamber from whence, even above the howling of the wind, came the boisterous laughter and coarse jokes of the men-at-arms at play.

A moment later the Wake stood within the archway looking down upon them. There were, he calculated, about fifteen men, wine cups in hand, some gathered around a table upon which a game of chess was in progress, the rest frolicking with two women whom he knew to be Althya's maids, Amalie and Bernardine. At first they all remained oblivious to his presence and swiftly his eyes ranged about the room, taking stock of his surroundings; the narrow windows to the south; the swords and armor hanging on the wall to the left; to the right, the steep stone steps leading below to the wine cellar, its massive, iron-clad door ajar, the key in the lock. But one by one the men began to be aware of the tall Englishman blocking their archway and a tense hush fell as they stared up at him, too astonished to speak. The captain, who was just about to checkmate his opponent, found the silence more disturbing than the noise and looked up in annoyance. Then his chin dropped.

"You!" he gasped.

"Once again, at your service."

The captain leaped to his feet and snatched his sword from the wall.

"Stand back, men," he ordered. "This is my affair!"

"Aye, leave your captain be, lads." The Wake spoke pleasantly, but there was a tension about his mouth that belied his tone. "He and I are old adversaries and 'tis a matter of honor with him to take me singly."

Scarcely had he finished speaking when the captain lunged, thinking to catch the Englishman off guard, but Hereward sprang aside, unsheathing as he did so. For a full moment thereafter they were content to parry, each man watchful, each testing his opponent and measuring his skill. Hereward was distinctly at a disadvantage in that, despite the captain's orders to his men to stand aloof from the fight, he dared not turn his back upon them. Furthermore, he soon discovered that the Norman was an excellent swordsman, lithe and strong, and exceptionally nimble of foot. But he was conceited, too, as was evidenced not only by his belief in his own ability to win the blood money for the Wake's capture singlehanded, but by his affected grace of movement in action which could only have been acquired by long years of practice. Such a man could perhaps be led into error by subtle deception.

Accordingly, therefore, the Wake fell back, giving ground with seeming reluctance, retreating step by step until he was almost backed against the wall. The men-at-arms watched their captain with admiration, unsparing of their compliments. But yet the Norman was too wary and too experienced a swordsman to permit himself to be distracted by the applause of the audience. Moreover, he was keenly aware that the Englishman was on the defensive and could retreat no further and he kept a shrewd and calculating eye upon him, parrying, cutting, biding his time, until, after a clever feint, he sprang forward in a lightning thrust at the heart. The men-at-arms, anticipating the kill, sent up roars of delight which rebounded among the roof beams, then died abruptly, as, with a thrust too swift for their eyes to follow, the Englishman sent their captain's sword clattering to the floor. An instant later the point of the Wake's blade was pricking his astonished opponent's throat, drawing from it a thin trickle of blood.

"Do not stir, men, or your captain's life is forfeit." The pleasantness was quite gone from the Englishman's voice and from the look in his eye he would have ripped open the Norman's throat without compunction.

The men-at-arms glanced uncertainly at the captain, seeking some directive. They quite obviously had not yet connected this yellow-haired Englishman with the brown-haired potter of the summer past, having no such good reason as the captain to remember his features. To them it appeared that their superior had some personal grudge against the stranger for which he desired a personal vengeance, though he for the moment was showing concern only for his neck, which he found it expedient to stretch to its fullest in an effort to escape the rude proddings of the blade.

"Bid your men retire to the cellar—and the women, too," the Englishman was saying.

Only for an instant did the captain waver. His fury was such that he would have ordered them to snatch their swords from the wall and charge instead, had the stakes been other than his own throat. But as matters stood he was blinded to alternatives.

"Retire to the cellar," he ordered.

In a state of mild curiosity as to the Englishman's intentions, the men and their female companions turned and filed slowly down the steps. They did not disappear from sight, however, but halted just beyond the portal, crowding together like a flock of tractable sheep and watching the proceedings with interest.

"Now," continued the Wake to the captain, "go to the window and summon the guards—both of them."

Slowly the captain moved to obey. Upon reaching the window, however, he hesitated, casting desperately about for some means of alerting the two sentries.

"Come," snapped the Wake, with a gentle prod which caused the blood to run anew, "do your scheming when I am gone. The quarry's afoot and must be run to soil. I have no mind to tarry!"

A moment later, therefore, in compliance with their captain's summons, the sentries came in on the run, their hands resting on their sword hilts. They stopped short at the sight of the Englishman holding their superior at bay, but after some slight indecision obeyed the latter's instructions to join their comrades below.

The Wake now turned his undivided attention to the captain. "I could kill you," he said, "save that I would not want my hands needlessly stained with blood on my wedding day. Wherefore I am disposed to make a bargain with you. I shall spare your life; you will apprise me of the arrangements for your lady's wedding."

The captain appeared to be considering the matter, but with no great degree of concentration. Indeed, his thoughts seemed to have winged away to other matters; to the nearby wall at which he was so intently gazing, and to the weapons hung thereon. But the Wake quickly broke in upon the formulation of any plan and his voice had a sharp, warning edge.

"Speak or, as God lives, I'll rip out your scandalmongering woman's tongue!"

The captain shrugged and surrendered. "Sir Guy has taken her to Gedney in the Deeping Fen," he replied.

"Who is to wed them?"

"The Norman priest in the chapel there."

"How long ago did he leave?"

"But a short while since—about the hour of noonday."

"How many men did he take?"

"Twenty or more."

The Wake relaxed the pressure of his sword tip against the captain's throat. "Then by the terms of our compact I leave you your life," he said, "which, however, I shall soon enough return to claim if I find you are lying. Now get below with your men!"

The captain obeyed promptly and the Wake locked the door upon him and slipped the key in his pouch. A moment later he had quit the house and was speeding back across the courtyard through a driving rain, whistling for Swallow as he ran. She heard his call and broke from the duskiness among the willows, her long mane whipped by the wind, her flanks wet and glistening. "Come, girl," he urged, as he leaped into the saddle, "there is little time!" and the great white beast set her nose to the wind and raced away across the fens toward Bourne.

The last of his men had just arrived when he reached old Godrith's cottage. He found them gathered about the fire holding their sodden brogans to the flames and watching the vapor arise, whilst Edgitha, the old man's granddaughter, passed among them with horns of steaming ale. They hastily replaced their footwear when Hereward entered and stood and listened without surprise as he explained the purpose of the mission, for not one among them but knew of their leader's tender feelings for the lady Althya.

"I have ascertained that the wedding is to be held in the chapel at Gedney-Deeping," he informed them. "De Lussac will have had a goodly start, but this we can substantially narrow by quitting the road at Tatten and following the driftway by Devil's Dike."

"But Gedney Isle is low and flat and gives an unobstructed view of the open fen for miles around," warned old Godrith. "There is no way in which a dozen mounted Englishmen can come upon it unobserved. De Lussac cannot fail to have posted lookouts, and by the time you reach the isle he will have for you as fine a reception as ever we prepared for a Norman convoy on the Lincoln road."

"Which is why," replied the Wake, "one man only shall appear to be approaching—and he afoot."

"And what of the chapel," inquired Eadric, "is it small enough to be surrounded by a dozen men?"

"Surrounded it need not be. It has but a single door."

"Can they not fire upon us from the windows?"

"The windows are too high for use as arrow slits; too narrow for egress."

"And what are the numerical odds against us?"

"Two to one, though it argues more in that we will be the attackers, and perhaps without cover."

"Cover or no," cried Eadric, "we will soon enough reverse the balance if you but find a way for us to come upon them unsuspected."

" 'Tis what I count upon," said the Wake. "But now let us get gone with all speed, lest we arrive to find them already wed."

"Should that befall," quoth Eadric lightly, "then more pity for de Lussac, in that propriety would compel us to widow his bride ere another man could wed her!"

As they drained their horns and reached for their sword belts and cloaks, Edgitha, who had been listening intently to the conversation, approached Hereward, a horn of steaming ale in her hand.

"My lord," she said, "it is not much our cottage can offer you, but since your clothes are rain-soaked and the ride to Gedney is long, my grandfather's brew might well help to safeguard you against ague and chill."

Impatiently Hereward waved aside the ale and was about to brush past her when his attention was arrested by something in the upturned face so startlingly resemblant of another's countenance that involuntarily he halted. How swift had been the passage of the years! Here was Hugh's child, Edgitha; this blossoming lass with sun-ripe hair and eyes as deep and mystic as the summer meres; for whose cradle he had tracked the rime-fox to his lair and bereft him of his snowy pelt; for whose childhood joy he had netted and tamed the wood thrush with the crystal voice. And now, so soon, she was grown to lovely maidenhood.

He ignored her offering, but touched a hand to her cheek and gazed deep into her face. "God keep you, little one," he said. An instant later he was gone and Edgitha stood in the doorway, horn in hand, and watched him ride away through the blinding rain.

The tiny isle of Gedney lay flat and solitary in the Deeping Fen, its handful of low, reed-thatched cots blending somberly with its bottoms and marshy meadows. There was about it a subtle air of malaise, as though instinctively it shunned all kinship with air and sun and sky, and would rejoice to be reclaimed once again by its natural element, the sea. Only its ancient stone and flint chapel rose to any noticeable height above the surrounding fen, though it, too, seemed somehow ill at ease in its new guise as a place of Christian worship, where once men bent the knee to the likeness of the dark god Tiw, to meet whom was death.

This melancholy spot, with its aged yews and moldering burial yard, seemed infinitely better suited to a funeral than to a wedding, but unlike any other community in the fens, it offered to de Lussac two unique advantages. Not only was it presided over by a Norman priest, but by a priest who, being of gentle birth but questionable fortitude, had embraced the ministry more to evade the perils of warrior life than for reasons of spiritual inclination, and who therefore could be induced for a small consideration to ignore any protests the bride might chance to make during the ceremony and to mis-hear any negative replies.

It was midafternoon of this wild April day before the wedding party reached Gedney. Sir Guy had taken no chances of arriving at his destination to find the lady Althya once again escaped. This time she traveled on horseback in plain view of all, hedged in by men-at-arms, her mount being tethered to that of Sir Guy, who rode beside her. By the time they reached the chapel she was in a state of exhaustion from having battled her abductors all the way from Orchard Isle, yet still it took three of them to drag her from her horse and full many a well-aimed blow she landed in the struggle. But at last her strength was spent and they lifted her up and carried her into the chapel. Sir Guy bellowed to the priest in the sacristy to come out and begin his reading, then, having set two sentries to guard the chapel door, he slammed it shut against the storm.

Left outside on such a day, the two sentries exchanged glances which more clearly bespoke a growing mistrust of one another than the bitter resentment they were feeling toward their master, then silently they turned their attention to the landscape over which they had been assigned to watch. From the chapel steps one could normally survey an illimitable expanse of marshland, but today the view was so shortened by rain that even the islet's fenny shores were vague and indistinct. The two men shivered and pressed back against the door in an effort to avail themselves of what little shelter was afforded by the lintel above. Inwardly they cursed the wind. They cursed the icy rain that seeped through their hauberks and wet them to the skin. They cursed the soldier's lot and their own especial misfortune at having fallen henchmen to Sir Guy de Lussac of Cruc Maur. And if his boast was true that no man, once employed by him, ever quit his service, it was true only because de Lussac made it true; because those who were rash enough to signify a desire to be quit of him invariably vanished.

"If Jules managed to effect an escape after all," one of them remarked somewhat furtively, "he will be the first among us ever to do so."

The other considered the point. "I doubt he got clear away," he replied. "How far could he travel afoot? How long can a man keep going with a tattered hide?"

"Mayhap a fenman found him and gave him succor."

"An Englishman succor a Norman! Ha! More like, seeing he already had one foot in hell, they helped him across the threshold by throwing him in the marsh."

"Jesu, man, you may be right. That would certainly account for our having found no trace of him—dead or alive. In any case, it will go hard on the fellow who left the filer handy if Sir Guy ever learns his name."

"Aye, that it will—that it will."

They fell silent, listening to the wild plunging of the weather and the still wilder outbursts issuing from the chapel. Sir Guy's verbiage was particularly diverting today, abounding in colorful allusion and contrasting effects, but still this ceremony gave no promise of being the speedy one he had planned. The wench was evidently remaining stubborn in her refusal to be wed. Mille tonnerres! Had they not even got her to the altar yet? They could hear her just the other side of the door grappling with the men. But she would soon grow weary as a hunted doe, and the sooner the better for all anyone cared. They wanted only to get gone from here. It was none of their concern whom their master wedded, or what maniacal plans he had in mind for his new bride.

Their musing was interrupted by a faint sound coming from out of the gloom over by the dikeside. They stepped from their shelter and peered intently in that direction, listening. The sound had the harsh, repetitive insistence of the cry of a stricken bird, but as it grew nearer and more distinct they took it to be nothing more than a creaking wheel. And so it proved to be, for in a little while a huge white mare emerged from the dusk, drawing a wain of hay. She was a massive brute who clearly set at nought the wild buffets of wind and weather. So, indeed, did the tall fenman who strode alongside her, his sodden tunic cleaving to his skin, his long hair streaming with rain. He seemed to be in a vast hurry, for he came on at rapid pace and there was about his countenance an expression so stern and resolute that instinctively the Normans dropped their hands to their sword hilts. But he paid them no heed, gazing straight ahead and casting never a glance in their direction, as though his business was of such a pressing nature that he had failed to take cognizance of their presence, or even of the long row of Norman mounts tethered to the chapel wall.

The sentries relaxed and returned to their shelter, shaking the water from their metal casques and indulging in many an obscene oath as it seeped beneath their hauberks and made icy runnels down their necks. They looked up again just as the fenman passed them by, and the wain came abreast of the chapel door. They noted with mild curiosity that the hay atop the wain was slowly being displaced, not so much, it seemed to them, by the capricious action of the wind as by the sure design of some more determinate agency. But their leisurely speculations were ended abruptly as a deadly arrow hail was leveled at them from the direction of the wain and they dropped where they stood, their last futile cries being swallowed by the storm.

An instant later the Wake's men sprang from cover, shedding hay as they ran. They were all fully armed, save Hereward, who lost no time in possessing himself of the dead sentries' weapons, then, with a signal to his men to follow closely at his heels, he flung open the chapel door and entered.

"Do not reach for your weapons! Turn and stand easy!"

The order was rapped out so sharply that the Normans heard it above the shouting of the hurricane and swung around to find the

Wake's men already ranged along the chapel's rear wall, their long-bows poised, shafts drawn to head. The Wake himself, after a swift glance at Althya, had moved on down the aisle and now halted mid-way, and though a few of the Norman men-at-arms could not fully comprehend an order issued in English, they needed but a single glance at the bowmen to be certain of its meaning. Only one man made to draw his sword and he was instantly dropped with a shaft through the windpipe. The priest did not stir. De Lussac, who had somehow managed to step behind Althya, remained motionless, one hand gripping her forearm, the other concealed behind her back.

"De Lussac, let the lady come forward!"

De Lussac made no motion to comply. Instead he swore lustily. "At him, men!" he cried. "At him! 'Tis the Wake! A fortune for his capture!"

Still the men did not stir, save to shift their glances from their master back to the stalwart English bowmen. They seemed to be estimating their individual chances of surviving an assault in the face of a deadly volley of shafts, which chances they apparently found none too encouraging.

"Aye, men," said the Wake, following their thoughts, "dead heroes reap no benefits other than their women's tears and prayers. My men would drop a round dozen of you the instant you moved in my direction, and those of you who were left would be outnumbered, and likely outmatched. Wherefore stand aloof from this quarrel and no harm shall come to you, that I vow."

"Fools!" cried de Lussac, seeing them won over. "Fools! Would you chance an Englishman's honor?"

"Better," snapped the Wake, "chance an Englishman's honor than an Englishman's longbow. Leastways, they are not so certain to die."

For some reason this latter observation had a magical effect upon de Lussac. It seemed to recall to his mind something he had over-looked, something of a pleasurable nature, something to his advan-tage. His wrath dissipated as vapor in a breeze. He smiled.

"Aye," he said, "death comes hard to all, but especially to the young—the very young."

His words were too honeyed not to possess a lethal content and Hereward froze. Now, for the first time, he noted the position of de Lussac's partially hidden arm and understood its significance. So that was it. Rather than give up Althya, he would kill her! A single false move and de Lussac would drive home the blade!

Instinctively Hereward retreated a pace and for the first time in his life he knew what it was to be possessed of an icy fear. Doggedly he strove to think above the turmoil in his brain, but violent, meteoric flashes blocked out all ability to reason or act. He knew that de Lussac was speaking once again, but no sound came to him over the pounding in his own ears. The chapel, the men, all faded from his vision and he was aware only of Althya's eyes fixed upon him; of her white face; of her hair, disheveled and clinging damply to her cheeks. This was how he most often thought of her. This was how he had first seen her, wet and tired and very frightened.

It was Althya's mute terror that shocked him out of his apathy and forced him to overcome the wild disorder in his brain. He must find a way. He must think! He must think! He must wrangle, argue —fight for time. Slowly, as if from out of some vast hollow space, de Lussac's voice began to come back to him and with a mighty effort Hereward tore his gaze from Althya's face and struggled to understand the words.

"—and if you are thinking," de Lussac was saying, "of rushing gallantly down the aisle in an effort to halt my blade, pray desist. The lady would be dead before you reached her. Nor, since I stand behind her, can your bowmen level their shafts at me without first killing her. You see, Sir Wake, I am not a man to easily relinquish my rights once they have been firmly established. The lady Althya is my legal betrothed, would at this moment be my wife had you not interrupted the ceremony. But your appearance was perhaps providential, for since you love her, as indeed you must to have rushed so precipitously to her aid, I will set a condition whereby you can free her of all my claims for all time. I will exchange her life, Sir Wake—for yours."

The Wake's face was expressionless. He appeared now to be cool and composed and had taken up his customary stance, legs apart, thumbs hooked in belt. He needed no time to deliberate de Lussac's proposal. "Fair enough," he said.

De Lussac regarded him incredulously and not a little suspiciously. "Perhaps you do not understand," he said. "This time you will find no opportunity for tricks or stratagems. I shall require you to dis-arm where you stand, to step up here and take the girl's place betwixt myself and your bowmen, then to voluntarily and without delay present your breast to my dagger."

"I am agreed."

"Nor shall you attempt either to retaliate, or to evade or displace the thrust. You will surrender yourself passively and unresistingly —the lamb brought to slaughter. And to bind you to these terms, and as a warranty for your good faith, I shall require you to swear to abide by them, upon your knightly honor."

This latter stipulation, in view of de Lussac's former disparagement of English honor, brought a brief smile to Hereward's face. "I do swear to abide by them," he said, "upon my knightly honor."

"Then our bargain is made. After you have taken the girl's place, she may go free."

Hereward unbuckled his belt and dropped it to the floor, then moved on down the aisle, his eyes on Althya's face. De Lussac was still retaining his grip on her arm, reluctant even now to keep his word and release her, but in a moment Hereward had pried loose the viselike fingers. "Go, my love," he said softly. "Wait outside. Eadric will come to you there." She seemed not to hear, standing uncertain and frightened, her face drained of color as she struggled to put some question into words. And he, seeing her so overcome, sighed and smiled down at her and with ineffable tenderness stroked the damp hair from her brow. "Go, my little love," he said again. This time she heard him and, reassured by his calm, turned to do as she was bid. And Hereward waited, facing de Lussac, listening to her footsteps recede down the aisle and fade away as she reached the open.

"Now," he said.

De Lussac smiled, making no effort to hide his soaring elation. Beneath his sleeve the muscles writhed as he gathered strength and raised the dagger above his head, his practiced warrior's eye marking out the spot that held the living heart. Then, just as he was about to strike, he hesitated and a frown creased his brow. His gaze drifted thoughtfully past Hereward, coming to rest on the long row of bowmen poised to loose their shafts. "But what," he inquired, "of them?"

"Them?"

"The bowmen."

The sudden revelation of de Lussac's problem brought a twinkle to the Wake's eyes. "Aye," he said, "I conceive you, but 'tis your dilemma, not mine. I have agreed to let you kill me and am here awaiting, whenever it pleasures you to strike. But you required of me no post-mortem assurances and once I am dead there will be nothing to hinder my men from filling your hide with shafts."

An angry flush mounted slowly to de Lussac's brow. "What you are saying is that I will have to spare your life, if you are to be in a position to protect mine."

"Nay, man," laughed the Wake, " 'tis you who are saying it. I am offering no solution to your problem, though obviously such an arrangement as you suggest would have advantages to us both."

De Lussac's eyes blazed, but for once, because he could not endure complete humiliation before his men, he contained his wrath. Slowly he resheathed his dagger, but when at last he spoke his words were low and thick with the brutal fury that could not long be held in check.

"Hereward Leofricsson," he said, "you may depart from here alive and free, but go in the knowledge that when at last your luck runs out my vengeance will reach you. 'Tis not a clean dagger thrust will await you then, but the fate which even the bravest man, fearless in face of death, holds in mortal dread—the eternal darkness of the dungeon cell. For within the narrow confines of four walls there are ways to reduce the sturdiest frame to a shattered hulk, yet still preserve that precious flicker of life which chains the unhappy spirit to earth. You, Sir Wake, are like to lose your own identity beneath my prolonged treatment, and develop instead strange and abhorrent characteristics. An eagle loses his nature when his wings are clipped."

" 'Twill be a day," quoth the Wake, "when the eagle is captive to the kite."

He turned and with unhurried stride made his way back down the aisle, pausing midway to retrieve his belt and buckle it about his waist. The Normans and English, having been out of earshot during the entire conversation, were puzzled by this new turn of events and stood watching in silent curiosity. At the door the Wake turned and signaled his men to exit, himself standing aside to let them file out. When the last of them was gone he halted an instant in the doorway, his tall frame silhouetted against the gray sky.

"You had best all remain here a space," he said, "for so long as we are within range, our shafts shall greet any man who attempts to quit the chapel." So saying he closed the door.

Outside he found Swallow already freed from the wain and fitted with a Norman saddle. He set Althya on the mare's broad back and mounted behind her, then, after his men had commandeered horses for themselves and dispersed the remainder to hinder pursuit, they all thundered away from Gedney Isle and were soon safe among the unfrequented bypaths of the fens.

At a crossroads in a wood Hereward drew rein, pausing under cover of an oak to wave farewell to his men and watch them until the last one was out of sight beyond the trees. Then he looked down at Althya and tightened his arms about her.

"Dear one," he said, "I'm a sorry choice of a husband for any girl, with scarcely a silver penny in my pocket and not an ell of land in all of England I can call my own. Yet despite it, this summer past you were willing to wed me. If you will have me still, let me hear it and I'll swear to love no other woman from this day forward."

He waited anxiously for her answer, but Althya, who had oft-times wept because Hereward would not wed her, wept now because he would. So he took her face between his big brown hands, and setting to with a will, kissed away her tears.

"Come," he murmured presently, "we will find us a monk to marry us."

He turned Swallow's nose to southward and once again they set off into the hurricane. The rain turned the landscape into a misty waste and the wind howled across the vast open spaces, trampling the reeds, wildly tossing the sallows, lashing at the trees and cracking their limbs, so the whole fen seemed to cry aloud in agony. The air was black, lighted occasionally by brilliant lightning flashes, and even to Hereward, with his uncanny knowledge of the fens and his fenman's discerning eyes, the way soon became difficult, for the hidden paths were washed out and he found it necessary to dismount and lead Swallow by the bridle, seeking solid footing beneath the floods.

Walking thus beside Althya, he thought back upon their first chance meeting; of her bitter words at York and her unwitting retraction of them at Belsar's Hill. He thought of Toustin whom she had loved, and he had killed; who lay buried away beyond the Humber, far from his lifetime loves and lifetime ties. He thought of everything Althya had to lose by marriage to him and cheerlessly he pondered the wisdom of his present action. Was he not, in binding her destiny to his, also binding her to a way of life in which the obstacles to be overcome loomed larger with every passing day?

And when at last they reached the monastery isle and he lifted her down from Swallow's back, he held her thoughtfully in his arms and pressed his rain-drenched cheek to hers.

"Althya," he said, "I am a man with a price upon his head. Are you sure you won't regret it?" And when her negative reply swept away all his doubts, he said no more, but led her up the steps to the chapel where he found a monk to wed them.

The monk, an aged man, was wrestling with an obstreperous window shutter that had escaped from its lock and was banging back and forth on ancient and querulous hinges. So engrossed was he in his efforts, and so hazardous the task of holding his perch on the high sill against the persistent efforts of the hurricane to dislodge him, that he was left in ignorance of the approach of the bridal couple. He leaped like a trout when they suddenly appeared below him as if from out of a thunderclap, and when Hereward explained the purpose of their visit he courteously concealed his surprise that they had hazarded the fens on such a night to be wed. Such eagerness on their part seemed contradicted by the bride's red eyes, for she looked as though she had wept all day. Also he noted that she was a Norman noblewoman and he the English rebel leader who reputedly misliked all Normans. But the holy man had acquired a certain wisdom along with his gray hairs and refrained from questioning them. Instead, he busied himself with the necessary arrangements, even lighting, with paternal kindliness, a few tapers on the altar to relieve the starkness of the humble chapel and give it a festive glow.

But his kindliness was unavailing, for such was the splendor of the hurricane that no sooner had he lighted the tapers than they flickered and went out, so the ceremony was performed in darkness. As the storm increased, the wind rushed with such force through the chinks in the wattled walls that the monk's kirtle was almost reft from his frail form, rain poured through the cracks in the shutters, and lightning lit the chapel bright as day.

"Do you, Althya, take this man . . ." The storm carried the rest away.

The monk paused to give Althya time to answer, but what her answer was the good man never knew, for at that moment the chapel door fell in and the long arms of the willows reached right inside and clutched at the silken garments which clothed the Virgin's image. Hurriedly, therefore, the holy man finished the ceremony and blessed them. Delicately he offered them shelter for the night, and when this was refused, he bade them "Godspeed" and hastened away.

Then once again the Wake lifted his bride upon the broad back of Mare Swallow and, breasting the hurricane, the great white beast headed back across the fens and Hereward sought shelter for the night in the secret, hidden labyrinths of the Gronnaswald.

Chapter Eighteen

THE LAST FORAY

IT WAS the dull roar of the surf upon the beach below that first broke upon de Lussac's consciousness. He lay still awhile, listening, straining unsuccessfully to identify the sound. He opened his eyes and stared up at the ceiling, then, finding something familiar in the ornate oaken beams, he let his glance drift slowly across them and on down the walls. His attention quickened as he made out a man's head hovering in mid-air without a body to sustain it. Curious sight, a human head without a body! And how gray was this face, how cruel, how terrible in its impassivity. De Lussac felt an unpleasant chill creep through his limbs as he lay motionlessly contemplating it, returning its fixed stare. Then, in a transport of relief, he saw that the head had horns. A la bonne heure! That was better—more natural! He had seen this thing before. But where? Ah, the stone bas-relief in the wall at Cruc Maur. That was where he must be then, in the Hall of his own castle by the sea.

Painfully he raised his head. He was sprawled out upon a tapestry which he guessed he had wrenched from the wall in a moment of savage frenzy. His blue silk tunic was filthy with the vile spewings of a prolonged debauch, and his customarily immaculate chin was now beclouded by a dark stubble of several days' growth.

God damn! God damn!

He pulled himself together and struggled to his feet, standing there with legs apart like a mariner braced against a heavy sea, waiting for the calm, waiting for the room to cease its crazy teetering. He looked about him, cursing again at the sight of the devastation he had wrought; the massive table, usually requiring two strong men to move, overturned by himself alone; the broken stools and benches; wine flagons scattered everywhere, one, by some happy chance, still standing upright. He eyed it thirstily, then stumbled toward it and fell upon his knees. But he had misjudged its distance and was forced to stretch full length upon his stomach to reach it. When at last his trembling hands seemed about to close around it, it tipped like a drunken thing and fell on its side, its crimson contents spilling out over the floor. De Lussac lay still, staring at it in spellbound fascination, seeing not a pool of wine but a pool of blood.

The Wake's blood!

Aye, that was what he was running from. His memory was clearing now, rekindling his anger with a ferocity that made his vitals squirm. Gedney—Althya—Hereward Leofricsson! How many months had passed since then? Three—three cursed months and still he had been unable to devise a plan to trap the Wake. He had sworn to do it; he had sworn that if there was a way he would find it. Yet instead, this was how he spent his nights and days, seeking forgetfulness where he should be deliberately remembering, scheming, plotting.

God damn! God damn!

His men watched him curiously as he stumbled from the Hall, climbed the sea wall and crossed the beach beyond. Here he disrobed and lay down at the water's edge, letting the cool waves wash over him, feeling the early morning sun relax his taut nerves and melt the stiffness from his limbs. "Fool!" he muttered. "The man's a fool who lies sodden on the floor and leaves his enemy claim the field." Thusly did he ponder. And in a little while, having sung a requiem to his own inertia, he returned to the castle where he had himself shaved and donned fresh clothing, then he ordered the Hall to be set to rights and a large repast prepared.

He breakfasted alone in brooding silence, ignoring the wine flagon set conveniently at his elbow and sipping instead, in superb sobriety, a cup of fresh spring water.

How was it possible, he reflected, for so large a body of horsemen as the Wake must command to so perfectly cover their traces, to come and go across the open fen unseen? Did they travel by night? No, such a system would be too hazardous, would involve the loss of too many men. But then, nor did they travel by day. This de Lussac himself had ascertained by setting spies to watch the fens after the first convoy had been attacked last spring, spies who watched in relays night and day without ever setting eyes on the Wake and his men. How, then, if the rebels held out in the Gronnaswald, could they operate along the Lincoln road without crossing the fen? By what route did they come and go? Therein lay a riddle, and the man who unriddled it would have served his king well.

And what of the Conqueror in these past months? What had he been doing? There had been no further word of him since rumor had it that he reached Lincoln with his escort badly mauled, so no doubt he was still holed up in that enfamined city; no doubt he, too, had learned that there was no traveling the Lincoln road while the Wake was free to roam it at will. One thing was certain, William had shown exceeding poor judgment in heading for Lincoln in the first place. If a way was ever to be found to trap the Wake it would not be found up there. It would be found right here in the fens where were to be found men who had known him from boyhood, men who knew his ways, men who had his confidence, men who knew the countryside as well as he and therefore knew the secret of his comings and goings, men who . . . Dear Jesus!

De Lussac halted his knife midway to his mouth and stared intently at nothing. Ha! To think that so simple a solution could have eluded him so long. But now how clear—how damnably clear! His knife clattered to his plate. Leaping to his feet, he rushed like a madman down the steps to the court and bellowed for his horse, his men-at-arms and Hubert, his tracker, then, without vouchsafing any explanation, he led them all off at top speed in the direction of Bourne.

"Nay, my child," old Godrith was saying, "you exaggerate the case. I think 'tis less of spiritual love you feel for our young lord, and more of earthly passion. But no matter. Unrequited love is doomed to infecundity as surely as the fruit bud that withers on the bough."

"You have lectured me at length, dear Grandsire," Edgitha replied, "and I have listened dutifully, bearing in mind your love for me and how you counsel me out of the wisdom of your years. But yet, though I could will it otherwise, your words have brought me neither solace nor enlightenment. For what I feel in my young and injudicious heart has still the power to outargue all your logic."

"This stupidity, child, is like to lose you a good husbandman. I fear Letwold will tire of waiting and seek a wife elsewhere. Wed him, Edgitha! Wed him now. He understands and will be patient. You will come to love him when you see his likeness in the face of your suckling babe. You will come to look back in time and say, 'This is love; the other was but sweet infatuation.' "

"Indeed, Grandsire, you may be right. But do not press me yet awhile, I beg you. Would you have me so dishonor this good Letwold as to carry to his hearthside the image of another?"

"Child, child," murmured Godrith in distress, "your own heart takes part against yourself——"

He broke off suddenly and cocked an ear as the clatter of horses' hoofs resounded from afar. He crossed to the window and peered through the chinks in the shutters, waiting there as the sound increased and the horsemen came into view. He expected them to ride on past his cottage, but instead de Lussac and his troop drew rein directly in front of it and the old man turned from the window, his face paling.

"Quick, little one," he said to Edgitha, " 'tis here they come. Haste, haste, back into hiding—and see you leave behind no trace of your presence."

The girl obeyed instantly, first retrieving her spindle, then starting up the ladder in the center of the room to the loft above. Godrith watched her progress anxiously. Just as she reached the top and climbed through the open trap, a heavy knocking sounded on the door. "Open up! open up!" came de Lussac's voice. "Open up, in there!" Swiftly the old man removed the ladder, setting it down inconspicuously in a corner, then, with a last hasty glance ceilingwards to make sure the girl had shut the trap, he raised the oaken bar from the door and flung it open.

"Forgiveness for the delay, my lord," he said, bowing respectfully. "I am an old man and move more slowly with every dawning."

De Lussac made no reply, only pushed past him and entered, followed by some eight or ten of his men. He glanced keenly about the solitary room that comprised the old man's abode, then, slamming shut the door, he nodded to two of his men who stepped smartly up to Godrith and with deliberate roughness pinioned him from behind.

"Old man," de Lussac began, "there are some questions to which I want answers, but first let me warn you that I have long had you under surveillance and consequently have a more intimate knowledge of your activities than you suppose. Wherefore it should be obvious that you have nothing to gain by attempting further to conceal them, and everything to lose—including your life. Think of that, should you feel the urge to start lying. Now to begin with, and to help you clear your conscience, let me hear you admit frankly that you are one of the Wake's men."

"I, my lord? One of the Wake's men?" Old Godrith's face was contorted with the pain of the unrelenting pressure on his arms, but he answered unhesitatingly and with well-feigned astonishment. "How would that be possible, my lord? He has use only for the young and strong, whereas I——"

"Merde!" screamed de Lussac, and raising his riding whip, he lashed the old man a dozen times across the face, leaving great welts and gashes in the flesh. "Bastard! Answer my questions! How does the Wake travel betwixt the Gronnaswald and the Lincoln road without traversing the fens?"

"My lord, I do not know——"

"You are a forester!"

"Aye."

"And reputedly know every inch of the countryside hereabouts!"

"Aye, but——"

"Then you know the answer to my question. Out with it!"

The old man stubbornly shook his head. "My lord, this is different. I know nothing of the Wake's——"

Again the whip lashed out, cutting the old man back and forth across the face until the blood oozed from the open wounds and his knees buckled. "Release him!" The supporting hands were withdrawn and Godrith slumped heavily to the floor where he lay moaning softly. De Lussac screamed his threats and swore and kicked him in the stomach, then suddenly, apparently quite without cause, the blows ceased. The cursing stopped. The room was hushed. Thinking perhaps de Lussac's frenzy was spent and that he was preparing to depart, old Godrith peered hopefully between swelling lids, to find instead that the trap above had been reopened and now down the ladder a Norman soldier was making his triumphant descent, preceded by Edgitha.

Godrith gasped in horror. He watched the gratified smile creep over de Lussac's face as with slow deliberation he inspected her young person; the pearl-pink complexion, now somewhat paled from keeping to the indoors; the golden plaits resting on her bosom; the loose-fitting dress girdled at the waist whose simple lines served to accentuate each gently swelling curve beneath.

"A true Saxon beauty!" he exclaimed at last. "Who are you, my dear?"

The girl was trembling visibly. With an effort she dragged her eyes from her grandfather and focused them on de Lussac. "I am Edgitha, granddaughter to Godrith."

"Well, well," said de Lussac, "and all the time we thought him kithless. Now why do you suppose the knave kept you hid away out of sight? Flowers thrive best in the sun. Mais tant pis!" He turned back to Godrith and poked him playfully with the toe of his shoe. " 'Twould be right wicked to mar such frail beauty, eh, old man?"

"For pity's sake, my lord," but Godrith spoke dully, like a man without hope, "spare the girl! What will you gain by hurting her?"

"A quick answer from you, for one thing. Ha! You think not? Well, do not take my word for it. Wait and see how my method works. Prop him up against the wall, men, so he can properly witness the proceedings."

Godrith was instantly dragged across the room and set with his back to the wall. At a gesture from de Lussac, two men proceeded to strip off the girl's clothes, whilst a third went outside and returned a moment later with Hubert, the tracker. The burly Angevin carried in his hand a multitailed whip into whose leather thongs were knotted at intervals sharp metal hooks designed to claw the flesh of the victim. The naked girl shrank back at the sight of him and struggled frantically to escape the grip of her captors, but a blow from Hubert's massive fist sent her sprawling to the floor, where at the first stroke of the whip all further resistance vanished and she succumbed to the will of her tormentor.

Old Godrith sat stupefied by the scene, unable even to avert his gaze. In a little while he became vaguely aware that the girl's screams had thinned and died away, that her writhing had ceased. He saw the Angevin straighten up and raise a hand to wipe the sweat from his face. Without seeing who spoke, he recognized de Lussac's voice: "Why do you stop? What are you waiting for? Allons!"

"My lord, the wench is unconscious."

"Then revive her, fool! Revive her!"

Hubert took up a nearby pail of water and reversed its contents over the bleeding body of the girl. She stirred and opened her eyes and de Lussac bent solicitously over her.

"Come, my dear," he said, "since the old man cares not a whit for your pretty body, you perhaps know a few things which would help us loosen his stubborn tongue. Speak up! Tell what you know and I will spare you further punishment. You are not yet so badly hurt that you cannot heal. Save yourself! Confess what you know of the Wake and his doings."

Edgitha stared silently back at him. He could see that she had sufficiently recovered consciousness to comprehend his meaning, but she made no effort to reply. Instead, and despite her excruciating pain, there was a dull defiance in her glance which enraged de Lussac and he struck her savagely across the face and resigned her to Hubert.

By now Godrith was sobbing quite openly. He had finally succeeded in wrenching his eyes from the girl and sat looking wildly about him, quivering in every limb. Repeatedly he signed himself with the Cross and prayed half aloud in desperate urgency, "If the child must die, let her die fast; let it be now, dear Lord, before it is too late, before my courage fails, before I talk to save her!" But his prayers proved of slight avail, for there was no blocking out the terrible sounds that filled the room, and as, for the second time, they trailed away into silence, his rising frenzy overwhelmed him like a deluging tide.

"Stop! Stop, my lord! Stop! I will tell—I will tell—I will tell!"

Hubert suspended his labors, whilst de Lussac came slowly over and stood before Godrith, smiling down at him, hands on hips. "Tant mieux!" he said. "But what you tell had best be the truth, be warned of that. Now to begin, how is it possible for the Wake to come and go unseen across the fen?"

The old man's sobs made speech difficult. "My lord, he does not cross the fen."

"Never?"

"Leastways, not on forays."

"Then there is another route connecting with the Gronnaswald?"

"Aye."

"Where is it located?"

"South of Lincoln."

"South of Lincoln!" De Lussac's incredulity slowly gave place to astonishment. "You mean the forest that is visible beyond the Witham River?"

"Aye."

"Jesu! So that is it! And is there a bridge across the river?"

"Nay. At some miles eastward there is a ford."

"Is that the only ford in the vicinity? Is he forced to always effect a crossing at the same point?"

"Aye, always at the same point."

"Wherefore the wooded terrain beyond the ford would be admirably suited to an ambush?"

"Aye."

"And what information have you concerning the Wake's future plans? Is he considering an attack upon Lincoln?"

"Not immediately."

"What do you mean by 'not immediately'? Eventually? He plans first to weaken the garrison—to bring about a diminution of their stores? Is that it?"

"Aye."

De Lussac leaned forward, his voice tense. "Are you certain of this? You must be aware that Lincoln is not entirely dependent upon the Lincoln road for provisions. Its main supply depot is Torksey, an outpost only seven miles distant and connected to Lincoln by canal. Therefore when you say 'not immediately,' you would seem to indicate that first he intends to destroy Torksey."

Godrith said nothing, only sat with bowed head.

"Is that it? Answer me—is that the plan?"

"Aye."

"And when is Torksey scheduled to be attacked?"

Again the old man said nothing.

"Revive the girl!"

"Nay, nay, my lord!" Godrith raised his eyes and their expression was like that of a man in the last physical agonies of crucifixion. "The attack is scheduled for today."

"Today! At what time?"

Godrith's voice was barely audible. "At sundown."

De Lussac remained silent a moment, excitedly pursuing his own thoughts. "Then if the Wake is occupied today at Torksey, it follows that he cannot at the same time be making mischief on the Lincoln road. Today a man might ride through to Lincoln unmolested, eh, old man?"

"Aye."

De Lussac indulged in a sound somewhat resembling a laugh and turned swiftly toward the door. "Two of you, Roger—Alain, stay here to keep guard. Let the old man tend the girl—I may need her. Do not let anyone communicate with them. When I am safely arrived at Lincoln I will send back instructions for their disposition." So saying, he quit the cottage and an instant later was riding swiftly away in the direction of the Lincoln road.

Old Godrith sat staring at the door, listening to the hoofbeats fade away into the distance; hearing, as in delirium, de Lussac's voice questioning, his own replying. "Torksey—at sundown." De Lussac's laugh. A knell of death! "Jesus forgive me! What have I done? I must get out of here and give the alarm!"

He struggled to his feet and began an uncertain journey across the floor, almost stumbling over the girl, who lay directly in his path. At the sight of her he halted abruptly, recalling what for a few blessed moments had escaped his overwrought mind. The two Normans, heedful of their master's instructions, made no motion to intervene as he dropped to the floor and gathered her in his arms, cradling her like a baby, rocking back and forth and talking in low, caressing tones. "Little one," he murmured, "my little one." She recognized his voice and opened her eyes and he saw they were dim with travail. He turned away his head, letting his glance wander thoughtfully over her almost fleshless body. Then suddenly he stopped rocking. For a long moment he sat quite still, gazing intently into her face, absorbed in some train of thought. Then, as he bent his head and pressed his lips to her brow, he drew his woodsman's knife and plunged it swiftly through her heart.

The town of Torksey derived its importance mainly from its command of the ferry across the river Trent by which supplies were shipped via canal to the citadel of Lincoln seven miles away. Though small, the town was well fortified, having stone walls of sufficient height and thickness to present a formidable barrier to an attacking force, most especially a force which, like that of the Wake, lacked both the numerical strength and the powerful mining and slinging engines necessary to the taking of a town by storm. But Hereward Leofricsson was fully cognizant of the military deficiencies of his rebel band and had therefore formulated a plan whereby he looked to gain peaceful admittance to the Norman-held town.

On that same July afternoon, as de Lussac sped in hot haste up the Lincoln road to carry his information to the Conqueror, the Wake and his men lay in hiding in a wood within sight of their objective. They had made the wide detour of Lincoln on the previous day, and had closed in and taken up their present positions only after nightfall cloaked the distances and hid the telltale dust cloud which would have warned the town of the approach of an unidentified body of horsemen. At present, therefore, Torksey lay basking peacefully in the summer sun, all in happy ignorance of the rebels' proximity. Above the town flew the hated Norman ensign. Upon its walls the Norman sentries went through the mechanical motions of pacing their beats, halting now and then to scan the surrounding countryside.

About midafternoon the quiet of the town was broken by the winding of a horn which re-echoed loudly through the streets and which was soon followed by the neighing of horses and the excited baying of hounds. In due course the gates were thrown open and from them issued forth a hunting party of some thirty Normans, accompanied by their attendants and preceded by a pack of hounds straining at the leashes of their keepers.

In the forefront rode the governor, Sir Ascelin de Valognes, a man of noble birth and striking appearance, the latter being generally acknowledged by his underlings, the former being a matter of frequent covert reference by himself. He enjoyed to the fullest the privileges and ceremonial to which his somewhat modest position entitled him and was reputedly one of the most sedulous followers of the fashions of the times, devoting to the adornment of his person much money and careful thought, shaving daily and being at all times wonderfully perfumed and impeccably, even foppishly, dressed. This by no means meant he was lacking in valor. On the contrary, he had played a hero's part at Hastings, having been among the first to penetrate the Godwinsson's entrenchments, an act of courage for which in his own estimation he had never been adequately guerdoned.

The Norman company came on, riding easily across the flat country leading to the wood. Scarce had the hounds come within the fringe of the trees than they picked up a trail and sped off, giving tongue furiously, leading the hunting party away from the open sunlit glades into the thickest part of the wood; racing through narrow paths in the tangled underbrush where wide-spreading boughs formed canopies to intercept the light. At length, on a level stretch of turf walled in by trees and bushes, the hounds lost the scent and circled about, whimpering nervously. The riders drew rein, halting in a group and waiting with ill-curbed impatience to continue the chase.

It was then they first became aware that they were not, as they supposed, alone in the wood. At the first sign of company they looked around in alarm, to find themselves completely surrounded by English rebels who had closed in noiselessly, some mounted for pursuit, the rest afoot. The Normans were so taken by surprise that the ensuing struggle was brief and bloodless. Sir Ascelin was unceremoniously pulled from his horse by an outlaw who threw him to earth and promptly sat upon him, planting his haunches on the governor's chest with a thud that knocked the breath from his body. With one hand he gripped the Norman's throat, with the other he whipped out his dagger and held it poised to strike.

"Your choice," he offered genially. "Surrender or die!"

"Diable!" panted the governor. "You handle your betters with churlish familiarity."

"Sir, how I handle my betters can only be a matter of conjecture to you. Now haste, man, make up your mind. Surrender or fight—live or die!"

"Surrender—and God's curse upon your soul!"

"Softly, softly! Let us pretend to the manners of the ideal knight. How are you called?"

Sir Ascelin said nothing, but lay warily deliberating his reply. Why were they not being slaughtered? he wondered. Why were they being taken alive? Was ransom the objective here? If so, as governor of the town, and a nobleman at that, it were better for him to conceal his identity as long as possible——

"Dainty sir," broke in the Englishman impatiently, " 'tis right pitiful to see with what little success you overtax your wits. When a man searches so long for his own cognomen, his reply is like to bear little resemblance to the truth. Wherefore let be with the name, then, and come with me."

So saying, he arose and pulled his captive to his feet, retaining a firm grip on the Norman's arm as he steered him through the melee to the other side of the glade. Most of the prisoners had already been rounded up and now stood lined against a wall of underbrush. They were being reviewed by the leader of the band, at first glimpse of whom Sir Ascelin started and cursed beneath his breath, for, like every Norman, he was familiar with the Wake's description.

"Ha!" he exclaimed, turning to his captor. "I begin now to comprehend. A rollicking joke, indeed! But permit me to point out that where base trickery is the stock in trade of any bandit, it scarce adds luster to a general's repute."

The Englishman's eyes were laughing. "Trickery?"

"You know well what I mean. It was not chance led our hounds direct to your covert. They followed a trail left for them by your infamously cunning leader."

"Your rancor, sir, does not offend me," came the good-natured reply. " 'Tis natural in a man who finds himself outwitted."

To this Sir Ascelin vouchsafed no reply, but having reached the spot where the prisoners stood, he took his place with the rest. The Wake moved on up the line, inspecting each man in turn, then passing silently on to the next. Upon reaching the governor, however, he paused and a light as of recognition came into his eye. For a moment he continued to study the man before him, taking note of the shimmering satin surcoat, the white linen undertunic delicately edged with lace, the blue velvet cap upon the sleek black head all beplumed with ostrich feathers, whilst all about him the air grew heavy with the unmistakable scent of violets. This, then, was the governor.

"Sir Ascelin," he said, "it must be apparent that there can be little help forthcoming to you from the town. You and your men would do well, therefore, to obey my orders without demur and I trust you will so advise them."

"That depends upon what it is you want of us."

"You must all disrobe, sir. We wish to borrow your attire."

Thus it befell that just about sundown the hunting party was seen to quit the wood and head back to town. The sentries on the walls watched unconcernedly as the horsemen crossed the rough heathland, riding in leisurely fashion like men wearied by the chase. But Holy Saints! Were their eyes deceiving them? The lordly governor was displaying rare cordiality toward his company today, even condescending to chat with them as they rode. Now what could have occurred to produce this metamorphosis?

Down below, meanwhile, the captain of the gate stood in readiness. He had long since learned that the soldier who looked to Sir Ascelin for promotion must know how to cater to his whims and anticipate his needs, sparing the great man such petty inconveniences as that of halting and demanding admittance to his own commandery. Now, in accordance with his established custom, he waited only until the governor drew reasonably near before giving the order to throw open the gates, whereupon in due course, and without the tedium of needless query and answer, Sir Ascelin and his party passed through the portal and entered the town.

But it chanced that standing by the captain's side was a young sentry endowed with considerably greater powers of observation than his superior officer. With creased brow and puzzled mien he continued to stare after the horsemen as they moved on slowly down the cobbled street, having noted that where Sir Ascelin generally returned the salutation of his inferiors with a haughty nod, today he had waved his hand in a friendly gesture altogether foreign to his nature. Furthermore, he was wearing his cap pulled down about his ears in a most undistinguished manner, while the few strands of hair visible beneath it were not black at all, but of a chestnut brown. This information he duly transmitted to his captain, together with the astute observation that there were many fair-haired men this evening in the governor's party.

The captain stared. Come to think of it, there was something strangely changed in Sir Ascelin's demeanor. If it were true, as the sentry suggested, that the governor was not the governor, then as gate captain it was his responsibility to take action. But what action should he take? He had never been given instructions as to how to proceed in such a case. Should he halt and interrogate Sir Ascelin de Valognes? Should he point a suspicious finger at him—and get a flogging for his pains? But no! By all the fiends in hell! This young sentry was surely sun-struck. The governor who just returned was the same man who had set out hunting this afternoon. Why? Because he was wearing the same clothes. And so, for that matter, was his entire company.

Thus did the captain conclude his deliberations and, by way of dispelling any lingering doubts, sent a resounding cuff across the face of the young upstart who had presumed to question the discernment of his superior. But even before astonishment at the unlooked-for attack had fully dawned on the green youth's countenance, the governor's party had wheeled about, longbows raised. The captain gave a hoarse cry and started running for the shelter of his tower, but long ere he reached it he fell to the cobbles, an arrow through his throat. The young sentry dropped where he stood. The watchmen on the walls were cut down at the first toll of the tocsin. And upon a prearranged signal the rest of the English, waiting ready-mounted in the wood, broke from cover and swept across the heath to the town.

Leaving Eadric the Wild to guard the gates, the Wake sped off through the narrow streets with the main body of the English, many of them bearing flaming torches. Their progress went unchallenged, for the Normans were like shepherdless sheep in the absence of their commanders. After peering from their windows and identifying the horsemen as rebels, they thereafter elected to look to themselves, remaining indoors out of danger's path and leaving the English to wreak what mischief they would upon the depot.

The Wake headed straight for the warehouses, a row of low wooden buildings at the far end of the town wherein were stored the precious supplies of grain and oil and salted beeves awaiting shipment by barge to Lincoln. The rebels needed no signal from their leader, but without loss of time loosed their flame-arrows into the targets. The shafts stuck fast and a hundred tiny tongues of fire licked at the seasoned wood. An instant later the roofs of the buildings burst into flame and the air was heavy with the odor of burning wood. Through the lowering dusk a few figures were seen to quit the warehouses and make off toward the canal, but they had thought only to save their own skins and the English paid them no heed. The flames were soon leaping madly, dancing midst billowing columns of smoke, and when at length falling beams ignited the stores below, an oily reek coiled heavenwards and there spread out to form a black pall upon the windless air.

The English backed away from the roaring furnace, their faces solemn in the lurid light. Methodically they started making their way back again toward the gates, destroying everything as they passed, leaving the ferry and barges afire at the wharves, shooting their flaming missiles into the thatched roofs of the houses until the roar at their backs was like the four winds of heaven united in a gale.

They picked up Eadric and his band at the gates and were soon on their way, but about a mile out from the town they checked their steeds and looked back. The Normans were in flight and appeared from a distance like black dwarfs fanning out over the heath. Their vaunted supply depot was one vast conflagration and for miles the night sky was ruddy with its reflected glow. Tomorrow, when the fires died down, there would be little left of Torksey, little beyond a host of smoking ruins within their scarred walls. Hereward smiled faintly and looked about him at his men. Their faces were black with smoke and streaked with the sweat of their labors; their eyes were red, their hair and eyebrows singed.

"Now Lincoln must look to herself," he said, and setting Swallow's head to northward, he rode on slowly through the dusk.

It was long after midnight by the time they made the detour of Lincoln and approached their secret entrance to the Gronnaswald.

The wind had died down to a gentle breeze and the moon was shining brilliantly, transforming the rough heathland into a smooth white waste. Carefully they picked their way across the marshy flats of the Witham, following a natural ridge of firm earth, cutting through an alder carr, skirting a mere from whose somber depths another moon stared up at the sky, then across a stretch of swampy ground where, among sheltering reeds and rushes, the water lilies floated with folded cups and waterside flowers gave off a fragrance that was stronger by night than by day.

Hereward rode on slowly, followed by his men. Before them now lay the river, its ripples glimmering as they caught the light. At the spot where boulders had been set to mark the ford, the shallows sang in the stillness. Up the riverbank and on, across a broad stretch of brushland and into the shadow of the forest. And when at last they moved in under the ancient oaks, the leaf-sky made a gloaming in which the tree trunks stood indistinct, looming like hairy giants in their mosses and as inconceivably remote as if their thousand years of living had left them a kinship only with the past. Hereward inhaled the moist forest air and knew he was home. Swallow knew it too. She had come to know the forest and all its vagrant paths and could find her way without direction. He leaned over and patted her fondly. "Good Swallow," he said, "good girl!" and laying the reins on her massive neck, he wearily closed his eyes.

After foraying for a week he should be looking forward to a space of rest and peace, yet he had no hankering to be back at the cave now that Althya was no longer there. How was she faring, he wondered, up in Scotland? But then Lightfoot would be back in a few days with messages from her. It was well to know, though, that she was in good hands and would be spared the hardships of forest life, at least until their child was born. Queen Margaret had an enduring love for her English homeland. She hoped one day to see it free and had sworn to care for the Wake's wife and child as she would her own kin. Aye, Althya was in good hands right enough, but how he yearned for the sight of her. Perhaps if they could take Lincoln before winter set in, he could ride to Edinburgh in December and be there for the birth. He might even bring her back with him if she were well enough to travel——

Suddenly his eyes sprang open and he gazed fixedly into the shadows. Something was amiss! It was quiet here—too quiet! He was acutely conscious of an odd, suspensive silence, as though the forest held its breath against an intruder. Where were the sentries who had lately been posted here to watch the ford? He did not recall passing them. And where was the churring of the nightjar? And the fluting of the blackcap? Something had disturbed the night creatures. They had taken fright!

He shouted a warning, but at that moment came the shrill blast of a Norman battle horn and the English were caught in a crossfire of shafts. They were too well versed in the tactics of ambush to halt and leave themselves as standing targets for an invisible enemy. Instead, they whipped out their blades and set spurs to their mounts, intending to break through the green barrier of shrubs and trees behind which the Conqueror's men must be massed. But the arrow hail was so thick that the foremost ranks went down as wheat before the scythe, while those who came after were caught in the press of struggling men; of wheeling, pain-maddened beasts and lashing hoofs. And still the Norman shafts blackened the air. There was no escape from the deadly iron hail. At a cry from their leader the fast-dwindling English, most of them unhorsed, bounded over the waste of corpses and struggled on toward the underbrush. But now, at a second blast of the horn, the Normans poured from their covert and closed in upon the last survivors of the rebel fighting force.

The Normans seemed numberless. There would be no breaking through their steel-clad circle. They closed in swiftly, showing white markings on their hauberks to identify them in the half-light. But the English stood firm, holding the swarming foe at bay, making up in skill and valor what they lacked in numbers, wielding their swords with such precision that each blow struck home. The wounded seemed scarce to feel their streaming wounds. The dying fought on till they fell. And when at last the English phalanx was reduced to a few score men, they fell back to close the circle of slaughter; loud-breathing, but highhearted still; tall and fearless as demigods and seemingly rooted in their English soil as the ageless oaks of their forest.

And de Lussac came striding through the melee, seeking the Wake. He found Swallow, dead, pierced by a dozen shafts. Her master, then, could not be far off. The English phalanx had been breached in several places and the shattered remnant had been forced to break up into pairs or small groups, thus to fight until they were annihilated or fell from sheer exhaustion. Somewhere among them, de Lussac knew, his search would end, for the Conqueror, his heart being set on taking the Wake alive, had issued stern orders that no vital blow should be aimed at his person. The king had further assigned FitzOsbern, Earl of Hereford, to formally accept the Wake's surrender in his own stead, FitzOsbern being—and here de Lussac sneered—a right fair and courteous knight.

He sighted the Wake at last, fighting back to back with Eadric. The two men were seemingly invincible, for their sword-sweeps, like glittering arcs, felled all who opposed them and already they stood thigh-deep in Norman corpses. De Lussac drew up, frowning, deep in thought. Now if, unbeknownst to the Wake, Eadric could be slain, then a man might come in at the Wake's back and take him captive. But how to get close enough to land the fatal blow? This wild man fought as fiercely as a wounded boar—and as unflinchingly. No Norman could come within sword's length of him. While he stood his ground, shielding the Wake's back, there was no taking Hereward Leofricsson.

De Lussac turned and made his way swiftly to the fringe of the fighting where from an archer he procured a longbow and quiver. Retracing his steps, he halted within shooting distance, taking up his position directly facing Eadric. He could not yet get a sight on his target, for the wild man was walled in by enemies, shouting at them in a kind of savage joy, "I would scorn to fight a single Norman. A man must needs take on a dozen to have some sport!" De Lussac raised his bow and waited, his arrow drawn to head. Soon another Norman fell at Eadric's feet and as, for one single instant, the wild man stood exposed to view, de Lussac released his shaft. Swiftly it winged away, straight and sure, biting through the ring mail and lodging deep in the flesh beneath. Eadric the Wild staggered and dropped his blade, then, striving vainly to pluck out the shaft, he fell heavily to earth.

Hereward, meanwhile, unaware that his back was exposed, continued to hold his half-circle. The Normans were crowding in upon him as hounds upon a buck, but ever he hewed down man after man; ever he slashed a limb or severed a hand or clove a skull, so that death came fast to his assailants and those who were left, being sore harassed, fell back repeatedly to evade the dazzling strokes. He seemed unwearied yet by battle, and though his mail was rent in several places and blood seeped through, overspreading the leather and ruddying the rings, his sword arm had as yet lost none of its striking power.

Only when he became aware of an apprehensive hush behind him did he cast a glance over his shoulder, but even as he did so a pair of Normans leaped upon his back, a dozen hands pinioned him, whilst at his side a courteous voice addressed him in English, "Your sword, Sir Knight. The fight is ended." Hereward relinquished his sword into an unseen hand to grapple with his assailants, throwing off their grip, cracking their skulls with his fists as he hurled them to earth and swung around in search of Eadric. He found him on one knee, struggling to rise to his feet, one hand feeling blindly over the sward for his sword, whilst the barb that defied extraction lay buried still in his breast, draining him of life and leaving its shaft to quiver like a reed blade in the empty air. Seeing Hereward turn, he raised his eyes, and even in the dim light they were lusterless with the agony of death.

"I failed you, Hereward," he gasped. "I failed to shield your back. Forgive——"

Hereward stooped, and picking up Eadric's sword, replaced it in his hand. "Nay, son, whosoever falls first is but the luck of battle." But even as he spoke he knew his words were lost. For Eadric had died as he had always willed to die, with his sword in his hand.

"Sir Wake," said the knight who had been standing by Hereward's side, "my name is FitzOsbern. The king has confided you to my care. I have been instructed to escort you to Lincoln Castle where King William himself will hold parley with you. But since it would sore distress me to have you manacled, your word alone will suffice to enable you to ride unrestricted."

Hereward glanced about. Scarce twoscore of his men remained. He himself was ringed in by Normans. "I bind myself only to ride from here to Lincoln," he said. "But upon that you have my word."

A short while later they were on their way, riding to Lincoln in the calm summer dawn. The sun was rimming the sky to the east, making the woodlands a fretwork of light and shadow. The pastures glistened with dew and the slow-moving forms of the grazing cattle cast long shadows on the grass. FitzOsbern glanced searchingly at his captive, noting that his demeanor evidenced none of the outward signs of defeat, for his head was stiff and unbowed; his eyes fixed, all unseeing, upon the roofs of the distant city. What was he thinking? Was he wondering who had betrayed him? Who had delivered England into the hands of the Norman? What was the price of betrayal?

He leaned over. "Sir Wake," he said, "relieve your mind on one score. No man betrayed you for gold."

But Hereward did not hear him. He heard only the other voice that came to him on the breeze, the voice of Eadric; Eadric the perverse and the wild of heart, but loyal and selfless to the end. "I failed you, Hereward. . . . I failed to shield your back. . . . Forgive——"

Chapter Nineteen

"MANSIONS IN THE SKY . . ."

IN HIS chamber at Lincoln Castle the king was being attired for supper.

He had spent the day abed, recovering from the fatigue of last night's encounter, and now found himself in rare good humor and filled with a sense of well-being. Success had crowned his every enterprise. One by one his enemies had fallen before him until now, amid the groans and tears of England, he stood as her undoubted Conqueror. Henceforth his authority would be acknowledged in every corner of the land. The realm over which he had taken formal possession five years ago was at last truly his. This called for a radical change of policy, for it was never good statecraft to stimulate native hatred between two races who must dwell beneath a single crown. He was resolved to work now to obliterate the dark and bloody stains of his early reign; to improve his knowledge of the English tongue and thus understand the simple formulae of his own charters; to go, like Alfred, to the farthest cities and shires to insure that his will was done, that those who ruled in his name refused, sold, or delayed justice to no man. And if he could not venture, like his predecessor, to bid his subjects love him with right truthfulness, he would at least earn their gratitude by engendering a measure of peace and mutual security betwixt Englishman and Norman.

But now the time was come to make final disposition of Hereward the Wake, a question to which, in anticipation of today, he had devoted years of careful thought. He had bidden the governor, Sir Herlwin FitzHugh, order a banquet for tonight. The sconces of the Great Hall would cradle a hundred festive torches. From the kitchens would come forth many culinary masterpieces; delicate meat pasties, whole kids browned upon their spits, quail and snipe stuffed with summer fruits and garnished with truffles. About the richly appointed tables his barons would congregate, standing idly about as they awaited his arrival, recalling among themselves incidents of the battle and hazarding many a guess as to this Englishman's projected fate now that he had finally been captured. That was the moment he, the Conqueror, had selected to make known his decision. There would be many sullen faces at the news, many discontented frowns and covert glances. Well, what matter? They had long known how little he cared either for their approbation or their censure.

His attendants finished shaving him and he stood while they commenced the robing, but at that moment any further ruminations were interrupted by a light knock on the door and Sir Guy de Lussac requested leave to be admitted to the royal presence.

"Sire," said Guy humbly when he stood before the king, "I beg to remind Your Grace that your promise to me regarding my proposed bride, the lady Althya, has not yet been fulfilled."

Such was the king's good humor that he only laughed indulgently at this. "Mon cher Guy," he replied, "you will admit that the matter is now somewhat taken out of my hands since the lady already has a husband."

Guy drew a step closer. "Sire," he pointed out, "this husband is a rebel who, according to the law of the Conquest, merits death by hanging."

"Are you suggesting that I hang him so that you can wed his widow?"

"Such an action would effect a twofold benefit, my liege," Guy replied readily, "the promotion of justice and the acquittal of your royal word."

But the king shook his head. "No," he said slowly, "the Wake was a good enemy. He will make a noble earl."

Guy started. His brown face flushed with anger. "Earl, my lord king?"

"There is in truth little I admire more than knightliness," replied the Conqueror. "I have set my heart upon the Wake's friendship."

"His friendship, sire?"

The king frowned impatiently. "What ails you, Guy? Can you do no more than echo the words I utter? Aye, this Englishman has fought well and fairly. He will serve me in the same way."

"Allowing the possibility of such an unlikelihood, sire," de Lussac said after a moment, "what of the lady you vowed I should wed?"

"The loss of the lady herself will not too greatly distress you,"

William replied. "As for her dowry, I shall undertake to find some way of recompensing you for the loss of it."

With that the Conqueror turned away, ignoring Guy's sullen silence. He motioned his attendants to proceed, commenting approvingly upon the splendid purple tunic in which they clothed him and paying special heed to the device of the Two Lions which was embroidered above the heart in gold thread and richly adorned with emeralds, rubies and diamonds. Satisfied with his appearance, the king seated himself, extending first one foot, then the other, whilst his plump feet and legs were clad in yellow silken hose and shoes of finest Cordovan leather crosstied with tasseled cords.

Such was William's apparent absorption in his attire that Guy found it necessary to cough softly as a reminder of his presence.

"Then I take it, sire, that the banquet scheduled for tonight is not intended to celebrate the Wake's capture," he observed. "Rather is it intended to celebrate the Wake's acceptance of an earldom in exchange for his fealty."

Something in Guy's crafty voice caught the Conqueror's attention. He looked up sharply. "It is," he admitted coldly.

He watched the change come over Guy's face. The sullenness lifted and was replaced by a furtive, guarded smile that puzzled even the astute William. But Guy said nothing more on the subject and a few moments later, after complimenting the king upon his appearance, he withdrew.

Meanwhile, in a solitary chamber high up in one of the castle's turrets, the Wake stood alone. From his window he could watch the hills and distant forest fuse into one vast infinity of darkness, could almost count the glittering specks in the illimitable dome above. But he was not conscious of the emerging stars, nor of the deep, impenetrable darkness. He thought of Althya.

What would become of her, he asked himself, if he were kept prisoner or executed? Anxiety made him stride about the chamber. In his mind there was not the slightest doubt that the Conqueror had already determined upon his fate. Nor did he doubt that whatever compromise the Conqueror was prepared to offer would be unacceptable. He knew suddenly that he could follow but one course. He had bound himself to ride peaceably only as far as Lincoln. Now that he was here he must quickly devise a means of escape. How this was to be accomplished in the face of the king's entire army was something only time and opportunity would determine. Equally certain was it that the freeing of his men also rested in the hands of Fate.

He crossed to the heavy oaken door with its iron bands and nail-heads and peered through a small grill in the upper panel. The guards outside had been supplemented by a dozen or more soldiers who sat at a table a short way off playing chess. Hereward hailed one of them.

"Tell me," he said, "where are my men lodged?"

The soldier laughed. "Too far off to be of any service to you," he replied, then, mindful of FitzOsbern's admonition with regard to courtesy toward the prisoner, he added a grudging "—sir."

"Are they here in the castle?"

"No, sir."

"But they were brought to the city?"

"Yes, sir."

"Are they being lodged in the city?"

"That, sir, I have not yet been apprised of."

This unsatisfactory conversation was interrupted by the sound of footsteps ascending the stone stairs of the tower. The soldier hastily returned to his companions, whilst Hereward retreated to the center of the room and waited. The footsteps came on, slowing as they approached the door, and finally halted directly outside it. The keys were turned in the locks, the bolts drawn. A familiar voice ordered the men-at-arms to await without, then the door was thrust open and Sir Herlwin entered the chamber alone.

"Sir," he said in a voice loud enough to be heard in the corridor, "the king has sent me to request your immediate presence in his private chamber." He did not await the Wake's reply, but drew close to him and whispered in a hurried voice, "I myself came to fetch you, Hereward, to caution you against continued defiance. The king is in a beneficent mood tonight. By humoring him there is much to be gained for your lady and yourself, perhaps even for your men."

"I have preached defiance to my men so long that they will expect nothing short of it from me," replied the Wake. "Knowing your friendship for me, my good Herlwin, I thank you for your counsel, but the day has not yet dawned when I must humor the Bastard."

"Surely you cannot still cherish the futile hope of ever displacing him?" asked Herlwin in surprise. "Are you so bereft of logic that you cannot discern your own good fortune? Hereward, the king holds you in such high regard that he is prepared to bestow upon you wealth and honors he withholds even from his fellow countrymen;

he is so set upon your fealty that in exchange for it he will be more than bountiful."

"Such bounty, when examined in the broad light of reason, can only disclose itself for what it really is—wealth and honors filched from other Englishmen."

Herlwin shook his head with a troubled frown. "It is indeed hard to follow your reasoning," he said.

He was about to turn and summon the guard to open up the door when the plaintive strains of a ghittern fell upon his ear. He stood still as awareness grew within him, then he moved over to the window. He could see the lights of the courtyard below, the flickering torches illuminating the city gate, but beyond that darkness cloaked the countryside, the same darkness that cloaked the player and made him safe.

Herlwin was conscious of having heard such music once before, at the Tower on the eve of Waltheof's escape. As he listened he could see again the green-clad minstrel soliciting a halfpenny from the earl. Was it possible that the Tower minstrel had been one of the Wake's men! Herlwin was startled by the thought that a rebel had dared penetrate the much-feared precincts of the Tower and the significance of his presence near Lincoln at such a moment was not lost upon him.

He turned quickly to find the Wake's eyes fixed upon him.

"Hereward," he said, "three months ago I resigned as governor of Lincoln, but as yet the king has not seen fit to replace me. This position, therefore, continues to impose upon me one paramount obligation. Those who, for whatever reason, dwell within its limits are neither my personal friends nor my personal enemies. They are all either loyal subjects, or enemies, of the king."

Hereward smiled down at him. "That was already clear to me, my friend," he said.

Herlwin sighed. The lines about his mouth deepened with his perplexity. "Yet to me it has ceased to be so clear," he admitted. "Indeed, there are times when right seems wrong, and wrong seems undeniably right. Come, I must take you to the king."

It was with a certain curiosity that Hereward entered the royal presence. With the passage of the years William was inclining more and more toward solitude, but at present he was still pleased to tolerate the occasional companionship of Montgomery, and more frequently that of FitzOsbern. It was these two who, perhaps by actual design, perhaps by chance, were closeted with the king upon Hereward's entrance. They made no motion to withdraw, simply rising respectfully to their feet as the king lifted himself from his chair and crossed the room. His movements were slow, hampered already by his increasing obesity, yet despite this he had yielded to the years no part of his commanding presence. Though the glory of his youth was gone, though his reddish hair had now retreated to the crown, revealing the immense domed skull, though the splendid shoulders stooped beneath the weight of countless unneglected duties, his incomparable energy and resolution dominated every scene of which he was a part.

In the center of the room William halted. A gracious smile curved his full lips and on his breast the splendid jewels of the Two Lions sparkled with his hastened breathing.

"My lord earl," he said, pausing just a fraction of a second for the Wake to grasp the implication of his words, "my lord earl, we have fought a fair and gallant fight, each one of us deserving of the victory, each one of us right according to his own pretensions. With peace established between us, England alone will be the victor, though I shall be the richer by a new-made earl and you, Hereward Leofricsson, by the wealth and honors attendant thereon."

William paused. He had already observed how rapidly the Wake's eyes roved over the room, taking in every detail. He wondered if Hereward had guessed that there would be no escape from this room, for behind the heavy drapes so gracefully drawn were concealed no less than twenty men-at-arms. But Hereward's eyes had ceased their roving. He looked down sternly at the Conqueror, his countenance stoic, unflinching, noncommittal.

"What of my men?" he demanded.

The king's smile lost none of its graciousness. "They, my lord, must garner the fruit of rebellion—the hangman's halter."

He paused again to give the Wake time to reflect upon these words and to perceive therein the neat noose that had been so cleverly drawn about his own neck. Two choices alone were offered and each of itself a penalty; to be hanged with his men, or, by his example of submission, to complete the despair of his fellow countrymen who had vested their every hope of liberation in him.

"Come," urged the king, irked by the prolonged silence, "a man would be a fool to put his own head in a noose."

Still Hereward's countenance showed no response. He vouchsafed no verbal reply. Upon their purple habitat the Two Lions of Normandy pompously flaunted their jewels as the royal breast rose and fell. To Hereward they represented more than the hated device of the Conqueror. They represented the despotic might of Normandy.

He took careful aim and spat full upon them.

The king looked down, his face gone suddenly ashen. He stood benumbed, watching the saliva trickle from the top lion to the second, then down to his belt. The silence of the chamber was pregnant with expectancy. Montgomery and FitzOsbern gripped their daggers; Sir Herlwin stood rigid. They breathed again as the king recovered his composure. With curt orders to the governor to place the prisoner in the castle dungeons, he turned upon his heel and left the chamber, and the three Normans who witnessed his departure, being familiar with the ruthlessness of the Conqueror's vengeance, knew the Wake was doomed.

At dawn the following morning the king departed from Lincoln, but before leaving he summoned to him Sir Guy de Lussac.

"Mon cher Guy," he said, "it seems that you were right in your estimation of the Englishman. I have instructed the governor to deliver him into your hands and shall now consider myself acquitted of my obligation to you."

Guy bowed to hide the smile of triumph on his brown face. "Your King's Grace is more than generous," he murmured.

No sooner had William taken his departure than Guy descended hurriedly to the castle's dungeons where he sought out the jailer. Having had previous dealings with him, the man was well known to Guy. He was a dark-haired Breton who, because of the immense breadth of trunk and shoulder, gave the impression of being squat. His face was fleshy, his features coarse, and the sprouting double chin resting on the bull-like throat was dusky with an unshaven beard. His dark tunic was covered by a leather apron which still bore many repelling evidences of his calling.

Guy spoke to him in low tones. "Have you done aught, yet, to promote the natural death of the prisoner?"

"Aye, my lord, as you shall see," replied the jailer with a satisfied smile.

Guy gripped his arm. "But he is not yet dead?"

The jailer looked at Guy in surprise. "No, my lord, though I calculate he could not be far from it."

"You fool!" gasped Guy.

"But, my lord, last night you said——"

Guy cut him short. "Aye, but this morning the prisoner is mine and I have other plans for him. Quick, take me to him."

Hastily the jailer fetched his lanthorn and requested Guy to follow him. Neither spoke as they hurried through the unlit passages. The reverberation of their footsteps seemed to fill the hollow spaces, and as the light from the lanthorn swept the walls it revealed in myriad colors the trickling beads of water that made runnels on the naked stone. Toward the end of their journey the tombal stench became more evident and soon the jailer halted before an iron door. Hurriedly he lifted the bars, and throwing wide the portal, stood aside to permit Guy to enter. Guy paused upon the threshold, cursing the darkness. The jailer behind him raised his lanthorn to shed a circle of light upon the far end of the dungeon. Within its aura Guy sighted the prisoner.

He stood naked in a pit, up to his chest in icy water. His wrists were suspended by chains above his head, whilst upon his shoulders rested a massive iron yoke. Already his body had grown limp beneath this crushing weight. His yellow head hung weakly on his breast, but the shackles at his wrists denied him any surcease.

"He would already be dead, my lord, save for the governor's particular interest in the comfort of this prisoner which brought him to the dungeons repeatedly during the night," said the jailer. "It was necessary for me to postpone the operation until it seemed certain that Sir Herlwin's attentions were otherwise engaged. However, a half hour more in that icy water will suffice. The other accouterments do but lend the operation additional speed by insuring continued immersion."

Guy turned upon him savagely, a large vein throbbing in his forehead.

"I have said that I no longer wish to compass his death," he said hoarsely. "Revive him immediately. Have him clothed and fettered. In an hour he rides with me to Cruc Maur."

The jailer reflected sullenly upon the promised reward, scowling that this sudden change of plan should deprive him of it. But Guy de Lussac recognized the worth of those who served him. He counted out three golden coins from his purse which he dropped into the Breton's waiting palm, then he strode away.

Herlwin, meanwhile, was pacing disconsolately through the castle, pausing here and there to inspect with listless inattention the count-

less objects that caught his eye. After a night spent in restless visits
to the dungeons and in tossing sleeplessly upon his couch, he had
risen to have his worst fears confirmed. The king had instructed him
to deliver up the prisoner to Guy de Lussac and Guy had lost no time
in making his claim. An hour from now he would set out for Cruc
Maur where his dungeons were already renowned for their ingenious
devices; where the Wake might be kept alive for years, suffering the
hideous torments devised for him by Guy's inventive brain.

Thus Herlwin brooded as he paced through empty rooms and passages, seeking vainly to unravel the tangled skeins of volition and
duty. There was little he could do to help Hereward—yet he could
do much; this was the king's enemy—yet this was Herlwin's friend;
the prisoner was guilty of treason against the King of England—yet
the prisoner was a loyal Englishman. Sir Herlwin sighed. Notwith-
standing his own sympathies, there was only one course of action he
could honorably pursue—a soldier must perform his soldier's duty
blindly.

True—all true! Then why, having reached what was unquestionably the right decision, could he neither eat, nor sleep, nor find a
moment's peace?

It was quite by chance that in his troubled pacing he paused at a
window giving out on to the courtyard and perceived the green-
clad minstrel taking up his position just outside the gate. As Herlwin
watched, the man unslung his ghittern and with a few simple pleas-
antries for the amusement of the guards began to beguile them with
his playing.

Herlwin frowned. This must be the man who had made his presence known to Hereward last night. This was unquestionably the
minstrel of the Tower! Then the seed of further recognition began
to stir. Though not in this guise, Sir Herlwin had seen this man again
since Waltheof's escape. But where? He leaned forward and pressed
his brow against the window bars to gain a closer view. Mentally he
invested the hollow cheeks with a thick black beard, then he gave a
start. Once again he was back in the Gronnaswald watching Letwold
teach his deaf-mute child to play the ghittern; seeing him raise his
face; recognizing the man who threw the knife at York—the knife
that killed his son! Here was that same man, daring recognition, daring now to approach the very gates of Lincoln Castle when he knew
full well that he, Herlwin, was governor thereof!

But stop! Letwold did this for love of the Wake. He was seeking a way to help Hereward Leofricsson. What if a way were shown him? But was there a way? Perhaps. Reluctantly, half-ashamedly, Sir Herlwin FitzHugh pursued the thoughts which against his will were inflicting themselves upon him.

His mind was made up before he himself realized it. With beating heart and hurried step he descended to the courtyard and crossed over to the gate. Letwold looked up as the governor approached and with an effort controlled his startled recognition. He continued his playing, though in spasmodic jerks, as though debating within himself whether it were wiser to stand or flee. But soon he discerned a strange urgency in Herlwin's manner, an intentness which aroused even the languid curiosity of the guards.

"We have no love of English music here," said the governor, addressing the minstrel in harsh tones. "If you have any esteem for your worthless hide you will remove it hence immediately lest you, too, accompany the Wake on his morning ride to Cruc Maur."

"To Cruc Maur!" gasped Letwold, then, aware of the guards' slackened pacing, he added, "But, my lord, you do me grievous wrong. I am no partisan of that scoundrel."

The governor gripped Letwold firmly by the shoulder and set him on the road south.

"Then you are a wiser fool than I took you for," he snapped. "Now get gone from here with all speed."

And Letwold knew there was not a minute to lose.

An hour later Sir Guy de Lussac set out for Cruc Maur, accompanied by his prisoner and a large body of seasoned men-at-arms. He smiled to himself as he passed beneath the city gate and followed the ancient Roman highway leading south. Indeed, he had reason enough to smile. He had taken no chances. The prisoner rode a short way ahead of him so as to be constantly under his personal surveillance, mounted upon a lame, slow-moving beast, and if the Wake had entertained any hopes of escaping en route they had been shattered by the chains which hobbled his ankles securely beneath his horse's belly.

The sun was shining and the sky was blue. Even nature had conspired to enhance the alluring thoughts that filled Sir Guy's mind. He reviewed from memory the various instruments housed in his dungeons beneath Cruc Maur. His own inventive genius had been responsible for some of them, whilst others had been vastly improved by his knowledge of mechanics. Lingeringly he dwelt upon the advantages of each, and with experienced precision calculated the number of months it would take to shatter so vigorous a frame and so resourceful a mind as that of the prisoner. For the hundredth time he eyed the broad back before him, whilst a new thought was sired by his cunning brain. Jesu-Maria! But that was right! He no longer needed the king's intervention with the lady Althya. He would see to it that, wherever she was, she was kept informed of the day-by-day details concerning the state of her husband's health, details which would be true of course, yet so skillfully contrived that she would shortly plead, nay, beg, to effect a bargain, offering herself in exchange for the speedy dispatch of the prisoner. Truly, things had resolved themselves to his advantage.

He was forced at length to suspend his pleasant ruminations, for they were approaching the strip of dense forest separating the highway from the fens. They turned east, following a rude trail which narrowed steadily until the horsemen were obliged to quit their formation and ride single file. As they journeyed on, the path became more rugged, being cumbered with boulders or sinking unexpectedly into large holes, till at length, coiling above a precipitous gorge, the riders found themselves flanked on the one side by a chasm, whilst on the other they were walled in by steep, broken crags which jutted out to screen off the riders who had gone before.

Sir Guy knew the path well. It was the main link between his domain in the fenlands and the highway, and he was therefore in no way alarmed at the systematic disappearance of his men as they rounded the crags at the opposite side of the gorge. The Wake, riding directly ahead of him, was already nearing the bend when a startled cry from one of the trapped men warned Guy of the presence of the outlaws. He drew up sharply, a string of curses falling from his lips. Sacré Dieu, was it possible! Another minute and the Wake would be beyond his reach. With eyes dilating in fury, he swiftly drew from his belt a long dagger and took careful aim. The missile sped through the air, glancing past Hereward and lodging deep in the throat of his mount. The animal reared, trembled on the brink of the gorge, then sank struggling to the ground, his blood spurting into the air like a scarlet fountain.

The English, peering from behind the boulders, were stunned. They perceived now for the first time that their leader's ankles were hobbled beneath his horse's belly. There was no way of removing

Hereward from the narrow pass without also removing the dying horse. Indeed, short of a miracle, there appeared to be no way of extricating him at all.

Then down from his gelding leaped the smith, Cynwric Hir, his long black hair in disarray, his bare chest shaggy with its dusky growth. In a voice that rebounded from the depths of the chasm he bade his comrades hold the narrow way, then, leaping forward, he raised his axe above the horse and swiftly hewed the living beast in half. None but the muscled arms of Cynwric Hir could have lifted the Wake; none but Cynwric Hir could have raised the vast and fettered form and placed him on the gelding's back. With a shout the English set their leader on his way. A moment later they had all swept down the forest trail and disappeared from sight.

With such rapidity had these events transpired that Sir Guy de Lussac came to life with the apathy of a man emerging from a coma. He rode apprehensively forward till he reached the mass of bleeding horseflesh, then looked up to view the empty trail. After another moment of indecision he ventured still further forward, riding up beyond the boulders where lay the mutilated remnants of his men. At the sight of them an ungovernable passion shook him. He cursed those who were left to him for weaklings; swore pitiless vengeance, then ordered them forward with threats that spurred on even the most timorous among them.

A half hour later, coming to a fork in the road, they drew up. Sir Guy hesitated, searching the road for signs of hoofprints. Behind him his men were already murmuring at the uselessness of pursuit, but Guy was scarcely aware of them. He had raised his head and was scanning the sky to the east where, barely visible in the distance, a thin wisp of smoke spiraled up from the treetops, writhing like a fine white veil against the summer sky. Guy smiled. This time the odds were his!

"On, men!" he cried, and spurring his horse, dashed headlong down the forest path.

After a short ride they came upon a clearing by the roadside, in the center of which stood an abandoned smithy. From the roof issued forth tiny puffs of smoke and within it they could see Cynwric Hir toiling feverishly over the anvil, freeing Hereward of his fetters. The task was just complete as the Normans swept in upon them. There was no time for the English to mount and flee. Swiftly they formed themselves into a battle ring, and drawing their long woodsmen's knives, faced the mail-clad Normans.

"By the Holy Crosse," cried Hereward, snatching a sword from an astonished Norman, "let us fight like men, and die like heroes!"

At a shout from de Lussac, the Normans closed in, spurring their mounts to drive a wedge through the English ranks, wielding their swords, smashing down to right and to left upon the compact mass of unhelmed heads. By Hereward's side, faithful in death, fell Letwold the serf of Harold. Then died Outy the Cobbler, mild-mannered and gentle, unskilled in battle, yet fighting with resolution and valor. And almost to the end, a giant among men, stood the mighty smith, Cynwric Hir, his axe rising and falling with the frenzy of a madman, hewing down at once both horse and rider, clearing for himself a path through the ranks of the oncoming enemy until the Normans recoiled before him as from a fiend. Only when his mighty breast was all bloodied with wounds and his mighty spirit was fled did he drop to earth, to be trodden and lost beneath the crush.

As the fighting ended, de Lussac himself sought out the Wake. He found him backed against the smithy holding off a dozen Normans. It was apparent at once that Hereward had not yet recovered from his ordeal in the water pit of the previous night, for his face was ashen and a feverish sweat beaded his forehead. His quickened breathing sucked in his stomach and sent violent spasms through his frame. From countless wounds his lifeblood ebbed, sapping his strength and shimmering in dreadful ruby drops upon the emerald turf.

Guy leaped toward him, motioning his men to fall back. With unalloyed relish he surveyed the quarry. In his own eyes his victory would not be lessened by the fact that his victim was already almost beyond recall. With savage, well-calculated precision Guy struck, piercing Hereward through the breast. The Wake's arm dropped to his side, his blade fell at his feet. As the surrounding Normans watched incredulously, he swayed, then crumpled upon the turf and lay still.

But Hereward knew nothing of his countless hurts. After a moment he opened up his eyes to watch the trees whirl above him, their leaves spinning like small black disks. From all directions they descended upon him, receding suddenly to vanish into the distance. Then from out of the quivering green among the treetops came

Althya's face. She smiled at him. His parched lips relaxed and he struggled to rise to go to her, but a swift and savage blow from de Lussac's brogue caught him full in the face and sent his lifeless body hurtling sideways to the forest floor.

The Normans stood above him, gazing down in wide-eyed disbelief at the legended form upon the turf. For a few moments their superstitious fears numbed them, creating an inertia which drained them of their power to move. Then, without knowing why, they all turned in unison, and leaping on their horses' backs, fled in terror.

But de Lussac, speeding after his terrified men, failed to notice the massive arm of an oak that overhung the roadway. It struck him a mighty blow upon the brow and he fell from his horse, one foot caught in the stirrup so that he was dragged along the road, his head bumping and bouncing crazily upon the cobbles until he was dead. And all unheeding, the horse sped on, snorting with fear, keeping pace with the rest until he had vanished into the distance.

The day passed and evening came. In the clearing, the squirrels chirped and chattered inquisitively, then subsided; the lynx saw, and went his way; the shy-eyed deer turned aside from the place of slaughter and all was silent. Then from out of the muted forest came the sound of trotting footfalls on the trail. At the clearing they paused, then came on, slowing here and there among the prostrate forms till at last the runner found his master.

Martin Lightfoot sank down upon his haunches, his eyes fixed upon Hereward's face. For a while he remained thus, making no motion, speaking no word. As the sun sank, soft red clouds floated above the trees, bringing a lifelike flush to the pallid face of the Wake. Then Lightfoot stirred. Stretching forth a gnarled and roughened hand, he gently combed the tousled locks and set each golden strand in place; gently wiped his master's face clean of the sweat of battle, clean of the green sod of England that clung to his cheek. Then he spoke.

"Peace has come to you now, lord, and it is well," he said, "for the woes of England were never meant to rest in the hands of one man, but in the hands of God. And since of him it is said that not even the smallest sparrow falls to earth without his knowledge, how, then, can England be forgotten?"

After that he spoke no more, but lapsed once again into his watchful silence. The moon arose, and waned, and darkness filled the clearing, black, impenetrable. This, too, passed and when at length morning came, casting its gray light aslant the trees, Lightfoot was gone, and the spot where the Wake had lain was empty.

But the fenmen said that at dawn, just after the rising sun split the mists that hung above the fens, Lightfoot was seen heading across them, making straight for the Gronnaswald. His shoulders sagged with weariness and grief. His tongue hung down, long and pink, bright against his shabby brown tunic and motionless save only for the awkward manner of his loping and the anguished twitching of his monstrous mouth. Like a man sleep-bound he picked his way among the familiar hidden paths, skirting the islets and the meres, stumbling on, seeing neither the fenmen who watched him pass nor the wild fowl that arose from the reeds and wheeled and screamed about him.

And the fenmen said that suddenly, like a man emerging from a trance, he paused and lifted his strange face against the wind that blew toward him from out of the Gronnaswald. And they, following the direction of his gaze, were also gripped with wonder at what they saw.

For beyond the blood-red meres the rising sun shed a scarlet cloak upon the Gronnaswald, lighting the tips of the trees like trees aflame and embracing within its fiery radiance a tiny hillock on the forest's outer fringes, upon whose summit stood Hereward the Wake. No hint of battle weariness clung to him now; no trace of fever parched the smiling lips. He stood with feet apart, planted firmly on his English soil. Before him he held his naked sword, both hands gripping its hilt as he leaned lightly upon it, and the brilliance of his ring mail rivaled the flaming sunrise.

And the fenmen said that, as they watched, Lightfoot sped forward to meet the Wake, though now the awkwardness had vanished from his loping and the anguished twitching of his monstrous mouth was stilled. For a moment they stood upon the hillock side by side, looking back across the fens, across the blood-red meres, across the oozing, emerald wastes. Then they turned away, and together they passed through the forest, and everywhere they trod their path was lit by the russet splendor of the morning sun.

AUTHOR'S NOTE

THERE is of course much that is fictional in this story, but the actual historical incidents have at all times been faithfully portrayed, having been derived from early English chronicles, from the works of Norman and Anglo-Norman chroniclers of the eleventh and twelfth centuries, and of course from those of later historians.

I have, however, taken certain liberties in the matter of time sequences. It is not known exactly in what years the Conqueror's sons, Robert and William Rufus, were born, but it seems unlikely that they had yet achieved manhood at the time of the story. Nor was Earl Waltheof executed as early as the year 1070. While this event actually took place some six years later, the extraordinary circumstances of his death were at the time held to be true and are to be found in the *Ecclesiastical History* of Odericus Vitalis, who, born in England in 1075, set himself the task of chronicling the Norman Conquest while there were men yet living who could recall the Battle of Hastings.

Then, too, the White Tower, which was in fact commissioned by the Conqueror, was not actually begun until the year 1078 and was not completed until the following reign. The Tower in which William abode at the time of the story, therefore, would have been the original tower which stood upon this spot; a tower believed to have been built by Julius Caesar upon the ruins of a primitive British fort, rebuilt by Alfred the Great, further enlarged and strengthened by the Conqueror for his own use, and later razed by him to make place for his historic White Tower. These dates, and those of several other events, I have shifted in the interest of my story.

In many instances legend and tradition have been invoked where history failed. But in all disputed matters, as in the proprietorship of the mythical vessel *Skidbladnir*, the origin of Charing Cross, or the death of Gurth, I have invented nothing, but have followed one of the several divergent theories.